ONE-EYED
JACK

OTHER BOOKS BY ELIZABETH BEAR

ONE-EYED JACK

JACK

ELIZABETH BEAR

PRIME BOOKS

ONE-EYED JACK

Prime Books
www.prime-books.com

For more information, contact Prime Books:
prime@prime-books.com

ISBN: 978-1-60701-406-5

For Scott, who daily confounds and revises the expectations of my narrative.

"You son-of-a-bitch, if you ain't heeled, go and heel yourself."
**—John Henry Holliday to Ike Clanton, around 1:00 a.m.
in the morning, Wednesday, 26 October, 1881**

One-Eyed Jack and the Suicide King.
Las Vegas, Summer, 2002.

It's not a straight drop.

Rather, the Dam is a long sweeping plunge of winter-white concrete: a dress for a three-time Las Vegas bride without the gall to show up in French lace and seed pearls. If you face Arizona, Lake Mead spreads out blue and alien on your left hand, inside a bathtub ring of limestone and perchlorate drainage from wartime titanium plants. Unlikely as canals on Mars, all that azure water rimmed in red and black rock. The likeness to an alien landscape is redoubled by the Dam's louvered concrete intake towers. At your back is the Hoover Dam visitor's center, and on the lake side sit two art-deco angels, swordcut wings thirty feet tall piercing the desert sky, their big toes shiny with touches for luck.

That angled drop is on your right. *À main droite.* Downriver. To California. The same way all those phalanxes and legions of electrical towers march.

It's not a straight drop. Hoover's much wider at the base than at the apex, where a two-lane road runs, flanked by sidewalks. The cement in the Dam's tunnel-riddled bowels won't be cured for another hundred years, and they say it'll take a glacier or a nuke to shift the structure. Its face is ragged with protruding rebar and unsmoothed edges, for all it looks fondant-frosted and insubstantial in an asphyxiating Mojave summer.

Stewart had gotten hung up on an upright pipe about forty feet down the rock face beside the Dam proper, and it hadn't killed him. I could hear him screaming from where I stood, beside those New Deal angels. I winced, hoping he died before the rescue crews got to him.

Plexiglas along a portion of the walkway wall discourages jumpers and incautious children: it's a laughable barrier. But then, so is Hoover itself—a fragile slice of mortal engineering between the oppressive rocks, more a symbol interrupting the flow of the sacred Colorado than any real, solid object.

Still. It holds the river back, don't it?

Stewart screamed again—a high, twisting cry like a gutted dog. I leaned against the black diorite base of the left-hand angel, my feet inches from this inscription—2700 BC IN THE REIGN OF THE PHARAOH MENKAURE THE LAST GREAT PYRAMID WAS BROUGHT TO COMPLETION—and ignored the stare of a girl too hip to walk over and check out the carnage. She checked me out instead; I ignored her with all the cat-coolness I could muster, my right hand hooked on the tool loop of my leather cargo pants.

With my left one, I reached up to grasp the toe of the angel. Desert-cooked metal seared my fingers; I held on for as long as I could before sticking them in my mouth, and then reached up to grab on again, making my biceps ridge through the skin. *Eeny, Meeny, Miney, Moe.* Eyepatch and Doc Martens, diamond in my ear or not, the girl eventually got tired of me. I saw her turn away from the corner of my regular eye.

They were moving cars off the Dam to let emergency vehicles through, but the rescue chopper would have to come from Las Vegas. There wasn't one closer. I checked my watch. Nobody was looking at me anymore, despite dyed matte-black hair, trendy goatee and the ink on the sunburned skin showing through my torn sleeveless shirt.

Which was the plan, after all.

I released the angel and strolled across the mosaic commemorating the dedication of the Dam. Brass and steel inlaid in terrazzo described moons and planets, stars: Alcyone, B Tauri and Mizar. Marked out among them were lines of inclination and paths of arc. The star map was left for future archaeologists to find if they wondered at the Dam's provenance: a sort of "we were here, and this is what we made you" signature scrawled on the bottom of a glue-and-glitter card. A hundred and twenty miles north, we're planning on leaving them another gift: a mountain full of spent nuclear fuel rods, and scribed on its surface a similar message, but that one's meant to say "Don't Touch."

Some card.

The steel lines described the precession of equinoxes and define orbital periods. They marked out a series of curves and angles superimposed across the whole night sky and the entire history of civilized mankind, cutting and containing them as the Dam cuts and contains the river.

It creeped me out. What can I say?

THEY DIED TO MAKE THE DESERT BLOOM, an inscription read, across the compass rose and signs of the zodiac on my left, and near my feet, CAPELLA. And ON THIS 30TH DAY OF THE MONTH OF SEPTEMBER IN THE YEAR (INCARNATIONIS DOMINICAE ANNO MCMXXXV) 1935, FRANKLIN DELANO ROOSEVELT, 32ND PRESIDENT OF THESE UNITED STATES OF AMERICA DEDICATED TO THE SERVICE OF OUR PEOPLE THIS DAM, POWER PLANT, AND RESERVOIR. A little more than ten years before Bugsy Siegel gave us the Flamingo Hotel and the Las Vegas we know and love today, but an inextricable link in the same unholy chain nevertheless.

I try to be suitably grateful.

But Bugsy was from California.

I passed over or beside the words, never stopping, my ears full of Stewart's screaming and the babble of conversation, the shouts of officers, the wail of sirens. And soon, very soon, the rattle of a helicopter's rotors.

The area of terrazzo closest to the angels' feet is called the Wheel of Time. It mentions the pyramids, and the birth of Christ, and the Dam. It ends in the year AD 14,000. The official Dam tour recommends you stay home that day.

Alongside these dates is another:

EARLY PART OF AD 2100

Slipped in among all the ancient significances, with a blank space before it and the obvious and precise intention that it someday be filled to match the rest.

Stewart screamed again. I glanced over my shoulder; security was still distracted. Pulling a cold chisel from my spacious pocket, I crouched on the stones and rested it against the top of the inscription. I produced a steel-headed mallet and measured it against the chisel's butt. When I lifted the eyepatch off my *otherwise* eye, I saw the light saturating the stone shiver back from the point of my chisel like a prodded jellyfish. There was some power worked into it. A power I recognized, because I also saw its shimmer through my right eye where my left one saw only the skin of my own hand. The Dam, and me. Both something meant to look like something else.

Card tricks.

The lovely whistlestop oasis called Las Vegas became a minor metropolis—by Nevada standards—in large part by serving gambling, whiskey, and whores to the New Deal workers who poured these concrete blocks. Workers housed in Boulder City weren't permitted such recreations within town limits. On Friday nights they went looking for a place to spend the money they risked their lives earning all week. Then after a weekend in Sin City, they were back in harness seven hundred feet above the bottom of Black Canyon come Monday morning, nine a.m.

Ninety-six of them died on the Dam site. Close to three hundred more succumbed to silicosis and other diseases. There's a legend some of them were entombed within the Dam, but that's a lie.

It would never have been permitted. A body in the concrete means a weakness in the structure, and Hoover was made to last well past the date I was about to obliterate with a few well-placed blows. "Viva Las Vegas," I muttered under my breath, and raised the hammer. And then Stewart stopped screaming, and a velvety female purr sounded in my ear. "Jack, Jack, Jackie."

"Goddess." I put the tools down and stood up, face inches from the face of the most beautiful woman in the world. "How did you know where to find me?"

She lowered tar-black lashes across cheeks like cream, pouting through her hair. The collar of her sleeveless blouse stood crisp-pressed, framing her face; I wondered how she managed it in one hundred-twenty degree heat. "I heard a rumor you meant to deface my Dam," she said with a smile that bent lacquered lips in a mockery of Cupid's little red bow. The too-cool teenager was staring at Goddess now, brow wrinkled as if she thought Goddess must be somebody famous and couldn't quite place who. Goddess gets that reaction a lot.

I sighed. Contrived as she was, she was still lovelier than anything real life could manage. "You're looking a little peaked these days, Goddess. Producers got you on a diet again? And it's my Dam, honey. I'm Las Vegas. Your turf is down the river."

Her eyes flashed. Literally. I cocked an ear over my shoulder, but still no screaming. Which—dammit—meant that Stewart was probably dead, and I was out of time.

"It's not polite to ask a lady what she does to maintain her looks, darling. And I say Hoover belongs to L.A. You claim, what—ten percent of the power and water?" She took a couple of steps to the brass Great Seal of California there at the bottom of the terrazzo, immediately under the sheltering wings of a four-foot bas-relief eagle. California's plaque was front and center among those indicating the seven states that could not live without the Colorado, and twice as big as the others. She tapped it with a toe. The message was clear.

I contented myself with admiring the way her throat tightened under a Tiffany necklace as I shrugged and booted my hammer aside. Out of my left eye, I saw her *otherwise*—a swirl of images and expectations, a casting-couch stain and a shattered dream streetwalking on Sunset Boulevard. "You still working by yourself, Goddess? Imagine it's been lonely since your boyfriend died."

Usually there are two or three of us to a city, though some places—New York, Paris—have more. And we can be killed, although something new comes along eventually to replace us. Unless the city dies too: then it's all over.

Her partner had gotten himself shot up in an alleyway. Appropriate.

"I get by," she answered, with a Bette Davis gesture.

I was supposed to go over and comfort her. Instead, I flipped my eyepatch down. Goddess makes me happy I don't like girls. Even so, she's still a damn hazard to navigation. "I was just leaving. We could stop at that little ice cream place in Boulder City for an avocado-baconburger."

A surprised ripple of rutabaga-rutabagas ran through the crowd on the other sidewalk, and I heard officers shouting to each other. Stewart's body must have vanished.

"Ugh," Goddess said expressively, the corners of her mouth turning down under her makeup.

"True. You shouldn't eat too much in a sitting; all that puking will ruin your teeth." I managed to beat my retreat while she was still hacking around for a suitably acid response.

Traffic wasn't moving across the Dam yet, but I'd had the foresight to park the dusty-but-new F150 in the lot on the Arizona side, so all I had to do was walk over and haul Stewart (by the elbow) away from the KLAS reporter to whom he was providing an incoherently homosexual man-on-the-spot reaction. He did that sort of thing a lot. Stewart was the Suicide King. I kissed him as I shoved him into the truck.

He pulled back and caught my eye. "Did it work?"

"Fuck, Stewart. I'm sorry."

"Sure," he said, leaning across to open the driver's-side door. "You spend fifteen minutes impaled on a rusty chunk of steel and then I'll tell you, 'Sorry.' What happened?"

"Goddess."

He didn't say anything after that: just blew silky blond hair out of eyes bluer than the desert sky and put his hand on my knee as we drove south through Arizona, down to Laughlin, and came over the river and back up through the desert wastes of Searchlight and CalNevAri. In silence. Going home.

~

We parked the truck in the Four Queens garage and went strolling past the courthouse. The childhood-summer drone of cicadas surrounded us as we walked past the drunks and the itinerant ministers. We strolled downtown arm in arm, toward the Fremont Street Experience, daring somebody to say something.

The Suicide King and I. Wildcards, but only sometimes. In a city with streets named for Darth Vader and for Seattle Slew, we were the unseen princes. I said as much to Stewart.

"Or unseen queens," he joked, tugging me under the arch of lights roofing Fremont Street. "What happened back there?"

Music and cool air drifted out the open doorways of casinos, along with the irresistible chime of the slot machines that are driving out the table games. I saw the lure of their siren song in the glassy eyes of the gamblers shuffling past us. "Something must have called her. I was just going to deface a national landmark. Nothing special."

Someone jostled my arm on my *otherwise* side, blind with the eyepatch down. I turned my head, expecting a sneering curse, but he smiled from under a floppy moustache and a floppier hat, and disappeared into Binion's Horseshoe. I could pick the poker players out of the herd: they didn't look anaesthetized. *That* one wasn't a slot zombie. There might be life in my city yet.

Stewart grunted, cleaning his fingernails with a pocketknife that wasn't street-legal by anyone's standards. Sweat marked half-moons on his red-striped shirt, armholes and collar. "And Goddess showed up. All the way from the City of Angels."

"Hollywood and Vine."

"What did she want?"

"The bitch said it was her fucking Dam." I turned my head to watch another zombie pass. A local. Tourists mostly stay down on the Strip these days, with its Hollywood assortment of two-dimensional mockeries of exotic places. Go to Las Vegas and never see it.

I'm waiting for the LasVegas-themed casino: somewhere between Paris, Egypt, Venice, and the African coast. Right in the middle of the Strip.

This isn't the city that gave Stewart and me birth. But this is the city we are now.

"Is it?"

"I don't know. Hoover should be ours by rights. But I'm convinced that empty date forges a link between Vegas and L.A."

He let go of my arm and wandered over to one of the antique neon signs. Antique by Vegas standards, anyway. "You ever think of all those old towns under the lake, Jack? The ones they evacuated when the reservoir started to fill?"

I nodded, although he wasn't looking and I knew he couldn't hear my head rattle, and I followed him through the neon museum. I think a lot about those towns, actually. Towns like Saint Thomas, where I spent a few very happy years around the turn of the century, before Laura and my old man died. Those towns, and the Anasazi, who carved their names and legends on wind-etched red rocks within the glow of my lights and then vanished without a whisper, as if blown off the world by that selfsame wind. And Rhyolite, near Beatty, where they're building the nuke dump: it was the biggest city in Nevada in 1900--and in 1907 it was gone. I think about the Upshot Knothole Project: these downtown hotels are the older ones, built to withstand the tremors from the above-ground nuclear blasts. And I think too of all the casinos that thrived in their day, and then accordioned into dust and tidy rubble when the men with the dynamite came.

Nevada has a way of eating things up. Swallowing them without a trace.

Except the Dam, with that cry etched on its surface. And a date that hasn't happened yet. Remember. Remember. Remember me.

Stewart gazed upward, his eyes trained on Vegas Vic: the famous neon cowboy who used to wave a greeting to visitors cruising into town in fin-tailed Cadillacs—relegated now to headliner status in the Neon Museum. He doesn't wave anymore: his hand stays upraised stiffly. I lifted mine in a like salute. "Howdy," I replied.

Stewart giggled. "At least they didn't blow him up."

"No," I said, looking down. "They blew the fuck out of Bugsy, though."

Bugsy Siegel was a California gangster who thought maybe half-way up the Los Angeles highway, where it crossed the Phoenix road, might be a good place for a joint designed to convert dirty money into clean. It so happened that there was already a little town with a light-skirt history huddled there, under the shade of tree-lined streets. A town with mild winters and abundant water. *Las Vegas* means *the meadows* in Spanish. In the middle of the harsh Mojave, the desert bloomed.

And there's always been magic at a crossroads. It's where you go to sell your soul.

I shifted my eyepatch to get a look *otherwise*. Vic shimmered, a twist of expectation, disappointment, conditioned response. My right eye showed me the slot-machine zombies as a shuffling darkness, Stewart a blinding white light, a sword-wielding specter. A demon of chance. The Suicide King, avatar of take-your-own-life Las Vegas with its record-holding rates of depression, violence, failure, homelessness, DUI. The Suicide King, who cannot ever die by his own hand.

"I can see why she feels at home here," Stewart said to Vic's neon feet.

"Vic's a he, Stewart. Unless that was a queer boy 'she,' in which case I will send the ghosts of campiness—past present and future—to haunt your bed."

"She. Goddess. She seems at home here."

15

"I don't want her at home in my city," I snapped as if it cramped my tongue. It felt petty. And good. "The bitch has her own city. And sucks enough fucking water out of my river."

He looked at me shyly through a fall of blond bangs. I thought about kissing him, and snorted instead. He grinned. "Vegas is nothing but a big fucking stage set wrapped around a series of strip malls, anymore. What could be more Hollywood?"

I lit a cigarette, because everybody still smokes in Vegas—as if to make up for California—and took a deep, acrid drag. When I blew smoke back out it tickled my nostrils. "I think that empty inscription is what locks us to L.A."

Stewart laced his arm through mine again. "Maybe we'll get lucky and it will turn out to be the schedule for The Big One."

I pictured L.A. tumbling into the ocean, Goddess and all, and grinned back. "I was hoping to get that a little sooner. So what say we go back to the Dam tonight and give it another try?"

The Russian and the American.
Somewhere on the Island of Manhattan, 1964.

A tap on the Russian's door: one he wasn't expecting but recognized. He lifted his head, checked the gas on the stove to be sure the noodles wouldn't boil over, and walked around the breakfast bar to the peephole. Shadows in the crack above the threshold told him one individual waited beyond; he checked the peephole out of habit and he threw both locks open, palming his pistol anyway before he slipped the chain.

Oh, he knew that look. The tilt of the head, the hopeful pout. The scent of expensive cologne and the fresh haircut and shave. The American's date had stood him up, and he had decided an evening with his partner was preferable to a Friday night alone. His words confirmed the Russian's suspicions.

"Can I buy you dinner, my friend?"

"I am cooking," the Russian answered, slipping his pistol back into his shoulder holster. "Your date stood you up."

"Am I so obvious?" The American slunk into the living room like a lean, self-satisfied cat, wrinkling his nose at the scents of charcoal and boiling pasta. "It's burning," he said mildly, turning to throw both locks and set the chain.

"No," the Russian answered, going back to the pasta and picking up a wooden spoon. "That's the charcoal."

"You're grilling in the living room, perhaps?"

The pasta had cooked. He drained it, clouds of steam wreathing his face and his broad scarred hands as he shook the colander. "Are you staying for dinner?"

"Not if it's, er, charcoal—"

"It is casserole," the Russian answered, and set about opening cans—cream of mushroom soup, tuna fish, green peas—while the American winced and turned away, picking a box off the counter.

"Kraft Macaroni? *Partner.*"

The Russian's mouth quirked at the disappointment in his partner's voice. He didn't turn, but kept one ear tuned as the American poked about his living room. "Clear off the coffee table," the Russian said. "There is clutter all over the dining room. We'll have to eat in the living room." He'd turned the stereo off and the evening news on before he started to cook, and the muted tones of Walter Cronkite underlaid everything he and the American said.

"Are you sure I can't buy you dinner?"

"And let this go to waste?" He scooped canned goods into the emptied pot, added a double handful of grated cheese, fresh chopped parsley, garlic salt, pepper, and dried oregano, and dumped the cooked macaroni elbows back on top along with the contents of the faux cheese package. *Stir well.*

He couldn't see the American's shudder, but he could visualize it. "Mad Russian. Is there *nothing* you won't eat?"

Ah, my friend. If only you knew. The American *was* remarkably worldly, for an American. But every so often the Russian was reminded of his friend's nationality, usually with regard to some squeamishness or naiveté. "I prefer tuna fish to rats," the Russian admitted, turning the flame down to low and covering the pot, knowing without looking that the American had glanced over his shoulder, considered the Russian's impassive back, and decided the Russian was joking.

"Everything you own is black, or white." An idle comment, following the sound of shifting clutter.

"Is it?" The Russian measured loose tea, but not yet into the pot. The British knew how to do some things properly, and tea was one of them. Of course, when it came to tea—*chai*—Mother Russia had advantages of her own.

"Are you sure I should be smelling something burning?"

"Absolutely," the Russian said, and carried pot and tea around the breakfast bar and toward the darkened niche that served him as a dining area. "My friend, would you get the lights in the 'dining room,' please?"

The American hit the dimmer switch without looking. And then turned at the sound of water running from an unexpected direction. Hiding a smile, the Russian watched the American's reflection in the darkened window; his eyes widened at the 'clutter' dominating the Russian's serviceable Formica table.

"Good lord," the American said with sudden reverence, as the Russian warmed the teapot and emptied the steaming water back into the top of the ancient, gilt-brass, red-enameled samovar that dominated the room. "Where did you *get* that?"

The Russian bit his lip to stop the laughter. "Greenwich Village, of course."

"Of course."

His partner strolled over as the Russian added the tea to the teapot and filled it again, setting it to steep. The American's lips were twitching. "It must be two hundred years old. How long were you going to wait to show me this?"

"I had thought," the Russian said, catching the American's wrist a moment before he could brush his fingers over the crimson enamel, "that I would give it to you when I returned home. Be careful. That's hot."

"Go—home? You haven't been recalled—"

The Russian didn't miss how the American's face paled when he said 'go home,' and it warmed his heart the way standing close to the charcoal brazier under the samovar did. "No," he said. "But if I am, I could hardly bring that back with me. Would you like some tea?"

"Very much," the American said, stepping away, although the American did not like tea.

The Russian fetched glasses. Two of them, ruby glass in gilt holders that matched the samovar. He shouldn't have bought it, of course. But he hadn't been able to resist. And it wasn't as if an agent whose housing was provided had all that much to spend money on, unless he was a clotheshorse. Like the American. "Sugar?"

"If I'm going to do it I should do it right, nyet?"

The Russian set the sugar bowl on the coffee table and filled the glasses with tea while the American turned off the gas and spooned their yellowish-beige dinner into a pair of unremarkable bowls.

"Spoon or fork?"

"Fork, please." He took a lump of sugar for himself and sat on the floor beside the coffee table.

"It's very red," the American said, settling down kitty-corner to the Russian and bending forward to examine the glass. He did not lift his fork, but reached for the sugar instead. The Russian stopped him a moment before he dropped the lumps into his glass.

"This is Russian tea," he said. "You put the sugar between your teeth."

"Rot your teeth doing that."

"A good communist will be provided teeth by the state as needed—"

"—stainless steel ones—"

"—bah. See? Like so."

Dubiously, the American followed his example, managing to sip his tea through the sugar without choking, much to the Russian's surprise. More surprising still, he smiled. "It's good."

"It's like home," the Russian answered. "Except not." He shrugged and picked up his fork. They did not speak again until they had finished eating.

"This is better than it looks," the American said grudgingly, setting his fork down and picking up his tea.

"Peasant cooking American style." But said without defensiveness, for once. The Russian leaned against the sofa. The tea had cooled enough to hold the glass between his hands instead of by the handle.

The American nudged his ankle with a foot. The American had always to touch people; he was also very European in that. Perhaps another reason the Russian felt comfortable with him. "Are you thinking about going home?"

I've really unsettled him. The realization delighted the Russian. "No," he answered. He stared into his glass, and leaned forward to fetch himself another lump of sugar. The American handed it to him without looking, knowing what he needed before he knew it himself. "The glasses *are* very red," the Russian said. He looked through the glass at the American, and then lowered it to take a sip. "You know, in Russia, red—*krasny*—also means *beautiful*. It is a very patriotic color, red. It reminds me of the Motherland."

The American looked up at him and grinned and shook his head, obviously not understanding the conversation. Which was acceptable. He was only an American, after all.

The Russian took the dishes into the kitchen when they finished their tea. He poured vodka into two glasses and brought one to the American, turned off the television, found an LP of *Monk's Dream*, and laid it on the turntable. Vigorous, intricate music: perhaps a little too intricate to support conversation, but the Russian did not think that tonight was a night for dreamy, drifting jazz.

He turned the lights up before he settled on the sofa, glass cupped in broad fingers, one knee drawn up. "Would you like to play chess?"

The American held his own glass between the flats of his palms and smiled. "Actually," he said, "you benefit by more than a dinner companion tonight. *I* am the proud possessor of a pair of tickets to *Fiddler on the Roof.*"

"*Fiddler on the Roof*?" The Russian couldn't stop the corners of his lips from curving this time.

"At the Imperial Theatre," the American said triumphantly. "On Broadway."

"I know where the Imperial Theatre is."

The American grimaced as he tasted his drink. "Go get your dinner jacket on."

～

They walked shoulder to shoulder through the weekending crowds, two handsome men, incongruous on foot in their mirror-bright shoes and velvety bowties. The American grinned at the women who turned to examine them more closely; the Russian pretended ignorance, but that smile wouldn't stop playing at the corner of his mouth. He laughed at the musical more than he had expected, and found the Rabbi's blessing for the Tsar particularly quotable, even as they left the theatre. "I don't suppose that will work on, say, some of our opposite numbers, do you think?"

"May God bless and keep all counter-agents—far away from me?" The American held the door for the Russian, chuckling low in his throat. "I'm not ready to go home yet. I don't suppose you're hungry."

"I'm always hungry," the Russian answered. "Make me a match with a gyro, and we'll talk."

"I don't suppose you know an all-night Greek deli?"

The Russian grinned. "Of course I do."

~

"I do not believe there was a conspiracy," the Russian said later, cupping a piece of lamb-stuffed flatbread in one hand, considering it more than he was eating it. He kept half his attention over the American's shoulder, and knew his partner was performing the same office for him. "I think Oswald acted alone."

The American laughed, swirling the dregs in his coffee cup. "Come on," he said. "The KGB made you say that—"

"No, no. You see, I met Oswald."

The American blinked. The Russian found it gratifying. "Met—" His voice trailed off. He tried again. "You *met* Lee Harvey Oswald?"

"In Moscow in 1962, when he planned to defect." The Russian shrugged. "He was unimportant. I was one of the officers assigned, because of my English. We spent a fair amount of time together." He took a bite of his sandwich, cucumber squeaking between his teeth, and chewed contentedly. "He was deemed . . . unsuitable for use."

The American had that look again, the half-curious, half-uncomfortable one he got whenever something reminded him that there had been a Russian before there was a partnership. Before there was the Russian and the American, inseparable. "Unsuitable. *Really.*"

The Russian grinned, and let the hand that wasn't folded around the gyro describe a lazy circle by his temple. "You have no idea. They sent him to Minsk, so he'd be out of the way. He tried to kill himself, because the KGB *wasn't paying him enough attention.* Is that insane enough for you?"

"It does indicate a certain, ah, *lack* of the self-preservation instinct." Pause, chewing. "Still, do you think he could have made that shot?"

The Russian shrugged and finished his gyro, licking his fingers for the last bit of sauce. "I could have." He enjoyed his partner's slow, thoughtful blink. "Come on," he said, standing. "I'll walk you home."

The American stood too, dropping money on the table. The Russian took his elbow to steer him out of the restaurant. "Walk me home?" Their eyes met. The American smiled, suppressed cleverness dancing in his hazel eyes. The Russian blinked and almost let go of his arm. *Oh, clever Russian. This time you outsmarted yourself.*

"There wasn't any date, was there?"

"Not one that stood me up, no."

"Oh." The Russian chewed that over for a little while as they walked homeward. This time, he did let his hand fall. He stole a quick glance sideways. The American's untied bowtie flopped lightly in the breeze. "If you wanted to spend the evening with me," he said, shrugging, "you only had to ask. Save the elaborate charades for those who are not—"

"My partner?"

"I was going to say—your friend—" The Russian looked up before they paused at the street corner. Force of habit; the American scanned the left half of the arc and the Russian scanned the right. Something glittered, halfway up the side of a brownstone, in a window that was both dark and open. The Russian's heart kicked hard in his chest— "*Duck!*"

ELIZABETH BEAR

He lunged against his partner's side, knocking the American sideways, trusting his partner to anticipate his action and to break their fall. Something sharp stung the forearm that the Russian threw up in front of his eyes; stung, not burned. He heard the ricochet whine and strike metal, and a split second later the flat report of the gunshot, followed first by silence and then shouts and running feet as the few remaining pedestrians caught on and vacated the scene. *No silencer, of course. He wouldn't want to sacrifice accuracy—*

They hit hard and rolled, the Russian lunging into a crouch, the cool crosshatched grip of his modified Walther P-38 heavy in his hand before he was even quite steady on his feet. The American sprawled in the gutter, using the curb for cover, his own automatic readied as well.

"Did you see him?"

"Window," the Russian hissed, crouched behind a blue steel postal box. He jerked his head, pointing with his eyes, ignoring the thin, warm trickle of blood across his hand. The sleeve of his dinner jacket was shredded. Concrete was chipped from the lampost base; the fresh gouge shone in the streetlight. "Any bystanders hurt? Any down?"

"I don't see any," the American answered. "I caught a glimpse of him hightailing up the fire escape when you took me down. He was aiming for you."

The Russian nodded, adrenaline like a blow to the throat. Feeling his partner beside him like a paired identity, left hand and right, two bodies but one animal. As if he knew what the American would say, how he would move before he did it. "He missed."

The American lifted his head from the gutter and glared at the bullet gouge, his luminous amber eyes narrowed as if it had done him a personal offense. He pushed himself to his knees under the cover of a Cadillac, sparing a moment of rue for the state of his dinner jacket before he settled into a runner's crouch. "You moved. That would have drilled your head. Think Oswald could have made *that* shot?"

"I could have," the Russian growled. "You didn't return fire?"

"With a *handgun*?"

"Good point. He'll be across the rooftop by now. Let's *move*. Go on go—"

"*Go!*"

He didn't wait; the American would be right behind him. He ran for the brownstone, scurrying crooked as a rat, and prayed the one with his name on it wasn't already in the air, moving faster than the sound of its own firing. He flattened himself against the wall—small overhang, smell of pavement and soot.

"You're hit," the American said, slapping stone beside him.

"A scratch."

"You lying?"

"Not this time. You said you caught a glimpse—"

"Tall," the American said. "Three, four inches on me, maybe—" the American was five-foot-ten, and the Russian knew he would have measured the opposition against the flights of the fire escape. "Slender. Cat blacks, dark hair, not so well-groomed as some." He patted his own forelock by way of example. "Nasty scar on the right cheek," the American continued as the Russian turned, brows rising, eyes intentionally cold. "A mean-looking scowl. Gray eyes, bit of a squint—"

"I recognize the description, but I must say, your eyesight is certainly acute—"

"*I'm* not the one too vain to wear his glasses except for reading."

"I'm farsighted," the Russian answered, holstering his gun as a few over-bold civilians began to emerge from doorways and under cars. "You noticed all this from several hundred yards, at night, my friend?"

"No." The American pressed his own pistol into the swing of his dinner jacket rather than put it away. "He's hard to misidentify. Even from a distance. But the question remains."

"Yes, my clever American?"

"What would an MI-6 assassin be doing gunning for a couple of lowly international law enforcement types on our side of the puddle, partner mine?"

The Russian swallowed, and raked both hands through his own bright hair. "Well," he said, as dryly as he could manage, "we know he has a taste for shooting smart Russians, neh?"

The Assassin on the Run.
New York City, 1964.

He couldn't remember the last time he'd missed, and now he'd done it twice in a row.

There was a reason for it, of course. He reminded himself of that as he scrambled up the fire escape—but reasons were not excuses, and his failure to kill both the English widow and the Russian secret agent would complicate matters, later.

Still, he hadn't expected them to be so hard to kill. Certainly not as hard to kill as *he* was.

Apparently he'd been wrong, and there was enough of their legends left to afford them a certain amount of protection. Plot immunity; the hazard of taking on a hero the world hadn't quite forgotten. At least it worked in his favor as well.

Which meant he would have to get closer, next time. But for the nonce, it meant he needed to lose them, because he had an appointment in Las Vegas, thirty-six years from now.

Tribute and the Witch Sycorax.
San Diego, Summer, 2002.

Sycorax smiled at me through the mantilla shadowing her eyes, eyes untouched by that smile. She lolled against a wrought-iron railing, one narrow hip thrust out, dyed red hair tumbling out of the black spider web of her shawl, looking like a Mac Rebenak song come to life.

The dead quickly grow thin.

She licked her lips with a long pale tongue and even the semblance of amusement fell away. "You're white, Tribute. No coup tonight?"

"Nothing appealed." Tribute wasn't my real name any more than Sycorax was hers.

She leaned into me, pressed a hand to my throat. Her flesh lay like ice against the chill of my skin. "I told you to hunt."

"I hunted." Backing away, red nails trailing down my chest. I hunted. Hunted and returned empty-handed. It's as much how you hear the orders as how they're given.

"If you wasn't a coward," Jesse said in my ear, "you'd do a bit more than not followin' orders. Even if you couldn't take *her* out, you'd take yourself out of the picture."

Suicide is a sin, I told the ghost of my conscience.

He snorted. Sycorax couldn't hear him, of course. "So's murder. And eatin' people."

She followed close on my steps, driving me before her. Ragged chiffon clung and drifted around her calves; she reached up to lace china fingers in the fine hairs at the nape of my neck. Her face against my throat was waxen: too long unfed. "You weaken me on purpose, Tribute. Give me what you have."

"Pansy," Jesse said.

Jesse, go away.

I still had the force of will to make him listen, as Sycorax pressed close. He went, growling. Somewhere down the alley, glass shattered. He was in a mood.

She needed me, needed me to feed. Old as she was, she had to have the blood more often and she couldn't take it straight from a human anymore. She needed someone like me to purge the little taints and poisons from it first—and even then, I had to be careful what I brought home. So sensitive, the old.

She caught at my collar, pulled it open with fumbling hands. I leaned down to her—chattel, blood of her blood, no more able to resist her will than her own right hand, commanded to protect and feed her. At least this time, I knew what sort of predator I served, although I had less choice about it.

I figured things out too late, again.

Sycorax curled cold lips back from fangs like a row of perfect icicles. Her jaw distended, unhinged like a snake's, and she sank her teeth into my flaccid vein and tried to drink. All that pain and desire spiked through me—every time like the first time—and on its heels hollowness. Sycorax hissed, drew back. She turned her head and spat transparent fluid on the cobbles. I smiled, spreading my hands like Jesus on a hilltop, still backing slowly away. I had made very sure that I had nothing to feed her.

Petty, I know. And she'd make me pay for it before dawn.

Down the narrow lane, a club's red door swung open and I turned with a predator's eye, attracted to the movement. Spill of light cut like a slice of cake, booted feet crunching on glittering glass. Girls. Laughing, young, drunk. I remembered what that felt like.

I raked a hand through my forelock and looked away, making the mistake of catching Sycorax's china-blue eye.

"Those," she said, jerking her chin.

I shook my head. "Too easy, baby. Let me get you something more challenging." I used to have an accent—down home Mississippi. Faded by the years, just like everything else I worked so hard to lose,

ELIZABETH BEAR

thank you very much. I suspected I sounded pan-European now, like Sycorax. Her lips, painted pale to match china white skin, curled into a sulk.

"Tribute. After a quarter of a century, you ought to know I mean what I say."

I tugged my collar, glancing down.

"Them." Sycorax twisted a stiletto-heeled boot, crushing the litter of cracked glass against the bricks.

She enjoyed the hunt a little too much. But who but a madwoman would have drained *my* living body and made me hers? Just fetching my corpse from the grave—

"I'm hungry," she complained. I sharpened my teeth on my lip to stop a malicious smile.

If I could buy a little time, the girls might make it to the street and I could lose them in the crowds and tangled shadows of the gaslamp district. Footsteps receded down the alley; I spread my hands in protest, cocking my head to one side and giving her the little half-smile that used to work so well on my wife. "Something with a little more fight in it, sweetie."

My wife was a hell of a lot younger than Sycorax. "Those two girls. Bring me their blood, Tribute. That's an order."

And that was the end of the argument. I turned to obey.

"Tribute."

Coming back around slowly, her gaze—catching mine—flat and pale. "Sycorax."

"I could spike your pretty eyes out on my pinkie finger and eat them, lovely boy," she purred. "Hazel, aren't they?"

"Blue."

She shrugged and made an irritated, dismissive gesture, hands white as wax. "It's so hard to tell in the dark."

30

The girls made it to the street before Sycorax ended the discussion, but I had to follow them anyway. I paced my ordained prey, staying to the shadows, the collar of the black leather trench coat that Sycorax had picked out for me tugged up to half-hide the outline of my jaw. I never would have bought that coat for myself. You'd think anybody who'd been dead for any time at all would have had enough of blackness and shadows. Sycorax reveled in them. If she were three hundred years younger, she'd have been a gothchick.

It was a good night: nobody turned for a second look.

People are always dying, and human memory is short. In a hundred years, I will probably be able to walk down any street in the world without raising an eyebrow.

As long as the sun is down.

Sycorax didn't bother to follow. I had no choice but to do as I was bid. It's more than a rule; it's a fact. I expected there were still a few women who would get a kick out of that.

My girls staggered somewhat, weaving. One was a blonde, brittle dyed hair and a red beret. The other one had glossy chestnut brown waves and the profile of a little girl. I tracked them through the district toward the ocean, neon glow, and littered sidewalks. A door would open and music would issue forth, and it wasn't long before I found myself mouthing the words to one particular song.

There's something gloriously ironic in a man charting a number-one hit twenty-five years after he's dead. *Otis Redding, eat your heart out.*

My quarry paused at an open-air patio where a live band played the blues. Girl singer, open coat, and a spill of curls like wicked midnight: performing old standards, the kind I've always loved. *Mama, tell my baby sister, not to do what I have done. I'll spend my life in sin and misery, in the House of the Rising Sun.* A song that was already venerable when Eric Burdon made it famous.

There's all kinds of whoredom, aren't there? And all kinds of bloodsuckers, too.

The singer nailed "Amazing Grace" a capella like heartbreak, voice sharp and gritty as little Mary Johnson doing "Cold, Cold Heart." I caught myself singing along and slashed my tongue with needle teeth before someone could overhear. Still no blood. I hadn't fed in a long time and it hurt more than it should have.

The girls sat down at a table and ordered food. I smelled beer, hot wings, eye-watering garlic. I suddenly very badly wanted a peanut butter sandwich and a milkshake.

Leaning against the high black iron fence, I watched the girls watching the band until a passerby in her fifties turned to get a startled better look at me. I stood up straight and met her gaze directly, giving her the crooked little-kid smile. It almost always works, except on Sycorax.

Trying to hide your face only convinces them they've seen something.

"Sorry," she said, waving me away with a smile. A moment later, she turned back. "You know you look like . . . "

"People say," I answered, pitching my voice high.

"Amazing." She nodded cheerfully, gave me a wide wondering grin, and continued on her way. I watched her go, chattering with her friends, shaking their heads.

The girls didn't stay for "King of the Road," although I would have liked to hear the singer's version.

Kids.

I almost turned away when they walked past. They stank of garlic-stuffed mushrooms and beer. The reek of the herb knotted my stomach and seared my eyes. I actually tried to take a half-step in another direction before the compulsion Sycorax had laid on me locked my knees and forced me back into pursuit.

They walked arm in arm, skinny twenty-year-olds with fake ID and black vinyl miniskirts. Cheap boots, too much eyeliner. The one with the brown hair broke my heart every time she tossed her head, just that way. I let myself drift ahead of them, taking a gamble on where they would cut across the residential neighborhood near the ocean: a dangerous place for girls to be.

I ducked down a side street to cut them off and waited in the dark of an unlit doorway. Sycorax's control permitted that much. I leaned against the wall, scrubbing my face against my hands. It felt like a waxen mask, cold and stiff. My hands weren't much better.

"Better you should go step in front of the Coaster, bro," Jesse said, a transparent figure gesturing with long hands toward the tracks and the commuter train. I ignored him.

I couldn't have done it anyway. Sycorax had given me other orders. And besides, I had a plan.

They didn't take long to catch up with me. I was unlucky; they picked the better of the two routes through the brownstones, the one I had been able to justify choosing, and just that innocently chose their fate.

The scent of bougainvillea and jacaranda filled the spaces of the night. I watched them skipping from streetlight to streetlight, shadows stretched out behind them, catching up, and then reaching before. The brown-haired one walked a few steps ahead of the bleach-blonde, humming to herself.

I couldn't help it. It wasn't one of my standards, but every blues singer born knows the words to that one. Hell, I used to have a horse by that name.

I picked up the tune.

I had to.

" . . . they call the Rising Sun. It's been the ruin of many a poor boy. And me, O God, I'm one!"

Their heads snapped up. Twenty, maybe. I was dead before they were born. Gratifying that they recognized my voice.

"Fellas, don't believe what a bad woman tells you—though her eyes be blue, or brown . . . " I strolled out of the shadows, ducking my head and smiling, letting the words trail away.

The dark-haired girl did a doubletake. She had a lovely nose, pert

33

and turned up. The blonde blinked a couple of times, but I don't think she made the connection. I'd changed my appearance some, stopped dying my hair black, and I'd lost a lot of weight.

The stench of garlic on their breath would have thickened my blood in my veins—if I had any left. I swallowed hard, remembering all those songs about wandering ghosts and unquiet graves. Ghosts that all seem to want the same thing: revenge, and to lie down and rest.

I smiled wider. *What the lady wants, the lady gets.*

"Oh, wow," the darker girl said. "Do you have any idea how much you look like . . . "

The street was empty, dark and deserted. I came up under the streetlight, close enough to reach out and touch the tip of that nose if I wanted. I dropped them a look that used to melt hearts, sidelong glance under lowered lashes. "People say," I answered.

And, sick to my stomach, I broke their necks before I fed.

It was the least I could do.

Poison roiled in my belly when I laid them out gently in the light of that streetlamp, in the rich dark covering the waterfront, close enough to smell the sea. I straightened their spines so they wouldn't look so terrible for whoever found them, but at least *they* wouldn't be coming back.

It was happening: my limbs jerked and shook. My flesh crawled with ripples like fire, my tongue numb as a drunk's. *I'm going back to New Orleans, to wear that ball and chain . . .*

Not this time. Struggling to smooth each step, to hide the venom flooding my veins, I hurried back to my poor, *hungry* mistress. I stole the brunette's wallet. I stopped and bought breath mints at the all-night grocery.

I beat Sycorax home.

One-Eyed Jack and the Fallen Angel.
Las Vegas, Summer, 2002.

The trooper shone his light around the cab and the bed of the truck, but didn't make us get out despite 3:00 a.m. and no excuse to be out but stargazing at Willow Beach. Right after the terrorist attacks, it was soldiers armed with automatic weapons. I'm not sure if the Nevada Highway Patrol are an improvement, but this is the world we have to live in, even if it is under siege. Stewart, driving, smiled and showed ID, and then we passed through winding gullies and out onto the Dam.

It was uncrowded in the breathless summer night. The massive lights painting its facade washed the stars out of the desert sky. Despite the mountains between here and there, Las Vegas glowed in the passenger-side mirror as Stewart parked the truck on the Arizona side. On an overcast night, the glow is greenish—the reflected lights of the MGM Grand. That night we had clear skies, and it was the familiar city-glow pink, only brighter and split asymmetrically by the ascending Luxor light like a beacon calling someone home.

I'd been chewing my thumb all evening. Stewart rattled my shoulder to get me to look up. "We're here. Bring your chisel?"

"Better," I said, and reached behind the seat to bring out the tire iron and a little eight-pound sledge. The sledge dropped neatly into the tool loop of my cargo pants. I tugged a black denim jacket on over the torn shirt and slid the iron into the left-hand sleeve. "Now I'm ready."

He disarmed the doors and struggled out of the leather jacket I'd told him was too hot to wear. "Why you always gotta break things you don't understand?"

I didn't ask for this job. I didn't go looking for this job, and I sure as hell didn't get to pick my father, or the way his blood linked me to

Nevada, or the way he paid my mother off and sent her south out of Carson City when her belly proved an embarrassment. Or the magic that rose up and bound me to a newborn city.

No.

I got to pick the manner of my death, however. And apparently that's enough for the fates.

They have a sense of humor.

"Because they scare me." I didn't think he'd get it, but he was still sitting behind the wheel thinking when I walked around and opened his door. The alarm had rearmed; it wailed momentarily but he keyed it off in irritation and hopped down, tossing the jacket inside. "It's got to relate to how bad things have gotten. It's a shadow war, man. This Dam is *for* something."

"Of course it's for something." Walking beside me, he shot me that blue-eyed look that made me want to smack him and kiss him all at once. "You know what they used to say about the Colorado before they built it—too thick to drink, and too thin to plow. The Dam is there to screw up the breeding cycles of fish, make it possible for men to live where men shouldn't be living. Make a reservoir. Hydroelectric power. Let the mud settle out. It's there to hold the river back."

It's there to hold the river back. "I was thinking just that earlier," I said as we walked across the floodlit Dam. The same young girl from that afternoon leaned out over the railing, looking down into the yawning, floodlit chasm. I wondered if she was homeless and how she'd gotten all the way out here—and how she planned to get back.

She looked up as we walked past arm in arm, something reflected like city glow in her eyes.

The lure of innocence to decadence cuts both ways: cities and angels, vampires and victims. Sweet-eyed street kid with a heart like a knife. I didn't even need to flip up my eyepatch to know for sure. "What's your name?" I let the tire iron slip down in my sleeve where I could grab it. "Goddess leave you behind?"

"Goddess works for me," she said, and raised her right fist. A shiny little automatic glittered in it, all blued steel with a viper nose. It made a 40's movie tableau, even to the silhouetting spill of floodlights and the way the wind pinned the dress to her body. She smiled. Sweet, venomous. "And you can call me Angel. Drop the crowbar, kid."

"It's a tire iron," I answered, but I let it fall to the cement. It rang like the bell going off in my head, telling me everything made perfect sense. "What the hell do you want with Las Vegas, Angel?" I thought I knew all the West-coast animae. *She must be new.*

She giggled prettily. "Look at you, cutie. Just as proud of your little shadow city as if it really existed."

I wished I still had the tire iron in my hand. I would have broken it across her face.

"What the fuck is that supposed to mean?" Stewart. Bless him. He jerked his thumb up at the spill of light smirching the sky. "What do you call that?"

She shrugged. "A mirage shines too, but you can't touch it. All you need to know is quit trying to break my Dam. You must be Jack, right? And this charming fellow here—" she took a step back so the pistol still covered both of us, even as Stewart dropped my hand and edged away. *Stewart.* "—This must be the Suicide King. I'd like you both to work for me too."

The gun oscillated from Stewart's midsection to mine. Angel's hand wasn't shaking. Behind her, Goddess strode up the sidewalk, imperious in five-hundred-dollar high-heeled shoes.

"I know what happens," I said. "All that darkness has to go somewhere, doesn't it? Everything trapped behind the Dam. All the little ways my city echoes yours, and the big ones too. And Nevada has a way of sucking things up without a trace. The Dam is a way to control it. You sink it all into Vegas until you want it."

Stewart picked up the thread as Goddess pulled a little pearl-handled gun out of her pocketbook. He didn't step forward, but I felt him interpose himself. *Don't! Don't.* "Let me guess," he said. "*The early part of 2100?* What happens then?"

"Only movie villains tell all in the final reel." Goddess had arrived.

Angel cut her off. "L.A. is built on failure, baby. I'm a carnivore. All that pain has to go somewhere. Can't keep it inside: it would eat me up sure as I eat up dreams. Gotta have it for when I need it, to share with the world."

"The picture of Dorian Gray," Stewart said.

"Call it the picture of L.A." She studied my face for a long time before she smiled. All that innocence, and all that cool calculated savagery just under the surface of her eyes. I wondered who'd she'd been before she died. If she'd worked her tail off for L.A., before L.A. claimed her. "Smart boys. Imagine how much worse I would be without it. And it doesn't affect the local ecology all that much. As you noted, Jackie, Nevada's got a way of making things be gone."

"That doesn't give you the right."

Angel shrugged, as if to say, *What are rights?* "All chiseling that date off would do is remove the reason for Las Vegas to exist. It would vanish like the corpse of a twenty-dollar streetwalker dumped in the high desert, and no one would mark its passing. Boys, you're not *real.*"

I felt Stewart swelling beside me, soul-deep offended. It was my city. His city. And not some vassal state of Los Angeles. "You still haven't said what happens in a hundred years."

Goddess started to say something, but Angel hushed her with the flat of her outstretched hand. "L.A.," she said, that gesture taking in everything behind her—Paris, New York, Venice, shadows of the world's great cities in a shadow city of its own—"Wins. The spell is set, and can't be broken. Work for me. You win too. What do you say to that, Jack?"

"Angel, honey. Nobody really talks like that." I started to turn away, laying a hand on Stewart's arm to bring him with me. The sledgehammer nudged my leg.

"Boys," Goddess said. Her tone was harsh with finality.

Stewart fumbled in his pocket. I knew he was reaching for his knife. "What are you going to do," he asked, tugging my hand, almost dragging me away. "Shoot me in the back?"

I took a step away from Goddess, and from Angel. And then Stewart caught my eye with a wink, and—*Stewart!*—kept turning, and he dropped my hand . . .

The flat clap of a gunshot killed the last word he said. He pitched forward as if kicked, blood like burst berries across his midsection, front and back. I spun around as another bullet rang between my Doc Martens. Goddess skipped away as I lunged, shredding the seam of my pants as I yanked the sledgehammer out. I had it up like a baseball bat before Stewart hit the ground. I hoped he had his knife in his hand. I hoped he had the strength to open a vein before the wound in his back killed him.

I didn't have time to hope anything else.

They shot like L.A. cops—police stance, wide-legged, braced, and aiming to kill. I don't know how I got between the slugs. I felt them tug my clothing; one burned my face. But I'm One-eyed Jack, and my luck was running. Cement chips stung my face as a bullet ricocheted off the wall and out over Lake Mead. Behind Angel and Goddess, a light pulsed like Stewart's blood and a siren screamed.

Stewart wasn't making any sound now and I forced myself not to turn and look back at him. Instead, I closed the distance, shouting something I don't recall. I think I split Goddess' lovely skull open on the very first swing. I know I smashed Angel's arm, because her gun went flying before she ran. Ran like all that practice in the sands of Southern California came in handy, fit—no doubt—from rollerblading along the board walk. My lungs burned after three steps.

The lights and sirens were coming.

Almost nobody *runs* in Las Vegas, except on a treadmill. It's too fucking hot. I staggered to a stop, let the hammer fall clanging to concrete as I stepped over Goddess' shimmering body, and went back for Stewart.

His blood was a sticky puddle I had to walk through to get to him.

He'd pushed himself over on his side, and I could hear the whimper in his breath, but the knife had fallen out of his hand. "Jack," he said. "Can't move my fingers."

I picked it up and opened it. "Love. Show me where."

"Sorry," he said. "Who the hell knew they could shoot so fucking well?" It came up on his lips in a bubble of blood, and it had to be *his* hand. So I folded his fingers around the handle and guided the blade to his throat.

The sirens and lights throbbed in my head like a Monday-morning migraine. "Does it count if I'm pushing?"

He giggled. It came out a kicked whimper. "I don't know," he said through the bubbles. "Try it and see."

I pushed. Distorted by a loudspeaker, the command to stop and drop might have made me jump another day, but Stewart's blood was sudden, hot and sticky-slick as tears across my hands. I let the knife fall and turned my back to the road. Down by my boots, Stewart started to shimmer. We were near where Angel had been leaning out to look down the face of the Dam. The Plexiglas barriers and the decorated tops of the elevator shafts started five feet on my right.

"One-eyed Jacks and Suicide Kings are wild," I muttered, and in two running steps I threw myself over the wall. Hell, you never know until you try it. A bullet gouged the wall-top alongside the black streaks from the sole of my Doc.

The lights on the Dam face silvered it like a wedding cake. It didn't seem like such a long way to fall, and the river was down there somewhere. A gust of wind just might blow me wide enough to miss the blockhouse at the bottom.

If I got lucky.

❦

From the outside northbound lane on the 95, I spotted the road: more of a track, by any reasonable standard. I dragged the white Ford pickup across the rumble strip and halted amid scattering gravel. It had still had Stewart's jacket thrown across the front seat after I bribed impound. Sometimes corruption cuts in our favor. A flat hard shape patted my chest from inside the coat's checkbook pocket, and the alarm armed itself a moment after I got out.

Two tracks, wagon wheel wide, stretched through a forest of Joshua trees like prickly old men hunched over in porcupine hats, abutted by sage and agave. The desert sky almost never gets so blue. It's usually a washed out-color: Mojave landscapes are best represented in turquoise and picture jasper.

A lot of people came through here—enough people to wear a road—and they must have thought they were going someplace better. California, probably.

I pitched a rock at a toxic, endangered Gila monster painted in the animal gang colors of don't-mess-with-me, and sat down on a dusty rock and waited. And waited. And waited, while the sun skipped down the flat horizon and the sky grayed periwinkle, then indigo. Lights rippled on across the valley floor, chasing the shadow of the mountain. From my vantage in the pass, I made out the radioactive green shimmer of the MGM Grand, the laser-white beacon off the top of the Luxor, the lofted red-green-lavender Stratosphere. The Aladdin, the Venetian, the Paris. The amethyst and ruby arch of the Rio. New York, New York. And the Mirage. Worth a dry laugh, that.

Symbols of every land, drawing the black energy to Vegas. A darkness sink. Like a postcard. Like the skyline of a city on the back of a one-eyed jack in a poker deck with the knaves pulled out.

It glittered a lot, for a city in thrall.

There was a fifth of tequila in Stewart's coat. I poured a little libation on an agave, lifted up my eyepatch and splashed some in my *otherwise* eye. I took a deep breath and stared down on the valley. "Ben Siegel, you son of a bitch. You fixed the chains tight, the ones the Dam forged. Didn't you?"

I drank a little tequila, poured a little on the ground. If you're going to talk to ghosts, it doesn't hurt to get them drunk. Ask a vodun if you don't believe me. And I had ghosts to call, that evening.

I like the plain, soft-spoken magic. A little offering, a few muttered words . . . and then deal with the consequences.

The American and the Russian.
Somewhere in New Jersey, 1964.

Three days—and a successful field deployment—after their rooftop chase of the MI-6 assassin had left them with nothing but a mouthful of feathers, the American wore a path from the sofa to the door, his pistol still in his hand, cursing the bare-boards safe house they found themselves in.

The Russian's clean, cluttered apartment—littered with its piles of books, and books used as bookmarks for other books—even *smelled* foreign; it smelled of tea and caraway seeds and most strongly of roses. Russia had never quite abandoned the medieval penchant for rosewater in favor of Western scents, lemon and pine.

He wished with all his heart he were smelling those roses now. *This* place reeked of dust and stale cat piss, and his pacing wasn't enough to cover the sound of his partner gagging behind the closed bathroom door as if he were trying to cough his heart up his throat.

Another particularly hideous retching fit. The American cursed and stopped pacing, tapped lightly on the flimsy hollow-core door. "Alive in there, boy?"

A pitiful moan, followed by an even more pitiful mumble. "Yes. Unfortunately."

If the Russian couldn't be troubled to dig up some wrath over being called *boy*, he was in worse shape than the American had thought. The American tried the handle: latched. "Open the door."

"Can't—" More coughing, followed by heartrending choking.

"*Open* the *god-damned* door."

A creak of floorboards that the American hoped was a shuffling step. And then the rattle of the latch, and a tired voice muttering imprecations before it was silenced by another coughing fit. The American opened the door carefully so he wouldn't strike his partner, but the Russian staggered back to the toilet and hunched over it again. *God, he looks terrible—*

The American crouched beside his partner and laced fingers through the Russian's hair, raking damp, streaked strands out of his face, ignoring the acid reek of vomit and the nauseous slickness of phlegm. The muscled body in his arms strained and twisted; the American held the Russian steady through another wrenching spasm. "It's all right," he said. "I've got you."

"I want to go home," the Russian said weakly.

"It's not safe to go home yet."

"Logic has nothing to do with it." The Russian shook his head gingerly against the American's hands, his strained neck obviously tender. "Next time, my friend. You will get captured and interrogated with the drugs and the beatings, yes? And I will take the pretty girl to dinner."

"Yes," the American answered, and closed his eyes in silent thankfulness that his partner was well enough to snipe.

"Delightful," the Russian said, and closed the Olsonite toilet lid so he could lay his forehead against the cool porcelain of the tank. "I'll hold you to that."

"We did learn something from your misadventure, however," the American said. He rose from his crouch and went to the medicine cabinet, rummaging until he found a cup and a new, wrapped toothbrush and a bottle of mouthwash. "There's no toothpaste."

"I'm not ready to stand up yet in any case," the Russian said. "What did we learn? I assume you don't mean about the availability of dentifrices."

"We learned that the assassin isn't working for our usual opposition, for one thing—"

"Or we wouldn't be here having this conversation, yes. I don't suppose there are any aspirins in that cabinet?"

"There's Dilaudid," the American answered, over the sounds of his own digging.

"And a sledge-hammer if we spot any cockroaches? At least head-quarters is prepared to help a man die in peace if he drags himself in here gutshot and bleeding, but I'm not sure I want to mix narcotics and veridicals; the result might be worse than a red-wine hangover. Is there aspirin in the wound kit?"

The Russian's voice was stronger already. Perhaps the truth serum—whatever it was—was wearing off without more severe after-effects. "That's in the kitchen. We'll check in a minute. I contacted the old man while you were sick—"

"—I'm still sick—"

"—and they're sending a pickup squad to bring us home safely. But moreover, you're not the only one the assassin has taken a pot shot at lately."

"Who else?" The Russian was interested enough to lift his head. The American poured mouthwash into a Dixie cup and unwrapped the toothbrush, tearing cellophane with his teeth. His partner wouldn't mind.

Much.

Wasn't in any position to protest, in any case. "A female British agent—well, one of their paid amateur investigators, a widow and a scientist, something of a crack shot, I understand—if you know their unaffiliated-agent program—"

"I do; it has some silly overblown name, like every other British or American intelligence operation. Is she alive?"

The American crumpled cellophane, hearing more than professional concern in his partner's dismissal. *Interesting.* The Russian had attended university in England—"She's expected to survive."

"So he attempted to assassinate another MI-6 agent?"

"Apparently."

"It isn't like him to miss. And even less like him to miss two targets in a row. Has MI-6 confirmed that he's gone rogue?"

The American let his expression answer the question, smiling at the Russian's wry flinch.

"Ah, the spirit of inter-agency cooperation."

"Something you should be intimately familiar with, my fine KGB spider—" The American tossed the toothbrush wrapper in the garbage and extended his hand to the Russian. "You haven't barfed in seven minutes, by my watch. Upsadaisy."

"I have run out of organs to vomit up, and my toes are too firmly attached," the Russian answered, but accepted the assistance and stood. The American guided him to the sink.

"Brush your teeth and I'll bring you some water and aspirin, and you can try lying down. I'll wait up for the retrieval team."

"You are a true friend."

"Don't let it get around." The American stood back, permitting the Russian access to the sink. "I'd really like to know how he knew where to ambush us."

"He had been tracking you and knew you had purchased the tickets?" the Russian offered. "That intersection is a natural bottleneck, and he had simply to lie in wait." He dipped the toothbrush in mouthwash and brushed hard, three or four times, before rinsing his mouth first with the remainder of the mouthwash and then with cold water, twice. He dashed handfuls of water on his face, and turned, forcing a game smile, droplets diamond-bright on water-dark lashes when he blinked. "I'm going to shower," he said.·

The American shrugged and turned his back. He didn't want to see the cigarette burns on his partner's chest. "Go ahead. I'll take care of the mess. And we can figure out what we're going to do about the assassin."

"Do we have permission to act?" The shower door slid. The Russian's voice rose over running water, triggering another coughing fit, but the American thought it was only a throat rubbed raw. "Or will it cause an international incident?"

"I was raised Catholic," the American said, crouching to pull the Lysol from under the sink. "I'm a big believer in forgiveness. And one of the girls at headquarters dropped me a hint; routine tracking has turned up the information that he boarded a plane to Las Vegas yesterday morning—"

"Wonderful," the Russian answered. "Las Vegas in July. Remind me to pack a sweater."

"Just be glad there are benefits to taking good care of the administrative pool," the American answered. "Other than prompt attention to our travel arrangements."

"Benefits other than the obvious, you mean? Pass me a towel, please."

"Only if you tell me what it is you find so obvious."

The Russian cleared his throat. The American laughed and lobbed a towel over the cloudy glass door, trusting the Russian to catch it.

"That's not a benefit," he said cheerily. "That's just part of the service, son."

The American and the Russian.
Somewhere over the Mojave Desert, 1964.

The Russian's hand on his shoulder awoke him on the Arizona/Nevada border. The passenger compartment of the aircraft was "darkened for night flying," but the Russian's reading light was on. He reached up to click it off as the American rubbed sleep from his eyes.

"Look, we're coming in over Hoover."

The American leaned over his partner to glance out the tiny window, down through the darkness to the spotlit face of the dam so far below. It was pretty, but he'd seen it a half-dozen times before. The Russian's well-concealed enthusiasm amused him. "You never get tired of flying, do you?"

"It's bourgeois to become jaded," the Russian replied, smiling. The American sat back as the Russian unfolded his newspaper. "We'll be arriving at McCarran Field very soon now."

"Good," the American answered, closing his eyes again. "Wake me up if you figure out what the hell we're going to do when we get there."

He couldn't fall back asleep, however, and found himself peering over the Russian's paper to catch a glimpse out the window as the plane swung over the mountains rimming the Las Vegas valley. A vast blackness lay below them, horizon to horizon, broken only by the grid-marked clump of lights ahead. The night air was clear and the valley flat enough that the American could make out the twin clusters of lights that were Fremont Street and the Strip. He spotted the Desert Inn, the Flamingo, the Dunes, and the Stardust as the plane made its turn to line up with the runway—and then he blinked.

Some optical distortion—a ripple in the window glass or a desert atmospheric inversion layer—caught and multiplied the lights of the city below. The American thought they extended from horizon to horizon, even the casinos impossibly magnified and reproduced, the colors of the lights shifting to greens and purples, the buildings seeming much taller and broader than they should have been. "Hey, you see that?"

By the time the Russian peered over his newspaper, the brilliant, ephemeral effect had passed. "See what?"

The American shrugged and sat back. "For a moment, it seemed like there were ten times as many lights as there should have been. It's gone now."

"How odd." The Russian did glance out the window, and shook his head. "Optical illusion?"

"I imagine." The plane touched down lightly and taxied toward the terminal under floodlights. "You know they allowed aboveground nuclear bomb tests north of here until last year?"

"I read it somewhere, yes." Then, as the plane rumbled to a halt: "When did McCarran start using jetways?"

"Jetways?" A definite thump: the extensible passageway struck the side of the aircraft, and the American glanced at his partner. "Jetways. What do you know? The last time we were here it was still the old rolling stairs." All around them, passengers were unbuckling seatbelts, standing, stretching after the long cross-continental flight. "Well, I guess we're here. Would you hand me my bag, if you don't mind?"

Tribute and the Scholar.
Las Vegas, Summer, 2002.

My plane taxied up to the gate at McCarran International Airport a little after 1:00 a.m. I'm limited to short flights for practical reasons; the good news is, the redeye is usually uncrowded.

I love Las Vegas.

Nobody ever notices me in Vegas. Now that I was on my own, I was thinking of staying on permanently.

Don't get me wrong. I never expected to survive. I thought I'd go down into oblivion with Sycorax, red stain of my borrowed blood on her lips and a fistful of my hair knotted in her hand. I never expected to see another sunrise. Not that I've seen one in twenty-five years, mind, but you know what I mean. But one minute my gut was clenching, twisting around my poisoned dinner, and the next Sycorax was staring at me in glazed shock, her pale hands fastened on her own wax-white throat as she sank to her knees.

If I'd known it would be that easy I would have handled this *years* ago.

If I'd known Jesse would leave me alone for half an hour if I did it . . .

Eighteen hours later, I was on a plane, and less than two hours after that I was stepping across the band of desert heat between the cool of the airplane and the air-conditioned jetway and following the cattle through McCarran's D gates to the tram.

There's a funny thing about Las Vegas. You keep seeing people you think you might halfway recognize. Some of them are minor celebrities, lounge acts, washed-up actors, and pop stars who were the Next Big Thing twenty years back. And some aren't.

So people turned to look at me, one or two, as I made my way from the tram over the gaudy carpet and down the escalators. But they weren't surprised, not at all.

I had no luggage to claim; we learn to travel light. But McCarran makes you exit through Baggage Claim whether you need to or not, and I had "Go Down Moses" stuck in my head, somehow—you know, *Go down, Moses, Way down in Egypt's Land. Tell ol' Pharoah, Let my people go*—and was concentrated on not singing it too loudly where anybody could hear me. Which is how I almost tripped over the spy.

I wasn't supposed to know he was a spy. I was supposed to see an athletic, black-haired white man in a polo shirt and khakis, turning to hand a cased tennis racket to his companion. The other cat was black, broad-shouldered, wearing his hair parted on the side and greased in ringlets in a style I hadn't seen since I was a *young* mortal man. They both reeked of Brylcreem.

It smelled like 1965.

I wasn't supposed to see the way their eyes met for a moment before they glanced over each other's shoulders, either, or to notice that their three-dialed waterproof wristwatches matched. But I've shot up a TV set or two in my time, and I noticed, and stepped wide to go around the pair rather than bumping shoulders with the athlete. A little faster, a little smoother than a mortal man should have managed, and the black man's gaze locked on me like a gunman's sights.

And he blinked, and tilted his head to one side, and then offered a wry, contemplative smile. "King," he said. "I didn't know you were in the game."

"I'm not," I answered without bothering to fix my voice. "I'm the real thing. More or less." And I showed him the fangs.

He stepped back: one, two—the racket case raised defensively in his hand—and I beat it for the exit while his partner was still turning to see what had caused his dismay. There was a taxi waiting.

I took it.

There's real, after all. And then there's *real*.

And if I was going to spend any time in Las Vegas, I was going to have to find out what was going on to bring two of *those* to the streets of Sin City. And not its native media ghosts, either.

No, a couple of strangers in town.

The Assassin and the Man Behind the Curtain.
Las Vegas. Summer, 2002.

There were two men already in the office when the assassin got there; one dead, and one alive. The dead one stood behind the live one. The living one was hunched over a laptop computer. The dead one was peering over the living one's shoulder, trying not to drip brains down his back.

Bugsy Siegel looked up when the assassin walked through the door, and frowned. For a dead man, he had an effective stare. He hadn't died pretty, and it still showed.

Ghosts don't heal, and when Bugsy was shot, the hitman put enough lead into the back of his skull that much of his face came off the front side when it exited. One eye was missing, the cheekbone shattered, the empty socket oozing clotted blood and matter. The back of his head was a pulpy mess; it contrasted vividly with his dapper charcoal double-breasted suit.

Even by the assassin's standards, what was left of him wasn't easy to look at. But the slow trickle of gray matter down his skull hadn't slowed him any. "You didn't get him," he said, and walked through the desk and the Mage whose laptop he had been frowning at to glower at the assassin from closer in.

"No," the assassin said. There was no point in denying it. "Hello, Felix," he said.

Felix Luray didn't look up from the computer. "It's the stories," he said, and flexed his hands together to crack his knuckles. "You'll have to find some way to work around it, so they *can* be killed. The bad news is their fans are still out there, keeping them alive. So they're real as . . . real as Robin Hood. Or the Easter Bunny. The good news is, capturing them should be no problem. That's in genre."

"I wouldn't have guessed," the assassin said dryly, and went to pour himself a drink. "And I can tell by the looks on your faces that Angel and Goddess didn't manage any better."

"Goddess is dead," Felix said. "The revenant John Henry Kinkead bashed her skull in with a sledge hammer."

Fumes stung the assassin's nose. The crystal was heavy in his hand, warming quickly from his skin. He sipped. "Well, saves me having to kill her, then. Who's 'the revenant John Henry Kinkead?'"

"The One-eyed Jack," Felix said. "John Kinkead was the third governor of Nevada. He died circa 1904 in Carson City. Fits the name and general description, and the timing's right."

"Huh." Felix was eyeing the assassin's glass speculatively. The assassin poured a second drink and passed it over; Felix poured half the measure on the rug, where it vanished, wicked up without a trace. Bugsy looked pleased. "What does his name win us, Mr. Luray?"

"Perhaps a little symbolic leverage," he said with a shrug, and tasted his drink. "We've got the dam, but a little more never hurts. Jackie gave Benjamin a run for his money a few years back, I hear—"

Bugsy turned his head and spat. It didn't leave a mark on the carpet. "That faggot's no match for a real Mage, Felix. Sure, he knows a little hedge-craft. But it ain't real magic, not the sort of thing you boys used to do."

"Still do," Felix said easily, and tipped out a little more vodka onto the floor.

"Well, yeah," Bugsy said. "But what I mean to say is, there ain't no more like you, Felix. No more like the Prometheans that built the dam, right? Or the railroad."

"No," Felix said, very quietly. "I'm the last."

Bugsy grinned, sending a thick clot of blood skating down his ruined cheek. "See? You won't have no problem with Jackie."

The assassin smiled tightly. He didn't mention his own research and experience, or what they had taught him about Felix Luray, and why he hadn't been invited to the war that had put an end to the rest of the Prometheans. A pity, the assassin thought; he'd found them useful allies in the past, despite their desire to feel that they were pulling all the strings.

Still, half a Mage—a failed Mage, if you preferred, a defrocked one—was better than none.

"So I take it our next objective is neutralizing the other genius, the Stewart boy."

"Not at all," Felix said, swirling his drink and savoring a slow, pleased smile. "Angel took care of that while you were busy in London and New York. Everything's under control."

The One-Eyed Jack and the Steel-Driving Men.
Las Vegas, Summer, 2002.

The John Henrys waited for me on the corner of Third and Bonneville, across the street from the chain-link around the construction site and in the shade of some old elms and a ragged toilet brush of a Mexican fan palm. The right-hand John Henry rested a twenty-pound sledge against his corded sweat-shining dark neck, his other hammer leaned up against the gray cinderblock wall behind him. He wore canvas pants and not much else, and if the girls giggling on the sidewalk in the sweltering heat could have seen him, they would have turned to admire the ridged expanse of his chest.

The left-hand John Henry, skeletal and paper-white behind a luxuriant growth of dark blond moustache and blazing tubercular eyes, treated his terrible cough out of the silver flask in his breast pocket. That hack around a chest full of bloody slime was so much a part of his legend he couldn't get rid of it even dead.

Like the silk cravat with the diamond stickpin, like the nickel-plated six-shooter concealed by the fall of his stylish gray coat. Stylish in 1881, that is. A little out of place as I crossed Bonneville against the light, walking through the wall of thermonuclear Las Vegas sunshine.

While I watched, he fumbled a twist of waxed paper from his waistcoat pocket and transferred a sticky-looking, dark-brown glossy candy to his mouth. The bitter ghost-scent of horehound followed when I paused in front of the dead men. They looked startled to be seen; as I hesitated in the gutter, a brunette in fuchsia short-shorts and not much else walked through the right-hand John Henry, head rocking in time to the beat of her portable CD player. The left-hand John Henry coughed into a silk handkerchief, leaving a spot like the dark heart of a snowy blossom of Queen Anne's lace, and turned to watch the girl wiggle away. I was scared enough of him that my guts turned to water in my belly, but I thought of Stewart and I made myself walk forward. *Ghosts. I called up ghosts.*

The right-hand John Henry puffed up his enormous chest and looked away, free thumb hooked through the loops of his pants. His thighs strained threadbare dun cloth, much mended, as he shifted the hammer on his shoulder. The left-hand John Henry folded the cloth to hide the thumbprint of blood and tucked it into his pocket— the one without the flask. He sighed.

"She's a lady of ill repute, Doc," drawled the right-hand one. I stopped in front of them.

"She's a woman who knows her own mind," the left-hand John Henry—Doc—replied in a rich slow voice like seasoned honey, and drew himself up to face me. "And as for ill repute, I have a little of my own. Some easy virtue, too. Do I know you, sir?"

"No," I said, holding out my hand. I felt them taking in my cargo pants, Doc Martens and earrings, my tattooed biceps, and the ring through my nose. The eyepatch didn't look so out of place in all that. A Cadillac crept behind me, wary of the construction dust. Pale eyes and dark tracked its purring glide. "But my name's Jack. One-eyed Jack, they call me." Neither moved to shake, and I let my hand fall to my side.

It got the smile from the left-hand John Henry I'd half-hoped for. A gambler. And a quick wit, too. "My given name's John, as well."

"It's why I called you back. You, Dr. Holliday. And Mr. Henry, here. You know—"

"I know I'm dead," John Henry said. He looked at the sledgehammer in his hand and set it down, leaned it back against the dust-colored wall. "Where are we?"

"Las Vegas."

"New Mexico? It's changed some." Doc Holliday leaned back on the heels of his shoes and looked up at the pale sky overhead, squinting after a jet contrail.

"Nevada." I shouldn't help but smile. "Around the corner from Fremont Street. And that's not the one you're thinking of either."

"Huh." He turned his head and coughed into his handkerchief again. "Named for the same John Fremont, though?"

I nodded.

"Then that's changed some too, I imagine. What did you bring us back from the grave for, son?"

He died at thirty-six, and I'm over a hundred. But I wasn't about to argue age and life experience with Doc Holliday. Even if I was something more than mortal myself.

"I need help," I said. I had a pretty speech prepared, but looking up—way up—into the frowning brown eyes of John Henry I was left with no room for anything but honesty. Might be because the man was a *symbol* for honesty. I swallowed and tried to turn my attention to Holliday, but it wasn't any easier to meet his eyes. "I'm the One-eyed Jack. The spirit of Las Vegas, its anima. Somebody shot my buddy, and I want to get them back. So I called you up. Namesake rite, tequila, and promises. But since there were two John Henrys who fit the bill, I got the both of you."

A pedestrian edged around me, seeing a ratty one-eyed homeless boy with a lightless dyed-black snarl of hair, standing on a downtown street corner talking to himself. We get that a lot around here: the straights are used to madmen out of doors in Vegas.

"What makes you think we can help with that?"

"You're—" *Who you are. New World demigods in the making, the Chuchulainns and Beowulfs and Yellow Emperors of the Americas. Folklore creatures.*

Like me. "You're Doc Holliday, sir. That there is John Henry the drillman. You're American legends, sir."

Holliday opened his mouth, but a coughing jag took him and he fumbled in his pocket for his flask and drank quickly, neatly, even when I thought he'd choke. The whiskey calmed his cough and he shook his head as he screwed the silver cap back on. "Jack, I never killed but three, four men in my lifetime. And every one of those bastards deserved to die."

John Henry shifted balance beside him, a mountain changing its stance. "I heard it was fifty, Doc."

"Stories grow in the telling, son."

I'd done some reading since Stewart got killed. "Wyatt Earp said you were the most dangerous man he ever knew, and the fastest gun."

Holliday laughed and stroked his moustache, straightened his cravat. "Wyatt never minded stretching a tale till it squeaked protest, and you know what the papers are like." He couldn't hide a pleased smile. "He was right about one thing."

"Doc?"

I was maybe three feet from Holliday. Before I could have moved, even shouted, his revolver was out of the hip holster and leveled at my chest. He cocked the hammer and pulled the trigger so quickly I didn't have time to close my eyes before the report boxed my ears.

So I *saw* the bullet hit my chest, go through, and pass without a whisper of sensation. Holliday laughed and spun his pistol back into his holster. "Ghosts," he said, and took another swig from his flask, squinting in pain. I wondered how the whisky tasted around the cough drop.

"Well," I answered. "I called you up with a task in mind, gentlemen. And you can't go back to rest until we figure out how to do it. So— immaterial or not—I suggest we go get a drink and talk it over."

"I can't drink your liquor," Doc Holliday said, as John Henry fell silently into step on my other side.

"I'll pour it on the ground."

I led them toward the Strip. Dead men don't mind the heat of the sun.

The American and the Russian.
Somewhere in the Desert Inn Hotel & Casino, 1964.

Bram Stoker—that Bram Stoker—said of Teddy Roosevelt that he was a man you couldn't cajole, couldn't frighten, couldn't awe. Some mornings, I wake up certain that the ex-president has somehow managed to get himself reincarnated as my partner. He won't be cajoled. Neither will he be beguiled.

Someone must have lied to him once. Someone I would like very much to find, someday, and talk to.

Because if he weren't so darned frictionless, I might be able to get him to talk to me a little more about what he said about Oswald—

"What are you writing?" the Russian said, toweling his hair as he walked out of the bathroom. The American crumpled the sheet hastily and dropped it into the wastebasket by his knee.

"A letter to my aunt, but it's not coming out well. Ready to go down and see if the café is still serving?"

"What's the expression? No locks, no clocks?" The Russian looked about for his shoes and sat on the bed to tug them on. "And then we need to try to figure out why the assassin's here."

"Because if we know what he's doing—"

"—we know where he is." Their eyes met, and a brief smile passed between them. "What do you plan to do with him if we *do* track him down?"

The American grinned, knowing he looked like a shark. *What do you mean if?* "Kill him. In cold blood. Preferably from a distance and from hiding. We'll work out a justification later."

"Excellent," the Russian said, stamping his feet into his black loafers. "Get your coat. And don't forget your concealed carry card. This is Vegas."

"Yes. They don't care if you have a pistol on your hip, but God forbid there's one under your coat." The American stood and followed his partner out, pausing for a second to hang the Do Not Disturb card and trap a strand of his own dark hair between the lockplate and the tongue. "Breakfast or drinks?"

"Both?" The Russian glanced over his shoulder hopefully, and the American nodded.

Halfway down the fire stairs, the Russian reached back and laid a hand on the American's sleeve, and the American glanced down to meet his partner's sidelong glance. His hand slipped under his coat, but he didn't draw the weapon, though his thumb rested against the safety lever. "Did you hear?"

"—footsteps?" The Russian flattened himself against the wall, one hand raised unnecessarily for silence. The American held his breath.

Always better to get trapped in a stairway than an elevator, if you have to get trapped. Of course, it could be a hotel guest, climbing for exercise.

Two hotel guests. Climbing quickly.

In complete silence, the American skipped four steps backward and crouched with his gun in his hands, covering his partner and the landing below them.

The footsteps came closer, hesitated before the turn. The American heard a noisily indrawn breath. "Gentlemen. If we promise not to draw our guns, will you put yours away?" A familiar voice, pitched in a light, ironical range.

"You tennis-playing son of a bitch," the American called back, delightedly. The Russian had already stepped away from the cinderblock wall and holstered his piece, and was moving forward as two tall, muscular men—one white, one black—gained the landing, shoulder to shoulder, and paused. The American looked from one to the other, at their polo shirts and skin-tight white jeans, a contrast to his own and his partner's sober suit jackets and monochrome ties. He burst out laughing, and was rewarded by a sideways, fleeting smile from the Russian. "What brings you two to Las Vegas?" He extended his hand to the tennis player, who clasped it heartily.

The black man leaned against the wall and crossed his arms, biceps bulging under the tight sleeves of his shirt. "The same thing as you two, I presume," he said, middle Atlantic accent and a light bass range. "Only a little more officially, if the rumors are true."

"We're here to see a man about a horse," the American answered, still grinning. The rational corner of his mind recognized the giddy relief as honorably discharged adrenaline, and his partner's second sideways glance told him the Russian knew it too. *I'm more worried about the assassin than I thought.*

"We're on vacation," the Russian elaborated, extending his right hand to the scholar. They clasped briefly, the scholar muttering something in a language the American didn't recognize, but which his partner apparently knew well enough to answer in. "We were just about to get something to eat. Would you care to join us?"

"Delighted," the athlete said, reversing course lithely. He grinned over his shoulder, and the American spread his hands in bemused acquiescence. Obviously the Russian thought it would serve some purpose for the four of them to be seen in public together, and the other agents were willing to play along.

"Do you, ah, need to head back to your hotel and get ties?"

The athlete shrugged, as if letting the suggestion slide off his back. "At seven o'clock in the morning, in Las Vegas? You don't suppose the Brown Derby's still open this late? Or open again this early?"

"There's a Brown Derby in Las Vegas now? I only knew about the one in Hollywood."

"Age of globalization, man," the scholar said, falling into step beside them. "Age of globalization."

One-Eyed Jack and the King of Rock and Roll.
Las Vegas. Summer, 2002.

I paused on the east side of Las Vegas Boulevard, near the flat rubble-graveled lot where the old El Rancho had stood vacant for so many years, and watched the ghost of Bugsy Siegel smoke a cigar while brains dripped down the back of his collar. Bugsy didn't seem to notice me, or my entourage, but I had the weirdest prickle as if he'd just been staring at me. Anyway, he wasn't the sort of thing I was used to seeing in broad daylight; I preferred the John Henrys, frankly, who followed along single file, barely wincing when the tourists walked through them.

Little ghosts don't interact much, but they can be a damned pain in the ass if they're mad enough, and powerful enough.

Doc Holliday cleared his throat twice before I realized he wasn't coughing. He just wanted my attention. "Speaking of ghosts and shadows, Jack—" He jerked a thumb over his shoulder, and I followed the gesture.

I've seen a lot of strange things. The ghost of an imploded hotel sitting healed and shimmering like a mirage in the evening sunshine wouldn't take a prize by any means, but it was enough to make me blink and rub my eye. *That* was what Bugsy'd been looking at; a parking lot filled with tailfinned Cadillacs and Buicks with five-body trunks, with Nash Ramblers and a '63 Corvette, candy-apple red, a pedestrian in a close-tailored gray gabardine suit coat and a skinny black tie slowing down to take a lingering look. I could see the rubble through his shoes.

"That's unusual," I said. John Henry grunted on my left side, and I chuckled a little nervously. "I hope I didn't call up every ghost in the city."

"If you did, you don't know your own power, Jack." Holliday ducked his head to light a cigarillo, in a logical move for a consumptive, shielding the flame of his Lucifer match with his hands. "That looks to my practiced eye like some sort of a *natural* supernatural manifestation, if you know what I mean. Where did you want to go to go drinking?"

"The Brown Derby," I said, checking the angle of the sun. It would be dark soon enough, and if we hurried we could hit the lull between the dinner rush and the post-show crowd.

If we hurried.

I beckoned the John Henrys along. We had a while to walk still, and I'd need better clothes for the Derby. Lucky for me there are shopping malls the length of the Strip these days. I hung on to my Doc Martens; they'd be fine if a little self-consciously trendy under a suit pant, but the damned things take a year and a half to break in right. I changed in a washroom and stuffed my old clothes in a wastepaper basket. I never liked that T-shirt anyway, and the cargo pants were torn.

We walked into the Brown Derby at 8:15 p.m. and were seated right away. Or, I should say, I was seated. The John Henrys followed, drifting through the table to take their chairs. It wasn't a bad table, in the smoking section with a view of the bar. I had just ordered a vodka martini and was hiding my small talk with the ghosts behind the menu when an Elvis walked past. Which is not unusual in Vegas, by any means.

Except he looked like Elvis Presley. *Nobody* looks like Elvis. I don't mean, nobody dresses like Elvis, or apes his hairstyle, or tries to move like Elvis. Because sure, people do.

I *knew* Elvis Presley. *Nobody* looks like Elvis—except his daughter, that is—and nobody moves like him, either.

And *this* guy wasn't *dressed* like professional Elvi dress. Soft sandy blond hair fell down in his dark blue eyes. Hair not dyed matte black, and not greased into a pompadour. He slunk across the gaudy casino carpet like a panther, total confidence and strength, with the collar of his black leather gothcoat turned up to hide the hammer-edged line of his jaw. He scanned the crowd as if he were looking for somebody, but he didn't quite know who, and it hit me with the force of a kick in the belly who he was. What he was. Who he had to be.

Elvis. Of course. I blinked hard. *Which means Stewart is really—*

—gone.

Surreptitiously, I raised my hand to flip the patch off my *otherwise* eye. And blinked harder, because the second I did it I could smell the old blood and the midnight on him, clots of darkness wound through his soul like so many slimy clumps of rotting leaves. Not what I thought he was, then. Not my new partner, my opposite number, my ally.

Oh, Vegas has enough problems this summer without one of those. Muttering an excuse to the John Henrys, I came around the table on a jagged line to intercept as he made for the casino. I trailed him casually, sidestepping MegaBucks and scurrying around the blackjack tables, trying not to move so aggressively that the eye-in-the-sky would spot me for a threat. I didn't mean to hurt him any; just warn him off. Tell him to head north for Chicago: the windy city's animae have always had a habit of taking in strays.

But I saw him stop, intent on something that had drawn his eye—a flash of golden hair alongside a strobing slot machine light—and my eye followed his, and I saw—

"Stewart?"

Walking hunched forward slightly as he made some sort of a point with his hands—*jab, jab, jab*—animated in conversation with three companions, the hairstyle different, longer, but the crooked nose unmistakably the same.

He didn't hear me. I wasn't close.

The vampire's gaze fastened on the four men crossing the casino floor, and he stepped back into the shadows behind a row of video poker machines, obviously eager that Stewart and his three companions shouldn't see his face. I glanced after the vampire as he faded from view, but Stewart took precedence. And if the bloodsucker chose to stay in my city, I'd run across him again eventually.

I hurried toward Stewart, making a mental survey of his companions as I came, trying to decide if an intercession was in order, or an introduction. Introduction, I decided. By the tenor of the conversation, these were Stewart's friends. Especially the shorter of the two strong-chinned, slender, black-haired men, who bore a superficial resemblance to one another. The final man was African-American, muscular and athletic, handsome in a rugged rather than a Tiger Woods sort of way. Familiar, too—but everybody looks like somebody famous, in Vegas.

"Stewart," I called, and held out my hand as the little group drew abreast of me and started to pass me by.

Stewart blinked and turned to me, a thin vertical line between his eyes. "I beg your pardon. Do I know you?" he asked, and my heart thumped once in my chest and went still.

It wasn't him. It could have been, from fifteen feet. From close enough to shake his hand, however . . . no. Not quite. Not the face, and not the faint European accent and subtle precision of pronunciation.

"No," I said, and backed away. "I beg *your* pardon. But you look very much like someone I—"

I used to know.

I turned on the heel of my Doc and went back to the restaurant, cursing myself for failing to follow the vampire instead. Cursing myself for the hope I'd felt, however briefly, and for the fresh sharpness of the broken ache in my chest.

I knew who they were now; the penny had dropped.

Not just not Stewart.

Ghosts. More ghosts, summoned up out of the collective unconscious, called up out of the soup of story. I shook my head, sat down in my still-warm chair, and looked up into the eyes of the memory of two dead men.

At least I'd thought of something the John Henrys could do to help until I figured out how to manage Angel, immaterial or not. I bet they could be pretty good at keeping track of a vampire, if they were careful, and stayed out of sight.

Meanwhile, I could try to figure out what it was that I'd summoned home to Vegas. A namesake rite wasn't supposed to work that way— and I shouldn't have had the power to do it, even if it did. I was starting to think I'd managed to call home every ghost—media, legendary, and the "little" ghosts, the ghosts of the unquiet dead, like Bugsy out there—with even the vaguest of connections to my city.

That could get confusing.

Especially if two or three Howard Hugheses showed up.

Tribute and the Streetwalker with a Heart of Gold.
Las Vegas, Summer, 2002.

It was full dark by the time I left the mint-green glow of the MGM
Grand behind me and walked north, counting the cracks in the
sidewalk. The desert itself was my enemy, but at least the mountains
ringing the valley gave me a long anticipation of sunrise and cut the
sun's descent short when it slid down the sky in the West. Headed for
California and points out to sea.

The skinny kid with the eyepatch troubled me, but I didn't know
why I ran. Hell, I didn't quite know what I was doing in the MGM to
begin with, other than staying out of the sun: they'd be unlikely to
hire an Elvis impersonator. I needed a club, a cabaret. Someplace that
wouldn't expect afternoon shows.

I could live by murder and theft. When I exhausted the resources
Sycorax had left me.

But that doesn't put you on a stage, now does it?

But the kid. Thousand-dollar suit jacket bought off the rack, and a
cheap high-school dye job. Scarred urban combat zone boots peeking
out from under his pinstriped trousers. Hell, maybe he was a rock
star. It wasn't like I'd been keeping track.

Except he'd been sitting at his table pretending not to talk to a
couple of mismatched ghosts, and he'd practically leaped over it to
give chase when he'd seen me. And then I'd run smack dab into
the media ghosts I'd seen earlier, and they'd been all buddy-buddy
with *another* pair, who *also* didn't belong in Las Vegas, all of them
dressed as if it were forty years ago and most of the country watching
television in black and white.

And I could swear I'd seen that eyepatch kid's profile somewhere,
before.

If I couldn't have a milkshake, I was ready to kill for an explanation. But since I didn't see a way to get either, I went out looking for gigs.

I got a little interest, too, even with my shift requirements. It was good to know, after so long, that I could still lay down a tune, and by the time I finished my third cold call I was feeling pretty good about myself. The manager stood me a beer, and I sat down in a booth beside the juke box to pretend to drink it and retie my shoes.

I found myself tidying the saltshakers while I watched a dark-haired girl who was far too young to be in a bar. Any bar, and the guy she was with wasn't quite old enough to be her father. He didn't look like anybody's father, anyway; in fact—

—in fact, he looked a lot like one of the media ghosts I'd ditched in the MGM Grand. The shaggy yellow hair, at least, and his profile when he turned just right. This one looked dazed, though, his eyes not quite tracking as he watched his skinny, no-doubt-about-it-hired-for-the-evening companion play with her French fries. *What kind of a stoner John buys a hooker a meal and watches while she draws in the ketchup?*

Maybe she was his kid sister, after all. Even if they didn't look a thing alike.

"She's trouble, Ace," Jesse whispered in my ear. But I ignored him, or pretended to.

I didn't like him to know how much of a comfort it was, having him there.

She looked up at me and lifted an eyebrow, then, and I saw the glow of city lights in her eyes. "Evening, King," she said. Soprano, no breath control.

"Name's Tribute." I abandoned my beer on the table when I walked over. The blond man scooted away from me at her hand gesture, and didn't quite offer a grunt by way of acknowledgment. He was all twisted up inside himself like macramé—any fool could tell—but when he tracked me with a scared sideways glance I could see the lights shimmering in *his* eyes, too. *Interesting.* They really didn't look like they went together, if you know what I mean.

"Funny sort of a name," she said. "I'm Angel. This is Stewart. He's a local."

"And you're not?"

Her eyes sparkled when she dimpled at me. She reached out and laid one hand on my arm. Her bitten fingernails were painted chipped, glittering green. "I'm from Los Angeles. And I hear you're looking for a job."

"I might be." I was trying to sound casual instead of wary, and I wasn't sure I succeeded. There were thirteen fries on her plate, and seventy-two sesame seeds on the bun of her half-eaten burger. I looked down and straightened the unused place settings. The last thing I needed in my recently simplified life was to get involved in some sort of a turf war between the genii of cities. My kind generally tried to stay out of the way of their kind. Them, and the media ghosts and race memories and legendary men and critters like the sasquatch and the squonk. I worry about spending time with any creature who is essentially a story made flesh. They change too much, too easily— and too many of them aren't even aware that a world outside their circumscribed reality even exists.

I ran into Dracula once. I'm hoping I never meet Buffy the Vampire Slayer. She'd kick my ass. "It would depend on the job."

"Bodyguard?" She smiled and reached out to take Stewart's hand when he curled himself back into the corner of the booth, drawing his heels up onto the vinyl like a child. He tugged his hand free and wrapped the arm around his knees, shivering. I couldn't quite tell if the look in his eyes was beseeching or simply flat blue madness, and I glanced back down at the girl.

"That's not really my kind of gig, baby—"

"King," she interrupted, tossing her hair over her shoulder. "Do you want to hustle in a dive like this for people who have no idea what you really were? Who'll think you're a *bad* imitation because they've stopped seeing how *bad* all the other imitators are?"

It was the wrong tack to take. Or maybe I was just tired of her coy, self-conscious gestures. Girls these days have an edge on them I don't remember from before; they were like cagebirds then, pampered doves, their naiveté the core of their charm.

Or maybe I'm talking about myself again.

"Take your time," she said, before I could say no. "Think about it. I'll find you again and we'll talk. Come on, Stewart."

I threw a twenty on the table to cover their tab, and stood up to let him follow her out.

The Russian and the Three Capitalists.
Somewhere in Las Vegas. 1964.

The Russian expected trouble. Which wasn't unusual: he always expected trouble. Although it was true that conditions for Americans who weren't white Anglo-Saxon Protestants weren't *quite* as horrid as he'd been raised to believe, back home, they were bad enough. And Vegas wasn't called the Mississippi of the West for nothing.

So he was surprised and pleased when they were seated immediately, and not even tucked away in a corner near the kitchen doors.

"Man," the scholar said as the food arrived, laying his napkin across his lap. "Did we order enough?"

The American grinned as the athlete and the Russian simultaneously reached for the fruit plate. "Have you ever seen my partner eat?"

"No," the scholar answered, hands deft as he sorted his silverware. "Have you seen mine?" He jerked his head sideways, at the rapidly diminishing pile on the tall man's plate. "I have no idea where he puts it."

The Russian, already chewing, kicked his partner lightly under the table. The American's mouth closed with an audible snap, and he stuffed a bite of bread inside it to keep the words plugged up. "So," the American said, when he'd washed his mouthful down with steaming coffee, "can somebody explain to me why we think it's wise for all four of us to be sitting in a public place when we're on the hunt for a rogue agent?"

"Simple," the athlete answered, without looking up from his plate. "We're bait. This Cobb salad is the best. And it's huge. You should try some." He leaned back from his dish, raising his fork out of the way as if he expected his tablemates to lunge for the salad like a pack of feral dogs.

"If we're bait, who's our backup?" The American leaned forward, interested now. "And how did we wind up drafted?"

"You were in the wrong place at the wrong time. Also, the Department briefed us on New York." A grin on the scholar's face as he lowered his voice—not to a whisper that might attract attention, but rather to a murmur. "The backup is classified, but they're from an agency that has an interest in protecting MI-6's reputation even if MI-6 won't do it itself."

"A team the assassin won't expect," the athlete finished for his partner, resuming his relationship with the Cobb salad. "Because he thinks one of the partners is badly hurt."

The Russian chuckled. "The English girl. It is good to hear she's on her feet again."

"We heal fast."

"So I've noticed. That doesn't answer the question of why we join you in serving as—*bait*."

The scholar nudged his partner, who gave him a dirty look from under a falling dark forelock. "You're not going to fit into your tennis whites if you keep eating like that."

"Perhaps we can play, later," the Russian said.

The athlete looked up, a predatory grin creasing his face. "Five dollars a game?"

"On my salary?"

"My partner is cheap," the American said, and the Russian rolled his eyes.

"Who is it that is always borrowing money from whom?"

"Cheap, but well-spoken—"

The scholar coughed, twining his fingers together over his plate. He had enormous hands, boxer's hands. "You wind up helping because your faces are recognizable. Your identities are public and you're already targets. And it's not like you two have to maintain a cover. So it doesn't destroy your usefulness if you're made."

"Our controller put you on to us, didn't he? We're supposed to be here on vacation; the home office takes no responsibility for this mission."

The scholar grinned around his buttered bread. "Our home office does. At least State is staying out of this one—"

"They can have it, if they want it. But it's not exactly their cup of tea. They're better with conspiracies." The American turned his fork in his fingers, contemplating the light reflecting from the tines. "I don't know how you two live undercover all the time."

"Oh, it's not so bad. See the world, meet interesting people—" The athlete spoke with his mouth full of salad.

"—and be captured and tortured by them," the Russian finished. "Are you going to eat the rest of that dinner roll?"

"No," the American answered, and pushed him the bread plate, then looked across the table at the scholar and shrugged as if to say, *what are you going to do?* "I don't suppose you know what the assassin is playing at, do you?"

"Our English friend has a theory." The athlete's fork described a trembling circle in the air as he washed his salad down with sparkling water.

The Russian poured tea from the little pot on the table, surprised at the quality. Most Americans seemed to think that adequate tea was a matter of dunking a paper bag full of fannings into water that had been allowed to over-cool. This was brewed properly, boiling water over loose leaves. Earl Grey. He softened his voice, holding the cup to his lips to conceal the outline of his words, and modulated his tone to hide any trace of concern. "Will we meet the English team?"

"Not until the affair is over, if everything goes according to plan." The athlete forked through his salad, ferreting out crumbles of bacon and egg. "With any luck, the assassin will think they're incapacitated in England."

"Tell me the theory."

The athlete offered them both a wry grin. The American put his fork down and reached across the table for the saltshaker, idly leaning it at an angle in a vain attempt to balance it. It wobbled and fell; he caught it and tried again.

"You're doing it wrong," the athlete said, before he could make a third attempt.

The American looked up. "Ah, excuse me?"

"You're doing it wrong." His capable hand brushed the American's square-fingered one aside; the Russian glanced up for a moment and saw the wry, almost patronizing twist of the scholar's lips. The Russian traded a quick flash of a grin with the scholar, sure their partners were too engaged in their ridiculous competition to notice.

The athlete lifted the saltshaker from the American's fingers and tilted it upside down, letting grains scatter on the tablecloth. He pushed them into a pile with his fingertips and angled the base of the shaker against it lightly and precisely. The Russian held his breath as the athlete opened his fingers like the teeth of a crane and lifted his hand away.

The shaker never moved.

"Bravo," the American said, softly, and the scholar slapped the edge of the table and made the saltshaker clatter down on its side.

"Oh," he said, "the wonderfulness of you."

The Russian hid his smile behind his palm until he got it under control, set his teacup down, and leaned forward, elbows on the table as he drew a licked finger through the tumbled grains. The hairs on his nape shivered; they were being watched. "You American spies are all alike."

"Pampered?"

"Pah." The tea got cold quickly in these little china cups. Glasses were better. "Americans know nothing of pampering—Smug, I mean," he said, interrupting himself.

"You were worried about the widow?" The athlete dusted his hands together, lips pursing.

"The Englishman's partner is an old friend. I was concerned." Ignoring his partner's amused, sideways blink. "Share the theory, if you would."

The scholar's expressive lips twitched. "We think it has a bunch to do with your partner, in fact." He darted a glance at the American,

ONE-EYED JACK

who choked on his coffee. "Your partner, the widow's partner, and my partner—"

"Why would she and I be the targets, then?" The Russian leaned forward, intrigued.

"The widow, you, and myself. Work with me, man."

The Russian glanced at the American to see if perhaps he understood. The American raised his shoulders and tipped his head in his trademark exaggerated shrug.

"Because the assassin works alone." The scholar's tone made it seem as if the answer was obvious.

The Russian pursed his lips slightly and shook his head. "I'm sorry," he said. "I just don't understand what that has to do with anything. He works alone, so he thinks other agents must, as well?"

"Sure, if he's going to consume them."

"Con—" The American set his coffee cup down with a rattle that betrayed the unsteadiness of his hand. "Like, 'Two Bottles of Relish'?"

"Munch munch. Yum yum." The tennis player's grin widened cartoonishly. "Our partners are too different. But you and I—" an eloquent gesture with his fork "—have a great deal in common. And in common with the assassin."

"And the Englishman," the scholar added.

Something still tickled the back of the Russian's neck, and he gave the appearance of paying rapt attention to the conversation while, in fact, his eyes flickered from one reflective surface to another. He sat back in his chair, gnawing on a fingernail as the American protested. "But what does that have to do with *any*—"

And then the scholar and the athlete exchanged a look that the Russian knew very well: it was a look he had traded with his own partner many, many times. And the scholar shook his head, and said, "Pal, they don't know."

The athlete's eyes got wide, and the fork moved back and forth again. *You-me-them?*

The American ran a thumbnail along his jaw. "We don't know *what*?"

The Russian cleared his throat as a flash of movement in a silver cream pitcher on an adjoining table finally resolved itself into the image he'd sought. The black-haired young man in the strangely cut suit who had accosted them on the casino floor. Watching over his shoulder from a dark table in the corner. "Gentlemen," he said. "Explanations may have to wait. I believe we are being observed."

The American glanced over his shoulder, abrupt and unsubtle. The Russian felt him about to rise from his chair and braced himself to stand, but the athlete reached out and placed a hand on the American's sleeve. "Talk to us before you talk to him," the athlete said, when the American's golden-brown eyes locked on his own near-black ones.

The American hesitated, glanced at the Russian, and shook his head. "I'm just going to go make friends," he answered. "You can stay here if you prefer."

Silence, and then the athlete shook his head and withdrew his hand. "I think my man and I had better be there to hear this."

John Henry Holliday and the Ghost of a Good Time.
Las Vegas. Summer, 2002.

The legendary ghost of Doc Holliday followed a vampire through the neon streets of Las Vegas and wondered—without really caring—how in the Lord's name he'd come to find himself here. On the other side of the Rocky Mountains, on the other side of the millennium, untouchable and alone.

Alone except the close-mouthed mountain of spiritual residue strolling along on Doc's left, his hammer hanging through a reinforced loop in his canvas trousers and swinging with each stride that made two of Doc's. Doc, hurrying to keep up, unwrapped a horehound drop and popped it into his mouth to stave off the cough. It seemed unfair that he still coughed, though he didn't breathe. At least he never ran out of candy.

The second spate of hacking made John Henry check his stride a little and glance around. "Begging your pardon, Mister Holliday," he said, "but the vampire can leg it." He stumbled over the word *vampire*.

Without breath for talking, Doc waved him on. He hadn't let consumption keep him from riding, shooting, or doing what needed doing when he was alive. That wasn't about to change because he happened to have passed on.

"Makes you wish for a medium," Doc said, when a traffic signal had slowed the vampire down long enough that he'd gotten his wind back.

John Henry gave him another unreadable glance, and Doc spat blood into his handkerchief.

"Ectoplasm," Doc said. "If we had some, we could drape it over our immaterial feet and trip him."

The steel driver had a good laugh, cavernous and resonant. "Do you think he might notice if we did that, Mister Holliday?"

"He might," Doc said. "He just might. But at least it would slow him down."

The Assassin is Troubled.
Las Vegas. Summer, 2002.

The assassin squinted through a telescopic sight that, for once, was not attached to a firearm, cursing convenience. *Too* convenient, rather, that all of his targets should gather in one place, at one time. Too convenient, and a bit unsettling that they had followed him successfully to Las Vegas.

He must have been careless. Carelessness would not do.

He would have to manufacture a convincing errand here in Sin City. The spies couldn't be permitted to discover the purpose of his visit, to discover his links to Angel. At least not before he could remove the Russian and the scholar, and . . . prevent their partners from reporting in.

He needed them. But he didn't need them here, and he didn't need them now. What he needed here and now was a sacrifice—and a ghost would not suffice. He pushed his forelock out of his eyes irritably and frowned.

"All stories are true," he muttered under his breath, pocketing the scope and fading behind a half-wall as the four men slid their chairs back and stood, as one. "But some stories are truer than others."

Which made him think about pigs.

Which made him think about the Russian, and laugh.

One-Eyed Jack and the Four of a Kind.
Las Vegas. Summer, 2002.

He didn't *really* look that much like Stewart. Not really, not now that I was studying rather than reacting. Broken nose, sure, but the jaw was different, and the way he moved, and the muscle on his forearms, and the exact shade of his hair—

I got caught looking, of course.

All four chairs slid back as if they were wired and all four men stood at once as if somebody had pulled on their strings. I didn't rise.

Instead I let the city lights shine in my eye and fixed their apparent leader with a stare. He didn't stop short, which impressed me. I can be pretty intimidating, when I try.

Instead he tucked his hands into the pockets of his trousers without bothering to unbutton his slate-gray suit jacket first. "We're still not whoever you thought we were," he said, an American with a flat Midwestern accent. He slouched, dropping his chin against his collar, his forehead wrinkling as he looked at me through his lashes. "But seeing as this is a second date, I thought it might be interesting to find out a little more about *you*."

The direct regard was meant to be unsettling, the body language disconcerting. He was good at it, and the blond with the accent hung back right where I would catch his cold blue stare any time my eye happened to slide off those of the spokesman. I wasn't about to let that happen, though.

I stood up and extended my hand. "I'm Las Vegas," I said. "But you can call me Jackie."

He drew one hand out of his pocket. His jacket pulled taut, momentarily, over the bulge in his left armpit, and I knew he saw me see it. "Las Vegas," he said, brow creasing more as he straightened and extended his hand. He glanced left and right, as if looking for the cameraman. "You're named after the city?"

"He *is* the city," the black man said in educated tones. "That's what my man here was going to explain to you before you got all hot and bothered."

The American's clasp was dry and callused, and he didn't flinch, although he angled a disbelieving glance at the taller men. Obviously, he thought he was used to getting some pretty strange things in his breakfast cereal.

"Pleased to meet you, Las Vegas," he answered, eyes meeting mine again as our hands dropped apart. "I'm the Wreck of the *Hesperus*. Now that we're acquainted, do you mind explaining why you're following us?"

Oh, what the hell. These are the good guys, right? Always the good guys, modern day knights in their modern-day armor of suit coats and shoulder holsters. That's why the world remembers them, hummed under its breath like the rhythm of a rhyme learned in childhood after half the words have been forgotten. A little something to kick the darkness back.

Sin City's not afraid to talk turkey, even to ghosts. Little ghosts— the real unquiet dead—can be a problem; a lot of the time they haven't got much of themselves left, and the ones that do are generally real angry about something or another. They might not even be people anymore: just collections of energy patterns. Legendary ghosts, like the John Henrys, are strong because they're made up of so many layers of fact and myth and memory. Media ghosts are really just modern legendary ghosts, but they're usually not as powerful, not having been . . . *laminated* out of the stuff of story for so many years. On the other hand, based on their games with the saltshaker, apparently media ghosts can do what legendary ghosts cannot, such as lay hands on things.

And interact with normal mortals.

And like Doc Holliday, all four of these carried guns. "Well," I said, keeping my hands in sight, "how much do you gentlemen know about animae and ghosts?"

"Animae?" the Russian asked, just as the scholar glanced over his shoulder at his partner and said, "some," out of the corner of his mouth.

"Geniuses," the athlete said, his eyes very dark. He held out a hand and I took it; his had ridged callus, like somebody who spends a lot of time holding a golf club or a tennis racket.

The scholar shook his head and shrugged apology at me. "*Genii* is the word the tennis bum is scratching his head over."

"Hey, man—"

It was a game, I realized—and the other pair knew it too, from the sly communicating smile they shared. The Russian stayed a little behind the American, covering his back, as the athlete stepped away. "All right," the American said, scratchy tenor voice and an arched eyebrow. "I'll play the idiot child. What are animae?"

The scholar coughed, and licked his lips. "This was the thing we were just going to explain before we came over here"—he shrugged, and looked helplessly at his partner, and tugged the American's sleeve a little to turn him away—"y'see, you and me, man . . . all of us, really. We're not exactly real."

The American and the End of an Era.
Somewhere in Las Vegas. Summer 1964/2002.

The American looked at the Russian, who crossed his arms and tilted his head before nodding slightly—a gesture that encompassed a fifteen-minute conversation, brought them into concord, and formalized a plan. *We're not exactly real.*

"You have five minutes," the American said. "Go."

The kid knotted both hands in his strangely cut hair. "It'll take more than five minutes, sir. Look—can we maybe sit down? Join me at my table—"

"We have to settle the bill," the athlete said, with a glance back at the spies' own table.

"I run a tab. I'll pay for it. Please. Just sit." He stepped aside and tugged a chair away from the table, turning it to display its seat. "You see, I think it's half my fault you're all here in the desert, and I've got problems of my own. And I'd like to buy you a drink and sort things out."

"My man doesn't drink." The athlete glanced over his shoulder.

The scholar wasn't smiling, and his brow had furrowed a little deeper. He leaned forward and crossed his arms. "I'll take a coffee," he said, and placed himself very definitely in the chair Jackie had drawn out.

"I'll take a coffee too." The Russian sat down across from the scholar.

The American watched, unsettled. *We're not exactly real.* He pulled out the chair beside his partner, while the athlete retrieved one from an empty nearby table, tilted it, and spun it around. The American leaned forward on his elbows once everyone was settled; the chill in his gut wouldn't slack. "All right," he said. "So, Las Vegas. You're the whole box top. Let's, ah, hear it. Explain to me why we're not—"

"—exactly real?" The young man smiled, showing even teeth above a pronounced jaw. "When it comes right down to it, I'm not exactly real either. We're conjured beings, embodiments of the collective unconscious, if you will."

"*Die Zeitgeist*." The Russian, sounding unwilling, but fascinated. The American shot his partner a look; he shrugged. It wasn't an apology. "Funky."

"Prove it," the American said.

"Well, for one thing," the scholar said, leaning back in his chair and stretching his legs, "there was no Brown Derby in Vegas in the sixties—"

"You say 'in the sixties' as if it's something else now."

"It's two thousand and two," the athlete said. "Don't look at me like that, man. I only know 'cause they woke *us* up again. We were walking through all the old ghosts and dreams same as you, caught up in our story."

"Who's they?" the American asked.

The athlete gestured broadly, taking in the restaurant patrons, the casino beyond it, the city and the world. "The ones who tell the stories," he said. "And your next question is going to be, 'What do you mean, ghosts and dreams?' Isn't it?"

"Yes—"

"Take an example." The athlete glanced up at the ceiling. "The MGM Grand wasn't here in the sixties. There wasn't anything here in the sixties. And the Desert Inn, where you're staying—it's a ghost as well. They imploded it. You guys are sort of a memory, something that got left over, created by the world's collective memory of the stories that were told about you."

"Jetways." The Russian, and the American knew that focused tone in his voice very well. It was the tone that meant a clue had just snapped into place, revealing a much larger section of the puzzle. It was a tone he trusted, although he couldn't always follow the twists that brought it on. "Jetways, jetways."

The kid—*Jackie*—was looking at the Russian, a thin smile playing with the corners of his mouth until the American couldn't take it any more and snapped, *"What?"*

"There are no jetways at McCarran Field—"

"There *were* no jetways at McCarran Field," Jackie said calmly. "It's McCarran International Airport now, and the seventh busiest in America."

"The lights I saw when we were flying in." The American's gut gave one more squeeze of denial, and then it settled down and let him think. *When you've eliminated the impossible—*

Hell, it wasn't as if his career hadn't spanned UFO.s, killer robots, and radio controlled vampire bats. His own nonexistence wasn't such a big stretch, after that. "You're telling me I'm a fairy tale? Make-believe?"

He ignored the Russian's sharp, offended stare. Whatever his partner had been about to say was cut off when the waitress arrived, was roundly charmed by the assembled, and departed with their orders. The American looked at Jackie again as Jackie shrugged, one-shouldered, and lit a cigarette. "I'm telling you what I know."

"Fine. All right. I believe you—" He could almost be amused by the surprise his friends evinced at his willingness to believe what they were telling him. Mind control rays, earthquake machines, being told one's life was a mass hallucination: all in a day's work. The coffee came, and he picked up his cup to hide the way his hands wanted to shake. "—now on to the interesting question, Mr., ah—"

"Just call me Jackie."

"—Jackie." Smoke curled around the young man's fingertips and outlined the patch over his eye as he raised the cigarette again, but didn't puff.

"The interesting question. You said you summoned us."

"Yes."

"How? And to what purpose?"

"Ah," Jackie said, and dropped the cigarette in his ashtray before he reached for the creamer. "That's what makes the question so interesting, you see. I'm not exactly sure. But I have a couple of propositions to make, if you like." He locked gazes with the American. Neither looked down.

The mug was burning the American's fingers. He lifted them to his lips and blew on them, and laughed at the back of his throat. "I don't suppose you play chess."

Jackie smiled hard. He was missing a tooth far back in his mouth. "Only for money, my friend."

Tribute Faces the Music.
Las Vegas. Summer, 2002.

Half an hour before dawn, I found my way back to the room I'd rented at the Motel 6 just off the strip. It had enormous windows, but the blackout drapes reached floor to ceiling, and I made sure to overlap them and pin them in place with the chair. One of the consequences of what I am is that I could make out the patterns on the hotel bedspread and carpeting, even in the dark, and so I spent more time than I would have wanted counting the awful repetitions.

The bed was that spongy texture only hotel mattresses have. I squared my shoes underneath, lay down on it and pulled the pillow over my face. It was a little bigger than King-sized, no matter what they called it; I could have laid three of me down side by side.

I couldn't sleep.

By sunrise, I was ravenous.

Sycorax and the poisoning had taken it out of me in more ways than the metaphorical, and I would need something that night if I was going to keep passing for a mortal. And feeding—

Isn't quite what the romantic fancies of novelists and poets and moviemakers would make it. The stable of willing paramours, the idyllic pleasures of the feast—

No.

It's not like that at all.

It didn't matter when I was with Sycorax. I took what she told me when she told me and tried to put it off as long as I could, and I mostly pretended I couldn't hear Jesse. Especially when he asked me to have him exorcised, to let him go.

But things were different now that I was on my own. I found I had qualms.

In addition to my qualms, I had questions. Like Angel and Stewart, and why Angel was out of her city. And why they were with each other, and not with their own partners. And what was *wrong* with Stewart.

I rolled over in the dark behind drawn curtains, keeping a healthy distance from the scalding brightness that glowed around the edges of the blackout curtains and contemplating whether coming to Vegas had been such a good idea.

It didn't have to be here. I knew that.

I wanted it to be here. Vegas had changed even more than I had; I barely recognized the place. But me and Sycorax had been traveling for the better part of three decades and it wasn't like I could just go home to Tupelo. I haven't got much good to say about Sycorax, bless her black little heart, but twenty-five years with her filled in the gaps in a public school education pretty well. And besides. Las Vegas was a place where I could perform, and nobody would find it strange that they never saw me out in the sunshine.

I could *pass*.

There's nothing more pathetic than an insomniac vampire.

I sat up in bed, reached for the remote, and turned the television on.

Maybe forty minutes later, the corridor door opened. I'd heard the footsteps pause in front of it, but I didn't get off the bed, even though it didn't sound like a chambermaid. They usually don't wear military boots.

Once he opened the door, I caught the scent of leather and sweat and nicotine and the blood under his skin, and then I didn't need to turn. The black-haired kid in the suit and Doc Martens slipped inside and shut the door behind himself.

"King," he said, smart enough to stay in the narrow corridor with the bathroom on one side and the closet on the other and to keep his back to the door, "we've got to talk."

"How did you find me?" Not bothering to disguise my voice for once. Even though he had to be expecting it, he startled: fresh salt sharp in the cool musty air. His flickering heart kicked up a notch.

"I got lucky," he said, layers of irony lacing his voice. Something there I'd have to tease out someday. I didn't turn to look directly, but I saw him move out of the corner of my eye. He jerked his chin at the television. "You gonna shoot that?"

"Nah," I answered, thumb on the mute button. "It's too much of a pain in the ass when you haven't got a road manager to fill out the paperwork. Besides, I haven't got a gun. My next question is supposed to be how you got through the locked door, but that's easy. So—how'd you recognize me?"

The hurt in his voice was thick and evidently artificial. "You don't remember me, King?"

"I go by Tribute, these days." I left the remote on the bed when I stood up and tightened the covers. The rug caught at my socks as I turned to have a look at him. Just a mortal boy, but it would be cocky to let him get in between me and the window in daylight. "The King—that's somebody else. Where should I remember you from?"

"Vegas," he said, stepping forward so the bathroom light would fall across his face. One eye was covered by the eyepatch. The other one sparkled in a way I'd seen too much of lately. I squinted at the face, though—the eyepatch stood out, and there was no telling what color his hair was under a couple of gallons of Gothic black. He looked a bit like Dean Martin, maybe—a much skinnier Dean, with higher cheekbones and a thinner nose—and when I pictured him with shaggy dark brown hair or a slicked DA, I nodded.

There are always people around the entertainment business whose role is never made particularly clear. They're attached to somebody, or they know somebody, or somebody owes them a lot of favors or a lot of money. They're glad handers and compromisers and the sort of people who throw parties that nobody dares miss. I'd seen this kid before, all right, and I'd thought at the time he was one of those people.

A good-looking little pansy, nice enough, better conversationalist than me.

But he hadn't aged a day in thirty years, and gold-and-white streetlights shimmered behind his unpatched eye. Yeah. I knew his name. "Jackie."

"You *do* remember." He folded his arms and stepped back, leaning, the crease in his trousers pulling tight as he kicked one foot up and braced the sole against the door.

"Yeah," I say. "I think I gave you a Cadillac."

A quick look down, and he scratched his ear. "It wound up welded to a stand at the 15 and Jones a few years back, being used as a billboard. They painted it pink. Perfect symbol of Las Vegas, if you ask me."

"Yeah. Perfect. I didn't know you were Vegas, Jackie."

"Would you have treated me any different if you did?"

"At the time, I'd never heard that cities had genii and I didn't believe in vampires or werewolves, so probably not."

He didn't look down and his heart didn't skip when I smiled, and I smiled wide enough that even human eyes would catch the way my front upper teeth hooked over the bottom row. "You're here to run me out of town."

His breathing quickened, just a touch. The lines beside his eyes deepened. I almost heard the incidental music shift tempo, a little bit faster, a little bit louder. "I came to ask what you thought you were doing here."

"Just moving from Memphis to the Luxor," I said. He gave me the blankest look ever, and I sighed. No use wasting any jokes about the underworld on him either; he wouldn't get any more use out of them than I would have back in 1962. "Just looking for a place to stay out of the sun for a while."

"It seems unfair somehow that you didn't need my permission to be here."

"Walking into a city isn't like walking into somebody's house—"

"Las Vegas *is* my house. And don't you forget it, King—"

"—it's more like walking into somebody's hotel room." As dryly as I could pull off, and to his credit, he tipped his head to the left, acknowledging the hit. Hah. I wondered if I would have been that clever in the old days, if I'd given myself half a chance.

Probably not. As Ted Williams once said, if you don't think too good, it's best if you don't think too much.

"Touché," Jackie said. "We still have a problem, King. What are we going to do about you?"

"I've got no interest in hunting your city out, kid."

"I've got no intention of letting you hunt my city, King. And I'm older than you. I just aged better, is all."

What was his word? Touché. "Most people did. But that's all behind us now, isn't it? Tell me something, Jackie—"

I let it hang but he didn't jump in again, and he didn't uncross his arms. I wondered if he had a stake up his sleeve. Rowan and garlic, and a cross of silver threaded on a chain around his neck.

There was no shortage of crossroads near here to bury the body under. My lip twitched up; I wondered if I could go on down to one and sell my soul for the power to sing the blues, the way old Robert Johnson was supposed to have done.

He was smiling at me smiling, and so I smiled right back. "—what can you think of that belongs in Vegas more than me?"

He didn't blink. "Sunrise, King. I'll give you tonight to set your affairs in order and to get out of town. For old time's sake, I'll give you tonight. I'd head for Salt Lake. Not a lot of myth brewing up there, and those boys don't keep a very good eye on their town."

"Mormons taste like shit," I said when he hesitated. "All that clean living." His lip curled, but I didn't manage to crack him up.

"You can't stay here. I've got too much on my plate right now to even think about having a vampire in town."

I'm embarrassed to admit it took that long for the penny to drop. I should have listened a little better to old Ted. "Your full plate, Jackie . . ."

He nodded, his one eye gleaming in the shadows, his gaze locked on mine.

"Has that got anything to do with why your other half is running around Las Vegas with a genius from LA?"

Touché, indeed. *Now* his heart thumped, and I smelled the cold sweat on his skin as he came toward me. Too smart to walk out into the room, but he was just out of arm's reach when he stopped.

"What do you know about Stewart, King?"

"Call me Tribute," I said for the second time. "Give me your parole, Jackie, and I'll give you mine, and come sit down and we'll crack open the minibar, and I'll tell you."

"Your parole?" Incredulous: his rising eyebrows shifted the eye-patch enough to show a pale thread of untanned skin on his cheek. "You're going to promise me you won't hunt in Vegas? I don't really think—"

"Don't be dense. Of course I can't promise that." I stepped back, away. Closer to the window, but careful of the white-hot glow that still limned the edge of the curtain. "But I won't take any of yours, and I won't take anybody you'll miss."

He was watching, measuring, but I had the advantage. I could smell the eagerness on him, the need to know trembling on his skin. It smelled like a win.

I held my peace, humming a few bars of a Big Mama Thornton standard as I swung an armchair around, where it wouldn't be too close to the light.

He stepped into the room. "What do you know about Stewart?"

"It's not much, baby."

"I'll take it."

"I can stay?"

He stopped. His lips twisted, and he turned away to inspect the rack of bottles on top of the minibar. "Bit early for the hard stuff."

"Did you get any sleep last night?"

"This is Vegas. Baby. Nobody sleeps."

He waited for me to look. His decision hung on the air around him like the smell of blood, delicious and thick. He'd have liked to have hit me; his frustration was metallic, harsh.

"How do I know you're not jerking my chain?"

"If you don't like my peaches, Jackie—"

"It's not shaking your tree that concerns me."

He picked a mini and cracked the seal, a sharp, limited sound. The scent of bourbon filled the hotel room and I sneezed.

"All right," he said, and knocked the whole bottle back without bothering to dump it in a glass. He put it down and stepped away; I tidied it against the others. "Screw it. Tell me what you know, King, and I'll tell you if you can stay."

The Assassin and the Ghosts of Gods.
Los Angeles. Summer, 2002.

It had been a long time indeed since blood—with or without the trappings of authority—had bothered the assassin. He wouldn't flinch from the blood of a cop.

Not even the need to do it eye to eye, and hand to hand.

The assassin climbed the steps two at a time, the carpet sticky beneath his shoes where it wasn't threadbare. He paused at the landing and looked up. Caught the eye of Angel in a red pleather skirt, descending. Her hips swayed as she danced over worn treads to the industrial strains of Objekt 775. The music, loosely so termed, blasted from a chopped Honda Civic parked under a partially burned-out sign visible through the rain-streaked window on the landing.

The window was stuck halfway open. The sign read *Gilbert Hotel* if you added the shapes of the unlit letters.

Angel nodded, and the assassin nodded back. "He's in the room?"

She smiled, an expanse of pricey dental work, and held up a hand to show a buck fifty in quarters pinched between her finger and thumb.

"Two twenty-seven. I told him I hadda buy rubbers." She winked, scraping a platform sole across the edge of the stair to cock her hip, and then made doe eyes. "Fifteen minutes all you need?"

"It won't take longer," the assassin said, and turned around to smile at her derrière as he passed her on the flight.

She'd left the door unlocked. The assassin slipped on a pair of white cotton gloves and turned the handle silently. The cop was in the bathroom with the door just cracked; he hadn't thrown the chain.

If he'd had the opportunity to live more than a day or two, he might also have had the opportunity to learn better. "That was quick, sweetheart," he called over running water.

The assassin kept his back to the wall, his shoes shining despite the muddy streets outside, and slid his right hand under his immaculately pressed lapel to retrieve the Walther PPK from his shoulder holster. The silencer screwed down oiled threads like a kiss gliding down a woman's belly.

The assassin thumbed the safety off.

"Don't call me sweetheart," he snapped, and shouldered aside the door.

The cop had stripped his shirt and his bullet-proof vest off, and stood before the mirror clad in a white singlet and his uniform pants. A wad of money lay crushed up on the scarred bathroom counter; peeled silvering on the back of the mirror and the sickly overhead light gave the cop's reflected face the appearance of leprosy. He was half-bald, Caucasian, a small paunch doming his belly. The assassin caught sight of his own chiseled face in the mirror over his target's thickly muscled shoulder, his black hair drooping over one gray eye, his scar livid white against skin flushed with excitement. He leveled the Walther.

The cop half-turned, eyes wide, reaching with a knuckle-crushed hand for the automatic holstered at his hip. He never touched it.

The assassin grouped two bullets through his target's heart, then sank the third one in between his eyes while he was still falling, scattering blood and brains and bits of white like a dropped china bowl. The loudest sound was the crack of the bathroom mirror as a tumbling bullet exited the dead man's body and punched through glass to the wall behind.

The assassin met Angel in the lobby four and a half minutes later. The blood hadn't spotted his shoes.

"Did you get what we came for?" she asked.

He patted the pocket over his heart. "How did Los Angeles ever produce a *police officer* as her Genius?"

Angel smiled and took his arm so he could squire her down the steps and outside into the rain. The Bentley was around the corner. She squeezed his coat sleeve between long red nails detailed with tiny airbrushed unicorns. She stood on tiptoe to kiss the assassin's cheek. "He was on the take," she said.

The Russian Plays Roulette.
Somewhere in Las Vegas. Summer, 2002.

Jackie said he'd give them plenty of time to think about it, and the Russian didn't doubt he meant it. Still, the four spies didn't sit still long; the American and the athlete rose as one, the Russian and the scholar a half step behind. The American's hands were balled up in his pants pockets, ruining the line of his suit. The Russian was amused—as the Russian was often amused—to discover that he could now discern nuances in the gesture. This particular manifestation meant that his partner was thinking hard, and more than a little irritated.

"Where are we going?"

"Someplace private," the American said, shooting the Russian a sideways glance and then staring over his own shoulder at the athlete, a tacit request for permission. The scholar stayed at the athlete's back like a fetch, a frown carving the lines in his forehead deeper.

"If you're onto something, man, share the wealth—"

The American flashed the athlete one of his legendary smiles. "In a minute. I've got a question for you."

"Yeah?"

"Yeah. The Vegas my partner and I saw when we walked in here looked a hell of a lot like the nineteen-sixties." He gestured widely, an arc that took in the roulette wheels, the card tables, the croupiers and the dealers and the jangle and wheeze of slot machines in uniform ranks like light-up tombstones in a military cemetery.

"It did, didn't it?"

"Yes, and this—doesn't."

The Russian felt his own smile tug his lips wide. He nudged the American with his elbow. "You want to know if it will help us get any privacy to go back there."

The American didn't look at him, just the other two. "Would it?"

"Well—" They traded a familiar glance. The scholar shrugged. The athlete smirked. "It won't keep the assassin off. That's his time as much as ours."

"What about that Jackie fellow?"

"I can't rightly say." The athlete had a gangling, slouchy habit of motion that the Russian thought would reveal considerable power and grace when he chose. "Worth a try." He looked around, craning his neck to take in everything from the gaudy carpeting to the jangling machines and the high, light-patterned ceiling in one sweep. "Here? Now?"

"No time like the present," the Russian said, and laid light fingers on the crook of his partner's elbow before he closed his eyes and concentrated. He remembered the walk from the Desert Inn to the MGM Grand; the athlete or the scholar must have done *something* to move them from then to now?

Mustn't they?

He pictured the Strip the way he'd last seen it, the Hacienda and the Desert Inn and the shell of the El Rancho Las Vegas hunkered down, a fire-raddled hulk. Heat struck his face, a wall of it like an oven, a weight of it like a punishing hand on his hair. He opened his eyes, let his hand drop, and turned.

Desert stretched around them, flat, the Las Vegas Strip a black ribbon in the middle distance spangled with turquoise and black and silver Thunderbirds and Buicks and a single gleaming red Pontiac Tempest GTO with the top down, dust curling from under its whitewalls.

"Mmm," the American said, turning to watch the latter—and the blond hair that streamed out from under a green and rust scarf behind the driver's wheel.

"The car or the girl?"

"It's too far away to appreciate the girl properly," the American said complacently.

The Russian laughed. "Remember, I'm farsighted." He turned and caught the athlete's eye, and then the scholar's. "Voilà, gentlemen." With an expansive gesture: "I give you—nineteen hundred and sixty-four."

The scholar slipped a hand under his jacket and came up with a snub-nosed .22 revolver. The Russian eyed it warily, but the scholar just flipped it open and started checking the loads. Five were chambered; the big man dug a sixth from his pocket and thumbed it into the chamber. He snapped the assembly shut with a practiced twist of his wrist and let the hammer down easy.

"That's a pretty dainty gun for a big guy like you."

The scholar hitched his thumbs through his belt loops and smiled. "You require a big pistol, son?"

The American's eyebrows went up. He glanced from the scholar to the Russian and back again in patent disbelief.

The Russian bit down on his grin as the athlete cleared his throat, pointed back and forth between them, and said, "You won that one. I think he won that one. What do you think? Do you think he won that?"

"I think I burn easily," the Russian said, and marched forward. "The Hacienda is this way."

"The Hacienda's a dump!"

"They have a bar, don't they?" The other three fell in behind him without further argument. "Tell me—who do you expect to meet that you require more than five bullets for?"

"It's nineteen sixty-four—"

"We have observed that." Sharply enough that the American snorted and the athlete coughed. The scholar sent the Russian an amused glance; he caught it and sent it back. "Who do you expect to meet out here?"

"Just about nobody," the scholar admitted, tucking his gun into his belt. "Except the opposition."

"It's even too early for Kolchak," the athlete said.

"Who?"

"My point exactly." The athlete frowned at the American, leaning across the Russian's line of sight to do it. "All right, pretty boy. This is as private as it gets. Let's hear it."

"Easy," the American said, smoothing his forelock out of his eyes. "I think our new friend Jackie needs us a heck of a lot more than we need him."

The scholar smiled. "He thinks he summoned us."

"By accident. Along with a whole bunch of other . . . "

"Ghosts." The Russian gave his partner the word bluntly. It wouldn't look like empathy to an outsider, but he didn't care what an outsider thought. He shouldered the American, and the American shouldered him back, packmates communicating.

"Ghosts," the American said. "But we know what we're here for, and we know why we came."

"Yeah, MI-6 leaving us to clean up their mess."

The Russian snorted at the athlete. "In my homeland, they have a more efficient manner of dealing with disgraced former employees. One finds a pistol loaded with a single bullet on one's desk. One is intended to know how to address the matter from that point."

"I've wondered about that. Why only one bullet?"

"It is *not* expected that one Russian will make two mistakes."

Delightful, when they walked into it. It almost made up for the blistering heat on the nape of his neck and the packed earth under his soles cooking his feet in his shoes. One-handed, he loosened his tie.

"In any case, my partner is correct. Our friend Jackie may be a poker player, but he's no spy. And if he means to use us to get his vengeance on the . . . genius . . . who killed his partner, it would take little in the way of moral suasion for me to use him in return."

The Russian glanced up from his shoes as they touched the melted, sticking tarmac of the Strip. The Hacienda was appreciably closer, and if he turned left, he could see the "Drive Carefully" side of the "Welcome to Las Vegas" sign. He blew his hair out of his eyes, checked for oncoming traffic, and walked faster. The athlete and the scholar paced him easily, the American nearly trotting to keep up.

The athlete was nodding. He leaned forward one more time as they gained the western side of the highway. "So you think there's a way to use him to get to the assassin?"

"I think it can't hurt to give it a whirl," the American said, leading them up the driveway to the casino. "We're catching a cab back, gents—"

The scholar held the door for the rest of them, but the American balked a moment, glancing up. "No air curtain."

"You mostly get those downtown, where people walk in and out a lot. Come on; Uncle Sam doesn't pay you to air condition the Mojave."

"Uncle *Sam* doesn't pay me at all," the American retorted, but he stepped inside, and the Russian followed tight on his heels, breathing a sigh of relief as cool darkness closed around them. A moment later, and they were ensconced at the bar, the only four customers this early in the morning.

The scholar contented himself with orange juice. The American and the athlete ordered mimosas, and the Russian a bloody Mary. "So, what's your plan?" he asked his partner, when they'd each had a chance to get in a few pulls of their drinks, and suck on a couple of ice cubes.

"I'll let you know when I figure that out," the American answered. His eye lit on something over the Russian's shoulder, and he finished his drink in one long swallow and clinked the glass on the bar. "I'm improvising. Excuse me for a moment—" He stood, straightened his tie in the bar mirror, winked to his partner, and took off in pursuit.

The Russian checked his watch. "He'll either be back in fifteen minutes, or four hours," he predicted confidently, watching in the bartender's looking glass as the American strolled up to a pretty brunette near the one-armed bandits, exuding gallantry.

"What's his batting average like?" The athlete watched more openly, with a professional interest.

The Russian pursed his lips, working through the sports metaphor. "He swings at every ball," he answered at last. "He has to knock a few out of the park, yes?"

"What if we have to get in touch with him?" The scholar, looking less amused and more annoyed.

"He has his cigarette pack. I can call him if I must." A long sigh, and another sip of his bloody Mary. "So," he said, turning on his stool and glancing up at the athlete with calm interest. "About that tennis match—"

One-Eyed Jack and the House of the Rising Sun.
Las Vegas. Summer, 2002.

Vampires sneeze like cats. Who knew?

I concentrated on amusement to keep another image the hell out of my head—Stewart, alive, and bound to Angel somehow, drugs or magic or something else. It took a lot of willpower to walk down the stairs rather than stomp, but I thought I had my heart rate back to normal by the time I walked out into the parking lot. Both John Henrys waited by the front door of Jeremiah's Steak House. I paused in the shade as they crossed the asphalt and glanced over my shoulder, drawn by a whisper of breeze and the tang of ozone. Storm clouds piled up behind the Spring Mountains, not quite pushing over; another alleged monsoon season that was going to pan out mostly dry.

In ninety-nine, the rain nearly washed the whole damned town away. Just goes to show you never can tell.

In any case, the moisture in the air warmed the sunlight to a glow less like a welding arc and more like the sort of thing you might want to go out and walk around in and feel on your hair. It shone through the John Henrys, rendering them momentarily translucent, until they stepped into the shadow of the overhang.

"Did you find him?" asked the steel-driving man, shifting his hammer over his shoulder. Doc coughed into his handkerchief and reached for his flask.

I nodded and looked back up at the mountains remote behind a forest of power lines, billboards, and low-pitched roofs. I didn't feel like looking anybody in the eye, and the center of my chest felt like John Henry had caved it in with his hammer. "I found him. I want to thank you gentlemen for your help—"

"You know you can't dismiss us now," Doc said, and wiped his mouth on his sleeve. "Not 'til the business you called us up for is finished. And this isn't it."

"No. This isn't it."

John Henry's hammer didn't ring on the concrete when he set it down by his feet and leaned the handle against his bulky thigh. He hooked thumbs as thick as two of my fingers together through the belt loops of his canvas trousers and dropped his head, staring at the ground in between my boots. "Do you want us to stick around and make sure he leaves town?"

"He's not leaving town," I said. They fell into step alongside me, Doc on the left and John Henry on the right. "He's helping me find Angel."

Doc's laugh turned into a coughing fit, his bony elegant white hand pressed against his lips hard enough to blanch away the little color left in them. "Think he'll be any use?"

"I think so," I said. "Turns out Angel offered him a job."

John Henry tossed his hammer idly, letting it turn in the air, end over end, before he caught it by the handle again. His muscles slid and writhed under glossy skin. "What kinda job?"

Stewart.

"Protecting her from me."

The American, the Russian, and the Man Who Shot JFK.
Somewhere in Las Vegas. Summer 1964.

When the American rejoined the Russian some hours later, the Russian was cross-legged on one of the twin beds in their hotel room, his Walther disassembled on newspaper in front of him. His jacket was tossed carelessly over the foot of the bed. The black leather of his shoulder holster cut across an impossibly white shirt; the American made a note to find out what laundry he used.

"The mechanism won't rust in the desert," the American said, closing and locking the door.

"Sand," the Russian answered acidly, capping the bottle of gun oil without looking up. "You believe them."

"Don't you?"

"As much as I dislike admitting it." He reassembled the mechanism while the American leaned against the wall beside the yellow louvered closet door and watched. "Somehow, it doesn't surprise me that we would be the last to know."

"There are implications that could be worked to our advantage, once we understand the process."

This time the Russian did glance up, a flicker of a smile twitching his lips as he slid the magazine home. The click as it latched echoed with finality. "My thoughts exactly. I finalized some details with our colleagues while you were indisposed"—the American coughed—"and we are to serve as the primary bait. The other team will attempt to locate the assassin through more proactive measures."

"Tovarisch," the American said, delighted. "You've weaseled us out of the footwork, haven't you?"

"Weaseled may be an unfairly pejorative term."

"You have a better one?"

"Given how thoroughly you despise footwork—" The Russian rose from his place on the bed without using his hands, tucking his gun away as he fluidly stood. "I think you could manage politeness. You'll please remember this the next time you're sweating in the passenger seat of a Chevrolet, complaining how much your feet hurt."

"Still, your master plan leaves us getting shot at."

"All our plans leave us getting shot at."

The Russian ducked into the bathroom to wash his face and let cool water run over his arms, despite the air conditioning. His hair was still wet from what the American suspected was the latest in a series of cold showers. The American walked past him, crossed the garish carpet to the window, and flicked aside heavy drapes geometrically patterned in shades of rust and tan. "So, how do we play at being bait?"

"An endless succession of pricey meals and dinner theatre, leaving us ostentatiously exposed, would be too obvious a lure, unfortunately."

"Besides, we're not on an expense account." The American let the drapery fall. "Very frugal of the old man, getting us out here on our own nickel."

The Russian snorted. "He's nothing if not cheap."

"Pot."

"I am thrifty. I am also not eternally broke, like some profligate, bourgeois Americans I could name—" Their eyes met, and they both grinned in affectionate understanding.

"There's also the issue of Jackie," the American said, when the silence had lasted long enough.

"Ah, Jackie." The Russian snagged his jacket and shrugged into it, leaving it unbuttoned over his shirt. "Yes. He will expect us to pay his toll—and I admit to rather liking the fellow. If we can bring him this Angel person he described to us . . . spreading good will and so forth."

"Besides," the American said, "she killed his partner. And his partner looked like you. There's got to be an angle there somewhere . . . " The American looked down and fiddled with his pinky ring, attempting to conceal his second-hand wrath on behalf of Jackie, and Jackie's partner, and failing. "It, ah. It occurs to me—"

The Russian was looking at him, an expression playing across his face that would have been unreadable to anybody else. "You want to see if we can combine our tasks? Go back to two thousand and two?"

"I don't know," the American said. "How do you go about finding the genius of Los Angeles within Las Vegas City limits?"

The Russian looked at the American, and smiled. "Footwork."

❦

The Russian's feet baked in his shoes and his toes felt as if they'd been gone over once lightly with a carrot grater, but he'd never let it show on his face. Not when his partner limped ostentatiously behind, muttering under his breath. At least the malevolent desert sun had slipped behind the mountains. "We haven't talked about the... the spooky thing."

"Jackie mistaking you for his partner?"

"Did he seem a little innocent to you? A bit of *un naif* for his role?"

"His role as the spirit of Sin City?" The American craned his head back, looking up at the simulated skyline of New York City rendered in bright primary colors that lorded it over the south end of the Strip, wrapped in the yellow garland of a roller coaster reminiscent of something from a science fiction film. "Tovarisch, what could possibly be more naive than that? New York City with no crime, no grime, no Greenwich Village, no Soho, no Harlem—"

"—no jazz—"

"I bet the hookers even have all their teeth. Look at that place."

"I take your point. Venice without the toxic water. Remember how sick you got? . . . "

"Intimately." The American made a moue, and the Russian laughed at him, quite silently. It didn't matter; the American always knew when he was being laughed at. "You know, it occurs to me that our chances of finding one girl in all of Las Vegas when we have no photo, and the best description we have is 'brunette, five-three, one-ten, looks like an L.A. hooker who thought she could get a role in pictures' is probably a lost cause. We've been trying for hours. What do you say we call it a night?"

"Have we been shot at yet?"

The American checked his watch. "Not since 1964."

"Then we're not trying hard enough. The British team can't nab the assassin if we don't lure him into the open. Come on—three more bourgeois excrescences to go."

They walked in silence for a while. The American never seemed to sweat. The Russian mopped his brow with a formerly clean white handkerchief. The Luxor and the Excalibur yielded them nothing, and they wandered shoulder to shoulder, aimlessly, once they entered the tall gold building called Mandalay Bay. Some artificial scent on the air made the Russian sneeze. He dabbed his nose with the same handkerchief, and wiped his watering eyes. The place was huge, arched cavernous hallways oppressive as the sewers and catacombs of Paris. "Oh, brother. Is this the last hotel?"

"It's the last hotel on the whole goddamned planet—"

"Groovy. We haven't been shot at yet. Where to next?"

The American sighed and set his heels. "Did you just say *groovy*?"

"I like slang. Do you want to start on downtown?"

"What if I promised you dinner?"

The Russian bit back a grin. He'd been holding out for the trump card. "A casino buffet?"

"Bait," the American said, and pointed over his shoulder, back the way they'd come.

"A sushi bar in Las Vegas? Don't be ridi—"

"This is the millennium, tovarisch. There was a place in the last casino but one called *Hamada of Japan*. Looked promis . . . oh, my god."

"What?" The Russian turned, following the direction of his partner's shell-shocked gaze, his smooth-soled shoes turning on the shiny, dark floor without a squeak. Years of training kept his jaw from actually dropping.

"That's Lenin."

"Correction," the Russian said, starting forward. "It's Lenin—without his head. Funky . . . "

"Did you just say? . . . "

"I wanted to see if you were paying attention. It appears to be a restaurant. And the statue is a replica."

"That's a relief. I'd hate to think any real works of art got their heads knocked off. Even Soviet propagandist works of art." The American was still grinning when the Russian shot him the filthiest look he could muster. He continued, "We eat here."

"We do not."

"Don't you ever get homesick?"

Constantly, the Russian thought. *But not for this.* But he stopped anyway, looking up at the bulky broad-shouldered statue, encrusted with faux pigeon droppings, and said, "Vladimir Ilyich, where *is* your head?"

"It's in the vodka locker," a smooth familiar voice said from the restaurant's doorway. "Viva Las Vegas. I think you two have a bit of history to catch up on. And I hear you're looking for a girl."

The Russian and his partner turned as one, shoulder to shoulder, reaching for but not producing their weapons. The man leaned against the marble-framed entry, hands in the pockets of a voluptuous leather trench coat, dark blond hair fallen over his forehead, sunglasses concealing his eyes despite the dimness of the casino.

"Wow," the American said. "You know you look like—"

"Yeah, I get that a lot. Come on." He jerked his thumb in direction and turned his back.

Helplessly, the Russian exchanged a glance with his partner. They fell into step behind the stranger, who was carrying on a running monologue without bothering to glance over his shoulder and see if the spies were keeping up. "You're friends of Jackie's. And, unless I miss my guess, a little behind the times?"

The American coughed. "A little."

"American politics have been running downhill since the Kennedy assassinations, really. But the former Soviet Union's in even worse shape." The man in the leather trench coat shot a speculative glance at the Russian. "I doubt you'll be pleased—"

"Assassinations? Plural?" the American interrupted, at the same moment that the Russian said *"Former?"*

"Bobby Kennedy was shot in Los Angeles in June of 1968," the man who looked—and sounded—like the King of Rock and Roll said, checking his stride a little. The Russian hurried to keep up, matching his gait to the American's. "The Soviet Union dissolved its government peaceably in December of 1991, dividing into fifteen separate countries, most of which are still struggling, economically devastated, eleven years later. It happened just a little more than two years after the fall of the Berlin Wall. I was actually in Kiev when it happened—Ukraine's had a rough time of it."

"Ukraine always does," the Russian said, resignation in his breast. "Are there still roses?"

"Roses?"

"In Kiev."

The stranger stopped so short that the American almost walked into him. He paused and frowned. The Russian held his breath, his heart tight in his chest, and couldn't say why the roses mattered, except they did. His hands were sweating. He shoved them into his pockets, ignoring his partner's concerned glance. The man who looked like Elvis Presley pulled his sunglasses off, tucked them carefully into his breast pocket, looked the Russian in the eye and said, "There were in 1991. There's worse."

His partner's hand was on his shoulder. He leaned back against it, frowning. "Let me hear it."

"The power plant at Chornobyl—the nuclear plant—you know it?"

"The site had been chosen, but construction had not been started yet, the last I knew." The Russian dropped his chin, already knowing what the ghost of Elvis would say. His degree was in physics; he knew better than most that the proposed Soviet nuclear plants were an unsafe design. "There was an explosion."

"In 1986."

"Of course there was," the Russian said, and looked up, something that didn't feel like a smile twisting his lips. "It's the history of Ukraine, my friend. If it weren't ideologically questionable, I'd wonder if there were a curse." He turned on his heel and stalked back toward the maimed statue of Lenin, the *precieux* faux-Russian bar—he recognized the chandelier, now that he thought about it; he'd seen it in one embassy or another—and, most importantly, the promised vodka locker.

His partner, still visibly rattled by the news that Bobby Kennedy had been shot, was right beside him. He needed the steadying hand on his elbow more than he cared to admit. "I thought we weren't eating in the tacky nightclub."

"We're not," the Russian said, crisply. "We're drinking."

There was Ukrainian vodka on the menu, and they served it both in martini glasses and in samplers of shots frozen into blocks of red-dyed ice. The bar itself had a strip of ice like a hockey rink down the center, and the walls were cluttered with peeling propaganda posters. Coupled with dim lighting, the effect was overwhelmingly claustrophobic, but the Russian's partner leaned against the bar on his left-hand side and the stranger in the trench coat leaned on his right, and there was a certain comfort to be had drinking silently between acquaintances while the decapitated head of Vladimir Ilyich glowered down at him from its high shelf in the glassed-in freezer behind the bar.

The Russian toasted it silently with his second martini glass full of Zlatogor and breathed out through his teeth. He didn't need to talk; his partner spoke for him. "Did Jack send you looking for us? To bring us . . . up to speed?"

"Jack sent me looking for his boyfriend. Look, what do I call you guys?"

The Russian and the American exchanged glances and shrugged. "What do we call you?" the American asked.

"Tribute."

"What's your real name?"

"Baby, you know that already." Tribute smiled and swirled the vodka in his shot glass. He put it back on the ice without touching it to his lips and squared his cocktail napkin precisely. The Russian swallowed vodka hard, watching the curvaceous brunette bartender as she slunk from one end of the ice-topped surface to the other.

"So how come you look so much like the Suicide King?" Tribute asked, after the Russian had finished his second drink.

"Suicide King?"

"Jackie's boyfriend. The Suicide King. Jackie calls him Stewart. Jackie's the knave of spades, if you hadn't caught on."

"The one-eyed jack. Yes, of course. And his partner then would have to be the King of Hearts." The Russian glanced up as he spoke, then glanced down as Tribute pushed the untouched shot glass toward him. "Boyfriend, you say? I suppose that's something else that's changed." He took the shot glass with a sigh. "I do not know. Do you have any more bombshells to drop on my head?"

"Not at the moment. Although I'm looking forward to your reaction to President Ronald Reagan."

Tribute had timed it perfectly. The American choked hard, flinching as fiery alcohol bathed his sinuses. He grabbed a napkin and covered the lower half of his face. "Currently?"

"No, back in the eighties. You all are just too much fun."

The American winced, set his napkin down, and sipped his drink again. "So who shot RFK?"

"Supposedly, a fellow named Sirhan Sirhan, but there are conspiracy theories about that, just like JFK." Tribute shrugged, drawing circles on the ice with his thumb. A passing matron turned to blink at his profile, shook her head, and kept on walking. The Russian ordered another drink.

"My friend here thinks Oswald did JFK all by himself," the American said, angling his head to include the silent Russian.

The Russian snorted and looked down.

The American said, "Why did you come looking for us?"

"I didn't," Tribute said, swiveling his chair to catch the American's eye. "I was looking for Angel. Apparently, given that people were talking about two guys dressed funny and asking the same questions I was, so were you."

The Russian glanced down at the munchie menu to hide his smile. If Tribute had found them, then perhaps the assassin would too. He blinked at the card stock in his hand. "Russian nachos? What on Earth?"

"Blame Julia Child."

"I love Julia Child. On PBS." The American was laughing at him, but it didn't matter. The American never had believed he could cook. "I suppose she's dead as well?"

Tribute smiled as he shook his head this time. "Still going strong."

Odd, how that little bit of continuity eased the congealed twist of worry in the Russian's chest. "What does she have to do with Mexicanized Russian food?"

Tribute shrugged. "Fusion cuisine. The world's gotten a lot smaller since your day."

"Our day?" The Russian recognized that tone in his partner's voice. The American was still working on his first martini. "I'd have guessed our day was your day too. Aren't you a, what did Jackie call us, a media ghost as well? 'Cause you'd be, what, seventy or so?"

Tribute turned to them and grinned; the Russian almost startled back into the American's arms at the glitter of white inhuman teeth. "I died in 1977. And I'm sixty-seven, for what it's worth."

"Wampyr," the Russian said. "Well, well."

Tribute's eyebrow rose. "You're taking it well."

"We've met your kind before."

"Twice," the American added, and the Russian turned his back on the vampire—a foolish thing to do, but ten ounces of eighty-proof vodka on an empty stomach after twelve hours in the heat perhaps had dulled his instincts—and shook his head.

"Only once," he argued. "The other one we never actually met."

"I was thinking of the fellow with the bats—"

"—random madman. Not a real supernatural being."

Tribute laughed, drawing their attention back. "That's refreshing. The next thing people usually say is that I've changed. When they actually get to live long enough to figure out who I am, I mean."

The cold glitter of the vampire's eyes arrested whatever the Russian might have said in reply. Carefully, he pushed his martini glass back an inch, using just his fingertips, and then steepled those fingertips against those of the other hand. "But you aren't that person, are you? You're something else."

"A predator," Tribute supplied.

"A predator who remembers being that man."

The vampire snorted and picked at the ice of the bar top with his thumbnail some more. He'd worn a little groove, although it didn't melt where he touched it. "If you can call the person I remember being a man." He shook his head and cleared his throat. "So the One-eyed Jack's got you all looking for Angel too. Spreading his resources out a bit, I suppose. Look, I'm supposed to lead him to her—" The sharp-nailed hand splayed flat on the bar, as if he meant to stab between the fingers with a knife. A human's hand would have blanched in places and reddened in others, from the pressure. Tribute's stayed bland white, porcelain. "—I can lead you as well. After I get some business of my own out of the way."

The American leaned forward, clearing his throat. "Why are you helping Jack?"

"The likes of me?"

Vodka was making the Russian's head swim. He needed to eat. And not Russian Nachos. "Yes."

"Boy's got to live some place." The vampire's shoulders moved under the black leather coat, which draped in folds soft as cashmere. The dark blond hair drifted down into his eyes. "I like Las Vegas. I want to stay. I have to earn that from Jack."

"You're buying your way in."

Tribute showed the tips of his eyeteeth again as he stood. "Besides," he said, "I've met Los Angeles. One city like her is enough, don't you think?"

"Where are you going?" The Russian reached out to lay a hand on Tribute's wrist. The vampire suffered the touch; his flesh was cold, as stiff as wax.

"Hunting," Tribute said, one word full of potent venom. He stepped back, a sharply folded fifty-dollar bill appearing on the bar where he'd been sitting. "Drinks are on me. I'll catch you later, little spies; you don't want to come."

The coat didn't swirl as he glided toward the door and was gone. The Russian glanced at the American and waggled his eyebrows in a passable imitation of their superior. "Jackie's *boyfriend*?"

The American reached out, took the Russian's martini off the bar, and knocked the whole thing back in a gulp. "Times change," he said wryly, when his face unpuckered. "You think Tribute's told Jackie his partner's alive? Or do you think the genius of Las Vegas is lying to us?"

"I think it's going to take a lot of sushi to fuel the thinking process," the Russian answered. "Do you suppose our money's any good here?"

The American smoothed Tribute's bill against the ice. "Better than his money would be there," he said, and tapped President Grant on the nose. "Come on," he said, steadying the Russian as the Russian pushed himself to his feet. "Let's see if we can get ourselves shot in a restaurant."

"Don't forget our guardian angels," the Russian answered, casting a mysterious glance skyward.

"I never forget them. I just prefer not to make them work too hard."

The Assassin and the Lady Sowing the Dragon's Heart.
Las Vegas. Summer, 2002.

The assassin sat in a straight-back chair, polishing his shoes, while the genius of Las Vegas pressed his face into the pillow beside Angel's thigh and tugged ineffectually against the handcuff locking his right wrist to the bedframe. Angel stroked his hair; he turned further away.

"No."

Flatly, with an edge that told the assassin that the Suicide King was closer to his right mind than he'd been in days. Consent had to be given, and so he was no longer under the influence of the narcotics and witchcraft Angel had been using to keep him pliant.

"Come on, baby," Angel said, as the assassin slipped his foot into a gleaming loafer. "You have to eat your soup."

"Or what? I'll starve to death?" He snorted and rolled onto his back, using the short chain to haul himself up against the headboard. He sat beside Angel, his thin shoulders squared and his jaw working. He leaned away from her and she curled toward him like a mother coaxing a nauseated child. "If you want me to eat somebody's heart, why don't you start with your own?"

The assassin stood, making sure his suit coat hung flat over his pistol. He buttoned both buttons and smoothed his lapels with a flick of his thumbs, checking the look in the mirror. He'd picked up a bit of Las Vegas sun, bronzing his cheekbones. Angel lifted her head, careful to keep the mug of broth in her hand out of reach of the Suicide King. "What do you think you're doing? I need you here—"

"You're not going to get him to drink that tonight," the assassin said, finger-combing his hair. "We need bargaining power. Offer him his partner's life."

Stewart blanched.

The assassin blew Angel a kiss. "And in the meantime, love, I have people to kill."

She climbed off the bed and came across to him, leaving the mug on the dark wood desk beside an industrial-looking beige telephone. She lifted her chin and stared up at him, challenging; he kissed her for real this time, ignoring the Suicide King's snort of disgust. "Come home safe," she said, and laid a possessive hand on his upper arm. "I'd hate to have to find another partner with your qualifications."

"Never fear. And be careful of the poof while I'm gone, Angel." He winked. "You do look good enough to eat."

Tribute and His Cross to Bear.
Las Vegas. Summer, 2002.

Before I went to kill anybody, I took a walk through the Neon Boneyard. Las Vegas is a city without a history, but the history it doesn't have was piled up here, baking under the unforgiving sun.

It wasn't the old Las Vegas, of course—not the Vegas I lived in—but it was an echoing ghost of it, acres of boot-marked hardpan and a hodgepodge of metal and glass radiating the heat of the day back into the desert night. Cooling plastic ticked; signs were piled by signs, big ones, medium-sized ones—some of them two or three times taller than me. Familiar names: Sam Boyd's, the Silver Slipper, Joe's Longhorn, all fenced around with green-laced chain link, like the damned things might spook and stampede.

I stopped by the Aladdin's golden lamp, which sat in a protective sort of bay formed by the curve of the Gold Nugget sign, and cocked my head back to look up at it. Funny how it looked so dated, thirty-odd years later. *Quaint*, that's the word I want.

Somebody moved in the darkness, the drifting night air bringing me the rankness of tobacco and cheap bourbon and unwashed man. A lot of bums slept in the Boneyard; it was safer than sleeping on the street. Until I got to town, that is.

I thought about it for a minute. It would be clean, easy. I could do what I had to do and get back on duty following those ridiculously charming escapees from the idiot box around.

All right, it wouldn't be clean.

And I was hungry, but I could still afford to be choosy—and some down on his luck drunk wasn't choosy enough for me. Especially not when Jesse frowned at me translucently from the shadows, disapproval plain in his expression though he was holding his tongue. Most people in Vegas are prey, it's true; the city's got teeth.

But I wanted something that wouldn't keep me up days feeling guilty about it.

I slipped into the walkway between the Sassy Sallie's sign and the chain link, jumped over, and caught a cab downtown, looking for irony if I couldn't find evil. Jesse didn't follow, and I didn't blame him. I'd only get a lecture if he were there, anyway.

There were a lot of people sleeping on the street. I only had to spend a few minutes hanging around the courthouse and the bus station to get the feeling Vegas doesn't offer much in the way of safety nets. People slept rough on the grass or on park benches, or moved around looking for something to eat now that the heat of the day had pulled back a little. I killed five minutes watching happy couples being panhandled as they left the courthouse with their marriage licenses in their hands; the bureau's open 'till midnight weekdays and twenty-four hours on weekends. No blood test, no waiting, and all the papers on public record.

I could walk in there, pay a couple of dollars, and pull my own marriage license application, if I wanted it.

Yeah. Plenty to choose from, and easy pickings. Jackie kept his city clean of people like me. What he couldn't keep out were the people like people everywhere, because they made him as much as he watched them. And I comfort myself that there are worse predators in the night than me.

It's a lie, but I comfort myself.

There were still a couple of street preachers working the crowd. The true Las Vegas wedding experience; pick your minister from those on the sidewalk shouting their wares, like hookers jostling on the corner.

"Hey, mister," one said, as I wandered close, "do you want to get married tonight?"

God forgives us the sins of our mortal lifetimes, if we ask real nice. My religion doesn't talk much about the ones committed after you die. I turned around and looked him in the eye, and shrugged.

"My fiancée's just run back to the hotel. You wanna come with me to get her?"

"Sure," he said, and fell into step. Tall man, heavy set, his hair shaved close to the skull. We walked a few yards, and it was easy enough to grab a wrist and snake him into the shadows. They make it sound so pretty in the books. Tidy little puncture wounds, and orgasmic pleasure spiraling into death.

It isn't pretty. You wouldn't want to know. Still, plenty of blood in that one, and if I couldn't find a record producer, a man of God would do.

You figure they'll get home safely, right? And if they don't, it's their own damned fault.

I never could stand a hypocrite.

One-Eyed Jack Walks the Plank.
Las Vegas. Summer, 2002.

The John Henrys made good company, and I needed all the company I could get. Beside which, it was fun to watch them walk through the press of bodies on the boardwalk in front of Treasure Island—*through* it, quite literally, as I threaded between. Hard going; the pirate battle was underway, and the thoroughfare was jammed.

There was no possible way I was making the railing until the tourists wandered inside, but I staked out a spot between a stout couple arguing in Lithuanian, two California lesbians, and a tour group of Southeast Asians. Doc wound up standing more or less inside me, and John Henry bisected both the Lithuanians, but at least all three of us had a pretty good view of the pirate side. Of course, the problem with standing there was that when the powder magazine on the fiberglass cliff behind the ship "exploded," the heat of the special effects about singed my eyebrows off. I lit a cigarette and smoked it while I waited. The Californians edged away.

The bad guys won, the good guys sank, the British captain went down with his ship, and the tourists shuffled into the casino to feed their souls and their livings into the slots. I pressed forward against the fake pilings and ropes, a John Henry on either side, and dropped cross-legged to the boardwalk.

I wouldn't have much time before casino security came to roust me as a drunk, but everything I needed was here: fire, and water in the desert, and pageantry and illusion, and willing marks. Everything Vegas is built upon.

I flopped on my belly, wriggled under the rope and over the lip of the boardwalk, then stretched my hands down to the water, the cigarette still smoldering between my lips. Behind me, the gaudy-painted British ship started to rise from the moat, to be reset and do it all over again in ninety minutes.

I liked the pirate ship better. It had dragons.

Black water chopped inches from my fingertips, even when I writhed forward until my hips overhung the edges of the boardwalk. I'd changed into a black T-shirt emblazoned with a mushroom cloud and the legend "America's Nuclear City," a backup pair of cargo pants and the Docs. The boots counterweighted my upper body nicely, but I still couldn't reach the water and the ragged wooden edge of the boardwalk was doing a pretty good job of emasculating or at least disemboweling me.

Somebody shouted for help. I'd run out of time.

My cigarette hissed when I flipped it into the moat, but the ember stayed lit. The dull red light drifted through crystal-clear water, sterile as a swimming pool, and images blossomed behind it, swimming, not stable yet. A big blur of white, a swirling glow expanding around the light of the ember. Coughing, Doc crouched beside me and put a steadying hand through my shoulder. I didn't even feel a chill.

"The posse's en route, son. Better dive for it."

"Thanks, Doc." A hand clutched my ankle. Somebody yelped. I felt the grip skitter off leather as I grabbed a quick breath, shoved over the edge and followed the ember down.

Cold water—Christ!—and I hit it badly, but not as badly as I might have. It smacked me in the back like a kick in the kidneys, but I held on to my short lungful of air and stroked down until my fingers scraped the bottom and the cigarette swirled lazily in the countercurrent, the ember's glow flickering out strangely like the light of a much bigger fire. The glow spread through dark water like coils of ink, twining my hands, and I felt it brush my face with a warmth like fingers. Chlorine stung my eyes and burned my sinuses. I saw stars.

And between the stars I saw a vast winter-white wall, Hoover in the floodlights as it had looked as I fell past it, as a freak gust of wind had lofted me and thrown me clear of the power plant at the base of the dam.

Yeah, I know. Just lucky, I guess—

The dam bloomed up, whistled past, and suddenly that blossoming was underlit with the glow of the cigarette, red as a drunkard's nose, billowing—the dimpled membrane of a wall of desert dust, the wall of a storm, a towering thunderhead . . .

A mushroom cloud.

My shirt, of course. Oracles are notoriously easy to influence. Struggling in the water, lungs burning, I stripped it over my head and let it slip to the bottom of the moat. Darkness turned the ink into unhealthy mottles on my skin.

Hoover. It was right the first time; the dam, the water, the ancient, chained Colorado toiling oceanward, grooving the desert. Green filaments of strength ran through the water; life and breath in a thirsty place, the firefly flicker of old holiness. *Through caverns measureless to man/ Where Alph the sacred river ran* . . . or something like that.

Right. It's about the river. I knew that—

The oracle shimmered and nearly went dark; they get sulky if you snap at them. I coaxed as best I could with black lightning flickering behind my eyes. *Who?* I asked it. *What? Why?*

It showed me Angel, of course—her skyline, sunlit and then gleaming in the darkness, hungry and ragged as a row of tiger's teeth. It showed me a dark-haired man with a scar on his face wasting a cop in the bathroom of a by-the-hour hotel room, and then cutting his tongue and whatever was left of his heart out with tidy precision, the sheets from the bed keeping the blood off his shoes.

Then it showed me Stewart in a dark weird place, the feathered branches of tamarisk moving in the random beams of flashlights. The lights glared off Stewart's eyes and his teeth, and the scarred man standing before him with the same expression and the same knife. A glimpse of wings—hard bronze wings, the angry wings of seraphim—and Angel's touch on the arm of the man with the knife, a dirty kind of benediction.

"You were born to serve the dam," she said, and her voice went through me like the sound of a stripping gearbox. "And the dam was born to serve me. Your poor little ghost of a city, your mirage, your desert hallucination"—she blew across her hand—"pfft. Your power is my power, Las Vegas. If you won't serve me, you'll make someone who will."

There was more. There had to be more. Stewart reached for me, reached out, his back against seamed concrete, his eyes in a tight squint of panic. There had to be more, but my vision was blackening around the edges, and the thin stream of bubbles I let edge through my teeth wasn't enough, and I couldn't come up where I'd gone down. A flashlight beam whispered through the water, piercing Stewart, and he vanished just as I reached for him, all seaweed and ghosts. I stood in the middle of a silted plain, streaked sunlight falling through brown water, catfish flickering among drowned streets and foundations stretched around me like Atlantis. Unreal shells crunched under my boots, the last touch completing the vision.

There has to be more.

I hesitated one long second, and then kicked off against the bottom of the moat and swam under the boardwalk, stroking for the pirate vessel and a place out of the lights where I could cling to a rope or a piece of fake cliff and gasp for a while. If I was lucky, nobody would see a dark head bob out of dark water.

Minutes later, still shaking, I hauled myself from the water into the shadows one-handed, something hard and ridged pressing my other palm. Cumbersome soaked leather chafed my legs, and icy water squelched through my socks every time my feet squished them against the inside of my Doc Martens.

Those poor boots. Second time in a month. There wasn't enough saddle soap in Las Vegas to make it up to them.

Shirtless, the moat water already drying off my skin in the arid night, I edged under a street lamp and held out my hand flat to see what had made its way into it.

A sooty brown object patterned with white ripples, some kind of freshwater clamshell, water still dribbling from inside. I shook it around on my palm. The halves fell open, butterfly wings, a rivulet of sand left behind when the water ran out.

A transparent shadow fell over me. I looked up into the eyes of John Henry. Doc hovered at his side, long white fingers fretting the leather of his holster. "Whatcha got, Jackie?"

"I dunno," I said, and held it up so he could see. "Something from a dream."

The American and the Fine Kettle of Fish.
Somewhere in Las Vegas. Summer, 2002.

One of the great simple pleasures of the American's life was watching his partner eat. The process of conveying nutrition from the Russian's plate to his mouth usually continued unabated long after the American had been reduced to picking at tempting crumbs. Furthermore, the food was apparently metabolized directly into sarcasm, because not a trace of it ever appeared at the Russian's beltline.

But even the Russian eventually got tired, or full, or both. He yawned, pushed his stool away from the wreckage atop the sushi bar, and rubbed the back of his hand across his eyes. "I thought of something," he said. "The assassin—"

"Yes?"

"—he's not living up to his reputation, is he?"

"That's just it," the American said, pleased that he'd gotten there a little in advance of his partner for once. "You have a reputation too. And so do his other victims."

"Mmm," the Russian said, idly poking the remains of a heap of pickled ginger with his fingertip. "What do you suppose changed?"

"You mean why now?"

"Yes."

"Maybe we'll find out eventually. But I'm not sure it matters, given our immediate goals—"

"Staying alive? It might. If we knew what set him off—"

"—it might show us a weakness. Not bad. There's room to run in that." The American gestured toward the entrance, where Jackie had paused in quiet consultation with the hostess. "Shall we settle up? Our host is here."

The Russian pulled out his wallet and thumbed through it. "I assume I'm buying?"

"If you insist."

"I *assume*," he repeated, staring at the American through his lashes, "because *you* never have any cash. Besides, did you notice the prices? There must have been some impressive inflation at some point." He pulled bills from his wallet, but was stopped by a hand on his shoulder as Jackie leaned down and set a crisp hundred dollar bill on the sushi bar.

"My treat," Jackie said. "I happened to hit pretty well on a slot machine on the way in."

The American wrinkled his nose. The genius of Las Vegas smelled of wet leather and chlorine, and the shirt he was wearing was soaked around the hem where it rubbed the waistband of his pants. "Happen to you a lot?"

Jackie arched an eyebrow at him, and they grinned at each other for a short moment. The understanding that passed between them wasn't easy or comfortable, but it was *very* sharp.

"An archetype's gotta eat. It seems to me you get lucky a lot too."

"Sometimes," the American said, and finished his sake before he stood. A chill brushed his neck, as if he was watched, but a surreptitious survey of the sushi bar and the corridor over Jackie's shoulder showed nothing amiss. Still, if it was the assassin watching, that was to be expected. He slid a glance to his partner; his partner caught it and slid it back, as good as a conversation.

And Jackie caught it too. He was watching when the American looked back, quietly, from under beetled brows. "You gentlemen have some business of your own in town?"

"Nothing that should get in the way of helping you out," the American said, shrugging to settle his jacket.

"—as long as we don't get killed," the Russian finished, without making eye contact with either of the others. "You didn't tell us you had other operatives, Mr.— "

"Jackie. Other operatives?"

"Tribute," the Russian said succinctly. "I expect he'll be along shortly. He was . . . seeing to his supper."

A frisson brushed the American's nape at the Russian's deadpan bluntness. "Yes," he said, putting his shoulder to his partner's. "You do have . . . interesting friends."

"I have even more interesting enemies. So what did . . . Tribute tell you?"

"He told us your friend was still alive," the American said, watching Jackie's face for a reaction. The one he got looked honest.

"Yes," Jackie said, as they headed for the entry. "That's one of the things I meant to update you on. It's turned into a rescue mission—"

"What would Angel want with your friend?"

Jackie was guiding them back toward the main floor of the casino. The table games seemed curiously silent. The American found he missed the hum of voices, the buzz of excitement, but it was drowned out by the rattle, beep, and clang of slots. Casino carpeting hadn't gotten any better, either.

Jackie paused in front of a dollar progressive, and thumbed two tokens into the slot. "You play," he said, jerking his chin at the Russian.

The Russian stepped forward and examined the controls for a moment. The American wasn't sure he liked the way Jackie studied his partner studying the machine, and he remembered with unease what the vampire had said about Jackie's relationship with the Suicide King. *He'd better not be getting any ideas about my friend.*

The American cleared his throat. "It's not a marriage proposal," he said.

The Russian shot him a dirty look, and then his hand moved like a crane's bill stabbing frogs, slapping the *Bet One Credit* button twice and then reaching out to grab the handle still mounted on the side of the one-armed bandit, although there was a big square button labeled *Spin Reels* flashing on the console.

The Russian pulled the lever, and the images on the reels began to whirl. Lights flashed, bells whistled, and a cheerful chirping noise tracked the escalating number on the payout display. The Russian glanced at Jackie in amusement. Jackie shrugged, a quick one-sided jerk of his head. "That should keep you in sushi for a while."

"My identification says I was born in 1933," the Russian said. "In a country that doesn't exist any more. I can't cash the tokens."

"They won't card for anything under ten thousand," Jackie replied. He grinned. "After that, they have to report it to the IRS. Consider it a perk of working for the City. So to speak."

"You didn't answer the question," the Russian said, scooping dollar tokens in to the plastic bucket that the American held out for him.

Jackie hesitated, twisting the wet tail of his shirt in his hands. "If she controls Stewart, she controls a bit of . . . of me. Of the city. And there are ways to possess a genius's power. To take it away from him. They're not . . . very pleasant, and the simplest one involves consuming his essence."

"That sounds—" *uneasily familiar*, the American started to say, but something warbled, a commonplace sound that had the Russian and the American exchanging arched eyebrows. Jackie looked down, startled, and dug in his pockets with an expression of obvious distaste. The leather pants *were* soaking, the American realized, and when Jackie retrieved a water-streaked oblong from a pocket and flipped it open against his ear, he started laughing and couldn't stop.

The Russian looked from the American to Jackie as Jackie spoke into his portable phone, and started to laugh as well.

Jackie turned his back on them until he was done talking, and then glanced over his shoulder and frowned. "Tribute wants us to meet him downtown," he said, and then blinked at them. "What are you two laughing at? It's waterproof."

Tribute Talks to Ghosts.
Las Vegas. Summer, 2002.

Sometimes it starts to sink in that your social circle has gotten a little limited. And sometimes it's funny how everything seems to tie together, one thread knotting another until it feels like the whole world is being tied together by some Turkish rug-weaver.

The thing with my prepaid cell phone worked like that.

I'd given the number to the managers of the various clubs I'd cold-called the night before, pitching my services as a lounge act. One of them called me—not the one where I'd had the good fortune to run into Angel and her pet, but a sleazy little place off Main Street, just a few blocks from what we used to call Glitter Gulch. I made the mistake of walking through the abomination they've made of Fremont Street just in time for the Elvis light show.

Christ, those sideburns. Man, if I had it all to do over again—

Nah. Let's not worry about that just now.

In any case, one of the things about Las Vegas bars is they're *dark*. No windows, most of the time, and the lights kept low. Which is why I got lucky, I think, and when I came through the airlock of this particular hole in the wall, I smelled Angel—and Stewart—before she saw me. She was talking to the same manager who'd called, and he was nodding. I knew what he was telling her. She was looking for me. I was flattered.

The other thing about these all-night places: they usually have only two entrances; one in front and one in back, and after midnight, a buzzer to get in. I'd slipped outside, put my back to the wall beside the door on the hinge side, and I had called Jackie. The way things were going, I wasn't surprised to find out he'd hooked up with the spies. I settled back against the wall to wait. Loyal liege-man, servant to the rightful ruler of Las Vegas.

Whatever gets you through the night.

It didn't take them long to get there. Jackie had sprung for a cab, apparently, and he and the media ghosts—the American and the Russian—all piled out the rear passenger side door like clowns from a Mini Cooper, an impression intensified when the ghosts of Doc Holliday and John Henry the steel-drivin' man came with them, not paying any particular concern to whose limbs got tangled up in whom's.

"Cars have gotten smaller," the American complained to the Russian as they stretched and stood and Jackie paid the fare.

A mortal wouldn't have heard it, but my ears were good. "Get Jackie to tell you about gasoline rationing in the seventies. Besides, haven't you noticed all the suburban assault vehicles?"

The American raised an eyebrow, but played along. Another taxi purred past, but didn't turn into the parking lot; the headlights caught his eyes sideways and they sparked like amber held up to the sun. "The huge truck things? Yes. What do people use them for?"

"Taking the kids to little league," Jackie interjected, looking at me. "Less conversation; more action, please."

I almost choked on my tongue. He arched an eyebrow—teasing. I hadn't expected to be flirted with, but maybe flirting's like breathing, for some folks. Or some cities. The spies looked puzzled.

I said, "Thank you for coming so quickly, gentlemen. Jackie. Dr. Holliday, Mr. Henry."

"Dr. Holliday?" The American craned his neck, and I realized with a start that neither he nor the Russian could see the ghosts. Of course not—they weren't . . . supernatural. Just average guys who happened to be fictional characters.

Jackie gave me a look, a twist of his mouth that moved his nose to one side. "I'll explain later. In the meantime, we have a city to save. Move it along, kids."

I nodded and fell into step beside him, extending my left arm to herd the Russian and the American. The American gave me one more hard, questioning look, but he went, and the Russian stuck to his side like a coursing dog. I didn't quite touch the Russian's shoulder, but I sidestepped, dropping my hand, and turned toward Jackie just in time to see the ghost of Doc Holliday flip the hem of his natty gray jacket back, reach for his gun, and yell through his drooping moustache.

—and the asphalt reached up and smacked me across the face a split second after somebody's mule kicked me between the shoulder blades and ran. I straight-armed myself away from the parking lot, but my elbows didn't lock, and then strong hands took my shoulders and dragged me forward and I realized I'd been shot, shot in the back as I stepped sideways.

Angel had help.

So much for Sycorax's coat.

I looked up. Jackie was crouched over me, both hands locked in leather and straining the seams of my coat. The Russian lay flat on his belly half-under me and wriggling to get out. Accelerating footsteps told me the American was running for the edge of the parking lot, toward the gunman, whoever he was.

And then Doc's revolver boomed and the sweet sick reek of black powder burned the back of my nose, outcompeting the appetizing tang of blood. The Russian was hurt; I pinned him to the concrete with both hands. "Hold still, fella. Jackie, lie *down*. It's just a bullet wound. It can't hurt me."

And it's a good way to get shot, trying to drag your buddy under cover while the firefight's going on. The one-eyed Jack looked at me hard and dropped to the pavement a yard or so off.

"Not injured—" the Russian said, but he quit trying to squirm out from under me.

"I smell blood. And it's not mine. So if you'd just lie still, I'd be much obliged." My accent came back strong all of a sudden—stress, and the irritation of the wound through my torso starting to heal, a burning, itching kind of pain not all that different from rolling in a hill of fire ants. He didn't argue, but let me flip my coat over both of us, covering up too much yellow hair in the dark. He could be hurt and not know it. I needed a second to take stock. And I could buy that second, because by rights I should be dead—deader than I am already, I mean—and the guy with the gun knew it. If I weren't a predator, that shot would have killed me before I hit the ground.

So the sniper might think he'd gotten us both, if we just lay still. He couldn't have too high an angle of fire, either, or the bullet would have tended down going through me, and it had punched through pretty much straight and then done whatever it had done.

I'd only heard one shot. Thinking back, I could only remember one shot, but the Russian could have wound up taking the same bullet that punched through me. Which would make the Russian the unluckiest son of a bitch since the governor of Texas, if you believe such things.

I pushed against my elbows again. This time they locked. There hadn't been another bang, and Jackie still sprawled alongside us, breathing like a runner. John Henry stood over him, both hands on his useless hammer, and Doc was staring into darkness, ready to snap off another shot that couldn't hurt a fly. The American had vanished.

"You all right, son?" Holliday asked, without looking down.

"We're fine down here, Doc. You just take care of your own self. Can you see anything?"

"I can see that Yankee skulking around the back of the drug store over opposite. No shooter, though."

"Has Angel come out of the bar yet?" Jackie didn't lift his chin to ask. Holliday did. "John?"

The big, quiet ghost shook his head. "I ain't seen nothin', Mr. Holliday. You thinkin' maybe she got a friend?"

"I'm wondering if I have an enemy, Mr. Henry," I said.

"Nyet," the Russian said. "That was my bullet. Who is Mr. John Henry?"

Jackie cleared his throat. I could feel the Russian stretching himself, settling himself, ready to dig in and run. The asphalt was still warm under my hands. It stank of tar and spilled beer and urine. The blood smell was fading, at least. An old wound torn open again? Maybe the bullet *had* missed him.

Good, 'cause I didn't want my blood getting mixed into his.

"Did some unfinished business follow you to Las Vegas?" I asked.

"Actually"—he braced himself as I was braced, as Jackie was braced—"we followed him. Be careful with this one, my friends. He is dangerous."

"So am I," I said, and flipped myself to my feet facing in the opposite direction, and started to run.

The Russian Contemplates the Odds.
Somewhere in Las Vegas. Summer, 2002.

The bullet hadn't touched the Russian, although he'd broken his nose for the third time when Tribute fell across him and he got a little too intimate with the pavement. White-lit pain receded quickly into difficult breathing. The cool drip of *something* out of the gunshot vampire and the hot blood sliding across his mouth were sensations he didn't mind if he never experienced again.

Missed twice, he thought, and tried not to feel as cocky as he sounded to himself. It was luck, and luck could run out. Even his. Because if the stories kept him alive . . . it stood to reason that there must eventually be a story in which he died, correct? Perhaps many stories. Like Robin Hood.

That was good news as well as bad. Because if he could die, the assassin could die also.

He simply had to figure out how. But that was a task for another time, as was understanding why both Tribute and Jackie were apparently—no, definitely—carrying on a conversation with two beings that the Russian could not sense. For the meantime—

The vampire *lofted* to his feet, a movement sudden and effortless as a falcon extending its wings, and began to run in the direction that the American had taken. Toward the gunfire, which had not been repeated. The Russian picked his head up to look, caught movement in an entirely different direction, and cleared his throat. "Jackie—"

"Yes?"

"Your quarry is leaving the bar."

The Assassin Has a Sense of Déjà Vu.
Las Vegas. Summer, 2002.

The shot had been good, and that damned bloody bystander had fouled it. Still, they'd both gone down, and with any luck, the slug had punched through the man in the long black coat and done enough damage to the primary target to keep him down while the assassin found a vantage from which to finalize the shot.

He faded into the shadows, aware of the American moving toward his position, running recklessly. An easy mark, but the American wasn't the target. He needed the American alive.

Luck wasn't on his side, for once. It was a right pisser to discover that no matter how careful the setup, the fates would still intervene on behalf of his opponents as cheerfully as they would on his own. Still, he had time before the American found him—and once the American's partner was dead, it wouldn't *matter* if the American found him.

He backed against the rough skin of a Mexican fan palm, the rifle pressed to his chest to disguise its silhouette in the dark, and squinted toward the parking lot.

Just in time to see the man he'd shot between the shoulder blades leap six feet into the air, twist in place, and land like a cat. There was no hesitation; the dead man scurried toward the assassin's previous position, quick as a scorpion, leaving wet black footprints in his wake.

Maybe the American wasn't his most immediate problem after all.

One-Eyed Jack and the House of Cards.
Las Vegas. Summer 2002.

I started to run a second before the Russian managed to scramble to his feet and follow, and I kept my lead. I had a couple of inches on him, and I think that limp slowed him down a little. The bad news was that I hadn't bought socks when I purchased my T-shirt, and my feet sloshed inside my boots. Wet cotton slid and bunched under the arches of my feet, rubbing my heels until each stride felt like shoving flesh against a stove. I was going to have blisters on my blisters.

I didn't care. Because Stewart was half a step behind Angel, following her like a dog on a leash, and his eyes got wide and strange as I came barreling up. Angel's hand dipped into her shiny little purse—no sign at all of where I'd hit her with the sledgehammer, her broken arm healed as smoothly as if the damage had been painted on by a makeup team—and I knew she was going for that pistol.

Fucking L.A.

She didn't have it out yet when a bullet sizzled past from the wrong direction. I was guessing, but it sounded like it came from over by the palm trees, and it was a clean miss; it didn't touch me or the Russian. It seemed to lend him a little extra energy, though, as he kicked off and dove past me in a beautiful flying tackle.

I put the brakes on, trying to stay out of the Russian's way, and Angel sidestepped like a pro, making it look easy, a little bob and weave as she spilled her purse and got the flat-sided automatic out of it. The Russian piled into the wall beside the closed door, between Angel and Stewart, with enough of a thump to make me wince; it had been one heck of a tackle.

Angel was just Hollywood fast.

Stewart recoiled, a helpless hands-raised flinch that I didn't have time to watch and hurt for the way I hurt for it, because Angel was still sidestepping, her gun out and leveled, and the Russian was pushing himself to one knee, blood flying as he shook his head, and somebody was going to get shot if I didn't do something *now*.

They tell cops that fifteen to twenty-one feet is the inside limit beyond which an armed officer cannot safely control somebody with a hand-to-hand weapon. I wish I could say I made the considered, logical choice to put that to a test. Instead, a handgun barked twice somewhere behind me, days'-worth of fear and grief tumbling on me like somebody pulling the bottom card out of a fifteen-level tower. I rushed Angel like a pissed-off jackrabbit just as she was swinging her gun to try to cover me and the Russian both.

She put her back against the wall and pulled the trigger once, bracing her right hand with her left. As luck would have it, the bullet didn't even crease me; I grabbed for Angel's wrist and shouldered her into the wall, the impact hard enough to jar my teeth. She went under it before I managed to flatten her. She dropped and kicked out, using my grip as a fulcrum, and hooked my ankle with her foot as she swung down.

We landed on our asses, legs tangled together, all four hands pyramided over our heads as we wrestled for the gun. Her fingernails worried my left wrist like teeth. I heaved, got a leg under me, and threw myself at her, going for the pin. Something in my ankle creaked; sharp pain raced up my calf. I never even saw how she got her knee in the way, but the next thing I knew she was rolling out from under me while vomit tried to bubble up the back of my throat and out my nose.

Remind me never to get in a fight with a girl half my size.

I fell against the pavement, gagging, curled around the seasick agony of my testicles doing their best to vacate the premises. I had to get up. My arms wouldn't support me when I pushed, but I knew I had to get up, because Angel was up, and Angel had the gun—

A heave got me onto my back next to the Russian, who'd dragged his gun out of the holster and braced himself against the wall, spraddle-legged like a colt. Blood still ran down his face, a thick trickle that splashed my hand and arm as I pressed against warm concrete, trying to shove past the pain and use the wall, force myself to my feet. The Russian brought his gun up, staring Angel dead between the eyes, obviously half-expecting to get shot before he could pull the trigger and coldly unconcerned by the possibility.

Except Angel was pointing her gun at *me*.

"Jackie," she said, tilting her head so a lock of dark hair drifted across her eyes. "I wish I could say I was going to regret this."

In the movies, it would have been slow motion—the tightening, whitening of her manicured finger on the trigger, the hammer striking the primer, the bullet tearing itself free of the cartridge casing and flying down the barrel, wreathed in languid curls of smoke—

All I saw was a blur. Golden hair and black and red fabric, everything stark in the streetlight, as Stewart exploded out of *nowhere*, stepped in front of the Russian and me, grabbed Angel's fisted hand and yanked the gun muzzle up against his belly. The sound of the shot was muffled. The ejecting cartridge must have burned his hand, because he jerked it to his mouth and sucked it like a bee-stung child, his other hand pressing into the wound that dripped crimson below his sternum in front, between the shoulder blades behind.

He staggered. Angel swung the gun back toward me. The Russian chambered a bullet with a sound like a guillotine's blade. "Give me a reason," he said calmly.

And Stewart sagged to his knees.

I don't know how it happened next. I don't. I was up, somehow, up and then down, lunging to my knees to catch Stewart. And he was in my arms, eyes bright, teeth shiny pale squares between the blood staining the crevices between them, and Angel must have looked at me and looked at the Russian because she threw the gun in his face and *ran*.

He followed her about three steps and checked hard. I bent over Stewart as Stewart's eyes grew dull. His lips moved; there was no breath behind the words, but I knew what he was saying anyway. *Back in a second, Jackie—*

"Bother," the Russian said, as I closed Stewart's eyes, kissed the right one, and looked up. "That didn't go very well at all."

"Why didn't you chase her?"

"The assassin's still around here somewhere."

"Friend of yours?"

His eyes met mine, incredulous, and then he smiled and glanced down at his pistol, sliding the magazine out to replace fired rounds. "Something like that. And maybe working with your enemy, yes?"

Stewart shimmered into pixie dust and I brushed him off my hands. Stepping in front of a bullet meant for somebody else must count. Sweet boy. "Maybe is a mild word for it—"

"Come on," Stewart said, stepping out of the bar. He bent down and quickly kissed the top of my head. "Let's get the other one, if he's still out there—"

"—and my partner," the Russian interrupted.

"And Tribute," I finished, trying to sort my bones out enough to stand. "And let's do it before the cops show up."

The American Asks Questions Later.
Las Vegas. Summer, 2002.

The American was screwing the barrel extension onto his modified Walther when he marked his quarry again. Motion and a flash of light on glass caught his eye as the assassin lifted the long rifle, aimed it toward the parking lot, and sighted through the scope.

The American leveled and aimed his pistol, a hard-earned reflex that cost him no more thought than smiling at a girl. He hadn't had time for the scope, and the iron sights were less than perfectly accurate, but the Walther was almost an extension of his hand; he could reach out and place a bullet in a target without much more difficulty than he could reach out and tap the brim of a friend's hat down with a fingertip.

The weight was comfortable. The trigger pressed against his finger, resilient, eager. Twenty yards off, the assassin readied himself; the American could read measured breathing, relaxed mind in the stillness of his stance.

He'd only get one shot.

The snap of his pistol was lost in the staccato of the rifle. The American cursed, moving forward, already knowing he'd missed as he pulled the trigger—

A curvaceous shape clad in skin-tight black patent leather landed on the assassin's shoulders as if she'd materialized in midair. The assassin went with it, clinging to the rifle inside a shoulder roll that brought him to a tucked-in crouch. He ducked his attacker's first side kick and turned into the next one, using the rifle to parry an overhand blow.

The American ran. Concrete jarred his knees and hips and his suit coat tightened across his shoulders as his arms pumped. Not fast enough, though; the assassin knocked the woman sprawling. She jumped to her feet, ready for war, and they met again, in silhouette, an exchange of blows that even the American's trained eye could barely follow.

The woman was good.

The assassin was taller, heavier, had more reach—and he was armed with an improvised club, while she had nothing but her hands and feet. The assassin brought the blunt end of the rifle around and forward, a jab with the weight of his shoulder behind it and plenty of follow-through. He slammed the gun into the woman's gut. She doubled over, fists raised in an ineffectual face guard, and he whacked her again, a sidearm blow that nearly made the *American's* ears ring. She flew back, sprawled and skidding, a landing hard enough to knock the air out of anybody.

The assassin raised his rifle, a jerky unhesitating motion like a man about to shoot his own horse.

The Englishman's partner, the American realized, and stepped into the puddle of streetlight between the assassin and the girl. His gun rested in his right hand, a casual waist-level grip. His hair had fallen down into his eyes. "Pick on somebody your own size," he purred, and watched the assassin's eyebrow arch.

A calm voice, autocratic. "Step aside."

"Out of the question. I can't permit any harm to come to this young lady. My partner would never forgive me." The American permitted himself a coy little smile. "Besides, you can't shoot me, can you? I'm no good to you dead."

A moment of composed consideration between the two of them, the assassin testing the American for hesitation—and then the assassin's gaze flicked over the American's shoulder, and he frowned. He pursed his lips and stepped back, keeping the gun carefully— meticulously—level. "Enjoy it while it lasts," he said, and slipped back into the night.

The woman in the leather jumpsuit climbed to her feet and started brushing herself off. The American popped two shots after the assassin; he knew he hadn't hit anything, but he waited ten counted breaths before he lowered his gun anyway. He turned his head to glance over his shoulder; Tribute stood there, as he had suspected, one white finger thrust through the clean-punched hole in his calfskin coat, examining the damage.

Tribute glanced up, as if feeling the pressure of the American's gaze, and smiled. "Aren't you going to introduce me to your lady friend?"

The Russian, Through the Looking-Glass.
Somewhere in Las Vegas. Summer. 2002.

A brief acquaintance was all it took to prove Jackie's partner like nothing the Russian had expected. He'd seen Jackie's naïve charm, his brashness, his determination, his loyalty, and a certain street-tough grit and expedience that didn't do much to conceal Las Vegas's childish delight in excitement and attention, its basic decency on an individual level, and its unconcern for problems as they applied to people as classes. And the Russian hadn't expected this peculiar child-man's lover to be . . .

To be as he was. Flamboyant, teasing, sharp-eyed, dressed like a latter-day Rebel Without a Cause, with the minor addition of black tooled-leather cowboy boots. He hadn't expected extravagant, flaming, *camp* homosexuality coupled with the cool steely-eyed courage it took to step in front of a loaded gun.

Stewart was obviously the brains of the pair.

He was still contemplating that last—and watching Jackie with his arm around Stewart's shoulder like he'd never let go again—when he became aware of two sets of approaching footsteps, matched unevenly to three approaching people.

Tribute was forgetting to pass for human; he didn't walk, but *drifted* beside the American and a shapely brunette with a sharp-edged red spot darkening along one cheekbone.

The Russian blinked. And then felt his cheeks tug his mouth into a broad, welcoming grin that converted into a wince when it reached his nose. He pounced—brushing aside the American's restraining hand—and grabbed the widow by her upper arms, swinging her into the light.

"It's you!" She didn't flinch from the dried and still-wet blood splotching his face. Instead she swung with him, as if they were dancing, and planted a warm, uncompromising kiss on his mouth. Over her shoulder, the Russian read thwarted possessiveness in the American's glare. It delighted him, and he kissed the widow back.

"I'm overjoyed you came along." He stepped back, gave her arms one more hard squeeze. "And that you're in better health than reports had indicated."

Her smile tilted one side of her mouth higher than the other. "Dear thing. Shall we vacate the premises?"

The Russian glanced at Jackie, but it was Stewart who stepped in. "We need to get under cover now."

"I have a keycard for the California," Tribute said. "We can get cleaned up there."

The Russian felt his partner come alongside, and shot him a glance that probably wasn't reassuring, through streaks of blood. He looked back in time to see Jackie give the vampire a soft, level look with six inches of steel wrapped up in it. "Where'd the key card come from, Tribute?"

"I picked it up after dinner. Look, do you want to argue with me, or with Metro?"

Blunt, but it worked. Jackie turned in place, one sharp twist of his leather-clad legs, and stalked off, Stewart sticking beside him like a shadow. The widow hustled in pursuit, easy strides in her heeled boots bringing her abreast. She grinned over her shoulder at the Russian, who winked in return and felt the American stiffen.

The Russian leaned close and whispered in the American's ear. "Jealous? I *did* say I got the pretty girl this time—"

"You did," the American murmured, with ill grace. "You didn't say the girl would be quite so pretty. What do you think of Jackie's . . . boyfriend?"

"We don't look *that* much alike."

"Nobody looks at anything but the hair. That's why you should get it cut."

"I don't get it cut," the Russian answered, with infinite dignity, "because nobody looks at anything but the hair."

"Speaking of looking. Here, let me look at your nose."

"I don't trust you just to look," the Russian said.

The American placed two fingers on either side of the damaged appurtenance and pressed sharply; the Russian gasped, his vision shot through with green and white streaks, and ringed in black. He took a deep breath as the American stepped back, and smiled. "Hey. You got it straighter this time."

Some time later, clean and safely ensconced on the seventh floor of the California—an irony apparently not lost on Jackie—the Russian charged water glasses from a bottle of room-service Canadian Club and handed them around. Tribute took a glass, but declined to drink.

"Pour some of that on the floor," Jackie said, without making any effort to rise from the armchair he was sharing with Stewart. "Some people will appreciate the gesture."

The Russian raised an eyebrow, but obeyed. The whiskey splashed on the carpet and evaporated, center drying out to the edges. The Russian watched, intrigued. "There are ghosts and there are ghosts."

"How did you know?"

"I heard it from an old Gypsy once." He smiled, a controlled twist of his lips, and saw the widow smirk at him from where she leaned in the corner. Her eyes crinkled at the corners. He held her gaze for a moment before he glanced away. "Ghosts are thirsty. Are you going to introduce us to your friends, Jackie?"

Jackie grunted. "It's Doc Holliday, and John Henry the steel-driving man. You can't see or hear them, I presume, but Doc just tipped his hat and John Henry said he was pleased to meet you."

The American made about half an inch of bad whiskey vanish as effortlessly as the ghosts had. "Where'd they come from?"

"I called them up on purpose," Jackie said. "About the same time I apparently called everyone else up sort of on accident. Except it seems maybe I didn't call you up after all. If I understand correctly what was going on out in that parking lot." He cocked his head sideways, listening to something the Russian couldn't hear. "And maybe your problems intersect with mine."

"It seems that they might." The Russian tasted his whiskey. He didn't think much of the aroma or the flavor, but it set the right kind of fire going down his throat. He glanced from the American to the widow, waiting for one of them to shake him off.

"We're being hunted," the Russian said when neither moved.

"Or more precisely, *he* is being hunted." The American leaned forward on the edge of the bed, his glass dangling between his knees, and nodded toward the Russian. "Him and the widow, and the scholar. The rest of us are just—"

"On the menu," the widow supplied, eyes sparkling and the curled ends of her shoulder-brushing bob swinging forward. She stared at the American through her lashes. He blushed, the Russian noted with delight.

"On the menu," Tribute said. He'd been silent, his hands folded over one knee and his blue eyes half-lidded under his bangs. "Interesting way of putting it. One might argue that Jackie and Stewart here are on Angel's menu as well. I got the impression, though, that Stewart knew a little more than that."

He didn't drop his eyes from Stewart's when Stewart leaned forward, his thigh pressed against Jackie's in a manner the Russian found a little indiscreet. Jackie let go of his partner to permit the movement. He seemed unhappy about it, though, rubbing his right hand over and over the blue and black and red abstract tattoo swirling like a cross between a tornado and a tsunami up his own left shoulder. The Russian could pick out stylized hearts and spades and clubs and diamonds worked into the pattern, small enough to resemble rattlesnake scales more than playing card suits.

"I know a lot more than that," Stewart said. "Is your nemesis a tall Brit with black hair and cold eyes, by chance?"

"You know it," the American said. "Keep talking."

The Russian leaned back, arms crossed. If his partner was engaged, *his* work was done.

Stewart cleared his throat. "He's working with Angel. And I know exactly what they're trying to do."

The Russian loved dramatic silences. On his personal meter, this one ranked an eight point six. He traded a significant smirk with the American, waiting for Jackie to provoke Stewart to continue.

But Tribute issued the nudge. "Are you going to make us wait until after the revolution?"

"Funny you should put it that way," Stewart said, batting his eyelashes at the vampire. By the speed with which Tribute glanced down, he would have been blushing if he were mortal. "A revolution is exactly what they have in mind."

I flicked a few more drops of whiskey on the rug and watched, amused, as they vanished without a trace. The ghost of Doc Holliday tipped his hat at me and smiled. John Henry didn't seem to be drinking.

The American was, though. I got the feeling he wasn't exactly comfortable about something in the room, but whether it was the thoughtful looks his partner kept shooting toward the widow as she idled with her glass, or the way Stewart sprawled across Jackie's lap, I wasn't quite sure.

Stewart was looking at me, so I looked right back. So did the Russian, leaning forward with his elbows braced on his knees. But Jackie spoke, tightening the arm he had clamped around Stewart.

"They want Las Vegas," Jackie said. "They tried to buy Stewart and me, and then they tried to threaten us, and now—"

Stewart turned to him and nodded. "It's worse than that. They've moved beyond coercion, and into necromancy."

"Oh," Jackie said, and blinked. He looked down and then quickly back up again. "*Oh!* Goddess?"

"I don't know," Stewart said. "Somebody. I didn't . . . that is, they couldn't make me."

Jackie squeezed Stewart hard. "It's okay. If you had . . . "

"If I had," Stewart said, "I wouldn't be here, I think. Once they'd bound Las Vegas to Los Angeles through me, they—"

"Excuse me." The American, fixing Stewart with a bright-eyed look.

I hid my sigh of relief; I'd been afraid that I was going to have to ask. Much better to let one of the media ghosts look ignorant.

The American said, "I'm feeling a bit as if I walked in during the intermission, here. Let me see if I've got this straight. Now, Las Vegas is bound to L.A. in some sort of indenture arrangement?"

"You could say that, yes." Jackie smiled, not at the American, but because he had also seen Doc turn his head and spit impotently on the floor.

I flicked more liquor on the rug, without looking away.

Jackie said, "Las Vegas is, it's in L.A.'s shadow. It's sympathetic magic; power from other cities the world around—Venice, Paris, whatever—is drawn here, filtered, and then, through Hoover, metered out to Hollywood and L.A."

"Whoa," the American said. "Can we have that in English, please?"

The widow twirled a strand of hair around her forefinger. "That was English," she said, the rise of a sculpted eyebrow wrinkling her brow. "Would you prefer it in American?"

"You understood that?"

"Plainly." She let her hand fall to her lap and glanced at Jackie through her hair. "Correct me if I'm wrong. What Jackie—may I call you Jackie?—what Jackie is saying is that Los Angeles uses Las Vegas as a dumping ground for negative energy, meanwhile drawing metaphysical energy from other cities, using the themed casinos as the device to do so. Yes?"

"Precisely," Jackie said warmly. The widow sat back, not without a wink aimed at the American, who frowned.

I had to ask. "And Stewart, you suspect they want a bit more than that now?"

I'm not sure anyone else noticed the look the Russian shared with his partner. Lancing realization, and then the Russian looked down at the drink in his hands and smiled.

"Age of globalization, man," he said, with a wryness that made me think he was quoting someone. "Tribute—" without looking at me.

"Yes?"

"—is there still talk abroad of 'American Cultural Imperialism?' as exported by Hollywood?"

"It's not so much talk anymore as a fact," the widow said, breaking her amused silence. She let her glass click on the end table as she set it down, and pushed her hair behind her ear. "There's some pretty strident opposition to it, too."

She chuckled.

The American glanced up, not understanding the humor.

"First we take Las Vegas," I said, shaking my head. "Then we take Berlin."

"Something like that," the Russian said, obviously opaque to the reference, and gestured to his partner. *Continue.*

"Okay," the American said. "Now, my partner and I and our friends"—a nod to the widow, who tilted her head in acknowledgement—"are here because the assassin has been trying to consume *us* to make *himself* more powerful. That's the simple form. Needless to say, we're, ah, not particularly in agreement as to his methods. Now, if I understand you right, Stewart, this Angel, this avatar—"

"—genius—"

"—*genius* of Los Angeles intends to do much the same thing to Las Vegas. And the assassin is working with her."

"Right," Stewart said. "And I think you just gave me the puzzle piece I didn't have." He extended his hands and then pulled them toward his chest as if raking up piles of chips.

"Okay," the American said. He leaned back and crossed his ankle over his knee, showing a bit of white sock between cuff and shoe. Not the world's most fashion-conscious spy, apparently. "Now tell me about necromancy."

"That consuming thing you just talked about?" Stewart's brows went up, his hands spiraling in front of him as he leaned forward in Jackie's lap.

"Uh huh?"

"Well, if I'd done what Angel wanted me to do, I'd be making Los Angeles a part of me. Linking L.A. and Vegas that much more tightly. Sympathetic magic."

"Right."

John Henry looked up and ran a thick-ridged thumbnail across the head of his hammer. He didn't speak, just watched.

"Well," Stewart said, quickly, without flinching, "then if the assassin, say, were to kill and eat *me*, he'd become both a little bit of Las Vegas, and a little bit of L.A." He squeezed Jackie's hand lightly, quickly, and let his own hand fall into his lap. "And then if he were to become real enough—that is to say, more real than a media ghost—" He shrugged apologetically, mostly in the direction of the Russian, "—and then if he and Angel could get rid of Jackie—"

"The two cities become, symbolically, one. And he becomes the genius of both."

Stewart glared. "Who said you could step on my lines, King?"

"Sorry." I wasn't, particularly, but he laughed anyway and leaned back. "So what happens then?"

He pushed his hand through his shaggy golden hair. "It depends," he said. "I'm not sure how he'd step into the role of genius without being dead first. But if he could, Los Angeles conquers, and becomes the magical and symbolic capital of the world. May God have mercy on our souls."

"But we've got you back," Jackie said. "They're thwarted."

Holliday tilted his hat back and looked from John Henry, to me, to the oblivious media ghosts, to Stewart and Jackie.

"For now," he said, when Jackie looked down and Stewart didn't. "For now. You can be sure they'll have another plan in mind."

It lost some of its impact when I had to repeat it for the spies, but the American's eyebrows went up, nevertheless, his broad forehead wrinkling. He looked surprised for a moment before his expression sharpened and his eyes gleamed. "Where do these genii normally come from, Stewart . . . Jackie?"

Jackie lifted his chin from Stewart's shoulder. "The city makes them."

"How? I mean, ah, what if one of you got killed?" The American made a deflecting gesture, as if to soften the directness of his words. "Where would the new genius come from?"

"Someone would be elevated to the role." Jackie glanced at me and smiled. "When I saw Tribute, here, I thought he was Stewart's replacement."

"You did?" My turn to sound surprised. He shrugged and tossed his head to one side, showing off the curlicues of ink along the side and nape of his neck. I looked down at my hands before he could catch me staring at his throat.

Politics.

"Elvis and Vegas are practically synonymous," he said, with a shrug.

The American rose to his feet and crossed to the window, where he stood for a moment fiddling with the blinds. He turned around and stood hip-shot, hands in his pockets, shoulders leaned back, gangly as a baby giraffe. "How long does the elevation take?"

"Couple of days." Jackie looked to Stewart for confirmation.

Stewart nodded. "We're both original. I've never seen a replacement happen in person, but, you know. You hear stuff."

"Smoke," the American said, with a glance at the Russian.

The Russian, who had been engaged in some sort of silent communication with the woman, picked exactly that second to look up and met the American's eye. I caught the edge of whatever passed between them, and the blood in my veins was still hot enough that it made me shiver. I wouldn't have traded places with the assassin for anything, just then. Not a direct line to Jesus, and not a fried peanut butter and banana sandwich.

"Yes," the Russian said, as if he was speaking to no one else in the room. His face was expressionless, but I could hear the wink in his voice. "You hear stuff. My friend, are you suggesting that they will have to make their attempt quickly?"

"Technically speaking," Jackie said, "the new avatar has to be dead. Which is the sticky part, I guess. I've never heard of anybody trying to become a genius intentionally."

"Dead?" The American fiddled with his ring, as if unconsciously. I wished I believed that enough to call it a poker tell.

I got up and started straightening the glasses on the nightstand, keeping my hands busy while Stewart cleared his throat. "Genii don't get to be genii until we're dead," he said, with a flip of his hand. "I drowned. In Los Angeles, come to think of it. But they shipped my body home, and here I am."

The American steepled his hands, arching both eyebrows. "And Jackie?"

I heard Jackie take that breath and hold it, saw the flicker of Jesse's attention, the toss of his head. He leaned on my shoulder, cold, and didn't say anything.

Funny thing about Jesse. Nobody but me can see him. And for me, he comes and goes like the afterimage you get from staring too long at the sun. If you're not me, I mean.

"Shot myself," Jackie said, when he let the breath out. He tapped the eyepatch. "Ironic he's the Suicide King, isn't it?"

The American didn't look down, but he paused before he nodded and changed the subject fast. "If the assassin means to replace a genius of Los Angeles who has been recently killed . . . they'll have to act before the new one is elevated, correct?"

"Or kill him too," Jackie said. "Which gets awkward, running back and forth between Vegas and L.A."

"Angel doesn't strike me a patient sort," Stewart said wryly. "So they're on a deadline, although they can punt it if they have to. How do we lure them into acting?"

The Russian looked away from his partner, finally. His eyes weren't purpling at all; I suspected there would be no sign of the broken nose by morning. He ran one hand through his mop of wheatstraw hair, finger-combing it into a temporary parody of Stewart's gelled hairstyle. "Easy," he said. "We use me as bait."

The Assassin, Lucky at Cards, Unlucky at Love.
Las Vegas. Summer, 2002.

The assassin cleaned his gun and didn't swear at all. Not even under his breath. Angel wasn't so reserved. She paced the breadth of their new hotel room and cursed a streak so blue it was almost violet, in English and Spanish and sometimes both. The assassin reserved comment, but he was impressed; he hadn't heard the like often, even in his Navy days.

It was a good two hours before she threw herself on the bed, finally exhausted. She stared at the ceiling for several minutes while he pretended obliviousness, then rolled on her side, propped her cheek on one hand, and let her dark hair tumble across the synthetic pastel coverlet. "Back to the drawing board," she said. "You could have warned me that you wouldn't be able to hit the broad side of a barn when the media ghosts were involved."

He paused with the brush halfway down the barrel of his disassembled Walther, but didn't turn to look at her directly. "An unforeseen complication, it's true." He laid the barrel down and reached for the plastic squeeze bottle of gun oil. "You'll just have to kill them for me."

"Me?" A little bit of a squeak. She sat upright, abruptly, swinging her feet over the edge of the bed. The scuffed toe of her red snakeskin-print high heel showed the nap of tan leather through the dye. "But you're the assassin."

"You killed Stewart."

"That's true," she said. She toed off her shoes and stood, crossing to him. She leaned the curve of her hip against his arm. "Well, I shot him, anyway. He killed himself. But it's not like I can't shoot somebody. I just don't like it when they shoot back."

The assassin placed the bottle of oil on the corner of the unfolded pages of the *Review Journal* that he had been using as a work surface, and slid his arm around Angel's waist. "It's only fair, love," he said, pulling her into his lap. "After all, that leaves me with the One-Eyed Jack. And the vampire."

"Our plan's shot to hell, though." Her tone was as piercing as the sound of a wet thumb dragged across a latex balloon.

He grimaced. "We have fallback positions."

"It's going to be hard to get our hands on Stewart or Jackie again. They're ready for us. They know what we want. They know too much about our plans."

"Right," he said, and pressed a finger to her lips to silence her. "That's our advantage."

She watched him, eyes bright. She didn't speak, but he read the question on her face. *What do you mean?*

"You see," he continued, trying not to gloat too obviously, "they'll be hunting. They'll come to us, when and where we want. All we must do, love, is lay the right sort of trail. And if we can get rid of Stewart and Jackie—well. Your control of the dam is no doubt enough to bring something else under our power. Something that maybe has a little Hollywood and a little Las Vegas in it already, you see?"

He smile, when it dawned, was slow. "Yes," she said. "Yes, I think I see what you mean."

The American and the Only Girl in the Game.
Somewhere in Las Vegas. Summer. 2002, 1964.

In a lifetime of extraordinarily beautiful women, even the American had to admit this one was different. And not just for the way the Russian treated her—that combination of old-world courtliness and just-one-of-the-guys brusqueness that he reserved for the rare women he admired—but for the athletic strength she betrayed with every gesture and for the mocking, acerbic intelligence in her dark eyes. And for the way the Russian very carefully made sure that *he* claimed the middle seat in the back of the taxicab when they left Tribute and the genii of Las Vegas at the California and returned to their own decade, and their own hotel.

That *was* unusual. Especially since the woman wore a ring on her left hand—*of course she does; they call her* the widow, *don't they?*—and exuded the particular cognizant sexual self-possession that never failed to prick the American's ears. And pique his interest.

She took charge of them both when they arrived back at their hotel, took their arms and squired them upstairs, her black and white patterned boots almost skipping with pleasure. Not to their own room, but to the top floor, where she paused before a door like every other door, raised one fine-boned fist, and gave it a substantial rap.

A plummy tenor floated through the door—"It's open!"—and the American found himself trading a startled glance with the Russian as their escort pushed the door open and entered.

"Gentlemen?" She stood aside, holding the door, as a slender man dressed in a white shirt and an elegantly tailored gray three-piece suit with the jacket removed turned toward them. His dark, curly hair broke across his forehead, damp and recently combed, and as they watched he wiped the last traces of shaving soap from a determined chin.

He was not wearing a gun.

ELIZABETH BEAR

The widow waved them inside, performing introductions on the fly. "—I don't believe you've met. The other gentlemen should be along shortly, if I am not misinformed."

The American turned to glance at her. Her delicately plucked eyebrow arched in frank mockery.

"Delighted," the Englishman said. He tossed the towel over his shoulder, toward the bathroom. It landed draped over the edge of the sink as if he'd hung it there.

The other hand, he extended to the Russian, who took it without a smile. "Charmed." Murmured dryly, with a lift of the chin and a level gaze.

The American stepped forward and cleared his throat as the widow shut the door behind them. The Englishman's handshake was as dry and serene as his voice. The American gave back one just like it. "Do you always leave your door unlocked?"

"Of course," the Englishman replied, an arch lilt to his voice. Their eyes met, and the American thought, quite sanely, *a pox upon this man and his tailor, unto the seventh generation.* "Especially when we're expecting company."

"Anyone might wander in."

"A pity for them, then. Can I interest you in a brandy?"

"Yes," the Russian said, stepping between them with a cut-glass glare at the American. "I think brandies are in order all around. And then I shall tell you all about our night."

"You might as well wait until the Americans get here," the widow said, sharing an untranslatable glance with the Russian, who looked down and very carefully did not smile. "Otherwise you shall have to go through it all again."

"The *rest* of the Americans," the American reminded.

She sparkled at him, and turned to take her drink from her partner's hand. "Quite so."

❦

When the scholar and the athlete arrived, the other spies were still drinking. The widow let them into the room, and the athlete glanced around at the assembled agents and helped himself to a glass of brandy without asking.

The American, still nursing his first glass of liquor, watched the interplay between sets of partners with a new awareness while he brought them up to date, the widow interjecting as necessary. The athlete paced, toying with his brandy, asking snapshot questions. The scholar leaned against the door, shirt straining over folded arms.

Surprisingly, he was the one who spoke first, his mouth describing an arc that the American couldn't quite bring himself to call a smile. "Vampires? Black *magic*? Man. Yours is a weird genre, my man."

The American ran his tongue across his teeth. "You're taking it better than I expected."

The scholar's mouth curved up that much more. "Hey, I *know* who's fictional around here. It may not turn up every day, but you hear stories." He shrugged. "You hear stories. You know."

"Yes," the Englishman said, who had been so quiet, observant, standing by his partner's chair. "We all know, I'm sure."

•

The Englishman's room had a balcony overlooking the Strip. The American couldn't remember if the Desert Inn had ever had balconies or not; he suspected it hadn't, but he was beginning to understand that the city he moved through, especially here in 1964, wasn't exactly a real city. Rather, it was a fantasy of a city, a ghost, a land of make-believe. "Down the rabbit-hole," he murmured, toying with his brandy. "Alice's adventures in la-la land."

The sliding glass door to the room was open behind him. If he cocked an ear, he could hear his partner's voice rising and falling, well in command of the story he was relating to the Englishman, the athlete and the scholar. A hot breeze lifted the hairs at the American's nape and swirled the drapes into the room. It could have been the breath of a sleeping animal.

He raised the glass of brandy to his mouth, inhaled the fumes. He was unsurprised at the voice close by his elbow, but he feigned a startle anyway, because she would expect it.

"It bothers you," she said, and leaned her elbows on the wall beside his.

He shrugged.

"You're jealous."

The American laughed. "He's not my type."

"That's not what I meant." Her quiet, alert voice could have stripped him of guile, if he'd permitted, but he had a lifetime's experience in not permitting. "He's got secrets."

He touched her with a sideways glance. She returned it companionably. "He's a spy." *And so are we.*

"Yes," she said. "But you don't like it when the set of your life doesn't encompass the set of his life. You're greedy."

He opened his mouth to rebut, and nodded. "It's true. Greedy and jealous. And"—his number-one smile, medium wattage—"it appears I have reasons to be envious, too."

"Oh, do you?" Such patently false ingenuousness. Her lips looked amused, but when it reached her eyes it wasn't a smile. She turned to face him. "Someday you shall explain them to me."

"Someday perhaps I will."

The city breathed around them, the slow scroll of red and white lights along the Strip like the glow of countless flashlights revealing countless invaded spaces. That amusement flickered closer to a smile. "You are disingenuous," she said. "You knew what Jackie was talking about at the California. But you left it to me to explain it."

"I like being underestimated."

"And here I thought you were playing at chivalry."

"Never touch the stuff—"

"Ah-ah." Her finger rose like a schoolteacher's, and waggled precisely back and forth. "Shining armor," she said, and brushed the back of a fingernail against his lapel. That same fingernail slid under his coat and tapped the holster with a soft, foreign sound. "Magic sword. You wouldn't lie to a lady, sir knight?"

"Touché." He bowed, and she laughed and met his gaze directly, chin tilted up. He leaned forward, holding her gaze through his lashes. She did not look the sort to startle and back away, or slap.

"Where's the fiery steed, I wonder?"

"In the shop."

"There's a bit of good news in my having to come to your rescue," she said, so close he felt her breath on his lips.

"We've lost the advantage of secrecy," he murmured.

"And the requirement. So now we are six."

"Mmmm." She hadn't looked down. He leaned in and went for the kiss—and stepped back, startled for real this time at the flick of her finger against his nose, a gesture you'd use to chastise an impertinent cat.

"You wound me," he said, and she laughed and folded her arms.

"I'm going to fetch another brandy," she said. "And if you want to know more about your partner, the man of mystery—"

"Yes?"

"Ask him about Stalingrad."

Shocking. Not what he'd expected at all, although what he had expected, he couldn't have said. "Stalingrad?" he said to her back.

"Yes," she answered over her shoulder. "After all, it's where he learned to shoot."

One-Eyed Jack and the Knights of Ghosts and Shadows.
Las Vegas. Summer, 2002.

Tribute leaned in the window of the borrowed hotel room, slowly shaking his head. I stood against the wall by the door, watching him, listening to the water run in the bathroom. Stewart in the shower, and I couldn't say I blamed him, although I probably would have let Tribute have it first. The vampire smelled of old blood, and he was leaving rust-colored smudges on the carpeting. And still he stood there, staring out the window as if he could possibly watch the spies out of sight.

Even the Russian's hair didn't stand out that much in a crowd.

"Doc," I said, as Stewart wandered out of the shower with a towel wrapped around his waist. Holliday looked up from his cross-armed, bent-necked repose. He was slouched against the wall, half inside the nightstand-and-lamp between the room's two full-sized beds.

"What can I do you for, son?" His smile ruffled his moustache. He dug in his pocket for a candy and unwrapped it one-handed. The bitter, syrupy scent made me want to sneeze.

"Can you and John Henry go out again and see if you can locate Angel and the assassin?"

Doc sucked his teeth and glanced over at the drillman.

John Henry shrugged. "I ain't got no plans for the evening."

The twitch in Doc's lip turned into a smirk. "Don't suppose you'd care to make it worth my while, Jackie?"

"Sure," I said, and scooped the two-thirds-full bottle of Canadian Club off the table. Stewart ducked out of reflex when I hefted it, but I only threw it against the headboard of the right-hand bed. It showered glass and whiskey over the bedclothes and the floor. Doc closed his eyes and smiled, and the reek of liquor vanished from the air. I thought maybe John Henry had a nip as well; he leaned both hands on his hammer and shifted his weight forward. His shoulders rolled under his hand-sewn shirt, straining the fibers.

"It's a deal," Doc said.

"Be careful you don't let her get ahold of you."

Doc tipped his hat onto his head before he walked out through the wall. I thought John Henry winked. Tribute turned away from the window. He hadn't reacted to the crash of glass; not even a flinch.

"What's she going to do to a ghost?"

Stewart picked his way around the broken shards toward the closet. "King, you don't want to know. Whose room was this?"

"Somebody who won't be using it again," Tribute said. He crouched down to unlace his boots, more spider than man, all angles and flapping coat. Flaked blood sifted around him like pollen drifting off a branch.

"Good," Stewart replied, sliding open the closet door. "Then he won't mind if I borrow his clothes." Sometimes I forget what Stewart comes from. He hides it under layer after layer of artifice—but the camp persona he's inhabited since 1970 or so is built around the core of a young man who survived feud and range war, when Vegas was still the Wild, Wild West. It can be a little shocking when the gunslinger shines through.

A moment later, a faked gagging sound floated from the back of the wardrobe. "The murder victim was not a fashion plate."

Tribute stood and toed out of his boots. He tossed the trench coat on the bed, ignoring the shattered glass with strange determination, and stripped the bloody shirt over his head. His chest was heroin-thin, his skin translucent, blue as skim milk between smeared streaks of flaking blood. There wasn't a sign he'd ever been hurt in this life— or unlife, for that matter.

The sound of tearing fabric floated from the closet. "I'll try to kill someone better dressed next time," Tribute said, unbuckling his belt as he padded away in bloody socks.

Stewart laughed and came back out of the closet as the bathroom door closed behind the King of Rock and Roll, twelve-year-old-boy-adorable in rolled up, oversized blue jeans and a T-shirt with a Confederate flag on the front and the sleeves ripped off. He glanced sidelong at the bathroom door, and grinned. "You think it's safe to let him go in there alone?"

"*Stewart!*"

"What? Just asking—" He gave me the eyebrow, and I shook my head. It was so good to have him back that it hurt, even when I was worried—scared shaking—by Angel and the assassin and what they'd almost done to him . . . and even more scared of the temporary ally who was standing in the shower, washing blood off his cold, white skin.

Stewart came to me, real and alive and breathing, and leaned his forehead on my shoulder. His eyes slid toward the bathroom, and he shivered, then glanced back at me, too smart to say it out loud. The water wouldn't cover our voices where something like that was concerned. *Jackie, you grabbed a tiger by the tail this time, love.*

Stewart, believe you me, I know.

"Those spies of yours are good guys."

"They're *the* good guys," I answered, and kissed him on the mouth. "We got lucky with our allies there."

He kissed back, a dreamy little peck and then something deeper. For the first time in days, my heart beat the way it should. "We'll be fine." He smiled against my mouth as the water cut off. "We got through Bugsy, and we'll get through this."

John Henry Holliday and a Hot Night in the Old Town.
Las Vegas. Summer, 2002.

"Mister Holliday," John said, "can you feel him?"

Doc could. Not Angel, but the media ghosts had a kind of gravity: turning toward the assassin was like sliding down a greased slope to the low point. Once you started, you wanted to keep going as you'd begun.

"Maybe he'll lead us to the chippie," Doc said, digging in his pocket for a horehound drop. He tucked it between his cheek and gum, ignoring the dull ache of his ghost-teeth as the ghost-sugar saturated them. "Cherchez la femme."

They stepped out into a night full to saturation with heat. Heat soaked the air until the air felt like a strange dry fluid. Heat radiated from the pavement, wicked up into Doc's immaterial feet with each footstep. It took more, these days, before he felt it, but this was a desert heat, the *idea* of heat, and of course it could warm the idea of a man.

He chafed his hands together and glanced over his shoulder for John. John was there, a step back on the left. When Doc caught his eye, he nodded.

"Then let's wear some leather," Doc said, and moved himself.

The dead had their own ways of traveling, and they didn't need to go on foot. Las Vegas might be a big city, but it was an eyeblink across as far as Doc was concerned. He felt John alongside him. Within moments, they were amid the color and light of downtown, the press of people who shivered without reason in the heat and drew their shoulders around their ears when Doc and John passed.

The ghosts arrived just as the lighted canopy over Fremont Street was kicking into a sound-and-light display that stopped milling tourists in their tracks. Branching support columns like weird architectural trees reached up between ring-shaped white-painted dangles decked with black boxes, from which the music boomed. Doc would have covered his ears, but immaterial hands didn't do much to stop the thumping.

The assassin stood out in a crowd, in modern Las Vegas. His glossy black head poked up a few inches over most of the bystanders, and where they shuffled in Birkenstocks and T-shirts, he wore evening dress, the shoes shined so bright they shimmered. Doc watched as he emerged from the Golden Nugget's glittering archway and crossed through the press of pedestrians, not troubling himself to look up at the sweep of an animated fleet of balloons passing by overhead.

John chewed his lower lip, a frown creasing his high forehead. His scalp shone under the lights between cropped curls. "We ain't gonna lose him."

"No, we shan't," Doc said. "We'll hang back for now. See where he takes himself."

Where he went was to a taxi cab, which they followed without trouble, gliding above the traffic it threaded through. "I believe he's going to Caesar's Palace," John said, as the cab turned onto the strip.

"Is that a gaming hall?"

"It's a hotel. And a big one. Don't you watch movies, Mister Holliday?"

Doc had to allow as how, no, he really didn't. More's the pity.

John Henry turned out to be right. But as they were making the turn into the long circuitous drive, something caught Doc's eye. He checked, one hand unconsciously hooking the tail of his coat behind his holster, and John stopped beside him.

"Mister Holliday?" John could certainly see the other ghost, too— the one who stood arms folded on the street corner, one hand inside his bosom in the attitude of a man resting a palm on a concealed gun. He wore a gray flannel suit and smoked glasses, but the dark glass couldn't conceal the fact that he was very, very dead.

"Go on ahead," Doc said. "I'll catch up."

John gave him a doubtful look, but went. And Doc swooped down to land beside the gunman.

"Holliday," Doc said, extending his hand. "John."

The other dead man drew his hand from inside his waistcoat and touched Doc's with it, giving a quick firm shake. "Siegel," the man said. "Benjamin." He had hooded eyes under a crease-crowned hat with a broad black satin band.

"You're a Jew," Doc said, surprised.

The corner of Siegel's mouth curved up. From somewhere, he produced a slim brown cigarette and set it on his lower lip. Smoke curled from his nostrils an instant later. "I hope you won't hold that against me."

Doc set his handkerchief before his mouth, knowing the acrid weed would make him cough. When he was done, Siegel offered him a machine-rolled cigarette, the duplicate of his own.

Doc took it, and leaned in so Siegel could light the tip from his own. "I guess not," he said. "To what do I owe the pleasure?"

"You're working for the One-Eyed Jack," Siegel said. "I'm here to offer you a better deal."

"It's a damn poor son of a bitch who changes sides in the middle of a range war," Doc said, thoughtfully. The taste of the nicotine mingled unpleasantly with the horehound still in his mouth. "Why should I come and work for you?"

"You shouldn't," Siegel said. "You shouldn't work for anybody but yourself. Freelance. Nobody else is going to look out for you like you do."

"It sounds to me like you're implying that my loyalty's cheaply sold, Mr. Siegel. I don't suppose you'd care to explain why I shouldn't take offense at that?"

"What loyalty have you got in this situation? You were called up, weren't you? Summoned out of your rest, bossed around by living strangers, given a job with hardly a fare-thee-well. I could do a lot more from you." He smiled. "One American legend to another. You understand."

Doc took another drag on the cigarette, then flicked the ember regretfully off the tip and stepped on it. He dropped the butt into his pocket and frowned. The last sliver of horehound cracked between his teeth. "All I want out of you," he said, deliberately, "is ten paces out in the street."

Siegel seemed in no hurry to finish his cigarette. "Then I'll see you get it."

Doc wasn't surprised at all when he winked out like an occluded star. He sighed, covered up his gun, and went to find John.

The American Encounters the Single-Bullet Theory.
Somewhere in Las Vegas. 1964.

In the gray light of morning, the American and the Russian climbed downstairs, silently, side by side. The Russian wasn't quite weaving—it would take far more than a few glasses of brandy to make him stagger—but he was careful about how he placed his feet, and he kept one hand on the stair railing when he would have normally plunged down more or less headlong.

The American figured he would never get a better chance. He waited until the Russian was distracted, fumbling his key into their door, and cleared his throat to make way for his most casual tone. "I, ah—the conversation with Tribute, before the terrible Russian bar."

"Yes."

"You're from Kiev?"

"Let me guess," the Russian said tiredly. "You've *just* noticed that I'm an ethnic Russian from Ukraine."

"I just never knew where you were from."

"I never knew where you were from, either." The Russian shut the door tightly and made sure the latch was engaged before he shot the chain.

"Kansas," the American said.

" . . . oh." The maid had left their drapes open. The Russian went to twitch them closed, sticking close to the wall until the window was covered. "Farm?"

"No. My father was at Leavenworth."

"A prisoner?"

He felt his lips curve. "A legal advocate." He jerked his chin toward the bathroom. "You want it first?"

"Go ahead." The Russian kicked his loafers off and flopped backwards on the bed.

The American went into the bathroom and spoke over the rush of running water as he washed his face and hands. He had thought about it, and the Russian was more likely to answer him if he couldn't see his face. Something nagged at him, that same twist of a hunch, the unsettled feeling that had haunted him ever since the Russian's off-the-cuff comment about Oswald, and he knew his hunches well enough to trust them. "So how did you get from Kiev to Stalingrad?"

The Russian was still silent when the American came out of the bathroom, drying his hands on a monogrammed hotel towel. Dark suspicion furrowed his brow. "What did she tell you?"

"To ask you about Stalingrad. That was all—"

"Why?"

The American shrugged and tossed the towel over his shoulder the way the Englishman had, already knowing he wouldn't manage the hole-in-one. "Because it's an interesting story?"

"What did she say about it?" The Russian stood and stripped off his coat, walking past the American, intent on the bathroom.

"That you were there."

"And?"

"That you learned to shoot there."

A chopped laugh rose over the sound of water. "You could say that." The Russian mumbled around his toothbrush.

"How did you get there from Kiev?"

Spit, and rinse. The sound of gargling. "Kiev fell, *tovarishch*."

"Oh—"

He expected the Russian to stop, but there was momentum behind his words now. They tumbled over one another as he reappeared in the bathroom doorway. "We fled with the refugees, my mother and I. My father was in the Army. Safe in Moscow, if anywhere could have been said to be safe."

"So . . . how did you learn to shoot?"

The Russian's blue eyes glittered under knit brows, but the thing on his lips was nearly a smile. "My mother was a sniper. She taught me."

"You must have been—"

"I was ten years old," the Russian said, with a shrug that slid his shoulder holster down his arms. "Big enough and old enough to fire a rifle."

"Yes," the American said, unbuttoning his own cuffs, his stomach churning and cold but his voice as level as he could make it. "I can imagine. So that's why you said you could have made Oswald's shot. That's how you knew."

"Yes," the Russian said. He folded his trousers over the back of the chair and slid into the right-hand bed in his T-shirt and briefs. "I know I could have made that shot—with that rifle, even, or one no better. I know because I have."

One-Eyed Jack and the Unquiet Grave.
Las Vegas. Summer, 2002.

Tribute came out of the bathroom wearing wet blue jeans and nothing else. He must have washed the blood out in the bathtub, and his bare, bony feet flexed on the rug as he stalked toward Stewart. Stewart was on his hands and knees, cleaning up shards of glass; like him, to worry that somebody might get cut. I was crouched behind him, shining a pocket Mag Lite around to make the bits glitter so he could find them more easily, and then he was handing me the splinters and I was piling them on the skirt of Tribute's trench coat.

"Let me handle that," Tribute said.

"Not enough." Stewart peered over the edge of the bed like Kilroy. "Oh, your coat. I'm sorry—"

"I don't care about the coat." Tribute put a hand on Stewart's shoulder to move him away from the broken glass, and started picking shards from the nap of the carpet with precise darts of his hands. "I didn't pick it out."

"Who did?" Stewart rose to his feet without using his hands, a controlled, powerful ascent to match the blunt question. He met Tribute's sideways gaze and didn't look down.

Tribute's mouth curled at one corner, a quick sardonic flicker. "My mistress."

Implications piled in my mind, and I found myself taking a quick inventory of anything in the room that I could smash to make a stake. Stewart looked ready for anything, too, but his voice stayed level. "Someone *sent* you here?"

No living creature could have been so still. Something—the rise and fall of his breath, the pulse at his throat—would have betrayed him. Whereas Tribute was like a wax model of himself, nothing moving but the hands. "No," he said. "I'm actually here troubling y'all because I'm a free agent now, and I don't want to live on the dark side any more. Which—to answer your next question, Stewart—is why I'm helping your partner. Because a lone dog can't hold a territory. It takes a pack."

"And you think if you help us we'll let you stay?"

Tribute shrugged and dumped a handful of glass on the battered coat. "Jackie said so."

Stewart shot me a look—number three, that translates *why wasn't I consulted?*

"You were indisposed," I said.

He sighed and blew his hair out of his eyes. "King—"

"Tribute."

"Tribute. Excuse me for putting it this way, but you're—" Stewart stopped, his hands working. "A bloodsucker, man."

"You gonna run all the boxing promoters out of town?"

Stewart looked at me and I looked at him. *Touché.*

Tribute shifted restlessly. "So I couldn't help but overhear," he said. "Something about Bugsy."

"Irrelevant," Stewart said. His tone prickled my hair.

"Are you sure?" And the vampire honestly looked uneasy. Tentative, jaw working as he sorted out whatever he meant to say next. "'Cause he brought Hollywood here, didn't he? I mean, to all intents and purposes? Before he got himself killed."

"Dammit." Of course it wasn't anything that I hadn't thought already. Half a dozen times. But Bugsy was dead. Dead, dead, dead.

The son of a bitch.

"It wasn't so much that he got himself killed," Stewart said, as Tribute finished with the glass and stood. The last handful tinkled onto the rest, and the vampire wandered around the room absently squaring pillows and smoothing coverlets. "As that Jackie and me got him killed. Kind of on purpose."

Tribute turned around, forgetting to look human again. He sort of floated, looking like he was made of silk draped over wires. "You shot Bugsy Siegel."

"No . . . " Stewart shrugged, and looked at me, helplessly.

"We made sure the Flamingo failed," I said. "That the patrons were lucky, and the dealers weren't. The Flamingo closed. And Bugsy couldn't pay back the money he'd skimmed from the mob. They have a policy about that."

Four bullets in the back of the head. Just about everybody's seen the crime scene photos. Grim.

"But the Flamingo re-opened," Tribute said. "And the mob moved in anyway."

Stewart coughed. "You ever hear the expression that runs, *well, we won the battle*? The mob must have suspected there was a hex on the place. They got a Promethean to protect it, adjust its mojo, symbolically speaking, and opened it up again."

"Huh," Tribute said. "And it did just fine."

"Those Magi had pretty good mojo," I said, trying to make a joke of it. "Look at Hoover. Big magic. Bigger magic than us. I don't miss 'em—"

"I was just thinking about that," Tribute said, and rubbed his palms against his legs before turning back to give the pillow one last fluff.

"You're not much like the legend," Stewart said.

Tribute looked at me rather than Stewart, blue eyes dark under the drooping forelock. "The jumpsuits were Liberace's idea, you know. And a few good weeks buried alive—well, buried undead—will change a guy. Bring him back to his Christian roots, if you know what I mean. Never mind the school of hard knocks since."

It caught me short. "*Weeks?*"

"Yeah."

"How—"

A shrug rolled his shoulders forward. His head dropped and he tapped the back of his knuckles against the bridge of his nose in a gesture nobody in the Western World could miss. "I don't know. She maybe wanted to drive me crazy. Send me back to the womb so she could bring me up all over again. Or maybe it was just that hard to get a crack at my grave. Whatever, it was October before she brought me out. They moved the grave after that to keep people from digging it up, but the body in the coffin wasn't me." He held his hands out as if that explained it, the fingers surprisingly fine-boned and slender.

Stewart and I just stood staring at him. He kicked away from the wall and walked over, bent over the bed, and started picking shards of glass off the coat and piling them on his palm. He dumped the first handful into the wastebasket and turned back for another one. "I haven't got any pretensions anymore," he said, without looking up. "I just want a place to hang my hat."

"I'm not about to trust you," Stewart said, very quietly.

"That's okay," Tribute answered. "I'm not about to ask."

The Russian Goes Undercover.
Somewhere in Las Vegas. Summer, 2002.

The Russian and the American spent the day holed up in their hotel room, watching television and playing chess on the American's traveling game board. In the evening, by previous arrangement, they did not reunite with the other spies. Instead, they showered and dressed in silence, locked the door behind them, descended the stairs, and stepped out onto the street thirty-eight years later, under a red sun slanting through the mask-faced buildings dotting the Strip.

After some discussion, the Russian decided it was worth the gamble to walk the short distance to the Venetian rather than taking a taxicab.

"I will trust to dramatic necessity," he said to his partner as they followed the curved sidewalk down to the street. "I do not believe a sniper can kill me. Actually, I begin to suspect the assassin can't kill me at all, which raises the interesting question of how *we* can kill him."

"If only we could find a story where he *was* killed. We'd know how to do it, then." The American's voice was almost flirtatious—the playful tone he got when he was on the trail of something, the master strategist concealed under his ever-so-slightly swishy, cuff-fussing exterior turning some puzzle-bit from the great game over and over again, looking for the place where it fit.

"Besides, he *can*, no doubt, capture us—and I'm certain the genius of Los Angeles *could* kill us. She cannot be bound by the same rules, can she?"

"And we've run into one too many taxicabs that aren't really taxicabs. Right, tovarishch?"

The Russian smiled slyly. "I shall kidnap you," he announced, "and bring you back to Moscow for testing in their ESP program."

"You and the Red Army," the American replied, craning his neck back to take in the facade of the Venetian as they strolled past reproduction wrought-iron lampposts. "It's a lot cleaner than Venice."

"No soot," the Russian said.

"No stink."

"There *are* pigeons."

"They're probably imported specially." The American pointed, shamelessly as a tourist. "Look at the windows on the 'Doge's palace.' They're the *right color*. That's . . . "

"Care to wager on whether the canals are chlorinated?" the Russian asked. They threaded through tourists and costumed resort employees and ducked inside the cool, indirectly lit hotel. Despite his theories on the efficacy of snipers where he and his partner were concerned, it eased the itch between his shoulder blades to be out from under all those sight-lines and all that sky. Their shoes clicked on marble floors; they strode beneath gilt baroque fripperies and geegaws, through arched chambers lit indirectly and frescoed with reproduction art. "Is that the *Triumph of Venice*?"

"Keep walking. No."

For once, the Russian didn't look at his partner, because he knew if he did he would dissolve into giggles. Which was what the American wanted, of course.

Jackie met them in the elevator. None of them spoke, but the Russian's lips thinned arched when the door that Jackie's key-card opened led to a luxuriously appointed split-level suite. Red daylight still glowed at the edges of the tightly drawn curtains, but the floor and desk lamps had been lit. Tribute sprawled on the cream-colored sofa, a remote control in his left hand and his stocking feet propped up on the arm, watching television with the sound turned off. Stewart sat on the right-hand of two beds, cross-legged in blue jeans, turning the pages of a tabloid-sized newspaper with apparently rapt attention.

The door clicked behind Jackie. Stewart glanced up; Tribute did not, but the Russian felt the shift in his attention like a prickle on his skin. "Are we ready?" the American asked, looking around the room.

"As ready as we'll ever be." Stewart flipped the paper shut—the *Las Vegas Mercury*—and unfolded himself awkwardly, stretching his legs out as his torso tipped over backward. He rocked to his feet and rolled off the bed, the Russian observing his movements closely. He didn't limp; that would be a problem, although the Russian could hide his old injury for short periods of time, when he concentrated.

Tribute looked up, glanced toward the door, and frowned—half a second before Stewart and Jackie echoed the gesture. "Welcome back, John," Jackie said. "Any news?"

"John?" the American said. "One of the ghosts?"

"John Henry," Stewart murmured. "Jackie asked Doc and him to go scout out the opposition." His attention was rapt on empty space just inside the door. Jackie was looking at the same spot, nodding his head slightly, as if he were listening very hard.

"What's he saying?" the American asked.

Jackie held up a hand—*wait a moment*—and Stewart rolled his eyes. "This is going to be a pain in the ass of biblical proportions." He stepped forward, interjecting himself physically into the conversation. "Mr. Henry, would you do me the honor of allowing me to play your horse for an hour?"

The Russian brought his lips to his partner's ear and whispered, "Horse? Voodoo? Loas?"

"I think so. Nothing we haven't seen before."

"I didn't know these ghosts could do that."

The American bumped him with a shoulder. "There seems to be a lot we don't know."

"Shhh," the Russian said. "I'm listening."

He could see the exact instant that the ghost of John Henry possessed Stewart's body. Stewart was slight, blue-eyed, with a tendency to slouch and slump. The Russian had seen his share of people brainwashed, mind-controlled, or performing a role, and he was a fair hand at disguise himself. The ghost's presence transformed Stewart just as assuredly; his spine straightened, his shoulders squared, and his lids half-hooded his eyes, transforming Stewart's bright-eyed mockery into patient contemplation.

"There," Jackie said, hitching his behind onto the railing between the beds and the sunken living room as Tribute flipped the channel again. "Please, John. Start it over, from the top."

John Henry folded Stewart's arms one over the other, took a deep, leveling breath, and said, "The assassin isn't just working with Angel."

Jackie, who must have heard it already, leaned further back against the railing and crossed his legs. "Keep going, John. You stayed away from Angel, right?"

"Yeah," Stewart said in the drillman's tones. "I figured if these two couldn't see me, then probably the other one wouldn't either, but Angel"—a big, expressive shrug—"well, you know."

"Yeah," Tribute said. He'd turned his head, but the remote still dangled from his fingers like a smoker's forgotten cigarette. "Where's Doc?"

"Mister Holliday stayed behind to keep an eye on things—"

"The assassin." Jackie's voice was gentle, his tone soft and level. It surprised the Russian. Left him guessing.

"I didn't find Angel," John Henry said. "But I picked up the assassin. I can kinda . . . there's a flavor to 'em, once you've met 'em. The media ghosts. They . . . taste like something." He shot an apologetic glance at the Russian and the American.

The Russian folded his arms over his chest. The American tilted his head and shrugged, eyebrow lifted, to all appearances frivolously amused.

"You followed him."

"Yeah. Mister Holliday and me."

The Russian stepped back, carefully. If his partner had been conducting the interrogation, he would have arranged himself behind the American's chair, glowering silently, so that every time the subject looked away from the American he would have to meet the Russian's eyes. But John Henry wasn't blocking them; he just wasn't used to talking much, and intimidation wouldn't help get the words out of him any faster.

"He met somebody, John?"

John Henry made a broad, helpless gesture with Stewart's hands. "We followed him from Fremont Street to Caesars. He met up with a white fellow, maybe fifty, fifty-five, with a tailored suit of clothes and a silver necktie. Mister Holliday said the clothes and the shoes cost a pretty penny."

"I bet," the American said, frowning. "Mr. Henry, did you hear what they talked about?"

"Enough to get a picture. The assassin was telling him more or less everything, and not just about us—about Angel too. Including that Stewart got away, and Angel was still, well, he said 'well under control.' Whatever that means . . . "

"Go on, Mr. Henry—"

"They were pretty damn pleased with themselves, Mister . . . er, Mister. 'Specially after the assassin told the other guy he had a new plan. Even though Stewart got away." John Henry followed the statement with an apologetic shrug.

"So your friend's serving two masters," Jackie said, raising one eyebrow at the American.

The American glanced down at his hands and self-consciously shot his cuffs, one at a time. His tone was arch. "It could be an MI-6 contact. Though that sounds like a pretty pricey suit for a government type. Unless he's got family money."

John Henry's smile was big and broad, and six times too wide for Stewart's head. Stewart's cheeks stretched trying to keep up with it. "Mister Holliday got his name off the card he used to pay for their dinner."

"Damn," Jackie said, quietly. "*Hot* damn. What was it?"

"Felix Luray."

The Russian had never heard of him. Judging by the quick sideways glance he shared with the American, neither had his partner, and Jackie looked to be drawing a blank as well. "Well, that's no help. Did the card have a name on it, John? Besides his, I mean. Like a company name?"

"It had some kind of a design. You'd have to ask Mister Holliday what it said."

Because John couldn't read it, of course. "Thanks, John," Jackie said. "I guess that will be all." And Stewart abruptly was Stewart again.

The hotel room fell silent except for the barely-audible click of Tribute flipping stations on the 36-inch television set. "No help," he said, swiveling to sit up and gesturing at the TV. "But amusing."

On the screen, a dark-haired man was being chased down a steel-railed walkway by a giant with glinting metal teeth. The Russian squinted at it; Tribute's amusement made no sense to him at all, but Jackie was snorting laughter, and, as John Henry released him, Stewart suddenly was as well.

Oh, the Russian thought, a few seconds after realization dawned across the American's mobile face. He reached under his coat and calmly brought his pistol out, checked the loads, and began screwing the silencer and flash suppressor onto the barrel.

The American cleared his throat. "Ah, that's not—"

"Indeed it is," Tribute said, lifting the remote control preparatory to changing the channel again.

"Doesn't look a thing like him," the Russian said, and calmly shot the picture tube out of the television.

Jackie and Stewart both jumped, Stewart making a grab for the Russian's hand that failed because the Russian was already disassembling his gun. "What'd you do that for?"

Tribute burst out laughing, dropped the remote, and pushed himself to his feet, still shaking his head. "Because it's *fun*," he answered, before the Russian had decided if he meant to trouble himself to explain.

The American cut through the following silence, suddenly all abrupt and focused business. "Well, as long as we know where to find them, let's get this show on the road, shall we? Stewart, take off your clothes."

The Russian almost caught his partner blushing when Stewart glanced up at him through his eyelashes and purred. "I thought you'd never ask."

Fortunately, he was well-versed in keeping his sense of humor to himself, and peeled off his own slacks and sweater without cracking a smile—although from the way the American was watching him, the Russian suspected *he* wanted to.

The Russian slipped into Stewart's clothes, which fit nearly as well as his own, and got the genius to fix his hair for him. It involved a blow-dryer, and palmfuls of goop even stickier than the Brylcreem the American smeared into his hair, and the end result was actually brittle to the touch. The American, of course, stood there and laughed.

Stewart gave him a pair of dark glasses and turned the collar of his borrowed coat up to hide the line of his jaw. "Not bad," he said, considering.

"We won't stand under any streetlights," Jackie said.

The Russian stood studying his changed appearance in the full-length mirror while Stewart adjusted the Russian's clothes on his own body, washed his hair quickly in the bathroom sink, and borrowed the Russian's frumpy tinted glasses. He stiffened his posture, shoulders back, head up—

"—limp," the Russian ordered, without looking away from the mirror. "No, not so heavily. From the hip. Yes, like that—"

"How did you hurt yourself?"

"A motorcycle accident," he said. "Not very glamorous. Show me again how you cross your legs."

He was conscious of pulling Stewart's persona over his own, conscious of how it paralleled John Henry settling over Stewart like an overlarge coat—and how it differed, as well. It fit comfortably, though—gestures softer, posture looser, gaze a little more flirtatious, a little less direct.

"Damn," Jackie said, when he looked away from the mirror at last. Tribute said nothing, but his eyebrow arched.

The American was grinning like a proud father, an expression that warmed the Russian's heart. "Good, isn't he?"

"Damn," Jackie said, again, and shook his head like a dog shaking off water. "I guess that's us, then. Let's go."

The Russian fell into step beside him and took his arm, boldly, as if it were the most natural thing on earth. The weight of his pistol was comforting in his armpit. The American leaned close to say, "Watch out for Rupert of Hentzau."

The Russian snorted. Jackie's and Tribute's blank looks only made it worse. Leaning on Jackie's arm, his mouth twisting with the effort of biting back laughter, he followed the genius of Las Vegas into the hallway, and from there to the heat of the evening outside.

One-Eyed Jack and the Wolf in Sheep's Clothing.
Las Vegas. Summer, 2002.

The most disconcerting part of squiring the Russian around was that, between the borrowed clothes and the hair gel, he even *smelled* like Stewart. But he didn't sound like Stewart, and he didn't feel like Stewart. I don't know how else to put it; the pressure of his hand on my arm was wrong, and the way he filled up the space beside me, and it took a conscious effort of acting so I didn't lean away from him, stiff and uncomfortable.

"You're doing fine," he said, as if he could read my mind, and squeezed my forearm in a hand that should have belonged to Joe Fraser. "Can you still see your ghost?"

I nodded. John Henry was just in front of us, glancing back anxiously over his shoulder as he paused at the corner of Carson and Casino Center to make sure he hadn't lost us. "He's right ahead."

The Russian nodded, thinking. You could see the wheels spin. "How do the ghosts find people, Jackie?"

"Well, they can find other ghosts. Media ghosts, little ghosts, whatever. Like calls to like, I guess—"

His next question floored me. "Why can't they find genii?"

"Because genii were real people once," I said, and shrugged. "I'll explain it to you sometime, as much as I understand it."

"May we all live so long," the Russian answered, and if I hadn't known better, I would have said it sounded like a prayer.

I had to agree; I didn't think too much of our plan myself, but it was the best we had on short notice, and the American seemed to think that its very audacious ridiculousness would work in our favor. "*Play to the genre,*" he'd said, and his partner had backed him up.

And let's be honest. Strategy is not my fucking forte, okay? I just hoped the spies were as good at their jobs as I had told Stewart they were. Because if everything had gone properly, Stewart, the widow, and the American were boarding a plane at McCarran right now—although the American had assured me that they would not be on the plane when it lifted, through some trickery he declined to explain.

I was getting used to that about the spies. They were all, to put it mildly, entranced with their own cleverness. And I couldn't hold it against them.

After all, they were written that way.

Case in point, the beautiful blue-eyed Russian leaning on my left arm. A distraction and a half, and I knew better than to try anything, on him or his partner, for all the American sent my gaydar into overdrive and Stewart and I have what you might call an understanding. 'Cause if you think the seven year itch is bad, try the seven-decade itch.

But they're from before Stonewall.

So I leaned on his arm and kept walking, hoping our backup wasn't on the way to New York City.

The American(s) in Paris.
Somewhere in Las Vegas. Summer, 2002.

The American had to admit, the gadgets had gotten better in the last thirty-eight years. Specifically, he'd need more fingers than he had to count the number of times he would have given his left nut for something like the GPS system upon which he and the athlete were tracking their co-operatives' progress through the streets of Las Vegas. And the GPS system wasn't even the best of it. Both the Russian and Jackie wore miniature wireless cameras that did a remarkable job of relaying at least a general picture of their surroundings to the American and the athlete, who could keep an eye on their progress without ever leaving the air-conditioned comfort of a room in the Paris, Las Vegas Hotel/Casino/Resort—an edifice in and of itself almost sufficient to make the American understand his partner's reservations about unbridled capitalism, and without even the redeeming feature of decent pain au chocolate.

The earwire headsets were far more subtle than communicators, the astoundingly light and durable body armor that the Russian and Jackie were both wearing practically science fiction. Yes, the toys were very good indeed. And they didn't stop the American from pacing in circles until the athlete looked up from the monitors and offered to remove his feet if he kept at it.

"Sorry." He paused, and frowned at the wall. "I don't suppose you play chess?"

The athlete gave him the same look that the Russian did, when the Russian was holding one half of a set of headphones to one ear and ignoring the American with the other. And then he smiled, abruptly, very sweetly, and said, "Try me and find out."

The American grinned back. "Ah, I think I will, then."

He was unpacking his traveling chess set when the athlete cleared his throat. "What do you think of the Englishman?"

"I hate his tailor. I'm thinking of having him killed."

"The tailor or the Englishman?"

Backhand, the way his own partner would have served it to him, and the American grinned. Maybe this wouldn't be so bad, after all. "Well, if I killed the Englishman, it would annoy our enemies; they need us all alive. But if I killed the *tailor*—"

"—what would he do for suits?"

"Exactly!"

They shared a grin before they fell silent, but the American still couldn't shake the feeling—the uneasy prickle at the back of his neck that told him he'd missed something, overlooked something, failed to take something into account. So he paced, but he tried to do it more quietly. He put his hands into his pockets. He took his hands out of his pockets. He straightened his tie. He checked his part in the mirror and re-combed his hair. He fidgeted, in short, and the athlete just glanced over from where he was setting up the chess set, frowned, and didn't even bother to swear. His partner was out there too, after all, and they both knew that the guy they were up against was as good as they were in every respect.

Maybe even a little bit better.

And the American was stuck in a hotel room, miles from the action, helpless if shooting did break out—relying on the English team, a dead rock and roll star, and the athlete's partner to keep his *own* partner safe. And that tasted wrong.

He was still fretting over it when the window shattered and a lumpy fist-shaped object rolled into the room hissing ghost-white clouds of gas.

Tribute and the Last Light of the Sun.
Las Vegas. Summer, 2002.

One of the things I like about Las Vegas is the short days. The ring of mountains around the valley makes for long twilights, dawn and sunset. You can watch the shadows crawl across the valley, a sharp demarcation between day and evening.

So I had no difficulty tailing Jackie and the Russian through the gloaming, though the red sunset still painted the base of Frenchman's Mountain and winked off the tile roofs and stucco walls of the houses there, and even painted brightness across the upthrust Stratosphere tower. The shadow of Mount Charleston stretched across the valley, and that long shadow protected me. And gave me the hope that, even if Angel and the assassin knew what and who I was, they wouldn't expect me to be on the streets so early.

Every little advantage helps.

Especially since, if the American was right about things, Jackie, Stewart, or I were the only ones who could do any lasting damage to the assassin.

The plan, such as it was, was simple—once you took the American's extended chess metaphor out of it. The spies—with the exception of the athlete and the scholar, because the assassin might not know they were in Las Vegas yet—had faked a return to the East Coast, as if regrouping to try a different tactic. Jackie and the Russian—disguised as Stewart—would attempt to lure the assassin out under the guise of trying to track him down, and the rest of the gang, myself included, would be handy to jump the assassin when he moved.

Simple. Clever. Dangerously full of holes and ways things could go wrong in a heartbeat, but not bad for short notice. And now there was the John Henrys' information, that the assassin had another employer.

It was a good thing I was too busy walking to stop and count on my fingers all the very many ways that something could go wrong.

The athlete's voice in my ear meant I didn't have to keep Jackie and the Russian in sight, which was handy, and the scholar's job was to keep *me* under observation. I caught the occasional glimpse or scent of him as I moved through the crowds, never more than a couple of hundred yards away.

Jackie and the Russian headed west past the old Debbie Reynolds—I can't recall what they're calling it these days—and caught a cab there, then took it to the Tropicana and switched to another one, as if they were trying to shake a tail. I waited it out in the middle of the big triangle they were driving, leaned up against a lamp-post, ignoring the occasional tourist doing a triple-take, watching the sky fade from ash to indigo and sorting through the smells and sounds of a thousand travelers from a couple dozen countries. I was close enough to get to them if there were any trouble, I hoped, God willing. The good news was that getting Stewart alive and keeping Jackie not dead until they could line up his replacement would tend to slow the bad guys down a little. And I was pretty fast, when I needed to be.

It seemed like a great plan, until a man in wraparound sunglasses and a gray flannel suit walked up to me and held up a cigar. "Hey, Elvis. Got a light?"

"Sure, man," I said, and dug under my coat. I've got no excuse at all for not noticing that I couldn't smell him or his cigar, even in all that crush of people. And when I looked down, somebody close by moved, sharply, and a patter like rain on window-glass fell all around my feet. Pale gold beads bounced on the pavement.

I was already moving, dropping to my hands and knees to count them, when I realized what they were.

Wheat. Grains of wheat.

Oh, so screwed.

"One," I counted, and picked up the first grain. "Two. Three. Four . . ."

The man in the gray suit pulled his glasses off, and the ropy blood behind them spilled down his face from a shattered cheekbone and an empty eye socket. "Five."

"That was almost too easy, King," the ghost of Benjamin Siegel said through his handsome, ruined face.

"Six. Seven. Eight." I picked up another grain of wheat, and heard screaming, people running on the street, and then as a white van pulled to the curb, a gun barked not far away.

And I smelled the scholar die.

The Russian and the Decadent American.
Somewhere in Las Vegas. Summer, 2002.

The Russian could only assume that Jackie wasn't leading him astray. *He* couldn't see their guide, or even hear John Henry's voice. All he could do was follow Jackie—first through their diversionary tactic, and then down the sidewalk towards a sushi place on Tropicana.

People turned to stare at them, and it wasn't just due to Jackie's scrawny-muscular flamboyance. It wasn't curiosity—or not just curiosity. There was sharp hostility in it, and a little bit of fear, and assumptions the Russian wasn't sure he cared for—much as he hadn't been sure he cared for the assumptions buried under the looks he got when he first came to America, before he'd schooled his accent into something more British than Soviet. Between his annoyance at that, and the way his worries about who might be tailing them kept him hyper-alert and on edge, it was no surprise that he almost walked into Jackie when Jackie stopped short on the sidewalk, and then led him jerkily through the parking lot, threading between shining sun-hot cars in prismatic colors such as the Russian had never seen. Jackie crowded him into a reeking corner behind the dumpster, and the Russian went, trying to make it looks like a quick assignation if anyone should happen to be looking.

The flies were terrible, and they seemed to like the smell of his hair pomade. But it was far from the worst thing he'd endured, and he gritted his teeth and kept his hands at his sides. "All right, Doc," Jackie said, staring into thin air. "What have you got for me?"

The Russian folded his arms and settled back against the wall to wait. There was a certain amount of entertainment in trying to figure out Doc's half of the conversation from Jackie's, but the Russian knew better than to give it more than half his attention.

This was a role he played well—the weather eye, rear-guard, while his partner's focus was on a subject. And if Jackie wasn't his usual partner, so be it.

He did pick up on Jackie's frustration, though, and from the angle of his questions he understood that Doc had made an executive decision to follow the stranger—Felix Luray—rather than to keep his tail on the assassin.

Which was good news, because he'd eavesdropped on a series of cell-phone calls and found out who Felix Luray was—and while the Russian had never heard of the Prometheus Club, the lift of Jackie's eyebrow when he mouthed the name made him think of another enemy from ages past.

"So he's in the sushi bar?" the Russian said, looking where Jackie looked, although he couldn't see anything. The heat of the sun on his hair made him dizzy. He wiped sweat off his forehead onto the back of his hand.

"Doc says yes," Jackie said. Slowly, and dripping with something the Russian couldn't quite identify. "Things have just gotten very complicated." And then Jackie pressed his fingertip against his ear, a gesture almost everybody had to be trained out of, when wearing a wire, and said, "Hey, base?"

Hands by his side, the Russian listened to his own earpiece, and heard nothing, not even static. "The dumpster," he said, and stepped out from behind it, gesturing Jackie to stay back. His sidearm was a comfortable bulk in his armpit. It didn't help his awareness of how exposed he was.

He didn't think it was the dumpster.

"Partner?" Nothing. Nothing at all, and it caught his breath up sharp. "Tribute, can you hear me?"

Adrenaline could still make his hands shake, even now. He slid one under the lapel of Stewart's jacket, touched the butt of his gun. He forced a breath through the tightness in his throat and called on the widow, expecting silence.

Instead, her calm voice came back to him before he'd even finished speaking. "I can't raise your partner," she said.

"Do you have us in sight?" He shouldn't have felt so relieved to step into the questionable shelter of the dumpster, but at least it appeared largely bulletproof.

"I did until you hid behind the rubbish bin," the widow said. "How badly do you think we've been compromised?"

"I think we've gotta assume Tribute and the scholar are in trouble," Stewart said. The wire crackled as he joined the conversation. "Lady, you've got your partner?"

"I never let him out of my sight without a note pinned to his shirt," the widow said sweetly. "We need to stop using this channel now."

She was right, of course. If Tribute, the American, the scholar, and the athlete were in enemy hands, their equipment had most likely gone with them. The Russian nodded and pulled his headset off left-handed, tucking it into the pocket of his coat.

"We've got other problems," Jackie said. "Let me tell you a little bit about Hoover Dam. And Hollywood. And the Prometheus Club, on the side."

"I'll bite," the Russian said, folding his arms. "Who's the Prometheus Club?"

"The association of Magi who want to rule the world," Jackie said. "Using massive symbolic magical emplacements to do it. Like, oh, Hoover Dam. To pick something at random. And who got very close to it, or so I hear, before they mysteriously disappeared four or five years back."

"And that's what were up against?"

"That's what I suspect Felix Luray is," Jackie said, and stuffed his hands into his pockets to sulk.

The Assassin, in the Wrong Movie.
Las Vegas. Summer, 2002.

In the normal course of events, he would have been betrayed by a beautiful woman by now. It actually worried the assassin a little that he hadn't been; it made him wonder if he had missed something, if Angel were better than she seemed. On the other hand, he thought, slipping a device that overrode the room's cardreader into the slot on the lock, this was hardly the normal course of events.

He made sure his breathing filter was in place, listened for sounds within—there were none—slipped his pistol into his right hand, and eased the door open with his left. The lights were on inside, the air warm and dry, a contrast to the air-conditioned hall and proof of a broken window. The assassin peered through the crack on the hinge side of the door and saw no movement.

He could smell the lingering traces of the anesthetic gas even through the mask as he slipped inside and shut the door. Side-profile, keeping a narrow target, he cleared and passed the bathroom—the shower stood open and there was no room behind the door for even a slender man—and edged into the bedroom.

Two men lay sprawled unconscious, one across the bed, the other on the floor. Neither one had had time to get to his gun. It looked as if the American had been going after the gas grenade and the athlete had just managed to destroy the headset he must have been wearing.

An inconvenience, but one more than paid for by the unexpected presence of the American. A presence that supplied a problem, because it meant he didn't know who was on the plane—

He was only just reaching for his cell phone when thunder of a distant explosion rattled shards of glass from the broken window, and the darkening sky beyond the shredded curtains smeared crimson and white.

One-Eyed Jack and the Best-Laid plans.
Las Vegas. Summer, 2002.

We regrouped under cover of darkness, in the loading bay of an office block across the street from the hole-in-the-wall where Felix Luray was eating sushi alone, except for the occasional company of his cell phone. I'd risked a quick look in the streetside window as I walked past, and from what I could make out through the blister-pocked stick-on window tint, my suspicions had been accurate. Luray wore a handmade suit tailored to fit, but what was interesting about him was the way the energies coiled and throbbed inside him and around him, drawn behind his hands when they moved, echoing every gesture.

I had half-expected I would recognize him, but this man was far too young to be the Mage who had given Stewart and me so much trouble back in the fifties. Just when you think you have everything figured—

Shit.

A linoleum-floored hole in the wall seemed like a weird place for the last Mage in America, but I guessed it was unobtrusive. Anyway, there he was, so we ditched our useless headsets and hooked back up with Stewart and the leftover spies, with Doc and John Henry waiting out of sight—even ghostly sight—where they could pick up Mr. Luray's trail should he come out of the restaurant.

Something was up with Doc. He had come over all quiet since we caught up with him, but he wouldn't tell me what it was about, except to shrug and turn his head away and say it wasn't my lookout.

The Russian wanted to go after his partner right away—"The ghosts can find them, right? So if they're still at the Paris, we head back—"

"What about Tribute?" Stewart would as soon leave him to hang, but I had to ask. He might be a bloodsucker, but he'd acted in good faith so far. "Besides, there's something more complicated going on here than we thought."

The Russian leaned back against the cinderblock wall between the loading dock and the street, folding his arms. "What could *be* more complicated?"

But Stewart's mouth twisted in acknowledgement. I had to admit, he looked adorable in the Russian's carelessly chosen clothes with his hair down in his eyes. "Jackie's right," he said. "Although, I dunno—it could just be more players, not necessarily new angles."

It felt good to have him standing there disagreeing. "Which is why a Promethean is in there—"

Something *bright* flared overhead, lighting the sky in red-gold like flame. My first thought was that the observation tower on the Stratosphere was on fire. It was about the right direction, and as I stepped around the wall to get a look—

Boom.

I actually think the Russian hit me before I registered that what we'd just heard was an explosion. I blinked and found myself flat on my back; the widow had sheltered Stewart much less dramatically, just pulling him into the lee of the wall and the refuge of her own body. The Englishman had simply ducked, though I noticed that he—weirdly—had his hat over his partner's head, rather than clutched to his own.

I thought my ears were ringing. A second later, I realized it was a car alarm. I tried to push the Russian off; he pinned my shoulders to the asphalt and looked up, scanning the sky.

"What the hell—"

A hard blink, and he seemed to snap back into himself as if some-body had released a stretched elastic. "Good grief."

"*What?!*"

I heard falling glass, more alarms, shouts of awe and denial. The Russian climbed to his feet as Stewart and the widow came apart. The widow helped me up, her partner dusting my shoulders, and we all followed the Russian around the corner of the building. It was still there, a twisted pall like the afterimage of a firework, like the nebula that remains after the death of a star, spiraling creases of smoke following the paths carved by chunks of debris as they plummeted through the sky.

"The plane," the Russian said, and put one hand out on the fender of a Jaguar that was shrilling disgust and alarm. "The unspeakable son of a *bitch* blew up the plane."

We stood there, clustered like fools, just looking up, while I tried to remember how many seats there were on a 737, until Stewart tugged gently at my arm. I realized that the pressure against my mouth was the back of my hand. I gave it to Stewart instead, and he clutched hard enough to pinch my fingers. "He was willing to cause that much collateral damage?"

The Russian shook his head, Stewart's hairstyle starting to fall into unmaintained crumples around his ears. "More. He was willing to kill my partner—rather than trying to own him—and one hundred and fifteen innocent bystanders to get me and her"—a jerk of his chin at the widow—"out of the way."

I swallowed. Trust him to know to the decimal point how many people were on that plane. I bet he even knew their names.

The Russian grabbed my elbow, leading me and Stewart away. The rest of the spies were already moving. I kept looking up at the fading smoke trail. I couldn't stop. I couldn't even turn my head away. Stewart kept me from falling.

"I don't understand," I said. "What does that mean?"

The Russian sighed and let go of my elbow, the better to scrub his hands through his hair. He didn't look like he had any idea how to explain.

The Englishman cleared his throat, tapped the crown of his bowler with a forefinger, and set it jauntily on his head, although his mouth stayed set in a grim line. "It means the game just changed."

Tribute and the Ghost in the Gray Flannel Suit.
Hoover Dam. Summer, 2002.

I woke in harsh light, on hard stone, and lay still for a moment, listening as hard as I could.

There are advantages to a heart that doesn't beat and lungs that don't need air. I could hear the gentle sound of trickling water, the patter of a human heart, and the rustle of soft cloth on skin. Not too much farther away, some giant machine or engine spun, its vibrations energizing the rock and metal under my cheek and palm. There was a heavy cuff on my ankle; I thought I felt a chain attached by the way the weight fell.

I drew in air, shallowly, and tested for scent, and did not like what I found, layered atop cold concrete and machine oil and water.

Angel.

She wasn't moving, other than breathing slowly, and she smelled *confident.*

Which didn't make me feel any better at all.

I rolled over on my back and sat up, blinking hard against the light. I rose facing in the wrong direction, crouched—one hand on the concrete, giving me an excuse to check out the chain on my ankle, and then pivoted on fingertips and the balls of my feet, turning to face her.

No reason to give the whole game away right at the top, and the drop-forged chain on my foot was good enough to keep even me from going anywhere Angel didn't want me going. And the chain might be the least of my worries; I was standing on a sort of artificial island. Water ran in a shallow trench all around.

Yeah, I know, it's stupid, but I had to get into the Venetian through the parking garage.

"Good morning, King," Angel said. "Welcome to Hoover Dam."

That explained the vibrations. Although not how she got us in here. The dam's guarded, inside and out, and access is tightly controlled. Still, I suppose genii have to have their ways that they don't share with the rest of us, necessarily. And this didn't look like the sort of room you'd expect to find in an industrial facility. The black stone mosaic under my feet was the first clue; it was inlaid with steel and brass in patterns that looked like a star chart, not unlike the one up on the dam's promenade. The ceiling overhead was vaulted, decorated with stars and so forth like the zodiac in the roof of Grand Central Station, and the details of the room were art deco, from the wrought-iron railing around the far side of the water trap to the furl like tall wings bracketing the brass door. Not a hastily constructed holding cell for an unexpected vampire guest, but something else, converted to the purpose.

"Angel," I said, and shook my hair back out of my eyes. "I didn't know you worked with ghosts."

"He won't be a ghost for long," she said, and grinned at me. *Interesting.*

"I meant Bugsy," I said, watching her face. Charitably speaking, I can't say I've worked with better actresses, but then, I wasn't in a charitable mood. A moment of sheer transparency crossed her features before she schooled them into arch, superior interest. I didn't think she had any idea what I was talking about.

Which was interesting, because Bugsy had Hollywood links.

The assassin was playing a *very* complicated game.

Jesse, are you there?

"Where the hell else would I be?" he said, scornfully, hands stuffed into his pockets. "It's not like there's much I could do, but I'm stuck with you."

"Bugsy's useful," she said smoothly, but I could see by the way her palms stroked her jeans that I'd worried her, even if a flash of fear didn't spike her scent, just then. "It's a pity we lost Stewart," she continued, unable to resist the role that had her gloating like a movie villain. "But it's fortunate we have you in his place. Has it been a while since you fed, King? Healing a gunshot wound is hungry work, I bet." She slid a little knife from the fifth pocket on her jeans and flicked the blade open with her thumbnail.

It cost me to keep it off my face when she stroked the knife across the back of her hand and let the blood run down her fingers to spatter on the stones. The scent was heady and clean; my stomach clenched in anticipation of the hot, ready stream that should follow.

No. I could handle it. I had a lot of practice handling it, when I was with Sycorax.

God have mercy on my soul.

I didn't look down at the droplets of sweet dark blood on the black stone floor. I didn't look away from Angel's smile as she wiped the blade on her jeans and folded it back into the little pocket. "Ciao," she purred. "I'm going to have to run, King. But I'll be back in a day or two. When you've had time to work up an appetite."

The brass doors were elevator doors, I saw; they split in the middle and she vanished in between them, leaving me alone with the hum of machines and the tang of blood.

It didn't last. Bugsy Siegel stepped out of the elevator a moment later, slicking his brains back into his skull with both hands. He was wearing the dark glasses again. It made him easier to look at. "Tch, King," he said. "I'da thought you had more cool than that."

"She's not supposed to know about you, Bugs?"

He showed me his teeth. His hand, red with the memory of his own blood, carved a gesture in the air. "You're not going to talk about it, are you, King?"

And no, I wasn't. Which scared me worse than anything else so far. I've never heard of a ghost working magic before. "So tell me a story, Bugsy. Is this about you and Hollywood, or is this about something else? Something personal maybe?"

"Don't you fucking call me that, punk. I'm Mr. Siegel. Ben if I like you. Which I don't. Anyway, it's my city. I got a right to maintain an interest. And this'd go better if you helped us. Better for you, and better for us. I never liked working with broads."

"Us?" I showed my teeth, too. Mine might have been sharper, but it was a near thing. "Not you and the assassin. Not in your league. And the *broad* doesn't know she works for you, does she?"

He shrugged. "Never tell 'em anything they don't need to know, that's my motto. King, we pull this off, it's the golden age of Hollywood and Vegas and America all over again. You can't say no to that. How could *you* pass up 1955?"

"You were dead by '55."

"Yeah," he said, and lit a cigar by looking at it. I couldn't smell smoke. "I was always sorry I missed it."

"Before I say yes—" His eyes lit up avidly. "—who's your partner, Ben?"

He smiled like a girl who got just the date she wanted for the prom. He puffed his cigar, and then stared at it thoughtfully, trickling smoke over his upper lip. "A Mage," he said. "A real live Mage. We've got some—muscle—too. You know, physical types." He wheezed laughter at his own joke, leaning his shoulders against the wall beside the elevator door. "The ones who helped out with you and your nigger friend."

Some of us haven't kept up with the times real well, I guess. "I always heard you did your own wet work, Mr. Siegel. Murder, Inc. and all that."

He shrugged, and put a hand on the railing. "A good leader knows when to delegate."

Not so useful. "If I agree, do the chains come off?"

"Not just yet," he said. "We require some evidence of good faith. Even from you, King. Sure you understand."

"Sure." My tongue was cold when I licked my lips. "What kind of a gesture do you want?"

"Take the broad up on her offer." He stuck the cigar between his teeth and slapped the button for the lift. I tried not to stare as the doors slid open, just as if he was flesh and bone. "We'll be in touch."

One-Eyed Jack, On the Lam.
Las Vegas. Summer, 2002.

We spent that whole damned night on the run. I was good. I was sharp.
I was doing all right—and I didn't kid myself that it had anything to
do with anything, except Stewart being there to hold my hand. Yeah,
I know I've got it bad. Stewart and me, we've been through a lot. He
put me back together again after Laura died, and my old man. The
one who never bothered to find out where I was, or if I'd even been
born all right. Funny to find out it mattered, after forty-odd years—

See, my old man was the governor. Not that I ever met him. He sent
my mother south, which is where she bore and raised me. And saddled
me with my father's name. I had good skin. I passed. Did fairly well in
the gold rush in Rhyolite, got well out of it before the crash, married
a good Mormon girl in Saint Thomas, and settled down. Heard my
father was dead in 1904. It didn't bother me much, I thought.

And I kept thinking it right up until Laura died, too. Oh, sure. I
don't much like girls, that way. But in those days that wasn't much of
a barrier to marriage.

So I thought I'd start over in Las Vegas. Population about thirty
back then, and there were railroad jobs that fall. The first train ran in
January, 1905.

I made it until May 15th before I got drunk on sour mash one night
and put a bullet in my eye. The city of Rhyolite was gone by 1907.

When the city claimed me, it came with Stewart. And Stewart was
a revelation to me.

Thirty years later, the dam came and Saint Thomas went under the
water, and I figured Laura and the house I bought her with Rhyolite
gold were just more ghosts at the bottom of the reservoir—

Anyway, the widow and the Russian thought the assassin would
be gunning for us, and though I vetoed the spies' plan to go back to

the Paris and look for their partners, I didn't see any reason that Doc and John Henry couldn't go looking, once we were safe, for whatever values of safe we could swing. They couldn't feel the scholar, which didn't make the Russian happy. But they could feel the athlete and the American. Half a loaf, you know?

I really wished, though, that there was some way Doc could dial a cell phone.

Better if we stuck together, I figured. Although that was going to take a pretty damn big car.

Fortunately, Cashman Cadillac is still there, and they still know me on sight. Funny story: Elvis used to go down there at three in the morning and buy cars by the dozen, and then give them away. It's where he got the one he gave me.

Doc's coughing made him easy to keep track of, if you were one of the ones who could hear him. It was a little creepy to look over and see him sitting *inside* the widow, though, especially when she was as oblivious to his presence as if he didn't exist.

Which, I suppose some would argue, he didn't

Anyway, Stewart drove, and Doc navigated, and the rest of us crammed in however we could, and it wasn't long before we figured out we were headed for one of two places; Boulder City, or Hoover Dam—there aren't a lot of way stations south and east of Vegas—and my money was on Hoover. A sucker bet, and if anybody had been willing to take it, I would have collected.

We drove across the dam to Arizona and then back to Nevada, just to make Doc and John Henry sure. Both of them agreed; they could feel the American and the athlete, and they were a little closer to the Nevada than to the Arizona side of Hoover Dam . . . and more or less straight down. The spies were awfully quiet. Especially the Englishman. Although the Russian did comment that he wasn't sure whether he was anticipating the opportunity to test his demolitions expertise on Hoover, or dreading it.

Fortunately, not while we were anywhere near the checkpoint.

"Well, it will be tricky," Stewart said, after we'd pulled into the parking lot of the Hacienda Hotel and Casino, a little south of Boulder City along US 93. The hotel and its environs crouched in a little clearing chiseled out of the canyon wall like a cavity in a tooth. The Russian wanted to know if it was the same company as used to run the Strip's Hacienda. He got very testy when I had to admit I didn't know. Maybe he just missed his partner, and was taking his worry out on the surroundings. Fucked if I know, but it did make me wonder if Stewart and I were that annoying about each other. I shot him a look to see what he thought, and cracked up hard when I caught him looking back, at just that second.

All right. Maybe only half as annoying.

The Russian got us checked in—or, actually, he got himself and the widow checked in, and they smuggled the rest of us in with their card keys—and we went upstairs to hole up and wait for nightfall. Because nighttime, of course, is just when you want to try to sneak into a government facility that's under military guard because of fears of terrorism.

But this was all in a day's work for the spies, right?

Right.

That's what I was worried about too.

The American in the Wrong Place at the Right Time.
Somewhere inside Hoover Dam. Las Vegas. Summer, 2002.

The American woke slumped against a wall, sitting. He had a headache and his hands were cuffed over his head, which made it—all things considered—a reasonably typical day. He was in an echoing room that smelled of damp concrete, which also wasn't too unusual, and there was a knee pressed up against his thigh.

That struck him as a bad sign, because the last thing he recalled was a shattering window, and the athlete diving for cover. He cracked one eye, saw the athlete drooping like so much dirty laundry, and sighed. It took a certain amount of effort not to mouth the words along with Angel when she spoke . . . from a safe distance, of course. "So good of you to join us."

"Not at all. I can't think how I would have refused."

His neck ached horribly, the best clue so far as to how long he'd been out. Six or eight hours at least, he estimated, which was bad, because it meant at least another fourteen hours before Tribute would be able to follow their scent to wherever they'd been taken. A lot could happen in fourteen hours.

On the other hand, his partner wouldn't quit looking for him, and neither would the athlete's.

Angel smiled coldly, right on cue as she swam into focus. She wasn't alone. They never were, when it would be convenient, and the American didn't bother trying to charm her. He didn't think that it would work this time. Instead, he turned his attention on the assassin who stood beside her, narrow-eyed and thoughtful, and enjoyed Angel's wrath that she wasn't his focus.

"Here to eat me?" the American asked, raising an eyebrow, forcing himself to move as if he wasn't in pain. He nudged the athlete's knee

205

hard as he straightened his legs in front of him, and had to assume that the assassin noticed.

"Unfortunately," the assassin said, "that particular culinary adventure will have to wait. Unless you'd care to tell me where you left your partner."

"It would be out of character," the American admitted.

"So is fighting on the wrong side," the assassin said. He glanced at the athlete and then at Angel; his eyes met the genius's, and she nodded and turned away. The American tracked her until she ducked down an open corridor. He wished he found the lack of a cell door more reassuring.

"Self-defense is the wrong side?" He thought he caught a change in the athlete's breathing, but couldn't be sure. He stretched against his chains, easing his shoulder and incidentally jostling the athlete's elbow. Yes, a definite catch in his breathing.

It would have to do.

"You know," the assassin said, coming a few steps closer, "it would be out of character for me to pick the wrong side, too. I'm not one of the bad guys."

"You're not one of the good guys either," the American said, as the assassin crouched by his feet—just out of range, if he slid down to the limit of his chains and kicked.

"I supposed that depends how you define the good guys." He checked his watch, dark hair brushing his eyebrows.

"Seems like if the whole world is on the other side, it might be time to ask yourself if you picked the right horse." The American didn't lunge, for all the temptation. He pressed his back and his skull against the concrete and stretched, a loud click announcing the realignment of his neck.

"Alternately, didn't someone once argue that if a thousand people said one thing and he said another, it was a thousand to one that he was right?" A slow grin creased the assassin's face around his scar.

The American decided he hated the assassin's tailor, too. "Someone even more arrogant than me?" he said.

"I think your partner's rubbing off on you. He's got you pretty well fooled, doesn't he? How does it feel to be in bed with the Soviets, comrade?"

"You know," the American answered, smiling sweetly, "I hear a rumor there are no Soviets any more. And I'd rather deal with a loyal enemy than a down-home traitor, any day."

It would have worked, in the movies. But the assassin knew that as well as he did, and just stood up and stepped back, smoothing and buttoning his coat. "He's told you about Dallas, then?" Smooth, testing, voice like the flicker of a snake's tongue testing the air.

The American tried to keep his expression calm, superior, but the cool words rocked him. And the flicker of the assassin's smile told him the assassin knew. "Funny guy. Why don't *you* tell me about Dallas, and I'll see how the versions mesh up?"

The assassin shook his head and clicked his tongue sadly. "Pity you're so credulous. Get taken that way a lot, do you? Why don't you tell me where to find him, and if I manage to bring him in alive, you can listen to his answers yourself?"

"Because you're noted for bringing them in alive."

"I believe you Yanks would say, 'takes one to know one?'" The assassin gave him a wry shrug. "Ah, well. I tried."

"And a very nice try it was." The American knew how to get an awful lot of condescension into his voice when needed. "Now?"

"Now," the assassin said, squaring his shoulders before he headed for the same passageway that had taken Angel away, "we wait. Or rather, you wait, and I go have dinner."

His footsteps clicked away on concrete. When the echoes had died, the athlete raised his head stiffly, turned to the American, and said, sotto voce, "So. Tell me about Dallas. Do."

The Russian, Underground.
Somewhere in Boulder City. Summer, 2002.

Somebody had to come up with a plan, and swiftly. Before the assassin took care of the athlete, and came looking for the rest of them. There was no guarantee that even a simple plan would work, but the Russian had always liked machinery. Which is why he knew about the hardhat tours of Hoover Dam—"Simple," he told the other spies, Jackie, and Stewart. "We go on the tour, we slip away, and we find my partner and if we're lucky, and we get out. We regroup here, and if we haven't managed to take the assassin or Angel, we figure out what we do next."

"That'd be okay," Jackie said, crossing his arms, "if they hadn't stopped doing the dam tours after nine-eleven. And what about Tribute?"

The Russian blinked. "What's nine-eleven?"

"Nevermind. It'd take too long to explain." Stewart stepped in, all efficiency, one hand on Jackie's shoulder. Jackie leaned against the touch. "If they've got Tribute at the dam, we grab him. But he might be dead—"

The Englishman cleared his throat.

"—more dead. Or they might have him chained up in a bathtub somewhere drinking blood from a coffee mug, for all I know. If he's not working with them after all."

"Based on his behavior," the Englishman offered, with a glance at the widow, "that is to say, based on what I've heard about his actions, I'm not sure what double game he could be playing that would benefit him."

"Agree," Jackie said. "So how do we get inside the dam? There's just the elevators and emergency stairs."

The Russian folded his arm and watched. This was where he preferred to be; a step back from the discussion.

"We do as my Russian friend says," the widow said, kicking one foot up as she perched against the windowsill.

"No tours," Jackie started, but the Englishman cut him off.

"There are tours in 1964."

Jackie's eyes opened a little wider, and he glanced from the widow to the Englishman for confirmation, and then at a space in the air that might have been John Henry or Doc. The Russian smiled at being so swiftly forgotten; he was accustomed to it. "Can you get us *all* back there?"

The Englishman straightened the carnation in his lapel, and the Russian thought he saw the echo of his own grief and unease in the gesture. One dead, three captured. No guarantees they'd be able to do anything to fix it. "We can't know until we try."

"Doc says he and John Henry can get down inside the dam ahead of us," Jackie said. He did look right at the Russian this time. "They can just kind of walk through it, and find the American and the athlete, and then come fetch the rest of us."

"Easy as pie," the Englishman said, and set his hat on his head. "Well, if we're going to 1964, we don't need to wait for dark after all, do we?"

The Russian nodded. The widow stepped forward, extending her hand. He was about to concentrate when Stewart grabbed his elbow. "Let's wait until we get to the dam, shall we?"

"Of course," the Russian said, embarrassed. "In 1964, we don't have a car."

"That," Stewart said, "and we're on the seventh floor."

The American, On Dying with Style.
Hoover Dam. Summer, 2002.

"They're taking their own sweet time about getting here," the American said, some hours after they awoke. The athlete snickered, and kept working on his manacles with a bent bit of wire extracted from the American's shirt cuff.

"They'll be along," the athlete answered over his soft, rhythmic raking at the lock. "Yours *and* mine. Have a little faith, mi amigo."

"Trust in God, but keep your powder dry," the American answered. He stretched against the chains, trying to keep his shoulders limber. They felt like somebody had cast them in hot lead and left it there to harden, despite everything he could do, and he had a great deal of respect for the athlete's continued determination as he manipulated the wire with fingertips that had to be numb, or prickling with pins and needles if they weren't.

Tribute started singing again, and the American couldn't hear the pick raking the lock any more. He edged his elbow sideways, to give the athlete something to brace against.

"Hah," the athlete said, a few moments later. The American felt the click as the athlete's manacle slid open. "Tah dah." And then the athlete groaned between his teeth, a heartfelt sound of agony as he brought his arm down. He flopped his hand in his lap. "It's like meat, except I can feel my fingers, and wish I couldn't."

"One down." the American breathed deeply, "three to go."

"Oh, you expect me to rescue you too?" The athlete wiggled his fingers, wincing.

"Funny guy."

The second lock went faster, and the sound the athlete made when the cuff opened was a little sharper. The American guessed the arm

210

with which the athlete had initially been working wasn't as numb, and hurt him more when the blood started flowing back into it. The American could imagine the sensation of heat like a scald, the sharpness like needles thrust into the skin. He winced in sympathy, but the athlete didn't let it hinder him.

He pushed himself to his feet, the wire pinched between fingers flushed with returning circulation, and reached for the American's manacles. "We'll have you out in a jiffy—"

Of course he would. The American grinned back, and turned his attention back to the corridor. As long as the athlete's attention was distracted, the least the American could do was watch their backs.

Which is why he saw the shadow moving in the corridor in time to warn the athlete someone was coming. "Hey," he whispered, and jerked his chin that way. The athlete looked up, slipped the wire into the American's hand, and slunk quickly across the close little room with its oppressive cement ceiling. He flattened himself beside the door, poised as a panther on a branch, and the American went to work on his own manacles. The wire was stiff and somewhat springy, long enough to give him good leverage against the tumblers as he raked. The manacles weren't easy, though; the lock was complex enough to make him frown in concentration, and the numb ache in his hands didn't help. Especially as he wasn't looking at his hand, but keeping his eyes front, trained on the corridor, as Tribute, somewhere down the hall in the other direction, started singing "Fever."

Their luck, it seemed, was determined to be universally bad. The assassin rounded the corner in the corridor and caught sight of the American as the same instant the American saw him—and he had to be able to see the lockpick, and also see that the athlete was no longer chained. The assassin met the American's eyes, coldly considering, and pushed his forelock back with one hand as he drew his Walther into the other. The American smiled, and didn't stop working on the lock.

You never knew. Some times you got lucky.

"He must be beside the door, then?" the assassin asked. "Left side or right, I wonder?"

The American kept his eyes straight ahead. He'd used the same trick himself. It wasn't any different from playing poker; half the game was influencing the opponent, and the other half was reading him.

"He went to help Tribute," he said, and let his eyes slide toward the other exit just as Tribute started in on the verse about Romeo and Juliet. "I'm sure he'll be back, if you just wait a minute."

The assassin just grunted, and cocked his gun. He raised it, and squinted through the iron sights. "*Do* hold still."

The sound of the gunshot was shattering in the confined corridors of the dam. The American flinched, eyes tightening, and felt shards of concrete pepper his hair. His fingers stung, shocked, concussed, as if he'd let a cherry bomb go off in his hand, and the lockpick was no longer in his grasp.

He looked up, expecting blood on his fingers, missing flesh. They looked uninjured.

Apparently, the assassin was still a very good shot.

And he moved like a snake on ice. As fast as the American registered that the assassin had shot the lockpick out of his hand without so much as scratching him, the assassin was in the room. He guessed wrong and glanced left; the athlete was on the right, and lunged.

Helplessly, the American struggled with his manacles. He got his feet under him and heaved himself into a crouch. The combat was too fast for him to follow. If he'd been in it, he would have been operating on instinct and balance and training, the reflexes that would let him anticipate and counter his opponent. As it was, he saw the assassin's pistol fall as the athlete slammed his hand into the wall. The assassin turned, got a grip on the athlete's arm and sent him flying with a twist of shoulder and hip.

The athlete rolled with it, fell well, came to his feet in time to duck the assassin's kick. The assassin closed, and the American lost what happened next in a flurry of strikes and counterstrikes. They fought silently, the only sound the scuff of shoes, the sharp smacking noise of flesh striking flesh.

The manacles scraped the American's wrists. He leaned on them; it was useless, of course, but he brought his weight to bear as best he could, chained into a crouch, put his head down and rocked hard, yanking. No good, no give at all. Nothing, and when he looked up again the athlete was down on his back, the assassin's hands locked on his throat.

The assassin's forelock dragged across his face, bright nail-scratches livid on his wrists as he pressed down against the athlete's hands. The athlete's mouth gaped open; he wasn't getting any purchase. His hips thrashed, feet kicked, but he couldn't shift the assassin's weight.

"By the way," the assassin said, very calmly, "your partner is dead." And then he pushed the athlete hard against the floor, one hand clenched on his throat, straight-armed, and pressed his palm across the other man's mouth and nose.

The athlete groaned, purple-faced, heaving in superhuman effort as his breath whistled against the assassin's hand. The American dropped his head and yanked on the chains, eyes closed, feeling the muscles in his shoulders strain and tear. His back screamed. His thighs cramped, ached.

The chains did not give.

When he looked up again, hot blood trickled down his forearms, soaking his cuffs. The athlete lay still. His eyes, half-lidded, gleamed through the lashes. The American gritted his teeth and made himself watch as the assassin wrenched the athlete's jaw open and reached into his mouth, roughly, hooking his fingers as he pressed down the unconscious man's throat.

The athlete kicked, twitching. The assassin dragged something out of his mouth, a small shining thing, pale blue, gleaming and wriggling in his hands like a goldfish grabbed from the fish tank. The assassin contemplated it for a moment, examining it as if to make sure it was complete, and popped it into his own mouth. He swallowed without chewing.

The American choked on bile, turned his head and spat, as the assassin stood, coolly, and dried his hands on his pants. The athlete lay still, unreal as a wax mannequin. The American forced himself to ignore it, to move on, to register nothing. No fear, no grief, no fury. Not now.

Maybe not ever.

He made himself look up, and meet the assassin's gaze. "And I'm next?" he asked, mildly.

The assassin raked his hair off his forehead and rolled his shoulders back, like a boxer ready to come out of his corner. He looked brighter, somehow. Sharper, more brilliant, more real.

Concrete.

"Not just yet," the assassin said, and collected his gun before he walked back around the corner. The American heard him on the call box there, summoning someone to deal with the body.

Of course they had minions. There were always minions. That wasn't the reason for the relief that eased his shoulders as he let himself slide back down the wall and sit. *Don't feel it*, he ordered himself, and watched the athlete's body twitch one more time and soften into death.

The assassin wasn't ready to consume him yet. Which meant that somewhere, out there, the Russian was alive.

Which was generally speaking a very, very good sign.

One-Eyed Jack and the Wrath of Gods.
Hoover Dam. Summer, 1964.

As luck would have it, the Russian's trick worked, and two hours later, Stewart and I were dressed up like 1964 and strolling through the bowels of Hoover Dam with a tour group composed of ten innocent bystanders, ourselves, and three spies with their baby blue hard hats pulled low. The Englishman amused me in particular, with his bowler in his hand and his umbrella hooked over his wrist, head tilted back in transparent amazement, ogling and pointing and nudging complete strangers in the most aggravating fashion imaginable.

If I hadn't seen his partner in action, I would have assumed he was a complete idiot and a danger only to himself. Which was, fortunately, what the tour operator seemed to assume as well—and he did keep her distracted from the rest of us.

The distraction was necessary, because Doc and John Henry couldn't walk through these walls. And weirder—it turned out they could affect things that were part of the structure of the dam. Push lift buttons, for example, and turn doorknobs. Weird and unsettling, and it made me wish I were a better magician, or I had a real, honest-to-Prometheus Club Mage around who would be willing to answer theory questions. If they hadn't been the guys who built the magic into this damned hunk of concrete in the first place.

Unfortunately, the only one I knew of was unlikely to agree to consult.

So anyway, the ghosts had accompanied a previous tour group down, and were supposed to meet us when they'd finished mapping everything they could, and tried to figure out where Tribute, the athlete, and the American might be held. And in the meantime, Stewart and I, and the Russian and the Englishman and the widow, got a tour of the cool concrete interior of Hoover Dam. And I kept my hands in my pockets so I didn't mistakenly reach out and muss Stewart's hair, or something else wildly inappropriate, and I kept reminding myself that it didn't matter how long things took us in the sixties—we could come back to the same instant in 2002 that we'd left.

For all the waiting made my palms sweat, the dam *was* pretty neat. Especially the vast humming powerhouse, with turbines as big around as grain silos spinning in their dark red and chrome housings. The whole of the upper powerhouse *surged* with the force of the water flowing through those giant machines; it shivered through my shoes, trembled in the railing when I laid my hand on steel. Under my feet lay the lower generator room, where the turbine shafts whirred ceaselessly, balanced fingertip on a single bearing. The tour would take us among them next.

Eight turbines on this side, the Nevada side. Nine in Arizona. The dam was completed and dedicated in 1935. And I couldn't begin to explain why it was that I had never come down here before, except—

Except I could feel in the thunder of the dam's enormous heart, in its chambers and its pulse, that I was not welcome here. This was not a place for me and mine: this was an immortal animal, constructed by mortal animals. It wanted nothing of mirage-born cities or their genii. Las Vegas was beneath it.

Goddess was right, when she said that this was not my dam.

I couldn't decide if the Russian was more entranced by the gigantic machines or if the widow was; they stood shoulder to shoulder, their ear protection leaned together as they peered through the viewport into the churning water inside. The Englishman, I noticed, was patently ignoring them, staring up at the chromed railings on the gallery we'd just descended from and twirling his bowler on the handle of his brolly.

He tapped a toe on the speckled stone floor, which was grooved with steel tracks for some sort of trolley apparatus, and turned to glance over his shoulder with a wink and a smile. For me. Not for the widow, and *definitely* not for the Russian. I was half-watching him and half-listening to the shouting tour guide when I felt a breath of coolness on my cheek and turned to face Doc Holliday.

"Find something, Doc?"

He opened his mouth. I tapped my earcovers and he nodded, and then doubled over into a wracking cough. I knew he couldn't possibly be getting worse—he was dead already—but it hurt to look at, just the same.

When he was done he straightened up, made a "circle the wagons" kind of gesture, and waited impatiently, crinkling candy wrappers, while I rounded up Stewart and the rest.

It made for an interesting game of charades, as it was much too loud in the powerhouse for us to hear each other without shouting even if we were stupid enough to pull off our earmuffs. Finally, the Russian held his wrist up and tapped the crystal on his watch, and when I nodded, the Englishman tugged my elbow and pointed with his umbrella. There was a little door in the corner, under the observation gallery.

I looked at Doc. Doc nodded, and coughed, and I passed the first part along.

The trick was going to be getting away from the tour guide. Or so I thought, until a hollow thudding, the sound of a good-sized chunk of solid steel slung rhythmically into concrete, caught my attention through the hearing protectors. I leaned around the turbine and looked—in unison with Stewart, which got a smirk out of the widow—down the echoing powerhouse.

John Henry stood on the catwalk along the top level of the powerhouse, his hammer swung overhand, ghostly chips of concrete flying from his ghostly steel. There was no damage to the dam itself— the real dam—and I could tell with one look at the spies and at the tour group that they couldn't see a thing.

But they could hear it, all right, and the tour guide was hustling people together preparatory to getting them out of the powerhouse as fast as possible.

I suspected the tour was at an end.

And our little group, as if informed by the same, sudden decision, hustled after the Englishman and his umbrella in the opposite direction, toward the door under the stairs.

It wasn't locked. Doc must have checked before he fetched us, and we filed through quickly and in order. Stewart double-checked once we were inside, in one of the greenly lit inspection tunnels, and made sure it latched behind us. The click, when I pulled my hearing protection off, seemed loud enough that I flinched.

I put a hand on the concrete wall of the inspection tunnel and felt it, felt the belly of the beast quivering under my fingertips. I snatched my hand back and stuffed it in the pocket of my suit jacket, and looked up to see the Englishman grinning at me as he dropped his hardhat on the floor, kicked it to one side, and settled his bowler back over his greased cap of curls.

"Further up and farther in," he said, and offered a bent elbow to the widow, who stepped up beside him in her two-toned boots and clicked her heels like a soldier coming to attention.

"That's not a reassuring comparison," the Russian said. "Jackie, I take it your spirit guides have reported for duty?"

"Doc?"

Wonder of wonders, Doc didn't cough this time, but he did reach for his handkerchief, just in case. "There's a room down here you need to see," he said, and tromped through Stewart and the Russian on his way to the head of the line.

"He says that way," Stewart translated, for the spies, and the five of us headed down in pursuit of the ghost.

Doc was right; we did need to see it. He led us through a regular maze of inspection tunnels that took us from the powerhouse to the dam proper, and then up inside the structure. Some of the tunnels vented to the surface of the dam, harsh sunlight and hot air drifting in through barred vents.

"We must be careful," the Englishman said, as we paused at a lift. "The opposition can get here too."

"1964?" Stewart asked.

"Further, even. He goes back a ways—up or down, Doc?"

"Down," Doc said, and Stewart pushed the button and then stared at his own thumbnail curiously, as if it had grown overnight. "Guns out?" he asked.

"Can't hurt." Which I relayed, because Stewart was looking away. I was surprised to see that the Englishman didn't have a weapon in his hand. The widow and the Russian were well-armed; I thought the widow's weapon was the one we took off Angel in the parking lot. And Stewart had his Colt, which I didn't think I'd seen since 1935 or so, when the West got a tad bit less wild.

You know, I never remember to pack a gun.

"Are we there?" the Russian asked.

"More or less," Doc said.

I glanced over at the Russian and nodded.

"Very well."

It was strange, but even in the bowels of Hoover Dam I could tell when he brought us back to 2002. The quality of the air was different, and there was thirty-eight years more grime and wear on the inlaid brass doors of the lift.

Doc pushed the button, seeming to revel in his ability to do so. The doors rolled open. We found ourselves in a narrow gray tunnel that should have been just like every other narrow gray tunnel in the dam. But there was something different about this one. The air was infested with the same thrumming sense of potential as the powerhouse, and I could tell by breathing that we—that Stewart and I—were just as unwelcome here.

"Feel that?" Doc asked.

"Yeah," I said.

Stewart said, "I see what you mean. Is your room through here?"

Doc led on. The room we came out into was little and square and bare, just as gray as everything else inside the dam, and lit with the same horrible green fluorescence. It was, however, notable for the presence of a dark-haired spy chained to the far wall. The American slumped against the wall, watchful, knees drawn up. Sleeping, or faking it: that's probably what I would have done as well, if I were blasé enough about being chained to walls to fall asleep.

"Rise and shine," the Russian said cheerfully. The American startled, and the Russian handed his gun to him; he used the leverage of his chains to hop into a crouch for enough slack to aim as the Russian bent over the chains with a wire in his hand.

"Where's the athlete?" the Russian asked.

The American shook his head, lips thin, and then looked up at me. "Watch the door."

Oh, right. Although I wouldn't do much good, compared to the spies, if anything did go down. The Englishman stood beside me, though, a steadying presence smelling of cologne. He spoke over his shoulder without turning his head, and I knew from the tone that it wasn't for me. "I don't suppose you—"

"We heard him singing," the American said, as his hands came free of his chains and the Russian retrieved his gun. The American groaned chafed his wrist with the other.

"Back on the Chain Gang?" Stewart asked, deadpan. The widow kicked his ankle hard enough to make him wince.

"John Henry," the American answered, pushing himself upright with considerable assistance from the wall. He looked at the Russian. "Did you seduce a pretty girl?"

The Russian's eyebrow went up. "I see no signs of drugs or torture. I don't think the bargain's settled yet."

"Damn." Groaning, the American managed to force himself all the way to his feet. "I don't suppose you brought a spare gun."

"Two," the widow said, palming a revolver to the American. He flipped open the cylinder, held out a hand, and slipped the cartridge the window handed him into the sixth chamber.

"The lift's moving," the Englishman—closest to the corridor—

reported. He glanced over his shoulder at the American. "Is there another way out of here?"

"Passage back that way." The American suited action to words, withdrawing through a low cement archway.

I went after—unarmed, I wasn't helping anybody pretending to play rearguard—and found the Russian at my shoulder. Doc was sort of in with the crowd; the widow, the Englishman, and Stewart brought up the rear. I wasn't too worried about Stewart. He's been handling that Colt since he was six or seven, and time was a man shot his own horse—and his own rattlesnakes—around here.

"How do we get out?" the widow asked, voice low.

"How do we find Tribute?" the Russian countered.

"And when we do, are we going back to get John?" That from Doc, who paused to cough, the ghost of his pistol lowered in his hand.

"Do we need to?" Stewart. "I mean, he's a ghost—"

"Huh," Doc said, and wiped his bloody mouth again. "You got a point there, son. How about the bloodsucker, then?"

"If they could hear him singing," the Englishman said, from the rear of the group, where he was walking backwards, "then he could hear us. But that would be unwise. Here's the lift."

"That's all right," the Russian replied, stopping so that I walked into him. "So is the opposition. Behind me, Jackie."

I obeyed. I couldn't see what happened, architecture-wise, up ahead, but the tunnel opened out into a brilliantly lit room—or maybe one of those ventilation shafts ran across it—and a figure had just stepped out into the bright bulls-eye. I didn't need the Russian's stiffly indrawn breath to tell me that the thing cradled in the assassin's arms was a machine gun.

"Gentlemen," the assassin said. "Lady. Please be so good as to put up your weapons?"

I expected somebody to open fire; he was framed very neatly. But I guess it does come down to superior firepower, and there wasn't anywhere for us to go. Stewart and all three armed spies meekly raised their hands, fingers slack on their pistols. I thought the rustle at the back of the group was the Englishman raising his umbrella.

"Very good. Come forward, please, single-file—"

We advanced, the Russian and then me, the American and Stewart, the widow and the Englishman. And Doc, more or less stepping where I stepped. We walked out into a big bright room; I heard running water and caught a glimpse of a wrought-iron railing. Tribute stood behind it, looking a bit the worse for wear. "Jackie," he said. "Stewart. Spies." Doc huffed into his moustaches, but didn't step out of me—just in case any of the bad guys could see him, I expected.

"King," I said, and put my shoulder to him as I turned to face the assassin.

He wasn't alone. Felix Luray was with him, all corporate polish except a Mage's iron ring on the thumb of his left hand.

Luray cleared his throat. "There's still time to work this out so nobody has to get shot. We just want to deal."

"Mr. Luray," the assassin said. "Do you mind terribly if I ask them to set their weapons down before we have this chat?"

"Not at all," Luray answered, all slouched insouciance. The spies and Stewart crouched down softly, while I held my breath, and laid their weapons on the floor, and straightened up again. And everything was quiet for a good long time, until it also occurred to me that everybody in the room—including Stewart—was looking at me. Well, duh.

Somebody had to speak for Las Vegas. I stepped forward just a bit, feeling insulted when the assassin didn't so much as tighten his grip on his rifle. I hadn't heard the elevator door chime back in the room where we'd freed the American yet, and I was starting to hope that the elevator's motion had nothing to do with us. It would be nice to have an escape route. "A deal?"

"Something that could help out you, and Las Vegas, and us." There was another brass elevator door behind him, and once the shock of being held at gunpoint subsided a little, I started to realize what else was weird about this room—like the black inlaid dolomite floor laced with brass and steel, the constellations and symbols. The exact image, dammit, of the thaumaturgic inscription on the terrazzo.

"Tell me about it," I said.

The Russian was tense beside me, his hands laced behind his head, his body almost trembling with fury—and as near as I could tell, it was all directed at the assassin. I felt Tribute leaning forward too, as if against a glass wall I couldn't see, but he didn't speak. *Interesting*.

And Luray noticed it too. "Yes?" he said, acknowledging the Russian with a wave of his hand. A little smile lifted the corner of the Mage's mouth, one I didn't think any of us were intended to see.

"Mr. Luray," the Russian said, with the air of a man rolling the dice, "your interest in this dam and its symbolism makes me believe you may be a patriotic American."

Luray's mouth twisted at the corner. I could tell he was playing up his English accent when he said, "I thought by your lights, I'd be a capitalist running dog."

"The two are not always dissimilar."

A risk, but it got a laugh out of Luray. "I do my best. Doing my best right now, if it comes right down to it—"

"I understand."

I could feel his tension on my other side, too, in the American. Feel whatever was about to happen vibrating between them, communicated without a touch, without a glance. I gathered myself. Whatever it was, I would be ready—

"I would think a patriotic American would be more concerned with the company he kept," the Russian continued smoothly, as the assassin stepped forward.

"That's enough," he said, in a reasonable tone. "Mr. Luray, may I suggest we get this lot under wraps somewhere, and question them at leisure? Where it's *safe*?"

Luray's eyes flickered sideways, and he nodded. "Sensible." But then he glanced at the Russian again. "The company I keep? Actually, patriotism has a good deal to do with it. You thought there were only two sides in this splendid little war?"

The assassin's weapon never wavered. It was trained quite plainly on the Russian now, and I felt the Russian's ankle pressed against the back of mine. He was setting me up for a leg sweep, and I wasn't too slow to figure out it was for my own good. The Russian's smile was cold enough that *I* felt it, and I wasn't even looking, but it was the American that spoke.

"Oh," the American said, softly, as if startled, and shot a look past me to the Russian. The Russian never turned away from the assassin and his spray-and-pray gun. "Camelot."

"Of course," the Russian said. "How foolish of me. The *other* dream of America. The one that is cultural hegemony rather than corporate imperialism. Of course that story had to be ended, for yours to persist—"

"Well," Luray answered, "not that I was involved at that point. Before my time. But you're very clever, aren't you?"

"You *know* about the Kennedys," the American said, and as Luray's lips parted to answer, the Russian's foot kicked my leg out from under me—but I was ready for it and went down tucking my head, trying to land on my ass.

You know, machine guns really *don't* sound like a sewing machine? Especially not seven hundred twenty feet under a pile of concrete and reinforcing bar. Cement chips spattered my hair for a second, and then the painful ringing in my ears was just ringing and not *gunfire*, and the American's hand was on my collar and he was yanking me to my feet, yelling *run, run, run!*

Tribute Sings the Blues.
Hoover Dam. Summer, 2002.

They came for me.

They didn't *get* me, but somehow that didn't change anything, because—in the middle of a repetitive conversation with the assassin, and a guy wearing a Mage's iron ring who just had to be Felix Luray, though he had smiled thinly when I asked—they *came* for me.

I didn't expect anybody to come for me. Especially not when I was starting to get hungry enough that I was thinking of allowing myself to be bought. And I didn't expect that, just before they vanished to wherever it is that they vanished to, the Russian would turn his head and catch my eye, and there was a promise in the look. Not that I actually *believed* they'd be back . . . but I hadn't believed they would come for me in the first place, either.

I rattled my chain, because I could, and crouched down on the inlaid floor as the Mage and the assassin stared at one another wildly, and then the assassin said, "Bugger," and winked out too. And Felix looked at me, and Bugsy wandered in from down the hall on the left, dripping brains.

I was starting to get the picture. Angel wasn't supposed to know about this. Angel wasn't supposed to know about Bugsy or Felix the Mage. Angel was only allowed to know about me because they needed her to own me, the same way she was trying to own Stewart. Because they wanted me to take his place as the link between Hollywood and Vegas; they wanted me to taste her blood, and become a part of both cities, so that the assassin could consume me and step into my role. Like an insane game of corporate mergers. Or the ancient tendency of big cities to gobble up little ones.

Oh, yeah. There was nothing new about this.

Hey Jesse, I said.

He shrugged and looked over. I thought he was examining the wall and the railing. "You got your own self into this, Elvis."

Well, yeah. Yeah, I did. I rattled my ankle chain a bit more, put my back to the railing around my castaway's island, and started to sing. "Viva Las Vegas," because I was bored with "John Henry" and "House of the Rising Sun," and because I hoped it might annoy someone. Besides, I was saving "Maybelline" for when I was alone and could really get into it.

I was out of practice, but being dead does wonders for your breath control. You wouldn't believe how good it felt to dig in and let go— actually, after a little while, I had to stand up so I could get under it, and you know, fifteen feet of drop-forged steel makes an okay percussion section if you stamp your foot just right—but it had been a long, long time. It's one thing to look like the King of Rock and Roll's forty-year-old illegitimate son. It's quite another thing to sound just like him, and one thing I've always had is a really distinctive voice— and before Momma died and I let myself get processed into a crooner, and all that crap I was shoving down my throat took its toll, I used to be able to hit my own high notes, too.

You know, I don't mind the fat guys in glitter jumpsuits and the ratted black wigs. I deserve that. I earned it fair and square. But it does make me sad that almost nobody remembers that I used to be able to *sing*.

And these days, I don't dare. I shade it off a little, like when I was playing Elvis Impersonator, and I don't get down *in* it. Don't fill up the dead lungs and let the dead throat and the empty belly swell, don't howl, don't resonate.

Except—being chained in a temple hidden in the belly of Hoover Dam gave me that back. What did I care if some tour group heard a dead man's voice resonating out of a ventilation shaft? So the ghost of Elvis Presley is haunting Hoover Dam?

I mean, at this point, what's one more crazy-ass white boy's fairy tale?

So I closed my eyes and sang, and when I was done with "Viva Las Vegas," I snuck a glance at the Mage. He was leaned up against the wall, watching me. Bugsy stood there too, fussing with the ghost of his cigar. He didn't look like he was paying attention, but the corners of his mouth were turned down hard. I guess he didn't like my choice of tunes.

What the hell: it wasn't like I had anything better to do, and if I distracted them here, it might buy the genii and the spies a little time. And with the assassin and whatever reinforcements he could dig up on their tail, they needed more than just time.

Besides. It had been a while since I had an audience. And the acoustics were fantastic. And it took my mind off the gnawing hunger in my gut.

I took a breath I wasn't going to use, except for singing, and started up "I Gotta Get Drunk," a Willie Nelson tune I never would have sung, back when I was a God-fearing man.

The irony hasn't been lost on me, all these years.

When I looked up again, the Mage and the ghost were gone, and I was alone except for Satan and all his angels, in the shape of the ghost of my dead twin brother, whispering in my ear. You get used to it, after a while.

The American in the Belly of the Beast.
Somewhere in Hoover Dam. Summer, 2002.

The American ached all over, but that didn't stop him from running. Not much could stop him from running, when he had a good reason—and being unarmed and encumbered with civilians, with a trained killer in pursuit, served as adequate impetus. At least he knew he could rely on the other spies to keep their heads in a crisis, but he really wished he had a gun.

Jackie led the rout. The American had been inclined to quibble at first, but Jack pointed out that he could see the ghosts and the American couldn't, so the American pounded along beside his partner, taking advantage of their occasional pauses at intersections to chafe his wrists.

The second time they drew up, the Russian shot him a look and said in an undertone, "How'd you learn about the Kennedys?"

"I haven't yet."

"But you said—"

The American grinned at his partner. "I *guessed*. Even I can pick up a hint that broad. But you're going to tell me the details, aren't you?"

"It's classified," the Russian said. The American glared at him. The Russian shrugged. Behind them, Stewart and the widow slid into place, the Englishman right on their heels.

"Ready?" the Englishman asked, glancing over his shoulder. The widow leaned around the corner quickly, glancing both ways.

"All clear," she said. "Where are we going?"

"Lower powerhouse," Jackie said, moving forward. "Can you all swim? The water below the dam is rough, but—"

The American sighed. He should have known that he wouldn't get out of this without getting wet. "Details," he said in his partner's ear, as they followed Jackie out into the cross corridor, watching the widow for hand signals and keeping their own eyes peeled as well.

The Russian snorted. They advanced single file, all four spies moving with machined precision. Jackie and Stewart kept up all right, but the American knew they weren't serious combatants. It was in the way they moved, the way they had to think about the pattern the others just fell into, like schooled horses performing dressage.

Concrete and more concrete, and the growing hum of the generators. They weren't descending any more, but moving fast and directly. They hadn't run into any dam workers yet, which was good; the American suspected they weren't where tour groups were supposed to be. He heard ringing ahead, though, growing stronger—a rhythmic pounding, over and over again.

"So," the American said, oddly comfortable with the answer he was sure he was going to hear, "who shot JFK?"

There was a long silence. The American looked over his shoulder to make sure their tail was intact.

"Before I tell you that, I have to tell you about Oswald," the Russian said, suddenly, so quietly that the American had to look at him to make sure his lips were moving.

"What about Oswald?"

"I was sent to stop him."

"*Stop* him?"

"Of course. We're not any more eager for Armageddon than the Americans are. Were. Whatever. An American president killed by someone who would appear to be a Soviet operative would be very bad for all of us, and it wasn't too hard to figure out what that boob intended—"

"But you failed."

"No, I succeeded." Jackie had stopped at another cross-corridor. They were out of the body of the dam now; there were rooms on either side rather than just solid concrete in five-foot blocks. It meant slower going, because anything could be behind those doors, which meant keeping a focused watch to the sides, and behind. "Unfortunately, so did the assassin—"

The American looked at his partner in disbelief. "No."

A brief curt nod was his answer. "But yes."

"Wow—" Sunlight, then, just a glimpse of it through an office window.

"Down here," Jackie said, reaching forward to catch the American's sleeve. He opened a fire door and gestured them down a flight of stairs.

The American went, with one more glance over his shoulder. They ran downward on toetip like cats. Above, the steel door clicked lightly. "—Why?"

"If we knew that," the Russian said, vaulting the last three steps, "I suspect we'd have a much better idea what's going on than we do. And before you ask why I never told you"—the American stopped with his mouth open—"because I didn't realize it had bearing, and because I am not permitted to speak of it in any case."

"So why now?" They flattened themselves on the right side of the door at the bottom of the flight while Jackie, Stewart, the widow and the Englishman descended the stair. Jackie lifted his eyepatch, and peered through the chickenwire-reinforced glass in the door.

The American felt the Russian's shoulder rise and fall. "Well, if I'm not real, and the assassin's not real—"

"—if he's not real, how did he manage to assassinate a president?"

"Don't interrupt me when I'm justifying myself."

"Sorry."

"No, you're not—"

"The powerhouse looks clear," Jackie said, and swung the door open before the American could stop him. He heard the widow's sharp intake of breath, saw the Englishman move to yank Jackie aside. Breaths held, waiting for the spit and ricochet—and nothing happened, except a thunder of machinery echoing up the stairwell, making the American flinch and wish for the discarded hearing protection.

"Okay," the American said with a sigh.

"Okay," the Russian answered. "That took a year off my life."

"Sorry." Jackie, in a small voice.

"Just don't do it again," the Englishman said. "Right, I'll go first."

"And I'll be in Scotland before you," the widow answered, and crouched, one hand on the floor.

The Englishman barreled through the open door as the American held it wide, peering around the edge. The Englishman's body stretched in a controlled dive. He rolled and came up in a crouch, body shielded by the massive blurring column of a turbine shaft, a polished steel tree trunk spinning at hundreds of revolutions per minute. Only two gray-painted railings and a sharp step up isolated it from the floor, and seven more like it spun down the length of the cramped, resounding room. The widow followed a split second later, a scuttling dash that put her back to back with her partner, about a yard apart.

The American took a breath and assessed the situation. The railings arced wall to wall; to travel the length of the generator room, they'd have to duck under them and rush past the green and orange-painted housings and shaft fittings. Close to the rotating turbine shafts. He turned and yelled to Jackie—"We need to go all the way?"

"John Henry says so. He found a fire exit. Take us to the surface and we can swim for it."

The Russian rubbed the back of his hand across his mouth. "It'll be rough water." He let his eyes flick to the American, who was trying not to think about how his shoulders still felt like the muscles had been laced with lead.

"If he can do it, I can do it." He pointed to the Englishman with his chin. "Come on. Let's go."

"Age before beauty," the Russian said, and grabbed the edge of the door.

The American ran.

As he dove into cover, he estimated that the most exposed portion of their transit would be around the middle of the powerhouse. And there were cuts—indentations—in the side walls that could conceal a gunman, or just about anything smaller than a tank, really.

The widow was suddenly behind him—he hadn't even heard her move—and then Stewart, with an awkward skittering rush. *Dammit*, he thought, realizing that his partner intended to go last.

"I'm going on ahead," he said in the widow's ear, and the widow nodded.

"Don't get strung out—"

"One shaft only." Which made the widow laugh, as he'd intended.

"I'll back you," she said. Her face was serious, lips firm, and he had no reason at all to doubt her capabilities.

"Let's do it—"

"Wait!" Jackie, falling heavily beside him, but a second too late. He was already committed.

He didn't vault the railings as gracefully as the Russian would have managed—or, for that matter, as the widow did—but he made it to the next turbine without breaking anything or getting shot. That cold prickle of anticipation hadn't left the back of his neck, however: an animal's knowledge of a trap.

He trusted his instincts. They—and his partner—were all he had. The widow joined him. When he looked over, he found her tucking a strand of hair behind one ear with her fingertip, her gaze trained over his shoulder, the single line of a frown creasing her pretty forehead. "Where do you think he is?"

She shrugged. "Waiting. Or rather, lying in wait."

He checked back the way they'd come, saw a flash of bright hair and a limp and knew the Russian was clear of the stairwell. A black business suit flapped, unbuttoned, the sleeves pushed up. Jackie dropped over the railing and crouched beside them, unsteady in his slick-soled dress shoes. The American reached out and caught his elbow, steadying him.

"Don't go," Jackie said. "I've asked Doc to scout." He looked strange with his eyepatch flipped up—right eye, in its paler triangle of flesh, aswirl with city lights and colored mist, like a time-lapse image of a nebula, left eye dark and worried and human. The American had expected scars, a hollow socket, not this vortex of lights and possibilities.

Jackie looked up and squinted, as if at somebody who would have been standing more or less in the gray-painted railing, and frowned. "Doc says he's here, all right."

"Show me," the widow said, as the Russian leapfrogged up to them and flattened himself on the damp steel floor. Jackie leaned over her shoulder and pointed, keeping his head low. "See that junction box there?"

"Yes," she said. There was something cold in her voice, something the American didn't like. He'd heard it before, somewhere: a tone he knew and feared. She turned and looked at him. "How far do you think his plot immunity would hold? And what would happen if something broke it?"

"His?"

"Or someone else's."

The American looked over at the Russian. The Russian was staring at his hands, rubbing a thumb across broad knuckles.

"I think if the . . . the genre expectations fall apart, they fall apart for all of us," the American said, very slowly. "I think we're all linked. If we weren't before, the assassin's hunt for the rest of us has tied us together."

"So if he kills one of us, his own immunity should go by the wayside," the widow said.

The American nodded. "I'll go. He wants me alive."

"No," the widow said. "I think his plans have changed."

"What do you mean?"

"He—" she paused, swallowed, eyes front, focused on the shadowed niche where the assassin waited. Where he had to be. "He blew up a plane. Our plane," she clarified, after a moment. "All souls."

"Christ," somebody said, very quietly. A moment later, the American identified the voice as his own. The athlete and the scholar were one

233

thing; the American mourned them, but he mourned them as warriors. They had been volunteers.

Civilians were something else. *All souls.*

"Hold that thought," she said, and pressed herself down on the floor, belly-flat, and began to wriggle forward. The American grabbed after her ankle; she was out of reach too fast.

"Christ," he said again, in a very different tone, but Jackie's hand was on his shoulder, holding him back, generous mouth compressed in a frown as he watched the widow slither under the railings.

"She's just as qualified as you are," he said, and the American sat back on his heels with a groan.

"My partner will kill me if anything happens to her."

"Your partner's unlikely to kill you," the partner in question said. "But he may be sorely put out. You couldn't have stopped her."

"He has a *machine gun*—"

"I know," the Russian said, his hand tightening ineffectually on the gray latex paint of the railing. He turned, met the American's stare, and shrugged helplessly.

"It wasn't my idea, all right?"

"Yeah," the Russian answered, after a minute, looking away. "I know it wasn't. So what do we do?"

"Back her play. And hope he's not insane enough to take his chances with ricochets in here," the American said, a little helplessly, and slithered under the railing himself, on the opposite side of the smoothly rotating turbine shaft. The others would follow him. Well, he was certain of the Russian, and he wasn't too worried about Jackie. The genius of Las Vegas might be a civilian, but he wasn't lacking intestinal fortitude.

The cold steel plates under the American's hands and forearms were spotlessly clean and dry. Rather than the grit and oil expected of a mechanical enclosure, every surface here was scrubbed like an operating room. The American crawled forward, head low, watching the widow's boots as she slithered under the next set of railings and paused in the shelter of the shaft housing, poking her head up enough to eye the distance and angle to the niche Doc and Jackie had identified as the assassin's point of concealment. She dropped again, wriggling forward—angled away from the assassin's hiding place and not toward it. Abruptly, the American understood her plan.

Even with superior firepower at his command, it wouldn't do the assassin much good to pick off one or two of them and alert the rest to his presence. They still had him outnumbered, and he couldn't be sure he had *all* their weapons, and the possibility that they would turn the tables remained too great. So he'd let the widow go past, the American guessed, and wait until the rest of the spies, Jackie, and Stewart were closer, and their guard was down—and he could take them all, more or less, with one well-aimed burst.

Besides, the assassin might be *willing* to kill his opposite numbers now, but that didn't mean he was *eager* to. The American thought he still had a use for them, if they could be taken alive. Otherwise, he wouldn't be there to crawl forward as if blithely into a trap.

He was just pausing to consider his options when he felt someone nudge his thigh. He glanced down, through the triangle made by his upper arm and body and the floor, and smiled when he realized that Jackie had recovered a three-foot pipefitter's wrench from somewhere and was passing it up. Still sprawled on his belly, heartbeat echoing so loudly he could hear it over the whir of the turbines, the American hefted the wrench in his right hand. It was balanced like a hatchet, all the weight at the outside end, but he'd thrown a hatchet or two in his time—

Gesturing the Russian past him, he hitched himself into a knee-dropped crouch behind the next shaft housing, and swung the wrench experimentally a few times to get the feel of it.

Not bad.

Not bad at all.

He rested one hand on the railing, peeked around the edge of the green-painted shaft housing, and held his breath. The Russian slithered across the long bolted-down tongue of the housing and paused there, while Jackie began edging forward over steel tiles and open floor, keeping the body of the next turbine between himself and the assassin's suspected position. The widow was opposite now; he'd have a clear shot at her whenever he cared to try.

A hell of a gamble, the American thought, and readied himself for a long overhand tomahawk-throw as the widow caught the railing on the third turbine with both hands and dragged herself up. Meanwhile, the Russian hoisted himself onto fingertips and toes and set himself against the nearest shaft housing like a sprinter against the blocks.

The vibration through the floor and railing was dizzying; the whole dam thrummed with energy, chained, directed, like the pacing of a beast on a lead. The American took his hand off the railing and shook his head to clear it, then forced himself to watch not the girl, and not his partner, but the narrow space behind the junction box.

Jackie caught up with the American, Stewart dogging his heels. The Englishman must be bringing up the rear, the American thought, but didn't turn to check. Something moved in the niche, and he raised his arm—

The widow seemed to come out of nowhere, just as the assassin was raising his gun to draw a bead on the American. The American's attention had been on the target, but she must have run up the railing on the shaft housing, turned a handspring, and come down in position to hook the assassin's wrist and snap the arm up behind his back.

He didn't drop the gun. The chatter and zing of bullets loose in the concrete-and-steel powerhouse sent the American ducking into the uncertain shelter of the turbine shaft. He heard someone yelp and hoped it was shock and not trauma. The assassin got off another three-shot burst; the American risked a peek around the housing and saw the widow down on one knee, both hands clutched over the assassin's as she wrestled him for the gun. She'd gotten the muzzle canted up, over her head, but not far enough up for anybody running to assist her to be safe, and the assassin was still too well-concealed for a tossed wrench to do much good.

Until the widow dropped her weight backward, got one foot up, twisted hard and set it in the assassin's midsection as she let the sudden shift in balance overset them both. She rolled on her back, the chattering rifle made the axle of a wheel, and kicked out hard with both feet as bullets whined and zinged.

The assassin went one way. The automatic rifle—not an M14, but something more modern—went another, and the widow went a third. The American snapped his arm back and threw, hard, as the assassin came to his feet, his pistol already in his hand, and turned the same second as Stewart lunged across bare steel toward the automatic rifle.

The turn saved him. He snapped off one shot in the same general direction as the widow, and then the hurled wrench struck him high on the shoulder and knocked him sideways. He lost the gun— the American heard it go—and dove after it, narrowly eluding the Russian's attempt at a scissors takedown.

The Russian fell heavily as the assassin bailed over the railing, vaulted the nearest shaft housing, and pelted down the length of the powerhouse, moving with a hurdler's grace. Stewart raised the automatic rifle; Jackie jumped over the railing and caught his wrist. "Wait! Ricochets."

The American didn't lower the rifle, but he turned to give Jackie a sideways glance and sighed.

Just as the Russian cursed—actually cursed, words the American hadn't known he *knew*—and dashed the width of the powerhouse. He went to his knees in the shadow of the junction box, swearing, and the American went after, swinging over the railing like an out-of-practice gymnast over a vaulting horse.

He landed beside his partner, the steel decking slick under shoes and knees, trying not to see the Russian's hands scarlet to the wrists—blood opaque as milk, his cheek and hair streaked with red where he'd pushed strands out of his face—bent over the widow and breathing into her open mouth.

The American felt for a pulse, felt for the heartbeat, straddled the widow's slim hips as his partner breathed for her and knotted the fingers of one hand through the other. He pressed his fists against her breast—

"No," he said, when he'd meant to begin counting, because his hands found the wound when they meant to find her ribcage, and he felt the sticky seep of blood and he knew. No chance.

Not a chance in hell.

"No," he said, and put a bloody hand on his partner's shoulder, and when his partner would have shaken him off, he grabbed and *pulled*. "No good," he said. "No, no good. Come on, it's over—"

The Russian slapped his hand away.

"God *damn* it," the American swore, and grabbed his partner by the shoulder, and yanked, and the Russian staggered back so hard he overbalanced and fell on his ass. "It's *over*."

"No," the Russian said, but looked at him, and when he nodded, closed his eyes. He put a bloody hand down on the steel, pushed himself to a crouch, left a stark print in sticky red behind. The widow lay sprawled, eyes open, one hand up as if to wave goodbye. The Russian looked for a moment, and then he wiped his bloody mouth on his bloody hand and turned away. "Give me that pistol," he said, and looked up to find himself staring into the Englishman's eyes.

"No," the Englishman said, checking the magazine with practiced hands, though he never carried a weapon. He counted the load, smashed the clip back into the Walther's grip, and chambered a round. "No," he said, as Stewart mutely extended the captured rifle toward the Russian, "this gun is mine."

"Come on," Stewart said, and laid a hand on the Russian's elbow. The Russian looked up, dazed. "Don't waste it. *Come on*."

One-Eyed Jack and the Rag-Tag Band.
Las Vegas. Summer, 2002.

We went into the Colorado downstream of the powerhouse, having recollected the legends and dragged them back in our proper time. Well, mine and Stewart's proper time. This was the new Colorado, tamed, stripped of its ancient mysteries; the only weapon left to its old treacherous soul was drought. But here, below the dam, the water was cold enough to be dangerous, turbid with perfidious undertows.

It washed the widow's blood away. Not much of a sacrifice to appease the river's lapping tongue, but all we had to offer. We swam, or stayed afloat, and let the current push us. There wasn't much by way of white water here, fortunately, and we dragged ourselves out at Ringbolt Rapids, wheezing.

I wasn't sure if I was more worried about Tribute, the Russian, or the Englishman. I mean sure, the vampire was chained up behind running water in some sort of temple hidden in the belly of Hoover Dam, but he could pretty much take care of himself. The Russian was almost affectless—face emotionless as he straightened his soaked shirt-cuffs and tightened his tie, socks squelching in his shoes. And the Englishman very carefully made sure his hat was tilted just right on his head, and then set about checking that the action on the assassin's Walther was only wet, and not fouled. He handled the gun with professional distaste, a frown tugging the corners of his mouth down.

It didn't reassure me.

The John Henrys dissolving into view on the riverbank were slightly better news. Doc wasn't coughing, for once, but his eyes burned fever-bright and I could see the pebbled river bank through his shoes. He stepped forward. John Henry stayed back; still happy to let Doc do the talking.

Stewart slung an arm around my waist, as if I needed help standing up straight, and maybe I did. It was good to lean on his solid warmth, anyway. So, all right, I barely knew her, and the spies were using us as much as we were using them. So that's how the game is played. Every time I looked over at the Russian, his drenched suit coat hanging on him like a tattered scarecrow draped over a cross made of sticks, my gut twisted.

I gave Stewart an extra squeeze, and turned my attention on Doc. "What's up?"

He rolled his dead eyes. Yeah, I guess even a ghost has heard that one plenty.

"John got a few words in with Tribute," he said. "He says it's not just Angel and the Mage. He says the ghost of Bugsy's in on it too. And Bugsy's probably a little ghost, but he's one of the angry ones. Unless he's a legend."

"If Bugsy's a legend, that's ungood," Stewart said. Characteristic, that knack for understatement. "'Cause he can probably track our ghosts same as we can track his."

"Thought of that," Doc said, and spat blood. "Not sure what we can do about it, though, 'specially as they've got a Mage."

"Running water," I said, and Stewart looked at me. Hey, you don't get to be a hundred something and genius of Las Vegas without learning a little about magic.

"We can't spend all our time in a canoe," he countered.

The American stepped forward, obviously following at least the audible half of the conversation. I held up one hand, and he hesitated, not too patiently, and then nodded, removed himself from the circle, and went after his partner.

"But you can get in to see Tribute. That's good, that means we can talk to him. Do you think one of you could kind of . . . hang around and watch his back? Come get us if anything changes, or if there's any news?" Doc nodded. I sighed, and rolled my shoulders back, and stretched my neck. "We've got to get back to town, Doc. We've got to figure out what's going on with these guys, and put a stop to it once and for all."

"Well, we found out about the secret heart of Hoover," Stewart said. "That's something. And we found out there's a ghost-dam that's just as real as the real dam, and that John Henry can put a dent in it if he gets a chance to swing his hammer a bit."

"And we found out where they're keeping Tribute."

"Until they move him." Stewart looked at me, bright-eyed, and glanced over at the spies.

I followed his gaze. The American had his hand on the Russian's shoulder, next to the strap of the assassin's machine gun, and if I strained hard enough I could just hear him talking, over the babble of the river. The Russian's head was down, his hair draggled in his face like a wet collie's. He turned the Russian so the Russian had to look at him—although the Russian didn't look up until the American physically took charge of him.

"How like you to take me swimming in my clothes. Alas, suit coat. I knew it, Horatio. A garment of infinite jest—"

The Russian's frown didn't shift, but he didn't step back, and I saw his shoulders rise and fall on a deep, conscious breath. "How come I'm relegated to Horatio?"

The American smiled. Even I could see it for sympathy, although his voice stayed teasing. "You'd rather be Hamlet? Poisoned, stabbed, and betrayed?"

"I'm not sure either of us taking on a role as Hamlet is wise, at this juncture." The Russian rubbed his face, looked down, and pulled himself together. Literally: it looked like a marionette straightening when skilled hands picked up the crosspieces and the limb joints settled into one another swinging. He turned, and stared his partner in the eye. "Besides, don't you see us in a more contemporary role?"

"Contemporary?" Deadpan, the consummate straightman.

"Frick and Frack?"

The American started laughing. "Partner mine, I don't think they're contemporary any more—" and Stewart nudged me, and I glanced at him, and took a breath that smelled like his hair, dripping swampwater in the sunlight, and let my shoulders ease.

"You notice anything about that?" he asked, leaning his shoulder on mine.

"They need each other?"

"They could be our evil twins, Jack-Jackie."

I squinted. Well, not quite—not really—but I saw what he meant. "Opposite numbers. Hang *on* a second." I glanced down at him again, and he frowned at me, and I looked back at the spies, and at the John Henrys standing side by side—"Sets of two. It's all sets of two. Except the assassin, but he's trying to be a set of two with Angel—"

"The Mage and Bugsy, yeah. But—"

"Tribute," we both said at once, and I grinned hard enough that my cheeks hurt, even though I didn't know what it meant. "Twin cities, twin destinies. Los Angeles and Las Vegas. L.A. didn't *really* hit its stride as a city until the nineteen forties. After World War Two."

"After Bugsy came to Vegas," Stewart said. "Tribute said as much at the California. Remember?"

We stared at each other for a few long seconds, and Stewart said, slowly, "You know—"

"Yes?"

"Elvis had a stillborn twin. Jesse Garon Presley."

"Shit," I said, and looked over at Doc. "Doc, get back to Tribute, would you please?"

"My pleasure." The ghost touched the brim of his hat. "Where can I find you if I need you, and I think I will?"

"I don't," I started to say, and Stewart stepped in between us. "We'll be at the old Kiel Ranch."

"Stewart?"

"Enough ghosts there to fuzz up anybody's sensors," he said, with a vague, dismissive gesture. "And there's a ground-fed pond out there too."

"Didn't you just say something bitchy about canoes?"

He reached out and patted my arm. "It's all right, sweetie. I'll do the thinking for both of us now."

I would have killed him myself.

If I hadn't been laughing too hard.

Tribute and a Shot in the Light.
Hoover Dam. Summer, 2002.

For lack of anything better to do with my time, I was still singing when the assassin came back, looking a little the worse for wear. One eye was purpling, and he limped as he walked to the far corner and sat down on the floor, his back against the wall between the elevator and the side passage. He crossed his legs and laid out the Entertainment section of the Las Vegas Sun on the floor, and put a semi-automatic down on it. Beside the handgun, he set up a squeeze bottle, a cleaning rod, the usual cotton patches, and flat-head screwdriver. I watched through lowered eyelashes as he released the magazine, cleared the chamber, and left the slide locked back.

Reassuring. It looked like he meant to clean it, rather than kneecap me before he took it apart.

When he'd fieldstripped the Walther into four assemblies, he put together the cleaning rod and threaded a patch through it, then reached for the bottle. I kept right on singing as he soaked the patch and threaded it through the barrel, then repeated the process. He never looked up.

He was meticulous. And he didn't notice in the slightest when Doc Holliday strolled around the corner, hands in his pockets like the American, and leaned against the wall by the lag-bolted staple holding my chain. "Stewart and Jackie wanted me to tell you they were coming back for you, King," he said, rolling a cigarette with long pale fingers. The tobacco vanished when it drifted to the inlaid floor. "And ask you to soak up whatever you could, and pass it on to me. I pass it on to John Henry, and—"

Smart. That couldn't be Jackie's plan. If you don't think so good, try not to think too much—

I nodded, because the assassin wasn't looking. His head was still

244

bent over his gun. "Also," Doc said, crossing his arms over his chest, "you might want to think some about Jesse."

Oh, sweet Jesus. It was just as well I was leaning into "Maybelline" until my gut ached, because I didn't quite choke, or flinch. But I did manage to shake my head.

"Stewart says it's about twins," Doc continued, implacable. He licked his cigarette paper, twisted, and thrust the rolled-up end between his lips. I wanted to tell him even a ghost cigarette was going to make a ghost cough, but you get a sense, after a while, of when you might just be wasting your time. "The city of Los Angeles. The city of Las Vegas. Conjoined, after a fashion. Born at one birth, you might say. Of one mother. Midwived together."

Just a little too true. I nodded and kept singing, the verse about the rainwater and the engine. It hurt.

Jesse.

My brother. My twin.

Who broke Momma's heart in Tupelo, Mississippi, on a cold January night in 1935. I always wondered—

If I hadn't been born with his death around my neck, if I hadn't had that to make up for, what might not have been different? What might not have been?

Doc didn't say another word, just smoked his cigarette until the song ended. I leaned forward, tugged to the end of my chain, rattled it hard to get the assassin's attention as he reassembled his gun. The moving water scorched my hand when I reached out over it, towards him. I jerked back and called, instead. "Hey, man—"

He looked up. He let the action glide closed.

"You know, where I come from, we don't take a gun apart without a little whisky. You know, to occupy the mind."

"I don't drink whisky. 'Man.'" He slipped the magazine back in his pistol, delicate as a man slipping a ring on a woman's finger. His eyebrow went up over the scarred eye and he smiled. "You hungry yet, Your Highness?"

"No," I said.

He leveled the Walther and fired two shots into my heart.

It doesn't work like in the movies, but the kick from a nine-millimeter's enough to convince you to sit down pretty good, if you're off balance, and almost everybody's off balance when he's just been shot. I sat down hard, left hand over the bloodless hole in my body, right hand still reaching out, just as it'd been knocked off the rail when I fell over.

The assassin grinned at me, stripped the magazine out of his pistol, and started to take it apart again. "How about now?"

The Russian and the Unquiet Grave.
Somewhere in North Las Vegas. Summer, 2002.

There wasn't much left of the old Kiel Ranch.

The Russian pulled their van over along the roadside near an apparently deserted lot. The site Jackie pointed to consisted of six or seven acres of broken hardpan and scrub alongside a corrugated metal industrial campus with broad blue horizontal bands on the sides. It looked like any other desert lot in Las Vegas—if anything, a little more forbidding than some. The seared earth was the color of moonrock, lifeless brown and gray, clotted with gray-green scrub anywhere it could pry a toehold. Behind that, a chain-link fence sealed off the rear third of the site, and everything looked gritty and forgotten and gray. A slumped tin roof peered from behind taller bushes behind the fence, breaked on the east and north by clusters of four or five world-weary trees.

"He says the highway dust is over all," the American muttered, laying a hand on the Russian's shoulder for a moment before he slid out of the back seat and stood, arching, both hands fisted in the small of his back.

The Russian was grateful for the contact, but wouldn't show it. He stole a glance at the Englishman, unsurprised to find him similarly impassive. Demonstrations changed nothing.

The Russian left the driver's-side door latched and scooted across the front seat to the passenger side, where the wheel was tucked against the curb, following Jackie out of the minivan. It was trickier with bucket seats than it would have been in an older car, but not significantly so. There was plenty of room.

The American bumped his shoulder like a worried dog. The Russian gave him a distracted smile and glanced away, making sure he knew where Stewart was. The Englishman caught his eye this time and frowned, and glanced down, adjusting the tilt of his hat with two fingers.

"Give me the keys," Stewart said. "We'll bring the sleeping bags and stuff in after dark. No point in giving the game up."

The Russian handed over the keys. "Where are you going?"

"Just moving the van over to the residential neighborhood back there before anybody thinks to come ask what we're doing. You can get everybody through the fence, sugar?"

Men didn't usually call the Russian 'sugar.' He arched an eyebrow at Stewart, and Stewart handed him a big, bright grin.

"We need to get you boys names," he said, and turned back toward the van, whistling.

The Russian shrugged, and turned around to see Jackie eyeing him, with frank speculation. "He likes you," Jackie said. "Come on. You heard the man. Get us through the fence."

It was a relief to have an assignment, even an easy one. They ducked behind the scrub and were through in ninety seconds—before the van even pulled away—and the Russian hooked wire to close the gap he'd cut, while leaving Stewart access. Then he dusted his hands on his trousers, straightened his tie, and walked over to Jackie. "What are these plants?"

"Mormon tea and creosote bush, mostly," Jackie said, leading the little band across dun-colored earth toward the trees. "Those are willows over there. The water will be down among their roots. That big tree's a cottonwood."

The Russian inhaled deeply, trying to smell the water, the way he'd heard you were supposed to be able too, in the desert. All he got was the scent of dust and automobile exhaust, and the air so hot inside his sinuses that it hurt.

"Give yourself a bloody nose doing that," Jackie said.

The Russian coughed on dryness, and made a note. "What's the feathery tree over there? The sort of purple-gray one, that looks like smoke?"

"Tamarisk," Jackie answered, and there was no mistaking the loathing in his voice. "Salt cedar."

"You don't like it?"

"It sets deep tap roots, sucks up enough water to lower the water table, and when the other plants die of thirst, it seeds over everything. Whole huge thickets, acres of it."

"So it's competitive."

"It's an invasive species. Non-native."

Unable to resist, the Russian offered, deadpan, "So are we," and grinned when Jackie actually laughed, and shot him a startled glance.

Good. The defenses were in place, were functioning. No weakness slipped through the chinks in the armor, and that was what was important. Oh, the American would know—the American always knew—but the American was different.

It was all right if he knew.

The Russian stole another sideways glance at the widow's partner, and caught him looking. They locked eyes for a moment, and looked down in unison.

Okay, maybe it was all right if the Englishman knew, as well. But he didn't want to think about it, one way or the other, so he turned back to Jackie and said, "Stewart doesn't want to be here, does he?"

Jackie didn't answer, but his lips tightened and he shook his head. He'd secured dry, modern clothes for all of them—and he was back in his signature leather pants and heavy laced boots. He limped, too— the mincing step the Russian associated with blisters.

The American knew how to pick up a cue. "Your partner has history here, Jackie? I overheard something about ghosts back at the river—"

"We both have history all over this town. That's how we got the job, you know. But you'll have to ask Stewart if you want to know about Kiel Ranch."

"Thanks," the American said, as they came around the scrub concealing the tin-roofed structure. A crumpled little house huddled under the meager protection of an open-walled shed banged together out of corrugated tin and salvaged wood. Once-whitewashed adobe had scaled down to the dun earth underneath, and one wall of the house had fallen, revealing a two-roomed interior no bigger than a garage. The whole thing was reinforced and cobbled together with planks.

"I think I will. Hey, there's shade."

"Don't go too near the house," Jackie said. "It's not safe. The foundation's fallen out from under it."

The American cocked his head to one side and shoved his hands in his pockets, regarding the house.

"Oldest structure in Las Vegas," he read off a dilapidated sign. "Why isn't it preserved?"

"Viva Las Vegas," Jackie said, as if that explained everything. "The Mojave eats its young."

"This doesn't match my understanding of a ranch house very well," the Englishman said, pausing beside Jackie. He had his umbrella propped open over his head now, an impromptu parasol. If the Russian hadn't been looking, he never would have caught the lines of tension beside the Englishman's eyes, or he would have thought them just a squint because of the sun.

"You've seen too many episodes of *Bonanza*." But Jackie said it with a wry sort of resignation, as if it amused him. "There was a bigger ranch house, but it burned down about ten years ago. The graves are still around here somewhere, though."

"Graves?" The American nudged the Russian, and the Russian very narrowly avoided kicking his partner as Jackie looked over and frowned at them both.

"Yes," Jackie said, as footsteps crunched up behind them. The Russian recognized Stewart's tread, dragging slightly as if weighted down. "The graves of the Kiel brothers. William and Edwin. Murdered in 1900."

"October eleventh," Stewart said, ignoring matched speculative looks from all three spies. "Some people say Edwin shot William, and

killed himself in remorse. Some people aren't so sure. We'll need this."
He crouched down to lay two gallon bottles of water on the ground.

"They had enemies?"

"Yes," Stewart said, looking up through bangs he still hadn't had
the time to gel into submission. "You see, some people also say their
daddy, Conrad Kiel, shot old Archibald Stewart down in cold blood.
Stewart had a wife and five children, the youngest born posthumously.
Well, according to legend, one day the Stewart boys got the Kiel boys
back."

The Russian cleared his throat. He didn't like unanswered
questions. Especially those that could affect his future well-being.
"And they're buried here?"

"Well, William and Edwin were, before the university came and
dug 'em up," Stewart said. "The grave's off that way." A broad gesture
with the back of his hand, and then he looked up at his partner, as if
excluding all else. "I laid salt around, Jackie; I'll do more after sunset.
That and the brothers ought to keep Bugsy from figuring out where
we are. Besides, this just isn't his turf—no way."

The Englishman tilted his improvised parasol forward and leaned
one shoulder on one of the peeled tree trunks holding up the shed
roof. "So, what do I do if I see a ghost?"

"Don't worry," Jackie answered, as Stewart walked off toward the
cottonwood trees. "They're little ghosts. Real people dead by violence.
They're more or less powerless."

"More or less?" the Englishman asked, just as the American said,
"You said Bugsy was a little ghost."

"Lotta people *believe* in Bugsy, though." Jackie shrugged. "He
might be—sort of half and half. I'm just not sure."

The American stared after Stewart. "Stewart's not his first name,
is it?"

Jackie's smile bulged his cheek under the edge of his eyepatch.
"No," he said, turning to watch his partner disappear around the
trunk of the much-maligned salt cedar.

"What is it?"

The smile went a little wider, but there wasn't any warmth in it, and Jackie didn't look at the American. The Russian dried his palms on his pants.

"Stewart's his only name, these days. If you want to know the other one, you could ask him, but I can't guarantee he'd remember it. We died a long time ago." And then Jackie looked down, as if recollecting himself, and swallowed hard enough to bob his Adam's apple in his wiry throat. "Come on; let's get settled so we can figure out where the hell we go from here."

Tribute and the Offer He Couldn't Refuse.
Hoover Dam. Summer, 2002.

I knew when the sun went down. I felt it hiss through my body, the night searing my veins, a surge of energy that should have snapped my eyes open and brought me upright, eager to hunt. Unfortunately, tonight, all it did was make me hungry. Hungrier.

If I were still alive, I would have been shivering in a cold sweat. Cold turkey, fingernails digging into my palms and my heart like a hammered steel drum surging to a calypso rhythm. I would have been curled in the corner, biting my fingers. Instead, I paced, dragging the rattling chain behind me. We don't get blurry when we're hungry. We get sharp-set, like hawks. The eye gets quicker. The hand gets faster. You strike before you know it—

My resources were low. I hadn't been taking very good care of myself. And Angel was leaning over the railing, her arms folded under her tits, cleavage augmented by a push-up bra, the smell of just-clotted blood still hanging around her. Whenever I caught her eye, she held out her arm gracefully, extending it over the water, until her fingertips just brushed the edge of my reach. She'd had to re-wound it to make the blood flow. It's good to heal like Hollywood.

I tried not to look at her too much.

Thank God for Doc. Inside my head, riding me the way John Henry rode Stewart, but a little farther back and a little farther out. I was still in control, but this way he could talk to me without Angel overhearing.

Not that he was doing much talking right then. A little muttering and a little swearing, that was all. It made up for the muttering and swearing I wasn't doing, either at Angel or at the assassin, who was standing a little further away, watchful, arms folded, shoulders against the wall as if he could stand there all day.

Angel must have seen something change, though, because just as I felt that spark of energy, need intense as sexual desire, she glanced from me to her watch, and then at the assassin.

"I'm going to get something to eat, baby," she said. "Do you want anything?" That last was a purr, as she straightened away from the railing and turned her back on me, dark hair draped in shining coils over her shoulders.

"No, thank you, love." His eyes flicked up to regard her for a moment, and his mouth curved on an artificial smile. I wondered if she couldn't see the coldness in it, or if she was just so used to playacting she'd forgotten what the real thing was supposed to look like. He let his eyes slide off her, and met mine. "I'm set."

"Suit yourself," she said, with a pretty flip of her pretty hair, and swung her pretty ass around the corner and away.

The assassin and I looked at each other for a moment, and he smiled. "Benjamin made it stick, did he? Capital."

"Keeping me quiet around Angel?" I nodded.

Doc was right behind me—well, right inside me—watching with interest. "See what you can pry out of him," he said.

As if I hadn't been planning that already. I crossed to the edge of the water barrier, the inside railing, and folded my arms over it, mirroring Angel's pose. If I kicked my ankle back, I had just enough chain.

I could still smell her blood, just a drop or two on the far railing, and it turned my stomach with need. I looked at the assassin and said, "I don't suppose you feel like explaining your plot to me?"

He laughed, outright, and then ironically. Down the corridor, I heard the lift ding and slide open; when they closed, the doors cut Angel's scent.

"You can't be serious. You're hoping I'll gloat?"

"Not really, but a little conversation would help pass the time." I smiled, and made sure he saw my teeth. "Besides. You may have noticed that my so-called friends left me here. And I know about

Bugsy and Felix, and I know you're running a double game with Angel."

"So why should I explain it to you?"

"Because I don't want to be a genius, and you do. So if you can promise me freedom and convince me it's not a wrong thing—"

"I'm injured," he interrupted, "that you would believe I'd choose the wrong side."

We all do, sooner or later. Doc laughed and lit a cigarette in my head. "Convince me," I said. "What do you want?"

"Freedom for my people," the assassin said. He tapped a cigarette from a pack, tucked the gold-banded tip into his mouth and lit it, cupping the flame in his hand to protect it from the draft. "What the slaves always want. If I'm in a position of power in Hollywood—a position of *reality*—I can do something about educating and releasing the other media ghosts."

"The way you plan on releasing the spies?"

He shrugged and dragged on the cigarette. Coal whitened to ash. "They're expendable."

"So what does that have to do with the Kennedys?"

"Oh, you caught that, did you?" He knew how to smoke a cigarette elegantly. It's nearly a lost art. Jackie more sucked on them. "You shouldn't listen to everything the Russian says."

"Professional jealousy?"

He glared at me through his lashes. "Pumping me for information is useless, King. You must know that."

"Don't think of it as information. Think of it as persuasion." I folded my hands in front of me, elbows on the railing. The fingers were wax-white, bony and fragile. We all look so elegant when we're starving. "You know what I think, you limey son of a bitch?"

That got a little bit of a smile. "Do I care what you think, Yank?"

"You tell me. I think you're running out of time. I think some or all of the spies got away. I think Angel might be about to catch on to your schemes and I think you're worried and in a hurry, and you don't want to be beholden to Felix and Bugsy either. I think you were honest just now—you want your freedom more than you want to run anything. And I think I can give you what you want, and you can give me what I want. But I need to know what I'm getting into, first."

He stared at me, openly, and rubbed his knuckle across the scar on his cheek. He looked down at his hands, and turned them over, as if inspecting the palms. His lip curled. I knew the look. "And if I tell you, I let you go and you help me?"

"No."

Oh, that had his attention. He seemed to glow when he met my eyes; just the corona of extreme hunger, identifying a meal. Ye of little faith—

"Then what, King?"

"Then I kill Angel for you, and give you what you want from me, and then you let me go."

"That's a big risk on your part, with no sureties."

I shrugged. "What do I have to lose? As I said, I can tell you're on a schedule. And I'd rather you didn't shoot me again."

He frowned and studied me carefully, and then nodded, slowly. "You want to know about Jack and Bobby."

It was hard to keep the relief out of my shoulders, but if my hands were shaking, maybe he would think it was hunger.

Doc, you ready to run this back to Jackie?

Soon as we know what I've got to run, he answered. *You know they may have to take you down if you do this thing?*

I knew. I'd cross that bridge when it caught fire on me. I looked the assassin in the eye and said, "It'll do for a start."

The Russian and the Naming of Parts.
Somewhere in North Las Vegas. Summer, 2002.

A little after sunset, when the light had faded, the Russian walked away from the rest of the group and found Stewart crouched behind a cluster of creosote bushes, his hands folded between his knees, his hair plastered to his forehead with sweat. His eyes were closed, and his lips moved silently. The Russian couldn't make the words out, so he waited a little, to be polite, and then cleared his throat.

Stewart cocked his head back and looked up. "Yessir?"

"They've decided to wait for Doc or John Henry to show up with intelligence," he said. "So we're here for the night, I guess. We should check the perimeter before it gets dark." He gestured to Stewart's loosely cupped hands. "Salt?"

Stewart turned both hands over, let the fingers uncurl, showed him the flat gritty winter-white crystals of Kosher salt. "How'd you guess?"

"It's what I do." The Russian stepped back and Stewart stood up. Carefully, almost reverentially, he spread salt over the ground in the form of a cross about two meters long and a meter wide, then stepped to the side and repeated the gesture. The Russian nodded to himself, understanding, and asked, very quietly, "*Did* you kill them?"

"It doesn't matter," Stewart said, dusting his hands on his jeans. "The legends say I did." He swallowed visibly and took a breath, and then squared his shoulders and looked up. "Make yourself useful; come help me sprinkle this water around."

The Russian took one of the jugs. Between them, they'd drunk what Stewart had brought, and been grateful for it, even though they were only sitting in the shade. Stewart had refilled the bottles from in the cattail-clogged rill under the cottonwood trees. Now the Russian flipped off the plastic lid and followed Stewart as he walked a circle around the shattered adobe hut and the spring, the other spies and Jackie. Stewart reached into a plastic bag in his pocket and cast thin handfuls of salt like Gretel sprinkling breadcrumbs, and the Russian splashed water into his cupped hand and scattered it after. The drops made little dark circles on the earth and vanished quickly. Any stain was invisible in the twilight.

"Do you have another name?" he asked, when they had come nearly all the way around.

Stewart stopped and turned around. The genius smiled at him shrewdly and pushed sodden hair off his forehead with his thumb. "A first name, you mean?"

"Yes."

He got a far-away look, as if he were thinking hard. His forehead creased between his eyebrows. "It used to be Hiram. But I don't use it anymore." And then he squinted through the darkness, with a fox-bright expression, and said, "That's it. Could I be dumber? Jackie!"

The Russian flinched from the raised voice, but the truth was, it wasn't a shout. Just a low, carrying call—and apparently it got Jackie's attention, because he unfolded lankily from his perch among the cottonwood roots and strolled over, hands laced behind his back. "Yo."

The Russian might as well have turned invisible. Stewart turned to Jackie and said, "What would it do to Bugsy maybe being able to find *them* if we gave them names?"

"Names?" Jackie blinked, and looked at the Russian. His mouth twisted thoughtfully, and he turned over his shoulder and glanced at the other two spies, who were still sitting in the shelter of the desperate little grove of trees. "Names. Media ghosts don't have names." A glance back at Stewart, his boots raising little puffs of dust as he twisted, and he said, "You want to do it?"

"Sure," Stewart said. He turned back to the Russian and pursed his lips. "How'd you like to be Nikita?"

"Krushchev? Not in particular—"

"No, just Nikita." Stewart grinned at him, turned around, tossed his last handful of salt in the general direction of closing the circle, and then bounced up on tiptoe to kiss the Russian on the cheek. "I dub thee Nikita," he said, as the Russian startled back. "Loyal knight and protector of the city of Las Vegas." And then he grinned, bright-eyed and delighted, and trotted off toward the American and the Englishman.

Jackie laughed low in his throat and watched Stewart run off, a smile on his mouth that the Russian—that *Nikita*—found almost painful to contemplate. He looked down.

"Nikita," he mouthed without breath, and then glanced up to find Jackie looking over his shoulder. Strangely, he didn't question Stewart's right to name him—or his right to dub him into service, either. "It's a ridiculous name."

"You'll get used to it. Hey, rock and roll—"

"What?" Nikita turned to look.

"John Henry's here," Jackie said. "Go let the troops know while I let him in the circle, would you?"

Looking after him, Nikita at first saw nothing but the glimmer of twilight, swiftly fading, as the purple mountains went black against the indigo sky. And then, unexpectedly, a dark outline resolved against the jagged horizon and the hunched shapes of scrub and stunted trees. A big man, a dark man burned darker in the sun, a red bandanna tied across his brow and a hammer slung over one shoulder, his deltoids and pectoral muscles straining the straps of a worn blue coverall. He was whistling to himself, a song Nikita didn't know, sweet and sad, and as Jackie walked up to him, he lowered the hammer to the ground and leaned on it, both gargantuan hands folded over each other. Nikita looked over at the others, saw Stewart laughing, and the Englishman raise his head in surprise as John Henry and Jackie nodded to one another and leaned close.

Let the troops know . . .

"I think they're aware," Nikita said, and closed the circle with the water he had left before he went to join the rest.

One-Eyed Jack and the Ghosts of Christmas Present.
North Las Vegas. Summer, 2002.

Around Stewart, you never know what's going to happen next. But you always know it's going to be interesting. So I wasn't sure what his little knighting and naming ceremony was supposed to accomplish— beyond breaking our trail a little bit more—but when I led John Henry across the dusty earth back to the campsite—charitably termed—I could see one thing at least. The media ghosts were noticing him, which was something a normal-type person couldn't do. Which meant Stewart's naming ceremony was about more than confounding genre expectations, somehow.

And that gave me a little bit of pause. Because if the assassin could turn real, and take on the aspects of a genius, what was to say the spies couldn't?

I wondered if Stewart had just hired our replacements. You know, it would almost kind of be a relief.

I could tell just by standing next to him that John Henry was surprised to be seen, but Stewart wandered into the middle of the circle and murmured a few words to the big ghost which seemed to make everything okay. At the very least, John Henry was leaning on his hammer again, and had swept the bandanna off his head to mop the sweat from his cheeks and brow.

"This is James," he said, gesturing to the Englishman, who like the Russian didn't seem entirely pleased with his new name.

"James?" I asked, while the newly christened spy was nodding to John Henry.

Stewart leaned against me and sighed, gritty, sweat-damp, and a bit wrinkled, but the most welcome thing I'd touched in a long time. "All Brits are named James if they're not named John, right? And we've got enough goddamned Johns for a quorum."

"Well," I said, as deadpan as I could manage, "that should keep Angel busy for a while anyway."

He coughed laughter. "I don't think she does that kind of work any more—"

"Mmm." I gave him one hard squeeze and stepped away. "You gonna introduce the rest of the gang?"

"Right," he said, and looked from John Henry to the remaining spies. "This is Nikita," he said of the Russian and then introduced the American as Sebastian.

"Sebastian?" John Henry asked, eyebrows rising as he settled the bandanna back over his close-shaved scalp.

Sebastian stuck his hand out and then pulled it back quickly, embarrassed at having forgotten John Henry's immateriality. "I didn't pick it out," he said with a little-boy shrug, and stuffed his hands in his pockets. "So tell us what you've got, Mr. Steel-Driving Man. Have you and Doc come up with a way to get Tribute out of jail yet, pass go, collect two hundred dollars?"

"That's Atlantic City, not Vegas," the Russian said, helpfully, and Sebastian shot him a dirty look.

"No," John Henry answered, squaring his immaterial shoulders.

"No, but you've some information?" James, his arms folded and his weight canted on one hip, watching with birdy intensity.

"Tribute bought a little something," John Henry said, obviously uncomfortable.

James seemed about to jump back in, but I brushed his sleeve with the back of my hand and he settled down on his heels, planted and solid. The quizzical look hadn't left his face, but I got the feeling it was a brushed-on thing, a mask concealing deep, implacable rage.

"Go on, John. What did he buy?" *And what the* hell *did he pay for it? But* that *question could wait. For a while, at least.*

"Some information about the, the Kennedy brothers?" Nikita's intake of breath was sharp, but other than glancing his way, John Henry gave no indication it meant anything to him. The big ghost kept talking. "Some boys the assassin is supposed to have killed about forty years back?"

"Just a president," Sebastian said, his flat Midwestern accent gone a little flatter. "And a presidential candidate."

"Brothers?" John Henry asked, and I heard Stewart, and Sebastian say "Oh," on a range of tones, simultaneously.

I turned around and looked at them, and Stewart held up two fingers. *Two.* Sets of two—

"Oh," I said, and looked at the Russian. At Nikita, I mean. Christ, this was going to take a while. Still, it was faster than translating for John Henry. "Another matched set."

"It's fucking thematic," Stewart started, and then settled back.

The Englishman, James, was very still, just waiting and watching, his eyes never leaving John Henry's face.

John Henry, who sighed and twirled the haft of his hammer between his hands and frowned. "Mister Holliday said to tell y'all we may have to do something about Tribute when this is done. He said to tell you Tribute knows it, and he don't mind."

King, what are you doing? But there weren't any answers forthcoming, and weren't likely to be for a while. "Right," I said. "What did he say about—"

"Tribute figured out how to let him overhear a conversation Tribute had with the assassin." John Henry rubbed the back of his hand across his lips. "Tricked him into thinking Tribute was on his side. And Mister Holliday says the assassin says it was about Camelot. That it's an old rivalry, old feud."

I think I was the only one who caught Stewart glancing off toward the graves. And then I caught Nikita looking at my partner, and reassessed. No, somebody knew.

I sucked my teeth. Well, all right. "Media rivalry?" I asked John Henry.

John Henry shrugged. "Tribute and Mister Holliday said tell you that the ghost of Bugsy is mixed up in it and the suit, Felix, takes a lot of cell calls. Is that right? Cell calls?"

"Yes." Biting back the itch that wanted to demand answers now. He really was doing the best he could.

"Anyway. Mister Holliday says the assassin said the brothers died because of Camelot, because they were a challenge to Luray's people. Because there was only room for one set of myths. He says Monroe died for them too. President Monroe?" John Henry said, hopefully.

"Marilyn Monroe," Sebastian answered, between gritted teeth. "That's so—"

"—fucking—" Stewart supplied.

"—fucking," Sebastian said, gratefully, "perfect. And it confirms my theory from the dam."

"Your theory?" Nikita, ever so mild.

"We've wandered into the middle of a war," Sebastian said.

"No." That was the Englishman, quietly, his head bent under the bowler as he checked the load in his confiscated gun. "We were soldiers before we knew it. All of us. Bred to it."

"Winner take all," Sebastian answered. "A war of symbols."

"And Las Vegas," Stewart said, not to be outdone, "is the central symbol. The key. Every continent rolled into one city that's under the sway of L.A. Sympathetic magic at its finest."

"Damn," I said, and tried to think it through. "So the Kennedys and Marilyn were killed before they could take control away from the Prometheans. And now the Magi are gone, and Felix wants everything that's left."

John Henry cleared his throat, obviously embarrassed to interrupt. The whole group fell silent, though, the way a group will when a quiet man wants to talk. "The assassin told Tribute they'd be going someplace for a ceremony, after he did what the assassin wanted him to."

"What did the assassin want him to do?" Sebastian asked, just as I said, "Where are they taking him?"

"They want him to kill Angel," John Henry said. "Kill her and drink her blood."

He swept his translucent bandanna off, and twisted it in enormous hands. Stewart took a step away from him, a step closer to me, and I slid an arm around his shoulders.

"And they said they were going to take him to Saint Thomas, wherever that is. And meet Luray there. I dunno where Saint Thomas is."

The steel-driver stared at me, and I nodded, *okay.*

I knew. I knew just fine.

James tipped his bowler back. "And Mr. Luray is the . . . "

"The puppetmaster?" Sebastian shoved hands into pockets.

"Or at least a pretty big string. I don't think Bugsy is in any more control than Angel is, no matter what he thinks." I paused for a breath, and no one spoke. They just let the silence hang there until I uncrossed my arms. "Wow. Seventy years of sympathetic magic. All right here."

"Pretty intense, huh?" Stewart asked.

"Yes," Nikita said. "And it's all my fault. I fell for Oswald, the red herring. And the assassin got through."

James frowned, thinking, and turned to Nikita. "But I don't understand. You were supposed to *stop* Oswald?"

Nikita coughed. "You think we wanted Johnson as president?"

"Good point. Okay, so when the assassin killed JFK, if you were there, why didn't you tell somebody? I can't imagine the Soviets wouldn't have wanted to throw a cog in the British-American alliance—" with an apologetic gesture at James.

Nikita smiled. It was almost as unsettling as Tribute's smile, and it showed a hell of a lot fewer teeth. "Because a Russian sniper's word would be so much more creditable than that of a decorated British officer?"

"Oh," Sebastian said, and glanced down at his shoes. "And it was classified anyway, wasn't it?"

Nikita said, "It still is."

Which was all nice, but didn't touch on the big thing. "Right," I said. "So how does this help us get Tribute back?"

"That's the problem," Sebastian said. "It doesn't."

"No." James slid the magazine back into his captured pistol, and tucked the reassembled gun into his pocket. "But it does tell us who the enemy is. So, I say we go back into the dam, and this time we get Tribute out. And do what we can about the assassin and Felix Luray in the process."

Nikita frowned at me. "I don't suppose you've had any brilliant ideas about how we get back in the dam?"

Sure. Ask the guy with no experience and no clue. "Shit," I said. "You guys are the spies. You figure something out."

"What will you be doing?" James asked.

I wished it didn't hurt so much to smile. "I'm going to be figuring out how to keep that mage Luray from kicking us from here to Salt Lake."

The argument lasted hours. I'd come up with my plan long before they were done hashing theirs out, and was pacing the edge of the circle of protection Stewart and Nikita had inscribed when the tone of the argument changed and I wandered back—a few hours before sunrise.

When Sebastian looked at Stewart and said, "Then we blow a hole in the dam," I was past being surprised.

"Breach *Hoover Dam*?" Stewart, incredulous. "The good people of California will thank you not to flood their homes and businesses, and the good people of Nevada and Arizona will thank you not to destroy their source of drinking water, I suspect."

Nikita glanced over at his partner, and said, "What if we only breach the *ghost* dam?"

Sebastian blinked. And looked at me. "Can we do that?"

John Henry said slowly, "I reckon I could."

We all turned to him, and watched as he swung his hammer up onto his shoulder. The ghost dam was as real as the real dam, and it was where the power was. And judging by what Goddess snarked at me, not very long ago at all, it was the second sigil—the one buried in the heart of the dam—that directed the power of the spell.

Break the ghost sigil, break the power of the ghost dam.

It was just a matter of getting there.

James looked right at me. "John Henry won't do us much good if Bugsy or Luray is there to stop him, if I understand the way these things work."

"You understand aright," John Henry said, slow and steady. He didn't look worried. He was about the only one.

James nodded. "What did you decide about Luray, Jackie?"

I didn't like what I'd decided. But there it was, and I didn't have anything better. "We meet him at Saint Thomas. We stop him, and we get Tribute back."

"What about Tribute?" Nikita. Ever so softly. Without looking at me. Almost as if he cared.

"Whatever I have to," I said, and they would have to be satisfied with that. It got real quiet then, and if we hadn't been in the middle of the fucking desert, you might have heard the drone of flies. Instead, there was just the swish of headlights, as another late-night commuter hurried past. It wasn't the answer I wanted to give. But if it came down to Tribute or Stewart—

No contest, man.

"Right," I said, because everybody—even the Englishman—was looking at me. "Let's get started, then."

And John Henry hefted his hammer, and smiled like he was never going to stop.

Tribute and the Hollywood Waltz.
Hoover Dam. Summer, 2002.

By mutual arrangement, I let the assassin put another bullet through me before he called Angel back down. Which is to say, I couldn't have stopped him anyway, and he aimed for the glancing shot rather than center of mass.

That trench coat was really taking a beating. Black fluid stained it front and back, and this time, the wound wasn't healing as quickly as before. I could feel the torn flesh creeping together, amoeba fingers of skin knotting and tugging, a sharp itching tickle. I leaned against the rail, wishing there was a wall on my island because I would have liked to prop myself against it, even if the fluids leaking down my back would have smeared it black in Rorschach blots.

Distantly, I wondered what vampire blood would do to the Promethean design under my feet. The Masonic symbols amused me, but the modern Magi are big believers in appropriating symbology. Symbology and appropriation; that pretty much sums up how their magic works, as I understand it.

Of course, I'm not a Promethean Mage. But then, I didn't think anybody was, any more. Just goes to show you how reliable my information is.

So I waited, and I bled, the blood—or what passed for it—wicking through the fibers of my shirt, adhering to the leather jacket. My skin felt like wax, and old brittle wax at that. If I curled my fingers too abruptly, I could crack the flesh across my knuckles and show dark meat within. The flesh was drawing back from the beds of my nails, and I imagined it was taut across my cheekbones, drawn tight and seamed as a mummy's. The corners of my mouth were starting to split; the shoulders of my trench coat were dusted with strands of sandy hair. It shed down my arms when I moved.

I tested my clawed hands on the railing. Hollow steel gave under the pressure. I felt *strong*. Strong enough to break the chain that bound me to the wall with a single hard yank.

Of course, that wouldn't help me get across the water. And that was still the major problem. I was going to have to wait for them to carry me out like they had carried me in.

I smelled her coming before the elevator door opened. The vibration of the motor and the creak of the cable seemed louder. Sharp set, yes. Like a hawk. The doors scraped as they opened; it sounded like the scrape of broken bones in my chest. I caught myself humming a Frank Zappa tune under my breath, and made it stop, tried to look fragile, tried to look broken. Slumped, head down on my hands, clinging to the railing. Dropped one knee.

Doc, I said, *I don't want any witnesses.* I felt his disapproval, but he went.

I dripped black blood on the tile and lifted my head only a little as she came over, a beaten man. Judging by the curl of Angel's beautiful lip, it was working.

She was clean, bathed, dressed in fresh clothing. Her glossy chestnut hair bounced against her shoulders when she turned her head to smile promise at the assassin as she walked past him. He lifted his chin and watched her go, lips pursed as if he was biting back a smile. The face was perfect: calm, proprietary pride as she crossed the cement floor and paused on the other side of the water.

If she could have smelled him, she never would have gotten close to me.

She leaned over the railing, her hair falling alongside her neck on either side, brushing the skin. Soft. Fragile. I could smell the blood underneath, hear her heartbeat. The pulse fluttered faster. Her pupils widened. Slowly, she unbuttoned the cuff of her raspberry-colored stretch cotton shirt and rolled the sleeve up, all the way to her bony biceps.

"My partner tells me you're ready to deal," she said, and smiled. "Don't you think you deserve better than this, King?"

I turned my face away and whined. Why did it never occur to me before that *King* is a name you call your dog?

I knew what she expected, what they always expect—the Dracula thing, swooning rapture, better than sex. I breathed deep, mouth open, lips curled back from my fangs, nose wrinkled at the hot richness of her blood as she drew a razorblade lightly across her left wrist. She glanced over her shoulder. Ostentatiously, the assassin drew and checked his gun, and chambered a round. Jesse wasn't talking to me.

I was just as glad.

And Angel turned and smiled at me, and drew a pistol into her right hand. "Play nice," she said. She stepped up on the bottom rung of the railing and extended her wrist across the water. I heard her heartbeat, the assassin's heartbeat—and another pulse entirely, the thunder of the Colorado like lifeblood through the veins of Hoover Dam, the great animal chained, the river itself—

The river itself, like blood.

Angel's fingers touched the railing. I dragged myself up, almost as wobbly as I pretended to be, and reached for her with crabbed, leaking hands. She watched with avid eyes, enjoying her power, enjoying my need.

"Try any rough stuff," she whispered, "and the assassin shoots you, if I don't first. No teeth. Just what's there. Be a good boy and we'll get you a real meal shortly. Understand?"

"Yes, Angel," I said, and she stretched a little farther, so I could take her hand.

My hand trembled. The skin was icy; she flinched from my touch.

"Ah," she said, and I turned her hand over gently, and curled her fingers into a fist to make the veins and tendons stand out more, and let the tip of my tongue run along the thick line of blood that curved down the heel of her hand.

It was already cold, no life in it, no use to me outside the body like that. There was still a little trickle running from the razor slice. It smelled so good my mouth ached, my hands shook.

I was a nice kid. Good kid. God-fearing, respecting my mother. Angel's luxurious little shiver when my cold mouth closed over her wound was enough to make my balls crawl right back up inside my body, even if I still had any use for 'em. Christ. The woman was sick. She watched avidly, breath quickening, eyelashes fluttering. I stared at her face while I nursed at her wrist.

Over her shoulder, the assassin smiled at me.

Easy, easy, easy. She couldn't have weighed more than a hundred and seven, and her weight was all leaned in my direction, the railing under her midsection as good as a fulcrum. She half-closed her eyes, purring, playing the scene as I began to suck.

And then shouted, panicked, when I surged to my feet and *yanked*.

She lost the gun in that first pull. I heard it hit the railing and then the water, clank and then splash. She shouted and threw her weight back, her free hand knotted on the railing, that sleek beautiful hair flying all around her as she struggled to keep herself out of the assassin's line of fire. "Son of a—"

She didn't know he wasn't going to shoot.

One more hard pull. I felt her arm come out of the socket, felt the running water burn my hands as they strayed out over it, held on for dear life and hauled. Strong, strong as I'd ever been, strong and getting stronger when I tasted her blood, her fury, her fear. I swung her through the air like swinging a rag doll over your head, and knocked her down on the stones. She screamed, high and scared now, a scream like a gutshot rabbit, and then her throat was against my teeth and her hands were pushing at my face, gouging eyes, wrenching ears.

Our jaws change along with the teeth. My lips skinned back and my mouth went around her neck as easily as my hand. Her larynx vibrated against my tongue as she shrieked, believing finally, too late, this was really happening now.

Better I killed her than Stewart or Jackie had to. Sin gets spread out if you do enough of it. What I mean is, murders are like birthdays.

When you only have a few, each one stands out. After the first fifty or so, they start to blur together.

One more wasn't going to hurt me any.

I closed my mouth, and the salt filled it, and her screams stopped as she strained into me, shoving, strong for someone so tiny, strong for someone so dead. Flesh parted, meat sliced with a ragged knife, and the wet blood covered my face and cartilage crunched between my teeth like a plastic water bottle clenched in your fist. Her hands locked, fists, helpless knee in my groin and she bubbled, the air slurping past my teeth rather than out her mouth because I'd torn her windpipe through. Arterial spray soaked my face, my coat, my hair, my hands. Her heart spasmed.

Her life filled my mouth, and I swallowed it down. She shivered and twitched, feet and legs and spine, and I wondered if she was seeing a white light and a tunnel, hearing the voices of the friends of whoever she had been, back when she was a real girl. Before she was a killer. Before she was a marionette.

Poor, silly kid. I bet the assassin told he she'd get a Hollywood ending if she stuck with him, and so she did.

A Hollywood ending. Sure. Just like Marilyn's.

Just like mine.

I stood up, when she'd stopped twitching, when the blood was all in me or on me. I stood up, healed and dripping scarlet, cold and sticky and itching on my face and hands, and I looked the assassin in the eye.

"My half of the bargain," I said. "Now what about yours?"

One-Eyed Jack, À Main Gauche.
North Las Vegas. Summer, 2002.

We meant to sneak down to the dam in 1964, avoiding Homeland Security. Unfortunately, Stewart naming the spies had a few side effects we hadn't anticipated.

I had an uneasy feeling we were going to miss the ability to time travel before we were done.

We parked high on the Arizona side. The lots were still closed for the night, but once you get up out of the canyon where the road is blasted, there are places to pull off. The hike back down is dangerous, especially if you're almost all stupid enough to be wearing black, so we put Sebastian in the back where his light-gray suit would stand out a little. And we tried to stick as close to the canyon wall as possible, although it was unnerving as fuck when a good-sized vehicle roared past, echoing and rattling and shaking dust and grit down on our heads. Stewart tended to flinch from the big trucks, especially.

I couldn't say I blamed him.

Still, we made it down to the dam without any fatalities. The long curved span was silent, and I was struck by the way the bathtub ring of calcification marking how Lake Mead's water level had fallen gleamed in the moonlight, chalky against the rocks of Black Canyon. The angels stood sentinel on the far side, guarding the Promethean sigil etched on the terrazzo, waiting—a chain on my ankle as surely as the chain that nailed Tribute to the wall in a little room far below us, if he was still there.

The Colorado ran down toward California on my left. I stared at the low cement wall, the Plexiglass panels protecting only the not-very-serious jumpers, the silent threads of power lines looped like silver chains across the red-gray desert. *À main gauche.* On the left hand—

Left hand and right hand. Hand of cards. Hand of . . .

My fingers curled, as if I were reaching for something, almost touching it, as if I were crumpling dollar bills in my fist. And then Stewart slid the fingers of his right hand through my left one and squeezed it tight, and I glanced over at Sebastian leaning over Nikita's shoulder as Nikita lifted a hand, fingers curled under, and pointed. James stood a little away from them, leaning on his umbrella the way John Henry leaned on his hammer, knuckles shining white in the moonlight.

Left hand and right hand. And one severed limb. "Stewart."

"Jack-Jackie?" He squeezed my hand again, and leaned his warmth into my shoulder.

I nodded to the spies. "If that were a poker hand, what would we have?"

"Three of a kind," he said, with a girly flip of his hand. "Which would tell me somebody's cheating. Actually, I'd say it's more like"— he eyed the spies speculatively—"we've got a two aces and two jacks, if we count you in: the knave of spades."

"And the king of hearts."

Stewart nodded and gave me one more squeeze. "Seven-card draw, obviously, and wasn't it a bitch to discard?"

"I wish I could have held on to that third ace." Which was precisely what was troubling me. "What about the other guys?"

He opened his mouth on something snarky and sharp and paused, hard. And closed his mouth, and thought for a minute, and swallowed. "Dueling metaphors. They're playing with, I dunno, a Tarot deck. The Mage and the Hanged Man, and the Ace of Swords, I'd say. And a Queen, or maybe the Empress. And they've discarded another Queen."

"And what's Tribute then? King of—"

"Cups," Stewart supplied.

"They've discarded both Queens," Doc Holliday said, close by my elbow. "Tribute killed Angel long about sunset. The assassin helped him do it."

"Well, shit." Somehow, I didn't think it was going to be to our advantage. Much as I wasn't going to miss the little bitch.

Stewart shifted his weight. "Do you really think it comes down to poker hands?"

"I think in a war of symbols, every little symbol helps. But I also don't want to play poker for Las Vegas." He grinned at me. I shrugged. "It's overdone."

"You'd rather pull a slot handle?" Stewart was ever-so-dry. He wasn't looking at me; he was watching the spies. But I caught the sideways flicker of his eyes under thick lashes.

Hey, it got a laugh. "Maybe an Elvis slot," I said. "No, actually. I've been thinking I'd rather play twenty-one."

Stewart leaned on me a little harder. He looked at the spies, lips moving as if he were counting under his breath. And then he looked at me and said, "There's only four aces in a deck. You're thinking you split, I take it?"

"Unfortunately, I have a feeling this one's dealt from a five-deck shoe, and there's a lot more face cards in play than we'd normally get. So I split and let him hit me." I waved at the spies, at Doc, at Stewart. "I've got a face card for each ace. Both hands, twenty-one."

"And as long as they've got Tribute and the assassin—a king and an ace—and they're . . . dealing, to extend your metaphor a little, it's a push, and nobody wins. Stalemate."

"Fuck, let's not take this into chess. Anyway, I'm not sure it really matters; it's just a metaphor."

"But with a Promethean around, metaphors are ammunition. We can't let this stay in stasis, Jackie. The balance of power has got to shift, and shift our way."

"You're saying we can't just drive them off."

Doc cleared his ghostly throat. "You never can, son," he said, and coughed into his handkerchief. "They'll just return and shoot you in the back when your guard is down. You've gotta end this now if you want to be free. Cut the cord."

"Right," said. "Let's get this over with. Have they taken Tribute out yet, Doc?"

"About an hour ago," he said.

"You seen John Henry?"

"Right here, Jackie." Apparently, the cliff walls weren't good for keeping ghosts out. Not the way the dam was, anyway—he showed up carrying his hammer, and with a plank-and-rope sling hung over his shoulder.

"What's that?"

"High-scaler's chair," he said. "The construction workers used them. I borrowed this one from the ghost of a man who fell building the dam. It'll get me to where I start hammering." He swung his hammer jauntily, lightly, a cheerleader twirling her baton. "Come on, Doc. Time for you to help lower me down."

Doc nodded, coughed once more, and tucked his handkerchief away before following the big ghost down the dam. He glanced over his shoulder as he walked away, and said, "You boys go on ahead and get the King out safe. I'll see John here off and catch up, if I can."

I hesitated, a weird sick sort of feeling congealing my gut, but Doc was obviously done talking. He winked, and covered a cough, and turned away. And Stewart was tugging my arm.

"I thought they'd need us," I said, finally, with a glance at the spies, who were shooting each other quizzical glances in between watching the John Henrys leave. "It's my city. My problem. I shouldn't just be leaving it to them—"

"They're legends. Let them handle it. They'll be okay." He shifted his grip to my elbow and turned me bodily away. "Come on," he said. "It's not long to sunrise now. And it's forty minutes, an hour to Saint Thomas. Let's go."

Tribute, Back On the Chain Gang.
Saint Thomas, Nevada. Summer, 2002.

When I woke up, it took me a moment to remember why I was asleep. Or unconscious. Then I lifted my hand and chains rattled and the memory of the assassin shooting me with a tranquilizer dart came back on a rush. Twenty-five years as a vampire, and I've never been knocked out. And now, twice in a row.

The union was going to hear about this, let me tell you.

"I apologize for that, Tribute," the assassin said. "It was necessary to transport you. In safety, you understand."

I didn't open my eyes, because the texture of the air on my face told me it was still dark, and the sun was a little way off. And the assassin was standing over me, but if he meant to kill me, he would have done it while I was out. No immediate danger, and I wanted a sense of my more distant surroundings.

It took me only a moment to realize that I must be in a tamarisk forest. I got the feathery rustle of the branches, the heavy, composted scent of the plant. I got the smell of water from a little ways off, and the cracked hard-packed earth under my back smelled rich and organic, full of rot. Not desert earth. More like something that had been dredged up from the bottom of a lake—or left behind as the lake drew back in the drought, slid down its shores and revealed what had been submerged so many years ago.

I smelled the assassin, heard his heartbeat, level and unworried. And another beat, with a racing edge; the scent that went with it was Luray. So the Mage was here. Here, but silent.

I was chained to the foundation of a house that had been given to Lake Mead and Hoover Dam seventy years before. *I commend these ghosts to the deep.* I smelled rust and dead fish and drying earth, and when I spread my hands out I felt hexagonal cracks in the mud under my back deeper than my fingers' length.

"I know you're awake in there," the assassin said, amused. "I can hear you rattle."

"I was contemplating my snappy comeback," I said, and sat up. Caked earth stuck in my hair, to my palms. Angel's blood flaked off my skin. "I told you I'd cooperate."

"I don't think even you would go willing to your own sacrifice."

I still felt good, at least. Strong, not too hungry. The assassin didn't need to know that, so I made sure I wobbled a little and used both hands to press myself up. As I stood, I palmed a rock. "You might be surprised. What good am I to you as a sacrifice? I'm linked to Los Angeles, not Las Vegas. I can't tie them together for you—where on earth are we, anyway?"

"Saint Thomas," the assassin said.

I turned until I faced him. He stood atop a foundation wall, balanced lightly, Felix Luray breathing avidly by his side. "A drowned town."

"Nothing lasts in this desert," Felix said. I kept my attention on him, let the chains rattle when I moved. Both hands manacled, pressing my wrist bones. Over the tamarisk, in the light of a rich orange moon, I could see a chimney or two, standing up crooked and tall. The space we were in was flat, open; the brush had been mown off it, and a low broken foundation wall bounded the whole. Steps rose on the side where the lake must be, and on the wall that had crumbled over them, I made out the outline of a cross.

Hallowed ground.

I swallowed, and looked down at my hands. No signs of damage at all. If I breathed, I would have taken a long, slow, thoughtful one just then. I was only half-paying-attention to the Mage. I was standing in a ruined church, and I wasn't screaming. And I didn't think that was a puzzle for another day.

"The Mojave eats her young," Felix reminded, as if it might be important.

"So what if she does?" I said, without looking up. "That doesn't get you any closer to a joint avatar for Las Vegas and Los Angeles. That *is* what you've been working toward, isn't it? A sacrifice that will tie the cities together, unite them?"

"Tribute," Felix said, "what could be a more perfect symbol than you? A vampire who was Elvis Presley, a twin who lived when his brother died, a man who is almost as much a symbol of Las Vegas as Las Vegas is a symbol of sin? A destroyer. A *consumer*, like the Mojave itself. The creature that eats blood and burns it into darkness. And the thing you've eaten, child of the night, is the symbol of Los Angeles herself—like the consuming desert you are. You couldn't have been more perfect for my purposes if I designed you."

"You don't need a genius." I tried to keep my voice level, smooth. *Breath control*, I thought, and almost giggled. I had no breath *to* control, unless you counted what I used for talking.

"You're *better* than a genius," he replied. "I should thank you for getting Stewart away from us. You're infinitely more suited to my purpose. You're my link, and when you're destroyed, it will be like a spell knotted into a handkerchief and burned. There will be no extricating L.A. and Las Vegas."

The assassin nudged him. "Don't gloat too soon," he cautioned, and Felix gave him a sidelong grin.

"Don't worry," he said. "No matter what happens, we still have the dam."

I shifted my grip on the rock carefully, so the assassin wouldn't see it. Something caught my ear. I couldn't quite name it, but it almost sounded like—"Hey, Felix?"

"King?"

"Do you hear that? Sounds like a big heartbeat? Maybe somebody hammering?"

Give him this much, he lifted his chin, opened his mouth, and cupped a hand to his ear to listen. "Just the waves, King."

It wasn't. But if he couldn't tell that, I wasn't about to help out any more than I already had. I shrugged under the blood-stiff coat. "So tell me about the church, Felix."

"It never hurts to layer symbols," he said. Then he glanced from me to the broken cross, and tipped his head particularly. "Oh, you mean why can you stand on hallowed ground?"

I nodded.

He smiled. "Easy. I've warded your chains. If they should happen to break, however, they won't insulate you any more. Of course"—he made a negligent gesture, and my hand tightened on the stone—"they won't protect you from the sun."

"Of course not," I said. We stared one another down for a minute, and I knew from the little smile playing around the corners of his mouth in the moonlight that I looked like a dog snarling on the end of a chain.

I let him have it. I looked down, and turned my back on the assassin and the Mage. "If you don't mind," I said, "I'd like to die in peace."

"As you wish," he said, and withdrew. The assassin didn't go; I only heard one set of footsteps.

I tightened my hand on the river-smoothed bit of rock in my fist, and tried not to smile. He'd gloated.

He'd *gloated*. I might die all over again in the process, but if we were still in genre, the son of a bitch might yet beat me to hell. If I could just get out of the church before the sun came up and burned me where I stood.

I was comforting myself with the very pleasant thought of feeling Felix Luray's throat shred between my teeth when the wind shifted. The scent of the lake gave way before the scent of ten, maybe a dozen strange men. The faint acid reek of gun oil followed it, and mixed up in those scents was a trickle of familiar ones. Jackie, and the American, and the Russian and Stewart, and the Englishman.

The chains on my wrists—the chains that were keeping me alive, if I could believe Luray and if I could call this living—brought me up hard before I went two steps. I almost called out a warning, and then

I closed my mouth on it, very carefully, and stepped back into the footprints I'd left when I first stood. If I were just here to burn when the sun came up, there wouldn't have been any reason to let me wake up. To *plan* on me waking up.

They were using me as bait.

I sank down on my haunches, until my head dipped under the level of the foundation wall, and tried not to look east, where zodiacal light smeared across the stars.

The Russian and False Dawn.
Somewhere in Saint Thomas, Nevada. Summer, 2002.

They parked at the bottom of the rise, beside the white minivan already stationed there, and walked up the little bluff overlooking the lake and the forest of thick-scented tamarisk trees. Before they got to the top, where they would be silhouetted by the rapidly setting moon, Nikita gestured the others to stay behind, dropped to his belly and crawled to the edge of the cliff. James came with him, and judging by the grim expression on the Englishman's face, it would have been more of a fight than it was worth to try to stop him.

They both knew it wasn't about revenge, anyway.

Well, not just revenge.

Despite the low bright moon casting everything below in strobe-sharp relief, all he could see over the wind-rippled sea of tamarisk was a few stark chimneys, limned white with precipitated calcium and mineral salts, and the black, clawed skeletons of waterlogged shade trees. No sign of the assassin, and no sign of Tribute, and Nikita didn't fancy a running battle through the head-high fronds of tamarisk, even though Jackie *had* managed to replace their guns.

Still—

He nudged James with an elbow and pointed, out over the shallow valley that must have been lake floor until recently. "What do you think that big ruin is, there?"

"Down by the waterfront? Er, present waterfront?"

"Yes. There's a reasonably intact chimney there."

"Yes. And something behind it."

Nikita glanced over at James, and James nodded decisively. "All right," Nikita said. "Let's get the rest."

"Steady on," James said. "I'll be right back." He slithered down the bluff in reverse, while Nikita wriggled a little closer to the edge and

281

craned his neck, trying to get an idea of the least exposed path down. Not the trail, obviously. They'd be picked off like ducks in a shooting gallery if they tried that.

Down the side slope then? Possible. He scooted sideways on his belly. The earth under his chest and hands still retained heat, re-radiating it into the night air, and it gave him a moment's pause to imagine the inferno this little valley would be under the desert sun.

If the sun caught them down there, there would be no saving Tribute. In fact, Nikita wasn't sure that the packing pads and Mylar blankets they'd hastily—and illegally—procured would be enough to protect the vampire, even in the shelter of the minivan. But they had little choice.

They would simply have to improvise as best they could. And besides, it was Sebastian's plan, and Sebastian's plans had a habit of coming out unexpectedly well.

He made his choice, and slithered down the side slope of the bluff, dodging thorned and unpleasant plants. This had been the shore of the lake when the water was higher, he realized, crouching just far enough below the edge to hide his silhouette. It was still a steep twenty or twenty-five feet down to the sandy bottom below, but he wouldn't proceed farther until the rest caught up with him.

Jackie was the real tenderfoot of the group, and Nikita decided that he would go with Stewart and attempt to free Tribute. Stewart didn't have Nikita's training, but he knew how to move and how to fight. James would go with them, leaving Sebastian and Nikita lightest and fastest, as the decoy team.

One by one, the other men slipped past him, pebbles rattling under their shoes as they scrambled down the bluff. The earth was soft—shoes sank into it to the ankle, which was just as well. It tended to keep one from skidding on one's behind all the way from top to bottom, and landing noisily and painfully on the man below.

When they were down among the tamarisk, Nikita explained his plan. And promptly ran afoul of James and Sebastian, who fell to arguing in whispers over details and assignments.

He should have seen it coming. Actually, he *had* seen it coming, and attempted to cut it off by supplying a plan of his own. Ah well. He folded his arms, traded an exasperated glance with Stewart, and sighed.

The run time was fine. The quiet time was bad. In the pause between heartbeats he had time to remember and to hurt. Fingers curled softly on the butt of his gun. The taste of grief was metallic, familiar. Almost comforting, after all these years.

It took the other men only about ninety seconds to sort things out to their satisfaction, while Stewart loaded a sixth cartridge into his revolver and Jackie paced and muttered under his breath, avoiding tripping over a sage bush in the dark as much by luck as skill. The division of labor they arrived at was almost identical to Nikita's, except Sebastian and Nikita would take Jackie and form the point team. Apparently they'd decided that Jackie's magical skills might be required if they ran up against the Promethean.

Nikita nodded, and shrugged, and pulled a black knit cap over his hair. Stewart had one too, and Nikita checked to make sure the genius had it on; bright hair was a liability none of the others had to worry about—except Tribute, and they'd sap that bridge when they came to it. Nikita blackened his skin with a kohl pencil, purchased at a twenty-four-hour pharmacy before they left Las Vegas, and ducked down to check the lacings on his boots. Just in case he had to run.

All in all, the odds looked pretty good.

The teams split and Nikita found himself walking point through thick, tobacco-scented tamarisk. Jackie followed two steps back and Sebastian wasn't far behind him—just enough that the shadows would hide him, and an observer might assume they were a two-man team.

They paralleled James and Stewart, who followed a blazed and clear-cut trail through the tamarisk. Probably cut by the state's historical society, or maybe archaeologists. James and Stewart snuck, but meant to be seen, if anyone was looking.

The earth under Nikita's feet was no longer sand. Instead, deep mud had dried hard as cement, baked in the unforgiving sun, and cracked in hexagons like honeycomb. Every so often, they stumbled over the buried foundation of a house, and after the first one, Nikita moved much more carefully, because the uncapped shaft of a well stood beside it and he smelled the rank, foul water underground.

Strange, because he would have expected the wells would be silted in also, but if he leaned far enough over the cement wellhead and extended his hand into the shaft before he flashed his penlight down—and what a great invention *that* was—he could catch the moving glitter of black water. No, not safe at all.

At least the foundations weren't too hard to find, despite the moonlight and the tamarisk, because the gaunt skeletons of trees stood over them, arched like sinister crones. *I wonder how many? Luray can probably afford a small army if they want one.*

Which made him wonder—where was that army, then?

He kept his breathing light, level, his eyes moving. The moonlight cast sharp shadows, made small movements seem like the stroke of broad wings and made large movements almost invisible in the knife-blades of light and darkness. The assassin could be anywhere, and so could the ghosts—or the Promethean Mage.

Whatever a Promethean Mage could do.

He sighed, as softly as a breath, and paused to get his bearings in the tamarisk. The same sporting goods store they'd raided for the Mylar blankets and hiking boots had yielded compasses, MagLites—which Nikita had instantly elevated to the head of his list of Advantages of The Future—snack foods, and ammunition. The pawnshop next door had provided a selection of firearms. It was unfortunate that the assassin's automatic rifle hadn't survived its dunking in the Colorado, but sacrifices had to be made.

It was to the compass—and a handy little pocket-sized object called a GPS locator—that he turned now. The setting moon provided enough light to read by if he tilted the compass just right. Nikita pointed slightly left and raised his eyebrows, first at Jackie and then at Sebastian. Jackie nodded. None of them were about to pop up over the tamarisk like a prairie dog to check their bearings; it carried rather too great a risk of being popped *off* like a prairie dog.

Nikita met Sebastian's eyes, and acknowledgement passed between them like an electric current. Nikita breathed another sigh. This one was relief; the connection between them lived. He had been afraid that it had died with their ability to jaunt back and forth between 2002 and 1964, although he would never have admitted to mourning the lack of . . . telepathy . . . for any reason other than the advantage it gave them. He trained his eyes forward as they started moving, wishing he could fall back a couple of steps and brush up against Sebastian's shoulder.

Just for luck.

One-Eyed Jack and the Moment of Truth.
Saint Thomas, Nevada. Summer, 2002.

Shells crunched like bones, and dry mud powdered my clothes. It all looked strange in the moonlight, even to my otherwise eye—alien, twisted around with thick heavy ropes of power I didn't recognize, heady strength binding and wrapping things in ways I didn't understand. It was power, though, and I tasted it, even if I couldn't use it. It was young, and tempered, and it sank deep and reached broad.

It occurred to me that I could be standing in the ruins of my own house, and I would never know it.

Creepy sensation, that.

We crept past uncapped wellheads and drowned foundations, past the corpses of betrayed trees and the rusted machinery fragments embedded like tombstones in the petrified mud. Sebastian had to crouch to keep his head under the tamarisk, and even Nikita couldn't quite stand up straight. I hunched uncomfortably, continually glancing at the GPS locator in my hand as if it would tell me where Stewart and James were.

Our footsteps were almost silent on the baked earth. I could hear the whisk of Nikita's inseams as he walked forward, and it occurred to me that someone from a more temperate climate would find the lack of droning insects spooky. That wasn't what drew me up—or the spies either, I imagined, although Sebastian had fallen too far back again for me to see if he checked.

No. Nikita and I froze with one foot in midair because I am the one-eyed Jack, and the dice roll sevens for me, and the one-armed bandits come up cherries. We froze because I'm the knave of spades now, whatever I used to be, and if I draw to an inside straight, baby, you can bet the ranch that the card I'll draw is the one I need.

We froze because somewhere in the darkness, somebody who wasn't one of us stepped on something that crunched.

"Drop," Sebastian hissed and I did it, face down on the mud, stems of tamarisk pressing my thighs, my flanks—

Mud grit under my palms and the thick, fermented scent of the trees, cordite, the showering of splintered tamarisk on my head, my shoulders, my hands before I ever heard the perk and whine of bullets searing overhead. The salt cedar parted, mown off, and tumbled on my head—and I didn't yelp, not quite, when a big hand closed on my ankles and *pushed* me forward. The tamarisk fell, interwoven branches covering us in a bullet-ripped bower, and I buried my head under my arms and tasted dirt as I swore.

But Sebastian was right there, right there, tugging my pant leg, urging me forward, and—buried in tamarisk, gouged by sticks, occasionally brushing Nikita's boot with the tips of my right-hand fingers, I went.

I heard a sharp yelp somewhere off left, where Main Street used to be, and bit my lip as the gunfire continued, dropping off to intermittent spits. It could have been one of ours or one of theirs; no way to tell, but it didn't sound like Stewart. I prayed it was anybody but him, then hated myself for the prayer.

Nikita didn't actually pick his head up, but I felt him pause and tense. I stopped crawling, grateful for the dark that hid us from the gunmen, worried about the source of a second sharp cry that came in conjunction with a burst of gunfire—this time, from only one weapon, and I caught the muzzle flash. Dammit. It was easier when I knew the spies couldn't get killed—at least, not by gun-slinging henchmen.

But now they were real, and while that might protect them from the assassin, it meant that the narrative would not longer protect them from the second-stringers.

Sebastian patted my ankle again and crawled past me, shoulder to shoulder with his partner under the tamarisk. They held some sort of conversation, mostly in touches and glances, with the occasional hand gesture, and then Nikita jerked his hand up suddenly, and Sebastian froze.

This time I heard it too, distinct and ghosty.

The rattle of chains.

Sebastian turned over his shoulder and caught my eye, and I nodded. Ready, yes. He pointed—*that way*—and I followed. On my belly, like a good spy. Clamshells scraped my palms and elbows, and I was glad that I'd found a pair of leather pants that nearly fit. Considering the pounding I put my clothes through, leather's not really tough enough for my purposes, but most places won't let you in to dine in armor plate, these days.

Well, except the Excalibur. But that's a special case.

We crawled toward the sound of metal on metal. Sebastian paused when he drew up next to a skeletal tree, got his feet under him, and slowly rose to a crouch, using the black trunk to conceal his black-clad silhouette. So far, the corpses of trees all marked houses. Even seventy years ago this had been the desert, and trees only grew where someone maintained and watered them.

Laura had rose bushes. Laura took care of the windbreak, too, six thick-boled cottonwood trees.

While Laura was alive.

I wasn't in love with her. I wouldn't demean her memory to pretend I was. But she was the only family I ever had that wanted me, before I had Stewart, and Las Vegas.

And you should have seen her roses.

I stayed on my belly, a body-length behind Nikita, but dared lift my head and peer in the same direction as Sebastian. The foundations we'd passed so far had been low, broken walls; this one was high enough that you'd have to stand right next to it and peer over to see what was behind it. And the building was bigger; tumbledown walls had scattered rubble through the tamarisk. It was the church, which meant we couldn't be too far from the receding lake, in the heart of drowned Saint Thomas. And the sky to the east was graying behind banded mountains.

Again the rattle of metal, and Sebastian pressed himself against the tree trunk, hiding his face against the bark, leaning forward and standing on tiptoe. I noticed Nikita wasn't looking in the same direction he was, but scanning the area around us. That seemed like a good idea, so I tried watching in the other direction, and caught Nikita flashing me a smile out of the corner of my eye.

Sebastian slithered back down the tree trunk and crawled back to us. His hands were scratched badly enough to show blood in moonlight; I winced. He seemed oblivious.

"He's in there," Sebastian hissed, and I glanced from him to the church in surprise.

"Alive?" Shaping the words more than speaking them, but even in the darkness, Sebastian picked them out.

He nodded, a sharp jerk of his chin. "Chained—"

"In a *church*?"

The spy blinked, and glanced at his partner. The Russian pursed his lips and nodded, thoughtfully, before he murmured, "Yes, I see your point."

"Luray must have done something to protect him," I said.

"Which means if we interfere, it could kill him, right? Tribute, I mean, not Luray." Sebastian frowned, as if trying to work through it.

"Yes." I wasn't up to testing my magic against a Promethean. Not face to face. "It's got to be set up that way."

Sebastian asked, "Can you protect Tribute?"

"From what?"

"The church."

"If we try to get him out," Nikita said.

"Maybe," I said, and looked at the foundation of the church, and looked away, and shook my head. "Maybe," I clarified, and I think the spies might have laughed at me if it wasn't likely to draw gunfire. "But I'd get shot trying to get to him."

Nikita propped himself on his elbows and grinned, hard enough that teeth flashed white in his blacked-out face. "We'll take care of that. Just stay down and get him out of there."

"What about you?"

I knew it was stupid when I said it, but I said it anyway. Sebastian just reached out and shoved my upper arm with the palm of his hand.

"We're expendable," he said. "And we're going to try to take out the assassin."

"What about Luray?"

He shook his head and grimaced, his elastic face scrunching as if he'd eaten something terrible. "Luray, I fear, is your problem, my friend."

And then Nikita turned his head, and cupped one dirty palm against his ear, and frowned. "Sebastian," he whispered, in an entirely different tone, "do you hear hammering?"

Tribute and the Voices In the Dark.
Saint Thomas, Nevada. Summer, 2002.

Nobody but me would have heard them talking. The American, the Russian, and Jackie, whispering almost under their breath, planning my rescue. Damn them.

And I had no way to warn them that wouldn't give them away. And the results of that—

Well. I'd heard the gunfire and the shouts. If you don't think too good, try not to think too much, as the man said, but I could extrapolate just fine. If you smell three spies and a couple of genii, and you know the bad guys are lying in wait somewhere nearby, and shooting breaks out—well, there's a limited number of conclusions a man can draw.

Although I had to admit, I was damned curious about that hammering. I could think of one obvious suspect, but—

Hell. If the spies already knew where I was, there was no point in going down quietly. And no way to keep them from exposing themselves coming after me other than removing temptation. And there was a definite rhythm to the hammering, if I listened hard, and it was getting clearer with every blow.

I wrapped my fists around the chains and leaned back against them. The steel links cut my palms, and I gave them one quick yank, just as a test, and then set myself and braced myself and rolled my shoulders under the jacket. I was strong, still sharp but full of blood, and I was ready to be done with all this. I opened my mouth and started to *sing*.

Loud.

At the top of my lungs, with all the belly under it that I could put there. And you know, God damn it, I could still lay down a note, and hold it up on the other end.

"Well, John Henry, he could whistle"—*yank*—"and John Henry, he could sing"—*yank*—"Went to the mountain early in the morning"—*yank*—"Just to hear his hammer ring!"

The chains snapped taut with a hellacious rattle every time I tugged them. It didn't sound much like the sharp clear tolling of John Henry's hammer, but it certainly made a racket, and that was what I was counting on.

Well, that, and I was honestly hoping I could pull the staples holding the chains down loose. It was old concrete, after all, waterlogged despite the rebar, and even masonry bolts might not be enough to hold me down.

I'm a lot stronger than I look. And "John Henry" has a lot of verses. I could feel the bolts slipping before I got to "Shaker, you'd better sing! / Throwing fifteen pound / from my hips on down / listen to the cold steel ring!"

With every fraction of an inch they gave, I heard John Henry's hammer ringing louder and faster, and I felt something burning along my arms and neck, a searing sunburn pain wringing tears down my cheeks. *And you can't drive steel like me, Lord, Lord. You can't drive steel like me.*

No mistaking it now. I was belting it out, singing at the top of my lungs, and John Henry's hammer rang on every downbeat. I looked up and saw the sky stained rose and gray, seeming to shiver with each yank on the chain, with every stroke of the hammer, with every beat of the song. I rocked against the chains, heard a bolt snap, felt the chain slip, felt the black blood run down over my hands as the muscles of my shoulders bunched and strained under the coat.

Just give me a cool drink of water 'fore I die—

The coat split at the center seam; I felt the abused leather give. Someone appeared at the top of the steps—the assassin. I saw him level his pistol, with the moment's glance I spared. And then the assassin was lifting his chin, turning, curious, as if he heard the hammer ringing down the lake, ringing out of the mountains.

I didn't linger for the bullet. I didn't have time to stand there and wait to be shot. Instead, I shouted the song, and doubled my fists, and *pulled.*

John Henry drove him fifteen feet and the steam drill only drove nine, Lord, Lord. The steam drill only drove nine.

A gunshot cracked flatly in time. I heaved. The bolts snapped and I fell backwards on my ass, skin bubbling, lips split and running cold blood down through the blood crusted all over my face, eyes tight shut in anticipation of the fire. Somewhere, not too far, a killer wave broke on stone and John Henry's implacable hammer came down and a second gun yelped—

My hands were burning. I couldn't see. I couldn't hear my own voice, to finish the song.

And he laid down his hammer and he died, Lord, Lord. He laid down his hammer and he died.

I would have sworn on my mother's grave that I felt the river break over me.

John Henry Holliday and the Exigencies of Narrative.
Las Vegas. Summer, 2002.

Atop the blockhouse of Hoover Dam, every stroke of John Henry's hammer rang like Gabriel's horn. Doc Holliday felt the terrible shiver through his palms where his gloved hands clenched on the weighty, pointed, iron rod John strove against. Each swing of the hammer was a wheeling overhand blow, a massive effort rolling up John's thighs and hips and through shoulders wider than some doors, the hammer falling like a meteorite, the mere task of supporting the (immaterial) spike enough to rattle Doc's (immaterial) teeth in his jaw.

It was a good thing ghosts were tireless. Because as much as it hurt, as tired as he got, Doc never had to let go and rest. Even dead, Doc couldn't swing any fifteen-pound hammer, but he could hold the spike and trust John not to miss, and together they could bust this dam.

John never missed. His face got shinier and sweat flew from his fists and elbows and chin with each roundhouse swing, and the chips flew and the cracks shivered wider and wider with each blow, until a trickle of water no wider than a pencil slipped inquisitively through. A moment later it was a geyser, finger-thin and jetting with enough force to cut a man in half, Doc thought, if he were unfortunate enough to step before it.

"John," Doc bellowed, and John pulled his hammer back again.

John hesitated. "The dam's not through, Mister Holliday."

"John, it's time to stop. The dam will take itself down now. All it needs is a crack. We need to climb out of here now." Doc took one hand off the spike, and let it sag. He put that hand out to touch the ropes of the high-scaler's swing they'd used to come down.

"It won't fall fast enough," John said, watching the edges of the crack he's made flake away in the running water. "It's gotta come down now." He hefted his hammer. "And Mister Holliday, this is how my story ends. Always has, always will. I win and I die."

Doc tossed the spike aside, heard it ring and saw it roll on cement before it settled. "You're already dead, you damn fool. I'm not going to be a party to you blotting yourself out because you think it's how the story goes. Maybe we need a better god-damned story."

"Mister Holliday, you better get on that high-scaler's chair," John said. "Jackie and the others, they're going to need you."

Unwillingly, Doc retreated. "John—"

"Mister Holliday, I'd get in that chair if'n I was you, sir."

"Dammit, John," Doc said. "Call me Doc, would you?"

"Give me a cool drink of water before I die," John Henry said, and turned away to raise his hammer.

Doc scrambled for the high-scaler's chair as John Henry brought his hammer down.

One-Eyed Jack and the Hungry Land.
Saint Thomas, Nevada. Summer, 2002.

Up at the Valley of Fire, there's an overhang called the Atlatl Rock. It was marked with a road sign by the Anasazi, when the Anasazi were still here—before the Mojave ate them, too. The archaeologists are very careful to explain that they don't know the meaning of the petroglyphs, but they seem pretty plain to me, and probably would to anyone who's ever studied a five-year-old's drawing.

They were meant to be plain.

The river is that way, it says, and it's a good long walk. Here is yucca, and here is desert, and here are men, and there is meat if you can catch it. Bring water. The sun is hot, and the desert will kill.

As I said, pretty plain.

As plain as Tribute's voice raised up in song, and the rattle of his chains in time to the ghostly thunder of John Henry's hammer, ringing the thirty or forty miles from the dam as loud as if he were hammering just up the bluff. The opposition had to be able to hear it; there were no two ways.

The spies went left towards Main Street; I scurried forward toward the church, trying to figure out some fragment of magic I could work to keep a vampire from smoking and burning on hallowed ground. I had nothing; calling up ghosts was just a matter of knowing how. Most ghosts don't mind being called, or they wouldn't be ghosts. It was working *with* the essential nature of things, rather than working against.

But hallowed ground rejected vampires for the same reason sunlight did—as the body fights infection. And the primal underpinnings of the universe weren't something I felt empowered to tackle just then.

I crouched against the foundation, nerving myself and thinking. If subtlety was removed, that left brute force.

Very well.

So mote it be.

Tribute's singing voice sounded strained, and the crack of the hammer and the rattle of the chains came faster. I edged up over the foundation and stole a quick look. He had a rhythm going, throwing all his weight against the chains, propelled by the strong muscles of butt and thighs. Putting his back into it, face squinched up with effort, grunting between lines of his song as the assassin popped up over the wall on the far side of the church and drew a bead. Not at Tribute. Past Tribute.

At me.

Tribute threw himself at the chain again. A bolt cracked and he sagged. He was grimy and smeared, black fluid running down over his hands, caked blood or mud or both plastered across his face and through his hair. He looked up at the assassin, gave a funny little shake of his head, like a cat, and heaved at the chains one more time.

Before I knew what I was doing, I was over the wall and running toward Tribute, trusting to luck because luck was all I had. The assassin's bullet stung my neck; I wondered if it had nicked anything important, but there wasn't time to worry about it, because Tribute's chains came free and he fell backwards, and I could smell scorching flesh as strongly as if flames were curling around him. Another bullet whined by, a different sound than the assassin's gun, and as I got my hands into the collar of Tribute's leather coat I glanced up and saw James standing there, sideways for a narrow profile, his confiscated pistol in his hand, firing as coolly and calmly as a cowboy laying out tin ducks at a shooting gallery.

The assassin ducked, and I got Tribute over my shoulder—and damn, he was light as a feather pillow, a leather sack of bones and knotted silk scarves and no flesh at all to speak of—and ran for the wall while James, frowning under his bowler, laid down covering fire. I felt something snap as I vaulted over the wall with the vampire slung over my back dragging chains, bouncing and rattling, and dove into the tamarisk on the other side. I couldn't have said what it was, just then, but it felt like—it felt like when you straighten a locked-up elbow, and it pops, and it hurts so bad, but somehow at the same second it feels better all at once, and the range of motion comes back like it was never locked at all.

Only on a cosmic scale.

James was beside me almost instantly, dragging Tribute under cover until Tribute got his feet under him and helped drag himself. "No good," the vampire said. "Sun will be up in fifteen minutes. But I appreciate the thought."

I thought of the Mylar and packing blankets back at the van, and cursed. Nearby, a machine gun rattled, and we all hunched down into the tamarisk, although not so much as a wood splinter grazed us. It's amazing how fast you can learn respect for automatic weapons.

James nudged me and said, "Did you have a look down those wells, Jack?"

"Wells?" Tribute looked up.

"More like cisterns," James said. "They've a narrow wellhead, but the underground chamber is perhaps four or five feet in diameter, judging by the echoes. Bigger than the well shaft, in any case—"

"Sir, I could kiss you," Tribute said, and smiled, showing chiseled teeth behind black, bleeding lips. And then he glanced at me. "You're bleeding, Jackie."

I swallowed and touched the graze on my neck. Slick fingers and a wet collar, but not much more than that. "It's not bad. Do you need? . . . "

"Lord, don't offer," the vampire said, and drew his knees up. "It ain't like in the movies, Jackie—and not with my mouth bleeding, even if it were. Already enough damned vampires in this town." A sad attempt at humor, and even he couldn't manage a laugh. He held his blistered hands up to his blistered face, and sighed. "Just a minute, I'll be fine. I'll stick around as long as the night holds—"

"Don't put yourself out," I said, and patted his shoulder.

When he lowered his hands, he looked better. "I've got to get these chains off," he said.

James crouched beside him, a bent thread of wire in his hand. "I can do that."

While he worked, Tribute struggled out of the shredded leather coat, and left it lying on the ground. "Did you feel the dam break?" he asked me.

I blinked. "Is that what that was?"

"John Henry, right?"

I nodded, and it struck me to wonder what the ghost of a river could do to the ghost of a man. "Yeah. I'm not sure—"

Well, I couldn't say I wasn't sure if he survived, now, could I? I bit my tongue, and shook my head. "I'm not sure."

The manacle on Tribute's left wrist opened under James's ministrations, and he grimaced and rubbed it with his right, and looked down. "I'm not sure either," he said, and then he hummed a note and murmured, "A man ain't nothing but a man."

And then something else hit me, and I looked over at James and frowned. "Hey. Wasn't Stewart with you?"

The American and the One-Shot Kill.
Somewhere in Saint Thomas, Nevada. Summer, 2002.

Sebastian didn't like the tamarisk thicket one bit. It covered smell and sound, the head-high feathery stalks as obscuring as August corn. You couldn't even crawl under it well; the fronds touched the ground and the stalks grew close together, so it was difficult to force a path between them and you couldn't quite see where you were going, anyway. The twigs broke into spikes; it was like pushing through a rose thicket.

But he was following his partner, and he'd cheerfully follow Nikita into hell.

They were still only halfway around the church when the gunfire started. Sebastian heard the hammering clearly by then, and he recognized and approved the defiance in Tribute's singing. He slid his replacement weapon into his hand as he came up into a crouch. It was a Sig P-229, an ugly, plastic-handled, rectangular chunk of metal as unlike his own elegant Walther as a tank was unlike a fighter jet, but Stewart had assured him it was also more durable and more accurate, and he wasn't going to complain about .40 caliber loads.

He had a feeling he was going to miss the silencer before the night was out. And he wasn't sure he was comfortable with the semiautomatic's lack of a safety lever, even as he took advantage of the rattle of Tribute's chains to squeeze the trigger once, cocking the weapon against immediate need. Oh, hell, it was probably just as well, with the unaccustomed way his hands were shaking. He glanced up to see his partner doing exactly the same thing with an identical weapon.

He grinned as Nikita's eyes came up and met his. He pointed left, around the foundation. Nikita nodded and gestured him on. "Age before beauty," he murmured, caressing the butt of his pistol with something suspiciously like affection.

"Got a new crush?" Sebastian asked as he sidled past, and Nikita snorted.

"It's a craftsmanlike weapon," he said. "I think we'll get along— Sebastian."

Sebastian froze with one foot raised. "Partner?"

Nikita pointed with his chin, and hissed. "*Stewart.*"

Sebastian peered through the gray predawn, and only picked out Stewart's black-clad form when he turned at Nikita's call and the whites of his eyes flashed in the dark. Stewart gestured them forward and down with an abrupt hooked gesture, and Sebastian went, Nikita crouched beside and slightly behind him half a second later.

"Where's James?"

"Covering Tribute," Stewart said. He had a firearm in his hand as well, a weapon that looked like it was manufactured by Tupperware, from a company Sebastian had never heard of. Still, Stewart seemed happy to have it.

"And you're covering James?"

The genius nodded. "Smart boy. Where's Jackie?"

Sebastian looked at Nikita for support. Nikita was studiously ignoring him. "He, ah—"

Gunfire cut him off, and before he could finish, Stewart said "Aw, shit," and rocked up on his toes, scurrying crabwise through the tamarisk without a sideways glance. Sebastian sighed and followed him, knowing Nikita would be at his heels.

He heard the opposition pushing through the tamarisk, secure in the killing potential of their automatic weapons, and wished he dared pick off a couple.

Yep, it was a fact. He missed his silencer, and the flash suppressor, too.

Stewart lead them toward what must have been the front of the church. They arrived in time to see a familiar figure swing down off the steps and bolt into the tamarisk, clamshells crunching under his shoes. Nikita dropped one knee, raised his pistol, and squeezed off two shots despite the danger. Sebastian didn't think he hit the assassin, but he did draw a couple of bursts of automatic weapon fire, for which Stewart cursed him good-naturedly as they flattened themselves once more.

Sebastian tasted chipped mud. Tamarisk bark showered his head; he caught a glimpse of muzzle flash through the thicket, peered through the fixed sights of the Sig and fired at the same moment Stewart did. A double-tap apiece, and at least one of them hit because the next burst out of that gun arced skywards and ended with the slumped thud of a falling body.

"Lucky shot," Nikita said, and wormed his way toward the foundation. "Sun'll be up soon."

His tone was conversational. Stewart snorted in answer. "Did Jackie get the bloodsucker out?"

"On three," Nikita said, and as Sebastian held his breath and watched for any sign of hostile movement in the thicket, he popped up, glanced over the wall, and dropped. A three-shot burst slit the vacated space. "Nobody in the church," Nikita said, as Stewart returned fire. "I want one of those AR-15s."

"M16," Stewart corrected. "A1, I think. We're lucky they're not A2s. The older flash suppressor doesn't work so well."

"I want one anyway," Nikita said, dryly.

Stewart barked a laugh. "Let's get you one, then. You saw where I drilled that guy?"

"Where *who* drilled him?" Sebastian asked. It was starting to feel right, again; he could sense the energy flowing, the banter, the adrenaline. His hands stopped shaking. He knew how to do this.

"Go on three," he said, for Stewart's benefit, not Nikita's. Nikita wouldn't need to be told.

He weighed the unfamiliar Sig in his hand and stood, laying down fire as Nikita gathered himself and ran. The second machine gunner stood, just a few feet away from where he'd been last time, and Sebastian unloaded what was left in the clip into his chest as Nikita dove for the first casualty's weapon.

This time, Sebastian was sure who got the bad guy, because Stewart was turned around the other way, watching his and Nikita's backs. "That's another M16," Sebastian said, and dropped down into the tamarisk to pop the spent magazine out of the Sig and slap a new one home. "I'm going to fetch it."

"Be careful," Stewart said, straining his eyes into a gray, growing light that illuminated nothing. "I just got line of sight on James for a second—they're on the other side of the church. I'll be behind you."

Sebastian gathered himself and ran for the gun.

Rounds slapped into the hardpan uncomfortably close to his heels, but he dove into the bushes and rolled sideways, Stewart beside him, and heard Nikita return fire, and lifted his head—

—to find himself staring into the three-leaved flash suppressor on the muzzle of an automatic rifle. His gaze traveled up the barrel, past the fingers curled supporting the weapon and into the eyes behind it.

His quick, startled breath was interrupted by the sound of a round being chambered, echoed a half-dozen times.

"Gentlemen," a smooth, English-accented voice said, "seeing as how my acquaintances have you outgunned, would you be so kind as to stand up, please?"

Sebastian was amused to notice that Stewart gave him exactly the same exhausted, exasperated look that Nikita would have done, just before he laid the rifle down, raised his hands, and stood up slowly into the gray pre-dawn. Sebastian followed a moment later, reluctantly allowing the ugly, blocky, comforting Sig to dangle limply from one finger as he did.

Tribute and the Angel of the Morning.
Saint Thomas, Nevada. Summer, 2002.

Jackie sat back on his heels as I got up, trying real hard not to show just how much I wanted to taste that blood soaking into his collar. The sky wasn't even indigo any more—it was solid gradations of charcoal and silver, bright enough to silhouette the feathery stalks of the tamarisk. There was a lot of gunfire north by northeast—judging direction by the bright stain on the sky—and the scents were all confused, tangled up in each other. Blood and gunsmoke, enemies and allies, the American saying something I didn't quite catch, and Stewart answering. Some of our boys still alive, anyway, and then I wondered when and how they'd gotten to be our boys. Or when I'd gotten to be one of *us*.

"What's the plan?" I asked Jackie, and Jackie shrugged as the Englishman cleared the pistol he was carrying and reloaded.

"Fuck if I know," Jackie said, and a figure sort of solidified beside him. He jumped, and turned on the balls of his feet, a swivel without breaking his crouch. "Doc," he said in relief. "We felt the dam—"

"It took John with it," Holliday said, and pressed his fist against his immaterial lips, white-faced in pain. "Washed him down the river. You should have seen the ghost of that river come pouring through. All that power shaking off the chains—"

"Damn." I scrubbed my freed hands across my face and felt the blood crumble and pill and drop away. "So we've beaten them? Does that mean we can go home?"

"That's the bad news," Jackie said. "They don't stay beaten. And there's still the assassin to deal with."

"I'll do it."

The Englishman glanced at me, caked mud on the knees of his impeccable suit, and the brim of his bowler dusted with tamarisk pollen. "What about Bugsy and the Mage?"

"What happens if we kill them all?" I was looking at the Englishman when I said it, but I was talking to Jackie, and Jackie knew it. "If you've broken the dam, you've broken their power base, haven't you?"

"There's still Vegas. And the California connection. We've got to—"

"Own it," the Englishman suggested, chambering a round.

"Yes." Jackie nodded. "Otherwise they'll just be back."

"So how do we own Los Angeles?"

He sucked his teeth out loud—unattractive habit, as my mother would have said—and cocked his head to one side. "Same way they wanted to own Vegas?"

"Build a dam?"

"Control the genii." He shrugged, ducking as another spatter of gunfire marked the dawn. "You killed—" Whatever he was about to say didn't quite make it out of his mouth, because I quick put a forefinger to my lips and cupped one hand to my ear, turning into the breeze. The assassin was talking—

—was talking to the American. And the American was—

"I think the bad guys have the drop on our friends," I said quietly, and glanced at Jackie. He passed the look along to the Englishman, and said "James, can you get a look at what's going on up there?"

"James?" I asked, but Jackie waved me irritably to silence as the Englishman half-stood, peering through the tamarisk, and dropped back down. *Huh. James.*

He made a face. "It looks like the assassin and some bully-boys have Sebastian and Stewart surrounded."

Jackie scowled. "Nikita?"

The Englishman shook his head. "No sign."

"He's by that cottonwood," Doc said, and shrugged when Jackie turned the scowl on him. "I saw him coming in. Can't feel a thing any more."

"Huh," Jackie said, as if remembering something. "I don't suppose you know where Bugsy is, do you?"

"As a matter of fact—"

I was sort of looking forward to hearing the answer. Unfortunately, that was when the wind shifted sharply, bringing me a scent I really could have done without. *Angel.*

And not a nice, safely dead Angel, either. Ah, no. Because she reeked of shit and decay, and my blood layered over her. Of course, and stupid of me not to think of my blood all over the place when I killed her, the bullet wounds, the cracked lips and hands, the saturated coat.

Stupid, stupid, stupid.

You don't usually get a chance to make two mistakes that bad.

I was just turning, croaking a warning to Jackie, when she knotted her fist in my hair and *pulled.* I was off-balance, crouched, and we're not exactly all there when we first turn. But hell, we're strong.

She sent me flying, tore a hank of hair out of my scalp. I sprawled, crashing through tamarisk. It cushioned my fall more than not, and as I shook blood out of my eyes I rolled and scrambled up, narrowly missed by someone's burst of gunfire. One bullet seared my back, but it didn't punch through, and I wasn't about to get distracted by a scratch.

I popped up, got a look at Angel with one hand knotted in Jackie's hair, holding the Englishman at arm's length by his obviously broken wrist—she must have wrenched his gun away—and took a breath. and yelled her name.

"*Angel!*"

Another spatter of bullets, and I ducked and got lucky again. This time one slammed into my shoulder and the other one creased my cheek and shredded my ear, but neither of those would slow me down. I popped my head up again, got a fix as Angel lifted her head, turning to the sound of my voice.

Yeah.

Just like Sycorax did me, long ago and far away. Just like Sycorax did me. "Angel! Put those men down."

A yelp—Jackie. She didn't dump him gently, but she dropped him, and the Englishman, too. I crawled, not toward her, but toward the assassin and his men. *Russian*, I thought, *I hope you're as good at picking up my cues as you are at picking up the American's.*

"Angel!" And I felt her, felt her response the way I might feel it in my hand. I didn't need to look to see what she was doing. I *knew*. "Angel, kill the assassin's men!"

I felt her leap, heard the rattle of the M16s, heard her land and bodies breaking around her. The men screamed; one of them kept firing, and I hoped the spies and Stewart had the sense to get their heads down and keep them there. I felt the bullets strike her body, tear her flesh, felt the blood fill her mouth and heal her wounds, heard someone cursing, and got ready to throw myself into the fight like that—

No need.

I prairie-dogged over the tamarisk, ready to pile into the assassin with everything I had. I was half a second behind the Englishman. His little semiautomatic snapped: perfect stance, firing with his left hand, his right one dangling, shattered, the arm pressed against his chest. He'd lost his hat somewhere, but that didn't matter; even from fifty feet with the growing daylight searing my eyes, I could see the narrowed concentration of his squint.

Pop pop. Pop.

The assassin still looked damned surprised when he pitched over backwards, two red circles on his chest and one right between the eyes, and the Englishman mostly looked tired when he looked down and slowly lowered the smoking gun. Nobody moved for either one of them. Everybody just kind of stared.

I didn't see Angel, but I could hear her feeding, down there in the bushes, and it was just as well they obscured the sight. Judging by the way the American and Stewart were backing away, it wasn't even as pretty as I was picturing.

I stood for a second, looking from Jackie to the spies to Stewart to Doc, and swallowed hard. There was still a Mage and ghost unaccounted for, unless there was something the rest knew that I didn't.

And my skin was starting to itch as the sky grayed towards gold. I needed to find that wellhead, and find it fast. And take Angel with me, unless I wanted to kill her all over again. I squared my shoulders and took two steps toward the spies and Stewart, and the sound of her slurping and crunching.

"Where's Nikita?" the American said.

Felix Luray walked out of the tamarisk, a hand on the Russian's arm, and said, "John Henry Kinkead."

Jackie's head came up and he pivoted on his heel, and Stewart turned with him and planted the other boot wide, a cowboy's swagger a boy raised up in a shotgun shack could never miss. "John Henry Kinkead," Jackie said calmly, hooking his thumbs over the waistband of his leather pants. He lifted his chin, looked Luray in the eyes, and curled his lip, one hand raised and back, forestalling the Englishman, who was taking very careful aim. "*Junior.*"

Felix tipped his head and the Russian moaned between his teeth, leaning against Felix's grip on his arm—and against something else, something immaterial that bound him tight. And I saw that he still had his gun, holstered in front, to the left of his belt-buckle, for a quick cross-body draw.

The American started to move; Stewart put a hand on his shoulder, and shook his head. The slurping sounds of Angel feeding, paused, and I heard her make a low, uncomfortable whine. The prickle on my skin told me I had seconds left.

God help me. I looked down at her face, at the blood smeared across it, for far too many of those seconds, and charity failed me.

And then I wondered how she died, the first time. I wondered what she dreamed, and fought for, and destroyed herself for. And maybe charity failed. But pity didn't, quite.

"Angel," I murmured, and she was beside me, flinching, crouching, hands over her face. I pitied her. I couldn't help it. How much better than her had I been, when I was mortal?

Not much. Not at all.

"What do you want?" Jackie asked, calm and swaggering, a redneck prince. Not far off, the Englishman covered Luray, still as a dog on point.

Luray skinned his lips back from his teeth. "I challenge you to a duel, John Henry Kinkead . . . Junior." The little catch there interested me. So Jackie *wasn't* who Luray had thought. "High noon on the high street, winner take all." And he nodded to the Russian, and said, "My champion against yours. Or, for that matter, you."

The itch on my skin was turning into a burn. "Come on, Angel," I said. "Follow me."

And hoping Jackie would understand, hoping I'd get a chance to learn how it played out, I abandoned him there and ran with Angel, aiming for the smell of water lapping in the underground.

One-Eyed Jack Bets the Ranch.
Saint Thomas, Nevada. Summer, 2002.

"I'll go," Stewart said in my ear, as Tribute crashed away through the underbrush and the sunlight grazed the top of the canyon wall. "I won't lose my nerve in a gun fight."

Sebastian shot him a searing look. "Don't believe for a second that my partner would turn, Jackie."

But I didn't need Sebastian to tell me something was wrong. The frantic look in Nikita's eyes, the way his hand twitched toward his holstered pistol, the way he leaned away from Felix Luray's long-fingered hand with its iron ring—

Casually, I reached up and flipped the patch off my *otherwise* eye. And grimaced, because Nikita's aura of guncotton and roses was tainted with something else, a swirl of rot and money and clotted blood that reminded me of the brambles wound around Tribute's adder-black soul.

"Bugsy," Doc said in my ear like a curse, and trailed his fingers over the butt of his gun.

And Felix Luray smiled, uneasily, as if he'd heard a ghost.

I squeezed Stewart's elbow before he could protest, and stepped forward. "What's your percentage, Felix? What do you hope to accomplish here? You've lost: we've taken down your dam, we've killed your would-be genius. You're not holding any cards. Why am I going to let you force one of my friends to shoot another one of my friends?"

And the Mage said what I'd been more than half afraid he'd say. "Double or nothing." He held up one hand. "If you handle the gun yourself."

The sun was swelling over the rim of the canyon now, a blinding bright slice that spilled long shadows across the tamarisk and the cracked earth underfoot, revealing shells chalk-white as broken bones. "So if I face your champion, Magus, you swear you'll leave Vegas alone?"

"I so swear," he said.

"And you'll honor—" I hesitated, and looked at Stewart. Stewart frowned. But I couldn't think of what else to say, although I saw the problem even before Sebastian cleared his throat. "—*our* claim on Los Angeles."

"If you step into the street yourself, Jackie."

I felt the flare of the truth, felt the oath take hold, saw it ripple out around him like the shockwave from impact. I looked into Nikita's eyes and said, "I'll do it. Personally."

The Russian's lids flickered shut; I read relief in his slack features even as Sebastian shot me a glare that could have blistered stucco.

"Aw, man," Stewart said. If he'd been three steps closer, I would have kicked his ankle.

Felix Luray smiled. "See you at high noon, then." He walked off through the tamarisk, toward the bluff and the vehicles, as Sebastian closed the distance between us and grabbed my shirt.

"He'll kill you," he said. "He doesn't miss."

I grinned at him, and flipped my eyepatch down. The world got a lot less bright, and a lot less complicated. "I'm counting on that. Besides, it's not just Nikita in there."

He blinked and let go. "Who else is it?"

"Bugsy," Doc said, while I was smoothing my shirt.

"Oh," Sebastian said. "How long 'til noon?"

Stewart glanced at his watch. "It's a little past five."

"Daylight savings, though," Sebastian said, and I saw the trick. Because if I weren't here at *solar* noon—high noon—for the gunfight, it'd be a victory for Felix.

"Sneaky son of a bitch," I said, and looked down at my boots. "What are you thinking, Sebastian?"

He glanced over at me, light catching in his eyes, and thrust his fists into his pockets, looking peculiarly dapper despite the gawky pose and the mud smearing his blacks. "I don't know yet," he said. "But I'll figure it out by noon."

"Right." I dusted my hands together, and looked after Luray, and Nikita until they went out of sight behind the tamarisk. Then I shoved *my* hands into *my* pockets and turned away from the group, towards where Tribute had run.

"Where are you going?" Stewart asked.

I shrugged. "Gotta see a man about a horse."

Tribute, Down the Well.
Saint Thomas, Nevada. Summer, 2002.

I really hate spiders. I hate spiders almost as much as I hate dark, wet, airless holes in the ground—but at least there was gray light filtering in, though I was up to my chest in cold water and up to my knees in sucking, silty mud, with cobwebs wrapped thick as a mummy's mask around my shoulders, face, and neck. That light would peel my flesh off my bones, but it was comforting even though I crowded back under the lid of the cistern, pressing Angel against the wall, both arms wrapped around her shoulders, holding her up out of the water not because the water would hurt her any, but because when you're used to breathing, it takes a while to get out of the habit. Because the light was freedom.

The light was the way out.

The light was escape.

And I held on to that thought as hard as I held onto Angel, down in the filthy water with the spiders crawling through my hair. She was making noises, horrible noises, little sobbing, sucking gasps through the changed shape of her teeth. Oh, and she deserved it, poetic justice. Don't tell me it wasn't. I know what she meant to do to Stewart, and I know what she meant to do to me.

And I still felt bad about it anyway.

Heck, that's my modus operandi. Screw the pooch and then feel bad about it.

Like feeling bad ever mended a broken heart.

Whatever. The fact remained, I hadn't killed her when I should have, and she was my responsibility now. And she was young, young and tough, but I was older and stronger. Not as old and frail as Sycorax yet. No, not for a long time. But we start off more mortal, and become more . . . undead as time goes by.

It was a trivial thing to restrain her, even without using my right of command. And eventually, the animal sounds gave way to sobbing, and the sobbing became words. They weren't coherent words, by any means, but they were words.

And I held her, and held her face out of the water.

Because I felt bad for her.

Unfortunately, she wasn't going to be much use for conversation for a couple of days. Which meant I was going to be stewing down this hole more or less alone until nightfall—

"Tribute."

Ow. Angel clawed at my chest. I pinned her back against cement. Soft as I could manage, I murmured, "Watch the echo, Jackie—" It boomed, reverberations shattered by rippled water.

"—sorry." He stepped back from the lip of the well and lowered his voice, but I could still see his shadow on the water, the sunlight falling around his shoulders in long, dust-touched rays. Angel whimpered; I wondered if she'd bitten her lip. "I need your help."

Well, *hallelujah.* "Help?"

"Don't rub it in, Tribute. Bugsy's riding Nikita, and I'm going to have to fight them both."

"Nikita? The Russian? You named them?"

"Stewart did."

Which explains that. "You made them real."

"Apparently." His silhouette shrugged, disarraying parallel rays of light. "It worked. James—the Englishman—got him. The assassin, I mean. Unless the widow getting herself killed broke his immunity— oh, hell. I don't know, King."

"I saw. Did you check the body?"

The shadow moved again; he was lifting and turning his head. "Stewart did. Is doing it now. And Sebastian's doing something about James's wrist. But that doesn't change the fact that at high noon, I'm going to have to shoot Nikita or get shot, and no matter what happens, Luray's going to double-cross us. Or Bugsy is. Luray's oath might just hold *him*."

"Wait a minute. Tell me what happened, Jackie. Word for word."

The cold water sucked at my chest and swirled between my legs. I ordered Angel to stay in the corner, and came as close to the light as I dared.

He took a breath deep enough that I heard it echo down the shaft, and slowly, without too many self-corrections, related what had been said. I stopped him mid-recital.

"You laid a claim on Los Angeles? In your own name?"

He shook his head. "I said 'our.' Us. All of us."

"Good," I said. "Because if it was you or Stewart, it'd just bind the cities closer together, and we need to break them apart. And now that Angel belongs to . . . us . . . we have as much leverage there as they ever had, with Stewart. Vegas lies in so many shadows—"

"It *is* the shadow," he corrected, and I couldn't deny it. "The shadow and the mirage. Not real." Something prickled in his voice that made me wonder whom he was quoting.

I swallowed my pride, and I swallowed my fear, down there in the dark with the walls pressing in on me. It wasn't like a coffin. Not really. More like a very unpleasant hotel room; once the sun went down, I had a way out. And there was something I could offer him.

Much as I'd rather pull out my fingernails with pliers. "Jackie."

He must have heard it, because he hesitated before he answered. "Tribute?"

"You're sure Luray has something up his sleeve, man?"

"So far, he's batting a hundred percent."

Yeah. I nodded in the dark, though he couldn't see me. "If you're calling up loas and ghosts and guardian angels, man—about time you called up mine."

One-Eyed Jack and the Voice of the Underground.
Saint Thomas, Nevada. Summer, 2002.

"Jesse," I said, as what Tribute was offering came plain. "You want me to call up your brother."

"I want you to cut him loose," Tribute said, and I didn't think the discomfort in his voice was just the daylight and cold water. "Think of it like a séance. Ouija board."

"Good Pentecostal boy believes in Ouija boards?"

"He doesn't believe in vampires either," Tribute pointed out, tiredly. "Will it comfort you if I call it glossolalia?"

I snickered. "What's he going to think of being cut loose?"

"He'll be so happy, he might have something helpful to say for once. But mostly I was thinking of the symbolism. Using Felix's own magic against him."

"All right," I said. "I need liquor—"

"The Englishman carries a flask," Tribute said.

"How do you know that?"

I couldn't see it in the darkness, but I could hear the smile. "I used to watch a lot of television."

"I'll be right back."

James did indeed have a flask, and he hadn't even drunk all of it while Sebastian splinted his wrist. I came back to the wellhead, the rest of the group accompanying me, and shook a few drops on the earth beside the cement pad.

"Jesse Garon Presley," I said. "A word, if you don't mind?"

I expected a ghost, of course, but the ghost of a newborn baby. Not a slender blond young man with a quick sideways grin and a forelock that tumbled down in his eyes and had to be tossed back, a gesture so reminiscent of the American that I glanced over at Sebastian to see if he noticed.

316

Of course he didn't; we never quite know what we look like from the outside, do we?

"I'm Jesse," the ghost said, and his voice had every bit of the drawl that Tribute had lost, or maybe shed on purpose. "What ch'all want?"

I heard a little splash from the well, as if Tribute flinched back a bit or took a couple of steps away from the sunlight. The spies watched, captivated; Doc shifted uneasily from foot to foot until Stewart nudged him with an elbow that went right through his ribcage, and then he settled down with his hands stuffed into his pockets.

I handed James back his flask. He took it left-handed, and made it vanish without so much as stealing a sip. I caught that out of my peripheral vision; I wasn't about to take my eyes off Jesse. "Your brother's been helping us out, Mr. Presley—"

"Jess," he said, and raked the forelock back again, with both transparent hands. The white Mojave sunlight fell through him, and when he reached out to touch my arm, half-curious, I felt a chill as sharp as the stroke of an ice cube down my spine. "And my brother ain't no godly man, Mister—"

"Jackie," I supplied, and took a breath. "Jess, you're right. A godly man he's not—hell, not even a man, these days"—I felt Tribute straining down in the darkness, as profoundly as if he leaned on my arm—"but he's trying. And I'm no godly man either, but I'm just trying to protect myself and those who look to me from—"

"I know who," Jesse said. "I ain't stupid."

"No."

No, he wasn't. The blue eyes were sharp, almost ferocious under the arched brows. He moved like a cat, an angry cat, a caged cat. Tail-lashing and ready to claw. His stare was direct and arrogant, self-possessed. Some ghost.

"Jess," I said. "Tribute wants to let you go. Wants to cut you loose."

His eyes brightened and his chin came up. "Really?"

"Really," Tribute said, from the bottom of the well. "Jess, I'm sorry. I've got some amends to make—"

"You've got more than amends to make," Jesse said. "I died and you lived, and what did you do with it? And what are you *now*?" He shook his head, his mouth twisting in disgust. "You've got a lot of work left if you're meaning to do better. And I ain't been too happy about watching your back these past twenty-five years, neither."

Doc's presence at my elbow was a welcome chill. Jesse stared through him as if he just wasn't there, but I didn't miss the way Doc's fingers hovered over the butt of his gun. *It's not like he had a choice*, I almost said, out of some weird loyalty to Tribute, but common sense made me bite my lip. Angry ghosts aren't all that forgiving.

"Before you go," I said, squatting down to pull a knife out of my boot, "I don't suppose you've got any brilliant ideas about how to thwart Luray without shooting this man's partner?"

Jesse frowned, and sucked his teeth, and turned his head and spat as I rested the steel point of my knife on the ground. "I hear the Colorado used to flood a lot, didn't it? Down the Imperial Valley?"

"That's why they built the dam," Stewart said.

"Well," Jesse answered, rubbing his nose with the back of his hand, "that's why they said they built the dam. You gonna cut that cord, Jackie, or am I going to stay sewn to my brother through all eternity?"

I sighed, and flipped my eyepatch up. What the hell; it'd been worth a try. The silver cord gleamed on the dirt under my knifepoint, winding Jesse and Tribute together. I severed it with a flick of my wrist.

By the time I looked up again, Jesse had faded out of sight. Just like the Cheshire Cat, his grin went last. "Well fuck," I said, and stuck the knife back in my boot. "That didn't do us any good."

"Oh, I'm not too sure of that," James said, without looking up from his inspection of the splint on his injured wrist. "Every little bit of symbolism counts. And it might make Tribute that much less useful to them."

"And anyway," Sebastian said at my elbow, where he stood half-inside Doc. "You don't have to worry. I have a plan."

The Russian Looks for an Angle.
Somewhere in Saint Thomas, Nevada. Summer, 2002.

The sun rose fast, and Nikita quickly found himself wanting nothing quite so much as a broad-brimmed hat. He squinted, shielding his eyes with his hand; from the top of the bluff he could see just the tip of a lime-caked chimney. There was no sign of his partner and friends moving below, as he knew they must be. Down there, there wouldn't be any shade except the tamarisk, and they had no clean water. If they had any sense they'd stay crouched in the bushes as much as possible, and maybe creep around the side of the bluff to get a look at the opposition's plans.

Not that the opposition had much in the way of plans.

Nikita wanted to smile a small, bitter smile, but his lips wouldn't do what he demanded. Instead, he stood in the blinding sun, sweating out the underarms of his blacks, cleaning his gun, because Bugsy was using his hands.

It didn't bother him as much as the persistent sense of his brains dripping into his collar, although the only thing staining his fingers when Bugsy let him wipe at the moisture was sweat. He also kept wanting to press his fingers into the socket of his left eye, just to make sure it was still in his head. He sighed, inwardly, and watched his body work, and considered what it would feel like to die. He wouldn't permit himself to think that he might live; it was down to Jackie or him, and he didn't want to live as Ben Siegel's puppet, in any case.

At least the gangster wasn't trying to make conversation.

The sun was only three fingers off zenith when Luray touched his shoulder and cleared his throat. Bugsy turned Nikita's head and stared at the Mage through Nikita's aching eyes. Blue eyes were not adaptive in the desert. It was good; the glare would blind him more than it would Jackie, and Jackie would have another small edge.

Nikita was trying to find every edge he possibly could.

"Time to go," Luray said.

"Locked up and ready to roll," Bugsy answered. Nikita found it strange to hear his own voice speaking English with that harsh Brooklyn accent. Bugsy seemed to like it, though, because he said, "We'll be home in time for supper," and gave Luray a big, broad grin.

It was a grin that worried Nikita intensely, because it made him think that somehow, as far as Bugsy and Luray were concerned, everything was going exactly according to plan.

"We'd better be," Luray said, quickly checking his watch. "I'm missing the assassin right about now, Ben."

"We'll be fine without him," Bugsy said. "We don't need him and we don't need the syndicate either. Stick with me, kid." He turned to Luray, slipping the freshly reassembled Sig into an improvised hip holster, and grinned even wider. Bugsy's expressions felt strange on Nikita's face; they were broad, but not very deep, and they made his cheek muscles ache.

"I'm stuck," Luray answered, and followed Bugsy and Nikita down the hill.

It looked different in daylight. The earth was washed-out, powder-colored, and it crumbled like too-dry cake under Nikita's boots. Small stones skittered, but the descent looked shallower; it wasn't long before they were off the bluff and walking over tumbled rock.

The dead gangster must have been nimble and quick, an athlete in life. He wore the Russian's form like a tailored suit, springing from rock to rock as gracefully as Nikita could have, while Felix stumped down after, skidding a little.

If they had any sense, Nikita thought, *they'd pick us off as we came through the tamarisk.* They wouldn't, of course; it would invalidate the bet, and Sebastian would want to stall to the last second anyway, on the long odds that somebody would find a way to pull Nikita out of it alive.

The hike down to the church was a little over a mile, over mostly flat terrain. Nikita could feel the heat on the top layers of his hair when the breeze ruffled them against his skin; it felt like a silk shirt out of the dryer. And apparently Nikita's companions at arms had been busy; somebody had haggled the tamarisk down along a fifteen-meter stretch of what must have been Main Street, not far from the foundation of the church. A cluster of men stood at the far end. James's hand was in a sling across his chest. The air smelled thick and herb-sap-bittersweet. Stewart was fussing over Jackie, lashing the holster of a six-shooter to his right thigh with a bit of rawhide while Jackie coughed against his hand.

Bugsy drew Nikita's body to a halt just as Sebastian stepped forward, away from James, and offered Jackie a clean white handkerchief. Jackie started to wave it away, but coughed again, and grabbed the cloth.

He got himself under control as Luray stopped beside Nikita. "Ready, Ben?"

Bugsy rearranged Nikita's face into a smile. "Ready as I ever was, Felix. Time for us to take over the world."

"You and me, kid," Felix answered, looking like he was quoting something, and Bugsy punched his arm.

"You need a haircut, son," Bugsy said to Nikita as he walked the length of the trimmed strip, pushing Nikita's hair out of his eyes again. "We'll see about that when we've got this dealt with, shall we?"

Over my dead body, Nikita thought, and heard Bugsy laugh.

"Not while I'm using it, son."

Jackie stuffed the handkerchief into his pocket hastily as Bugsy walked up, and moved away from his entourage. He met Bugsy in the middle of the mown strip and paused there, color high in his pale cheeks, his eyes burning with a feverish light. One handed rested on the grip of the six-shooter, with an elegance Nikita hadn't realized Jackie knew.

"You heeled, Mr. Siegel? Ten paces, turn and shoot?" Jackie asked.

Bugsy's lips twitched, but he didn't betray any surprise that Jackie knew who it was in Nikita's body. "You were expecting a fair fight?"

"If your friend wants to collect his wager," Jackie said, coolly, "I suggest you keep it clean." He showed his teeth. Nikita could picture him in cowboy boots, a scuffed vest hanging loose over a worn shirt, collar cinched with a string tie. He would have shaken his head to clear the image, but he couldn't, of course; Bugsy was still staring in Jackie's glittering eyes while Jackie stroked the butt of his gun.

And then Sebastian winked—not so much a wink as a flicker of his eyelid, and although Nikita couldn't lift an eyebrow in acknowledgement, he felt the energy jolt between them, the moment of communication and trust, and he relaxed.

Sebastian would make sure he didn't hurt anybody he wouldn't have wanted to hurt. No matter what else happened.

Sebastian would make sure it came out right.

"Oh, don't worry about me," Bugsy said, and pulled the Sig out of his holster to cock it before slipping it back, making sure it sat loosely in the leather. "I'm as clean as can be. And ready when you are."

Jackie stifled a cough against his wrist, and glanced at his watch, and then at the sun. "Well," he said, "it ought to be about time, son. You count. Bugs."

Calm and collected, he smiled, and turned his back, stealing the march on Bugsy. Nikita felt the gangster's surge of loathing at the hated nickname, and fought back his own interior grin. Jackie wasn't so bad, for a capitalist.

Simmering, Bugsy turned his back, squared his shoulders against Jackie's—Jackie was taller—and said, with sharp precision, "*One.*"

Bugsy paced forward, and judging by the crunch of weeds under his boots, Jackie did too. "*Two.*"

Nikita couldn't close his eyes, but he could focus himself. Focus his will and strength, visualize the sequence of desired events clearly—*three*—and without telegraphing his intent to Bugsy—*four*—imagine each step, each pace—*five*—imagine his own body ready for action—*six*—as his fingers arched, itching, around the butt of the gun—*seven*—and the cut tamarisk crunched under his feet.

Focus.

Eight.

Focus—

Nine. Step. *Ten*—

Bugsy planted Nikita's heel and spun, slapping leather like the professional he was, and Nikita, with every ounce of will he could muster, imagined his own hands grabbing Bugsy's wrist, wrapping tight, straining, slowing the draw. He almost felt Bugsy's wrist slipping through his fingers, fingers with no more substance than smoke. He *actually* felt the warm black plastic of the Sig slide into his hand, felt the jerk of trained muscles clear the gun and spin it up, as if Bugsy meant to shoot from the hip, and Nikita's trick must have worked because Jackie had his gun up and aimed and there was a lick of flame—

A pistol spoke, and it wasn't the Sig. Nikita knew the sound of a revolver, and he knew the Sig hadn't kicked—and suddenly, Bugsy wasn't holding him up any more. *Just like him to let me die alone*, Nikita thought, and looked down at his chest.

He'd been shot before, and he expected to feel something. Not pain; the pain happened afterwards. But the hard slam of bullet against flesh, the shock of impact.

Nothing, as the Sig fell out of his fingers and discharged as it hit the ground, and no dark stain spreading over his chest, almost invisible against his blacks, and no suck of air through the hole in a punctured chest. He blinked, and raised his hand to touch his chest, and looked curiously at his muddy but unbloodied fingers. And then he blinked again, and looked up at Jackie, and the broad matching grins on James's and Sebastian's mouths.

And Jackie pointed at the ground behind him.

Nikita turned, and grimaced. The once-handsome, dark-haired body of Bugsy Siegel lay at his feet, shimmering, transparent in the white noonday sun, brains and gore and bits of bone oozing from the wounds where bullets had exited his eye socket and his cheek. Those were no surprise; they were the wounds that had killed him.

The dark patch over his heart was new, and still leaked transparent red.

"If the ghost of a river can kill a ghost," Doc said, stepping out of Jackie's body and blowing the smoke off the muzzle of his gun, "then do you reckon the ghost of a bullet can kill a ghost as well?"

"Yes," Nikita said, glancing up with a smile. "I 'reckon' it can." And then he turned and looked at Felix Luray, and crouched down, and picked up his accidentally discharged gun. "You're going to adhere to your bargain, aren't you. Mr. Luray?"

Luray glanced aside, but Nikita imagined he didn't find a lot of sympathy in Jackie's eyes. "Of course," he said.

Jackie covered the twenty paces between them in a few quick strides, and draped one arm around Nikita's shoulders. Nikita didn't complain, although, technically speaking, Jackie was fouling his aim. "That's good," he said. "Because if you weren't going to behave, I'd have to take steps."

"Steps?"

Jackie smiled. "Yes. I'll do what Jesse suggested, and call up the ghost of the whole damned Colorado River, and flood the Imperial Valley from one end to the other. You think the ghost of a flood would have any effect on a lettuce crop, Luray?"

Luray held his hands up, showing them empty, and walked toward them out of the tamarisk. "So you'll be genius of Las Vegas and Los Angeles both now, Mr. Kinkead? You and your partner? I think we have some things to discuss, regarding how I can be of service to you in your new role—"

Something in Luray's voice—a concealed throb, the restrained anticipation of victory—triggered Nikita's threat sense, and he was already raising and extending the Sig when Jackie gave him a second little squeeze and stepped away. "Actually . . . " And Jackie glanced at Stewart and grinned. "I'm not interested in a job as the genius of Los Angeles."

"The wager?"

"I said *our*," Jackie said, and with a quick stoop pulled a knife out of his boot to clean his thumbnail on. "I've heard a rumor, though, that Tribute's planning on taking over, so if you wanted to talk to him about the job—"

Nikita wasn't sure he'd ever seen a face fall out of smooth and into worried as fast as Felix Luray's did. "Tribute?"

"Yeah," Jackie answered. "I hope you can see your way clear to work with that."

Luray's face fell, and whatever he might have said next Nikita missed it, because Sebastian grabbed him off his feet, and swung him into an airborne bear hug, yelling his name.

Nikita hugged his partner back, hard. And then Sebastian set him down, and Nikita grabbed his shoulder and turned him.

Luray stood among the tamarisk, frowning at his hands. Stewart had Jackie pulled down into a closed-eyed liplock. And James was picking his way through the tamarisk, walking away, twirling the assassin's pistol around his forefinger slowly, his black bowler hat shiny in the noonday sun.

Nikita turned toward Sebastian, ready to tug his sleeve to catch his eye. He didn't need to. Sebastian was already looking, and nodding slowly.

"Even if he says yes I still drive," Nikita said, grinning.

"Go get him," Sebastian answered. "It isn't like he's got a story to go home to any more either."

One-Eyed Jack and the Boy from Tupelo.
Las Vegas. Summer, 2002.

Two days later, I met the new genius of Los Angeles on top of the Rio Hotel, on the rooftop patio of the Voodoo Lounge, just before sunrise. Tribute leaned over the cement wall on folded arms, watching gray and gold silhouette the lumpy outline of Frenchman's Mountain like a man watching the glow from a nuclear meltdown creep across a dark night sky. The Strip shone green and blue and lavender below and around us, and the piercing white Luxor spot speared upward from the shiny black glass pyramid of the casino, transfixing the heavens.

He wasn't looking that way.

But I was.

"Hey," he said, when I came up behind him. "Figure Angel and I are clearing out tonight."

"Just keep her the hell out of my sight."

He coughed, disguising laughter. "We're going to work on her personality, never fear. Luray was awful apologetic and eager to be liked, by the way. What'd you tell him?"

My turn to chuckle. "I told him I'd kill him myself and then drown his ghost in the ghost of the Colorado if he gave you any shit."

"That's gentlemanly of you." He craned over his shoulder as the first sharp rays of light stroked the tip of Mount Charleston. It'd be a while before they reached us, though. "You seen Doc?"

"He's gone," I said. "Task completed, summoning over. You know John Henry didn't really die, don't you? His legend is still out there."

"Seems close enough to dying for me," he said. "Speaking as one dead man to another. Doesn't matter how many times you go through it. Hell of a thing, when your story says you got no other ending."

"Hell of a thing," I agreed, arms folded. "From one dead man to another. Maybe we need to find some better stories."

That was good for a few seconds' silence.

"Hey," I said, and pointed to the bat-shadows flocking through the Luxor light a half-second before it winked off for morning. Brightest light on earth, they say. You can see it from orbit, pick it out from all the other lights in Vegas. "You helped make my mirage come true."

He laughed, and shook his head a little. "What are you going to do about the spies?"

"I hired 'em," I said. "They can't go home—"

"No, Stewart saw to that."

The bitterness in his voice made me wonder when and how he'd gotten so protective of the media ghosts, but I wasn't about to ask. "You think going home's all it's cracked up to be?"

He shrugged. "How would I know?"

"How would any of us?"

He jerked his thumb at the Strip, rainbow lights glimmering out down in the valley as the sky grayed over it. "Your city, Jack-Jackie."

And when I followed his gaze, I couldn't answer. Because he had that right. So I just sighed and shrugged, and scratched my nose. "You're welcome to come visit, you know. And I'm sure you'll get used to L.A."

He snorted and turned back to the sunrise, the steadily brightening east. He took a long, unnecessary breath before he spoke, and paused, but I didn't let him make me fill the quiet. "Jackie. I never did ask you. Who the hell are you, man?"

He didn't look at me when I glanced over. I didn't really expect him to. I know what he was asking, though—how am I different from the media ghosts, the legendary ghosts, the little ghosts, the layers and layers of stories people tell themselves to keep things like him at bay all night? How *is* it that my city and I *are* more than a memory, a mirage?

He was asking if I had a name.

I turned around and leaned one hip on the cement. He looked up, then. "John Henry Kinkead, Jr." I stuck out my hand. "My old man was the third governor of Nevada, but I never did meet him. My partner's Hiram Stewart; his family's ranch is what the city's built on, more or less."

He looked at the hand, at me, back at the hand. "Never heard of you, man."

"No," I said. "You wouldn't have. Genii aren't the sort of people that stories grow up around, King. They're the sort of people who get consumed by the stories, instead."

"I know what that's like," he said, and he took my hand and gave it a quick cold squeeze and one firm shake. His hair slid across his forehead, a soft blond wing. Even in the predawn, his eyes were startling. "Elvis Aron Presley. At your service." And then he glanced back toward the mountain, and grinned his famous crooked grin. "Inside, if you don't mind."

I looked at the first broken rays of dawn roofing the valley; they'd slid down Mount Charleston and limned the red tile housing on the western valley in gold and red. By the time I looked back along the retaining wall, he was gone behind the blacked-out door into the bar, a lingering phrase of "America the Beautiful" hanging on the still-warm air.

Nice song. And good to hear him sing.

It's like "This Land is Your Land," though. Nobody ever makes it to the interesting verses. *O beautiful for patriot dream / That sees beyond the years / Thine alabaster cities gleam / Undimmed by human tears—*

I shrugged and leaned back against the wall, concrete snagging the shoulders of my jacket. The gray and golden sky was fading to a blue like turquoise. Desert dawns are over fast.

"Viva Las Vegas," I said, and spat over the wall before I went down to meet Stewart for breakfast in the cafe, humming a song of my own.

AUTHOR'S NOTE

This book was born and chiefly written during the time when I lived in Las Vegas, 1999-2006. Of course, it is a work of fiction, and where the likenesses of real or fictional historical people appear in its pages, I present but shadows of those folk—no attempt at reflecting reality, but instead an attempt to show how perceptions of history and art overshadow the reality of what existed.

Much as the Las Vegas version of the world is a theme park, so this novel's version of Las Vegas is a funhouse mirror reflecting and distorting even make-believe.

This is a book in large part about the history of Las Vegas, and Las Vegas is a city that relentlessly eats its own history. Because of that, *One-Eyed Jack* remains a period piece; I found it impossible to portray Sin City in a timeless fashion. It seemed more honest to anchor it in a specific moment in time. So in this book, it is eternally 2002... except when it is 1964.

I had a difficult relationship with the city when I lived there: Vegas and I were not a comfortable fit. *One-Eyed Jack* is the pearl that grew around that irritation—an examination of the parts of Las Vegas that I could learn to love or value.

This book and its metafictional aspects owe their existence in large part to the often-pseudonymous ladies and occasionally gentlemen of the *The Man from UNCLE* and *I, Spy* fan communities, whose insight into fandom and how it processes transformative works greatly influenced my creative process. Thank you all; your generosity with your time and expertise is incredible.

It also could not have been written without the assistance of Kit Kindred and Dr. Michael Green, my sources for a great deal of Vegas lore and history. I also owe a debt of gratitude to Steven Brust, who generously shared his skill and insight with me when we both lived in Las Vegas. I would also like to thank Hannah Wolf Bowen, Kat Allen, Jaime Lee Moyer, Leah Bobet, Amanda Downum, Solomon Foster, Emma Bull, Sarah Monette, Jodi Meadows, Charles Finlay, Rae Carson, Chelsea Polk, and all the other critiquers and first readers whose names are lost to my failing memory—and the depths of failed hard drives.

The entire loosely conceived Promethean Age sequence of novels owes an enormous debt to Jennifer Jackson, my agent; to Michael Curry, her able assistant; and to Liz Scheier, the editor who first purchased *Blood and Iron* back in two thousand and mumble. The current volume was utterly graced to be edited by Paula Guran, whose suggestions much improved it, and I am indebted to her.

Well, that's the book handled.

For support of the author, in addition to the above, I would also like to thank my mother, Karen Westerholm; Beth Coughlin; Stephen and Asha Shipman; Alisa Werst; Jeff MacDonald; Sheila Perry; and Heather Tebbs. And my brilliant and stubborn and startling Scott, who sustains me.

ABOUT THE AUTHOR

Elizabeth Bear was born on the same day as Frodo and Bilbo Baggins, but in a different year. She is the Sturgeon, Campbell, and Hugo-winning author of over twenty novels and nearly one hundred short stories. Her dog lives in Massachusetts and her partner, writer Scott Lynch, lives in Wisconsin. She writes on planes.